Pippa Roscoe [...] nd makes daily pro[...] y she'll leave the [...] he [c]ountryside. Sh[...] wasn't dreaming about handsome heroes and [in]nocent heroines. Totally her mother's fault, of course—she gave Pippa her first romance to read at the age of [s]even! She is inconceivably happy that she gets [t]o share those daydreams with you. Follow her on [T]witter @PippaRoscoe.

Jackie Ashenden writes dark, emotional stories, with alpha heroes who've just got the world to their liking [to] have it blown wide apart by their kick-ass [... s]he lives in Auckland, New Zealand, with [... an]d, the inimitable Dr Jax, two kids and two [...] she's not torturing alpha males and their [...] roines she can be found drinking chocolate [...]s, reading anything she can lay her hands on, [w]asting time on social media or being forced to go [mo]untain biking with her husband. To keep up to date [wit]h Jackie's new releases and other news sign up to [her] newsletter at jackieashenden.com.

Discover more at millsandboon.co.uk.

STOLEN FROM HER ROYAL WEDDING

PIPPA ROSCOE

A DIAMOND FOR MY FORBIDDEN BRIDE

JACKIE ASHENDEN

MIX
Paper from
responsible sources
FSC
FSC C007454

This book is produced from independently certified FSC™ paper
to ensure responsible forest management.

For more information visit www.harpercollins.co.uk/green

MILLS & BOON

First Published in Great Britain 2022
by Mills & Boon, an imprint of HarperCollins*Publishers* Ltd,
1 London Bridge Street, London, SE1 9GF

www.harpercollins.co.uk

HarperCollins*Publishers*
1st Floor, Watermarque Building,
Ringsend Road, Dublin 4, Ireland

Stolen from Her Royal Wedding © 2022 Pippa Roscoe

A Diamond for My Forbidden Bride © 2022 Jackie Ashenden

ISBN: 978-0-263-30084-0

This bo

For n

Printed

STOLEN FROM HER ROYAL WEDDING

PIPPA ROSCOE

MILLS & BOON

CHAPTER ONE

MARIT PRESSED A hand against the white corset of the wedding dress in an attempt to calm the unease sweeping across her stomach. Her heart fluttered in her chest, not with the nerves of an eager bride but with the fear that she was about to make a terrible mistake. Until she remembered exactly why she was doing this. The hand at her stomach formed into a fist. She had made her decision. It might be the last reckless act of the youngest Svardian Princess, but it was important. She knew what she was doing.

Liar.

The voice sounded very much like Freya's. Marit's heart thudded guiltily in her chest at the thought of the older sister who had been more like a mother to her than their own. No, Princess Freya most definitely would *not* approve of what Marit was about to do.

She looked at her reflection in the hotel room's mirror and clenched her jaw when she saw her lip trembling. Shouldn't a mother be present on her daughter's wedding day? Shouldn't family be gathered? Friends?

Inhaling slow and deep, Marit turned a critical eye on the off-the-shelf wedding dress she and André had bought in the Parisian boutique yesterday afternoon. The sweetheart neckline gaped a little and the dress looked too big for her. The skirt, made of layers and layers and layers of tulle, swamped her and there was something about the colour…the startling white made her look pallid.

It's not the dress, Marit.

When Aleksander, her older brother and King of Svardia, had called her to his office in Rilderdal Palace two weeks ago, she thought he'd found out about her secret project. That perhaps one of his palace spies had told him about her plans to create an inner city youth orchestra. Marit might not have been allowed to study music at university, but she could never have walked away from it. She'd kept the venture a secret because her family—her *parents*—would have expected her to fail. Just like they had ever since she'd been an awkward young princess tripping over her own feet, or spilling chocolate sauce on her gown just minutes before the yearly Christmas family photograph, or later, nearly causing an international incident because she had forgotten the correct etiquette with the Taiwanese delegation.

So, two weeks ago, Marit had sat in the King of Svardia's office—a jarring clash of the latest technology and original baroque interior design—mentally mounting a defence of the youth project she'd been working on for eight months since leaving university.

And when her brother had said, 'Freya will be stepping down. She has no choice. And neither do you. You will now be second in line to the throne,' she'd not heard him at first. But her heart had.

It understood, far more quickly than her brain, the precarious position she was now in and, caught between fight or flight, the organ had stopped. Her body's need for survival had been the only thing that forced a powerful, loud, crashing thud of a beat through her heart to restart it. Her brother's dominant gaze had needled into her awareness, forcing understanding through her shocked mind. There had been no choice. No discussion. It simply was.

She had met her sister outside her brother's office, tears gathering in Freya's beautiful amber eyes, and they had crashed together in an embrace that conveyed the depth and desperation of their love and their fears. Freya was the most loving and generous person Marit had ever known and that she would never be able to carry a child to term was devastating. But that Freya felt she could not remain second in line to the throne because she was not able to produce the spare heirs required to protect the future of the Svardian monarchy felt unbearably cruel. Freya loved what she did with a passion Marit could only ever compare to her own love of music. And Marit feared the loss of that role on top of the children Freya had wanted so much might just be too much for her sister to bear.

Marit's grief for Freya's loss was a seething dark, aching thing. But her greatest shame was the twist of selfishness within it that ached for her own loss: *her* freedom. Through the years it had been made painfully clear that Marit was surplus to requirements. She might have received the required royal training but no one had ever expected, or wanted, her to be involved in royal duties. And the role that Freya was leaving was frankly intimidating to the Princess who had been proclaimed The Rebellious Royal by every single international broadsheet. There had never been any question of her refusing her King's command. Marit would *never* abandon her brother or sister in such a way. But there was one last act of rebellion she had left to do. As second in line to the throne, she would have to marry a man with a title, a man of her brother's choosing.

But she just couldn't.

The thought of marrying a stranger, of being intimate with a man she'd never met… Her heart quivered in her chest as her breath stuttered around what she was about to do. Because she wasn't second in line to the throne *yet*. And if she was already married by the time she took her sister's place, then the legislation that had tied the hands of Svardian princesses for generations wouldn't apply to her.

Which was why Marit was standing in front of a mirror in the best suite in *Le Jardin Exquis* in an off-the-shelf wedding dress, about to marry André Du Sault. Her best friend from university, and the only reason she'd scraped a pass on the business degree her parents had insisted she took, understood why she was doing this. He had his own reasons and the rest, they'd decided in the short time they'd had to pull this entire thing together, they would figure out as they went. But now? Now it was time to get married.

The sound of a commotion outside the suite drew her attention to the door, ruffling the layers of the tulle skirt.

'*Monsieur, arrêtez!* Wait, *monsieur*! You cannot go in there. *Monsieur!*'

The panicked cries of the hotel's staff were all the warning Marit had before the door was flung open to reveal a figure in the doorway with silvery eyes and a determined jaw, staring at her as if he knew her.

Contrary to popular belief, Lykos Livas was not in the habit of kidnapping women on their wedding days. Not that he hadn't, on occasion, enjoyed the company of a runaway bride or two. But tracking down and retrieving a runaway princess in the heart of Paris on the morning of what she intended to be her wedding day at the behest of said Princess's brother was hardly a normal start to the day for Lykos. He checked the address in the message on his phone and returned the mobile to his ear, leaning back against his silver Aston Martin Vantage.

'Are you sure she's here?' he demanded.

'I'm sure that her *phone* is there, Lykos. As I'm currently in Norfolk patching drywall—'

'You're what?' Lykos frowned in confusion, unable to imagine Theron Thiakos, CEO of an internationally renowned security company, doing DIY of all things.

'Finally fixing the hole that Summer put in the wall.'

'*Adelfe*, if you and Summer are in the middle of—'

'*Ela*, Lykos, that's the mother of my child,' Theron groused.

'And she's perfect for you,' Lykos soothed in the most patronising tone he could manage.

'*Nai*, she is,' Theron replied smugly, ignoring Lykos's tease. Lykos was happy for the man he had all but grown up with on the streets of Greece. Straining at the constraints of the orphanage in Piraeus, the two had raised merry hell throughout Athens until they had been discovered by Kyros Agyros. That his success was even partly down to the man who had both mentored Lykos and betrayed his trust still stung. But it had been an important lesson to learn and one he'd never forget; the only person in this life that he could trust was himself.

'So, are you going to tell me why you needed me to track the phone of the youngest Svardian Princess?'

'It's a palace phone and the King of Svardia gave his permission,' Lykos replied without betraying the direction of his thoughts.

'I know that, but what kind of brother hires *you* to track down a twenty-two-year-old princess?'

'What is that supposed to mean?' Lykos demanded.

'It means, *adelfe mou*, I know you.'

'She is a pampered princess in the midst of a temper tantrum, she's about as far from my type as possible,' Lykos growled, indignant at the thought.

'What are you getting out of it then?' Theron needled him, clearly aware that Lykos wouldn't be doing this out of the kindness of his heart. Even the thought of it was laughable. 'If this has anything to do with Kozlov—'

'Get back to your drywall, Theron, if that's what the kids are calling it these days,' he interrupted, forcing a levity into his tone he didn't feel in the slightest. It was disconcerting that Theron had identified why he was willing to kidnap a princess.

'Lykos—'

He hung up the phone before Theron could finish his sentence, knowing his fellow Greek wouldn't understand the need driving him. Lykos pulled at his cufflinks as he looked up at the four-star Paris hotel where Princess Marit of Svardia intended to get married in little less than half an hour.

'*No amount of dressing up will erase the fact that you are, and always will be, nothing more than a street thief unwanted even by your parents, left to scrabble around for scraps.*'

The unwelcome memory of Ilian Kozlov's words sliced Lykos's focus in two. He'd come across the Russian when competing for controlling shares in a tech company three years ago. But besting the 'businessman' only seemed to inflame the elitist snob. Kozlov had started to come after Lykos's portfolio and when that hadn't worked he had crossed the line by impugning Lykos's reputation.

And why? Because Lykos was a threat. He was one of the few men in the world with enough financial acumen and backing to take Kozlov down.

So now Kozlov would have to pay. Personally.

The King of Svardia had finally agreed to sell him the shares Lykos needed to oust Kozlov from his own company. That was, Lykos had decided, the price to be exacted for the Russian's insult. And all Lykos had to do? Be the thief that Kozlov had accused him of being and steal a princess.

As he entered the hotel, Lykos thought of what he'd read in Theron's file on André Du Sault. He had enough money in the bank account so generously provided by his rich parents that he could have taken Princess Marit anywhere. The hotel, Lykos supposed as he marched straight past reception as if he were a guest with every right to be there, was quaint. Charming, he'd imagine it being described…but definitely below André's means.

Lykos added a little more steel to his determination. That was not how to treat a woman. Even if that woman was a spoilt princess who had run away with some university crush. He took the steps of the elegantly curved staircase to where Lykos guessed her suite would be, continuing until he reached the top floor.

'*Monsieur?*'

Lykos refused to acknowledge the hotel porter he passed in the corridor.

'*Monsieur!*'

His eyes narrowed on the suite at the very end of the hall.

'*Monsieur, arrêtez!* Wait, *monsieur*! You cannot go in there. *Monsieur!*'

Lykos's fingers wrapped around the handle of the door and pushed. Standing in front of a mirror in a dress that did absolutely nothing for her figure or colouring was Princess Marit of Svardia. And still she was the most beautiful woman he'd ever seen.

It was a moment of pure shock, the realisation turning him to stone. In the space of a single heartbeat he'd taken in everything about her. Blonde hair in angular waves made him think of the way the surf hit the beach at Piraeus. Slashes of crimson across her cheeks, harsh and bright against the pallor of her skin. Eyes, large orbs of hazel with flecks of gold and jade so bright he could see them from across the room. Her mouth, part opened in shock, was somehow the most erotic thing he'd seen in a lifetime of debauchery. He had caught her mid-turn, swamped by tulle, her waist seeming so small he'd be able to cradle it in his hands. But it was the scattering of freckles across her nose that drew him up short, their presence speaking of an innocence he should steer well clear of.

Lykos bit back a curse. Marit was barely twenty-two years old and he ruthlessly marshalled his body's shocking reaction to her with a severity that was near painful. By the time he'd controlled his startling response he looked up to find that golden flecks had transformed into hissing sparks.

Oh, she was *mad*.

Marit turned fully, kicking the skirts out of her way as she did so, fury and fear mixing potently in her blood.

'I take it my brother sent you?' she asked. But trying to contain the seething anger only made her sound imperious and she internally cringed as she thought she saw a curl of distaste pull at the man's lip.

'He would like you to return to Svardia.' His accent made her think of salt and money, strangely.

Instinctively she took a step back. 'I have every intention of doing so, but first—'

'*Un*wed,' the man all but growled, taking a single step towards her, returning the distance to what it had been.

Fire scorched her. *No.* She couldn't return to Svardia until she was married. If she was not, then Aleksander would have to choose a husband for her. A stranger. And she couldn't let that happen.

'No.'

'Yes.'

'I can imagine it easily escaped the notice of one of my brother's minions—'

'*Minion*,' the man repeated as if it were some great insult.

'But this is the twenty-first century and—'

Her words were cut short the moment he swept into the room, stalking towards her in such a way that had her stepping back again, or at least trying to. Her heel tangled in the hundredth layer of tulle and, swaying dangerously on the other, she was about to go down when the man appeared before her, bent down and, to Princess Marit of Svardia's utter shock, hoisted her over his shoulder.

'What on earth do you think you are doing?' she cried as her hands scrabbled down his back, desperate for something to hold onto as he bent again to pick up her bag and hook it over his other shoulder. She lifted her head, shaking strands of hair from her vision, trying to ignore the itch across her cheeks from the rush of blood to her head, and cried out for André. As they entered the corridor his door swung open and her fiancé rushed out to a stop.

'André! Please—' Her words were cut off by a wave of nausea as the man carrying her swung around, presumably to face her fiancé. Holding her breath, Marit strained her ears for the words André would surely say in order to rescue her from her captor.

One second, two.

Nothing.

Her heart sank as the man swung back to continue towards the staircase. Blinking back the moisture in her eyes, she glared at André, who refused to meet her gaze, a miserably mouthed apology on his lips. She clenched her jaw and tried not to think unkindly of the friend who had at least in some way tried to help her. It wasn't André's fault. It was her brother's. And the man carrying her over his shoulder like a…like a…

She growled. Actually growled. Anger caused her to lash out and pummel his back with her fists. Without even a pause in his stride, he flexed his back one way then the other, throwing her a little closer into the crook of his neck, the muscles across his shoulders and back rippling through the tulle and cotton of their clothes, whispering of a power that did shocking things to her core.

'Thank you, *glykiá mou*, I've been meaning to get a massage for some time now.'

Growling again, she tried to lever herself upright to respond when she felt his palm come down firmly against her backside, holding her in place.

'Stop it, Princess, or you'll fall off. And you're not a package that has insurance if it breaks.'

His words should have made her blush with anger. But that wasn't what had brought heat to Marit's cheeks or an ache between her legs. Embarrassed at the things she was feeling just from the hand holding her in place, Marit barely saw the bellboy who had brought the wedding dress to her suite only an hour ago.

'Your Highness?' He stared at her, shock clear on his face. 'Wait!'

Marit was surprised when the man beneath her stopped and turned.

'Who are you and what are you doing with Princess Marit?' the young bellboy asked, his voice trembling but determined. He couldn't be more than nineteen at the most, only a few years younger than her, but certainly many more years younger than the man carrying her over his shoulder.

She felt the subtle lean in the man's head, as if he were assessing the bellboy, and he grunted as if respecting the teenager for challenging him.

'Lykos Livas. Call this number,' he said, passing the bellboy a card from his pocket. 'If you are not satisfied, call the police.'

Lykos. A strange name, Marit thought. Greek, perhaps? *Wolf.* She thought of silver eyes and the power that arced through his torso as he moved, the lithe, easy grace of him. Yes. It was a name that suited him well.

'How do I know you are who you say you are?' she heard the bellboy ask, unable to see their interaction. But she most definitely felt the smirk of arrogance shiver through Lykos seconds before his answer.

'Google.'

Lykos turned on his heel and stalked from the building— the bellboy's interruption restoring his faith in humanity just a little. What kind of world was it that allowed a woman to be taken from her hotel room without her permission by a complete stranger, without a single person stopping them?

That he was the man doing the taking was neither here nor there. It was an outrage.

He adjusted his hold on the Princess over his shoulder, pulling the car keys from his pocket with his free hand, and clicked the button that released the locks. He went round to the passenger side, ignoring the wide-eyed looks from Parisian pedestrians, opened the door, threw the tote bag in first and then poured the Princess into the seat.

As he went to close the door he heard an angry voice demand that he 'watch the dress' from somewhere in the middle of all the…froth. Rolling his eyes, he swept up as many of the layers as he could, pressed them awkwardly into what little space remained and carefully closed the door. He returned to the driver's side and just as he reached for the handle a delicate wrist flicked out from amongst the masses of tulle filling the car and pressed down the lock.

'Really?' he demanded, flicking the lock on the keys.

And just as quickly she pressed the lock down again.

'Seriously?' he said, patience wearing thin.

'Seriously,' she said in that little half growl of hers that reminded him more of a kitten than a lion.

Turning his back to the window, he pinched the bridge of his nose. If Theron could see him now, he'd be in tears. Actual tears.

Lykos pivoted back to face the car. He couldn't see her through the layers of dress froth, but he'd expect her to be watching him closely. He pressed the key fob again for good measure and, as expected, she pressed down against the internal lock.

He looked up. 'Officer,' he said, shock marking his features, his hands raised in surrender. 'It's not what it looks like…'

He saw movement amongst the masses of material, hit the key fob and pulled the door before she could realise it had been a ruse, sliding into the driver's seat and slamming the door behind him.

'Officer! Officer!'

'Sorry, Princess. No police officer.'

'What? No!' The bridal dress shifted again, hands pressing the skirts down to reveal a mass of blonde hair that looked less bed head and more utter mess and two hazel eyes that bored holes into what little conscience Lykos had left. He shrugged it off and fired the car's ignition, the purr of the engine easing his irritation and putting him firmly back in control.

Before he put the car into gear, he turned to those hazel eyes still spitting fire. 'I know you've thought about it, but I'll ask you not to mess with the car while I'm driving. It's dangerous and you'll hurt yourself. Or worse, me. Your brother told me you were reckless, but not stupid. I'm counting on that.'

The cupid's bow thinned and her cheeks flushed, which only made the scattering of freckles across her nose and cheeks more prominent. He flexed his fingers around the steering wheel and took her silence for surrender. He nodded, satisfied, and pulled away from *Le Jardin Exquis*.

Driving in Paris was a lot like driving in Athens: crazy, stupid and the most fun Lykos had had in ages. The beeped horns, the curses, the raised fists. It forced him to focus on the restrained chaos of the roads rather than his feelings as he tried to ignore the push of his need for vengeance and the pull of the woman in a wedding dress beside him. Twenty minutes later he pulled into the underground parking beneath his apartment that was about as far from Athens as he could get, and turned off the engine.

'What happens now?' The question came from the

powder puff beside him, but the tone scratched against his conscience.

'We call your brother and arrange for you to be sent home.'

He saw the hand closest to him, slender and pale, form a fist that looked delicate more than dangerous. He could practically feel her need to rebel. To argue. But she had to know by now that it would be useless.

'Do we have a truce?'

There was silence. Eventually the tulle rustled as if she had nodded. Lykos exited the car and waited. But nothing happened. With a great deal of suppressed impatience, he walked around to the passenger side and opened her door for her. A silver-shod foot thrust from the skirts at the same time as a hand, which he reached for only because Lykos honestly couldn't see another way of her getting out of the car. But tugging gently on the hand brought her out and much closer than he had ever intended.

Large eyes stared up at him, shards of jade slicing through rich caramel, framed by long thick lashes. His gaze dropped to her lips, slick with gloss, but the cherry-red richness was all natural. The sheer vitality of her struck a note within him and vibrated into a chord of need that wound out from the deepest core of his being.

Until he remembered who she was. And who he was.

Marit's breath puffed from her chest into the space between them the moment the look in his eyes changed. Before then she'd felt... She shook her head. She'd felt nothing more than stress from the day's events.

But it had been the first time she'd been able to properly look at the man who had kidnapped her. His eyes were the palest grey, which was why she'd thought them silver earlier. His brow was low and made him look frustrated. Or it was simply the effect she had on him. High cheekbones cut into an angular face not softened by the swirls of artfully trimmed dark hair covering his jaw. He was taller than her by quite a bit and she felt tiny. As if everything about him surrounded and dwarfed her and for a moment it had been...delicious.

Until ice had formed in those silvery depths and she had to resist the urge to shiver. She cast her eyes over his shoulder to the exit sign. Maybe she could—

'Don't even think about it,' he commanded as his hand wrapped around her bicep and he guided her to a bank of lifts at the back of the car park.

They watched in silence as the lights counted down the floors and when the lift doors opened she couldn't tell who was more surprised, she and Lykos or the elderly couple disembarking.

'My child, are you okay?' The look of concern was unmissable across the woman's heavily wrinkled face.

The question pulled Marit up short. No one had asked her that since she'd been told she would be needed as second in line to the throne. No one had asked her that, even though her entire life was about to change, even though she'd never be able to continue with her youth project, given her new royal obligations, even though she would never be just *Marit* again. The empathy shining in the warm brown eyes knocked a chink into her armour and for a second she thought she might cry.

Until she was roughly tugged against the side of Lykos's lean torso, knocking the air out of her lungs.

'Oh, it's so very sad,' Lykos said, shaking his head and tutting as he pushed Marit into the lift. 'Jilted at

CHAPTER TWO

How dared he?

Marit knew that it was the height of ridiculousness to be mad at Lykos for—of all things—his comment about a dress she knew did absolutely nothing for her shape or colouring, but somehow that sent fire coursing through her bloodstream.

It was her wedding dress! Or at least it would have been if he hadn't shown up, hoicked her over his shoulder and kidnapped her. For the rather long ride in the lift to the penthouse suite she fumed, getting more and more angry as Lykos appeared less and less bothered.

No. Worse, he seemed to positively *enjoy* her ire.

Lykos moved with the doors as they opened, stepping directly into an apartment that was instantly and obviously breathtaking. Over the years Marit had visited some incredible places with her family on their diplomatic tours, but there was a sleek sophistication to this space that spoke specifically of the male beside her.

'You live here,' she realised as she watched him visibly adjust into the space. On any other man it might have looked as if he were relaxing into it, but there was nothing relaxed about the lines of tension in his body as he pulled sharply at each of his cufflinks.

'Sometimes,' he threw over his shoulder as he went

towards a discreet but clearly well stocked bar. While his response didn't tell her much about the strange sarcastic Greek, the apartment spoke volumes.

Arrogant. Rich. Male. It screamed from every single thing she could see.

'You're not one of my brother's men, are you?' she asked as the suspicion that she knew what was going on began to evaporate like steam from a coffee cup. This man, this *Lykos Livas*, was absolutely nothing like the security service men she knew from Svardia.

'No.' The single word held such a significant amount of hubris she was distracted by the sheer arrogance of it, until she realised what he'd said.

Fear turned in her stomach, forcing threatening thoughts through her mind. Had her brother even sent him? Had she just been kidnapped by some shady foreign enterprise hoping to cash in on her brother's new ascension to the throne? Her fingers fisted into her palms as she scanned the room for exits.

As if he'd noticed the turn in her thoughts, he sighed. 'You wait until I have you out of your hotel, off the streets and in my apartment and *now* you panic?'

Although the tone of his voice clearly showed how unimpressed he was with her self-preservation skills, he hadn't heard her scream yet and she was just about to open her mouth to do so when—

'Adagio.'

'What?' Marit demanded.

'Aleksander told me your safe word,' he said, waving his hand dismissively. 'Adagio. The name of your pet hamster when you were five. Something about it being ironic because he was fast?' The tall, dark-haired man shook his head as if bemused at the words coming from his own mouth. 'Your safe word,' he repeated, as if speaking to a child. 'So that you know he sent me for you.'

Marit closed her mouth but continued to glare at him until she worked out what he was saying. Only her brother and the close protection officers in the Svardian security services knew of her safe word. But then it was possible that someone in the SSS had sold that information. But why would someone use *her* to blackmail the King of Svardia? Unless they had discovered the truth about Freya...

'Okay, stop. I can hear your mind whirring from here.' Lykos sighed. 'Here.' He passed her his phone.

It was a video file, her brother's face paused at the beginning. She hit play, noticing that the phone was warm from where Lykos had held it.

'Marit, I trust Lykos. You can too. He will bring you back home and we will straighten this all out. For now, just stay put. And don't marry anyone!'

Marit felt awful, hating to see the dark smudges beneath her brother's eyes. He looked exhausted and, although his words had been half joking, there'd been a deep frustration that spoke of the weight of a new crown and the fear for his younger siblings. Marit clenched her jaw as shame drove nausea from her stomach.

All Aleksander was trying to do was ensure that Freya was protected. The fact that Marit might even be interfering with that was anathema to her. She really wasn't trying to cause problems for Aleksander, and certainly not Freya. Her brother would rule Svardia fairly and proudly and, even though he might have lost all sense of fun and joy in his late teenage years, he would do the best for their country. Always. It was just that...she had wanted to go into her new royal role with someone by her side. Someone there just for her. And that was now impossible.

She nodded, passing the phone back to Lykos, hating that he'd seen the video and despairing of what he saw when he looked at her. A runaway princess, spoiled and a royal pain. She couldn't meet his gaze so, instead, let herself be drawn to windows that looked out on an artfully designed rooftop terrace that surveyed Paris in a proprietorial way.

It was over. There was nothing left to do now but return to Svardia. That thought changed her heartbeat from two-four time to four-four, doubling in speed. What on earth did she know about the royal duties her older sister so effortlessly performed? She was grace and sophistication, where Marit was stiff and awkward. She always said the wrong thing under pressure and the only time she felt even remotely like the way Freya looked when she was performing royal duties was when she played the piano. How on earth would she survive, knowing that she could never measure up to her sister? That her family—most especially her parents—would always compare them and find her wanting.

The hiss of a machine and the scent of coffee drew her attention back to the man who would return her to all of that.

'How do you know my brother?' she asked, even now trying to put off thoughts of the future.

'Investments,' he replied, his voice moving behind her as she peered through the glass, beyond the large rust-effect metal containers displaying large green palm fronds, to the firepit and a single chaise longue that was large enough for two, sending wicked thoughts into her mind in an instant. Inside was no better. She glanced from wall to wall, every single furnishing was lush and textural: leather, fur, satin overlaid mahogany and black metal in every neutral colour imaginable.

Tactile.

The word came from the décor, not the man himself, she insisted mentally. And then she remembered the feel of his hand on her—

'Coffee?'

'Yes,' she answered too quickly.

Lykos resisted the urge to shake his head. How on earth had this woman been able to commit so much trouble when she had the world's worst poker face? Her gaze flickered from the coffee in his hand to the window, to the doors of the lift, until it rested beneath a frown, somewhere over his shoulder.

'Investments?' she queried.

'Yes.'

'With a sideline in kidnapping and extortion?'

'Where did you get extortion from?'

'I presume you're getting something in return?'

'Yes, Princess. In the real world that's called payment.'

Lykos clenched his jaw shut. He shouldn't have said that. He might not have a very high opinion of runaway princesses but that didn't excuse rudeness. He held out the coffee he'd made for her, waiting for her to meet his eye. He shouldn't have said it, but he wouldn't be shamed by it. And when she finally met his gaze steadily—going up a notch in his estimation—he wouldn't forget that Princess Marit of Svardia had absolutely no clue how the real world worked.

'I take mine—'

'Milk with two sugars?'

'How did you—?'

'Lucky guess,' he threw over his shoulder as he returned to make his own: black, bone-dry and unsweetened. How had he known? She was soft and pampered, that was how.

'So, what is the going rate for kidnapping a princess these days?'

'All your brother's shares in an oil company.'

A frown marred the smooth plane of Marit's brow when he turned back to face her. 'What oil company?'

'Does it matter?'

She narrowed her eyes, watching him for a beat. 'It does to you,' she observed.

His heart thudded and Lykos realised he didn't like that she'd been able to see that so easily. Like Theron. He shrugged off his discomfort but a small smile pulled at the corner of her lips and his attention snagged on it. By the time his gaze flicked back to her eyes he couldn't help but feel that she'd done the same thing, as if he'd felt the brush of her eyes on his lips too.

'Kozlov Industries,' he answered, anchoring their conversation in something far too boring for a princess. Paradoxically, Marit shifted her skirts a little and proceeded to collapse into the seat in a froth of tulle, her cup held high through the dramatic move, and looked for all the world as if she were ready for a story.

'What does Kozlov Industries do?' she asked when he refused to give in to her unspoken command to explain further.

He glared at her, unsure as to why it was of any interest to her.

'What?' she asked with faux innocence. 'I just want to know what I'm worth to you, is that so bad?'

He didn't like the way she'd phrased that: '*what I'm worth to you*'. The words crawled beneath his skin and slithered through his memories until they churned in his gut.

'What you are *not* worth to me is the giant headache that's beginning to form.'

'All you have to do is answer the question,' she she childishly, 'and I'll leave you alone.'

'I doubt that very much,' he growled, pressing a finger to his temple and rubbing at the place where, genuinely, a headache was threatening to form. But when he looked back to where she was sitting in the chair like Little Miss Muffet—one of the only nursery rhymes he remembered his mother whispering to him in the dead of night while his father was passed out—his mind emptied of excuses.

He knocked back his espresso, feeling the rich liquid burn his throat, before placing the cup back on the side. 'Kozlov is a Russian oligarch, with his fingers in far too many pies.'

Lykos thought of the man who he had first crossed paths with three years ago. The Russian thought nothing of buying up the competition and then breaking the company apart, smashing it on the rocks and destroying hundreds and thousands of livelihoods. He was a man without conscience and as such was dangerous. Lykos had known plenty of bad men. Kozlov wasn't just *bad*, he enjoyed it, he relished the misery of others.

'You don't like him?'

Lykos barked out a bitter laugh. 'No, Princess. I don't like him.'

The man was a bully and a snob who had lashed out even harder when he'd realised that Lykos wasn't as easily toppled by snide rumours or business deals as he'd imagined. Lykos was slowly forcing him into a corner and the man was getting desperate. It had taken Lykos years of painstaking hard work to acquire even a small portion of shares in the man's company. Shell companies, clandestine meetings with CEOs on the brink of financial collapse who, with their last breath, threw their lot in with Lykos just to take revenge against the shark in the financial waters of the world's most vital stock exchanges. But Kozlov had finally realised what was happening and had blocked any attempts Lykos could make to further his shareholding in Kozlov Industries. Until he'd discovered the identity of a very surprising shareholder.

'Your brother, however, has shares in his flagship company.'

'How?'

'I believe there was a poker game involved.' Because Kozlov would *never* have sold anyone such a large stake in the company that was his shining triumph.

'My brother doesn't play poker,' Marit scoffed, as if the idea was farcical. But Lykos had seen with his own eyes just how good a poker player Svardia's new King was.

'I could be mistaken,' he replied in a tone that revealed he didn't think anything of the sort. 'Anyway, I return you to your brother unwed, and in exchange I get his shares in Kozlov Industries.' Those, combined with his own, would finally oust the oligarch from the company he'd founded.

The man's reputation would never recover.

'You want to take his company? Kozlov's?' she asked astutely. 'Why?'

He stalked towards the chair she was sitting in, placed his hands on the arms and leaned close enough to see the gold flecks in her eyes sparkle. 'Because he's a nasty man and I want to take it from him. That, Princess Marit, is all you need to know.'

This close, he could see the curve of her eyelashes, the soft freckles across her nose and cheeks and the way her lips sloped in a straight rather than curved line. They looked as if she'd been nibbling on the fleshy centre.

He pulled himself back, realising that he'd leaned in too far only by the way that the jade shards in her eyes flashed in warning.

Twenty-two. She was only twenty-two.

He turned away, disgusted with himself and the entire situation, spinning on his heel and leaving the room.

Marit blinked and blinked again, trying to clear the afterimage of Lykos left long after he'd gone. The determination that had marked his features as he'd warned her of his intent had been electrifying, but nothing compared to what it had morphed into.

Awareness. She'd felt it—his awareness of her as a woman—and her pulse hadn't recovered. She hadn't recovered. It was as if he'd reached out and touched her, and her heart had responded by trying to climb out of her chest.

And Lykos had seen that and left the room.

'Lykos?' she called, suddenly feeling a million shades of awkward.

'I'm calling your brother, then taking a shower,' she heard him shout from behind a door at the other end of the apartment.

No *make yourself at home*, no *help yourself to a drink or whatever you need. The toilets are here, here and here, and the exits are...* She turned back to the lift.

'And you need a key for the lift, which I have, so don't bother.'

She turned to glare in the direction the voice was coming from, but it didn't make her feel any better. She stood up and started to pace the living area, feeling a restlessness she didn't want to examine too closely. The idea of Lykos and her brother talking made her chest hurt and she rubbed her sternum a little to ease the tension there.

Aleksander would understand her actions, surely. He'd understand why she'd wanted to marry someone of her choosing. He *had* to. He'd known what it was like for her growing up. When they were younger Aleksander had, like Freya, tried to share some of their parents' attention with her but it had only made things worse. In her excitement, she'd become overeager, her actions too fast, causing her to spill something, or her words too quick, saying something nonsensical, irritating both her parents. After a while it became so painful for everyone, her siblings stopped and she gave up trying to impress them. Gave up trying to be seen. It had cut her off from the family unit, leaving her sticking out awkwardly at the side. And she'd promised herself never to feel that way again. Marit swallowed the emotions thickening her throat. If Lykos was on the phone with her brother, perhaps she should speak to him and at least get the shouting over and done with.

She followed Lykos's voice down a white-walled corridor to a rich walnut door at the end. It was slightly ajar and she could just make out what Lykos was saying.

'Yes, I know. But she's here now.'

'And André?' her brother's voice asked though the speaker of the phone.

Marit held back a little then, unable to resist, she peered through the crack in the door to see Lykos moving about what must be a bedroom beyond. He was in the process of removing his cufflinks.

'Won't be a problem.'

'You know this for sure?'

Lykos huffed out a laugh. 'Yes.'

Marit felt her cheeks colour with embarrassment at how easily André had let her go. He'd not even uttered a single word to stop Lykos. It hurt more than it should, digging into an older wound, a deeper one. She looked up to find Lykos shrugging out of his shirt and her breath caught in her lungs.

Her hand flew to her chest as her heart thudded against her ribs, while her eyes traced every single line and plane of Lykos's body. The muscles on display weren't puffed from excessive exercise but honed, earned, lithe and powerful. As if Lykos knew how to use what he had rather than just rely on brute force. Even his body hinted at a lethal intelligence that seemed to run contrary to the strange cynical sense of humour she'd seen him display. Broad shoulders tapered into thin hips, the dusting of hair across his pecs seemed a handspan to Marit, her fingers flexing outward as if to test her guesstimate.

'And Marit? How is she?' The concern in Aleksander's voice caught Marit by surprise. It was years since they had been anything that resembled 'close'. And his ascension to the throne in the last three months certainly hadn't helped that.

Her gaze returned to Lykos, who had stopped with his hands on his belt, frowning towards the phone as if unsure what to say. She flattened herself back against the corridor wall when his eyes turned towards the door, her pulse pounding in her throat.

'She is…fine,' Marit heard him say and the snap of

leather told her he had removed his belt. Biting her lip, she was about to turn back to see if she could…

'Lykos, I need you to keep her.'

'What?'

What?

Lykos's voice had been as harsh and shocked as her own internal voice.

'Just for the week.'

'A week? Aleksander—'

'I will explain later.'

'I don't want her.' The explosive words cut into her like shrapnel.

'You would make a king beg.' It was less of a question from her brother, more of a statement.

'I will expect something very great in return,' she heard Lykos growl.

Nausea rose in Marit's stomach and the fingers that pressed against her lips shook.

He didn't want her here.

'I'll see to it that you have it.'

She turned to lean against the wall, her breaths short and puffy as she wilted down to the floor.

No one wanted her. Not unless they were paid for it.

It wasn't an unfamiliar feeling and she tried to tell herself that she should know this by now. She hadn't been the important sibling, she hadn't been taught the same things, treated the same way, wanted the same way. Loved. She had been unseen for so much of her life. Until now. And even now she wasn't really wanted. She was the only stand-in available. She was the worst-case scenario.

'What is it that you expect me to do with her for a week?'

'Just…keep her away from here and out of trouble.'

She bit her lip until a faint metallic taste hit her tongue. The sharp sting pulled her back to the present, her brother's words finally registering. He should have known better.

She heard Lykos sigh. 'She's a princess. How much trouble can she be?'

Poor man, Marit thought. He had no idea.

Water poured over Lykos's skin, the freezing jets raising goosebumps and thankfully not much else. He breathed through his nose, trying to calm the emotions swinging between resentment that he'd been lumbered with a spoilt princess, irritation that a brother would be so neglectful of his sister and frustration. Because that spoilt princess happened to be causing a reaction he'd not experienced since his teenage years.

He couldn't understand it. She was absolutely not his type. His preference leant towards brunettes that were his age or older, with sleek sophistication and absolutely no desire for a commitment he would never give. Marit was... He cursed. She was nearly ten years younger than him. The thought had him clenching his jaw. It didn't take a genius to work out that she was innocent too. The way she had looked up at him in the car park... There hadn't been an ounce of artifice about her or her reaction to him.

He shut off the water and turned for a towel before the memory of that moment could take hold of his body and lead to another twenty minutes in a freezing cold shower. He dried his body with harsh strokes, as if he could rid his skin of the desire to reach for her.

Stamáta!

Enough. He had more control over himself than this.

Wrapping a towel around his waist, he strode into the bedroom and stopped immediately.

For his entire childhood he'd lived in a constant state of hyperawareness. Firstly because of his father's fists and then at the orphanage, where fear and desperation were tools to be used against the weak. Consequently, he had a very specific alertness to his surroundings, especially his possessions, where they were and, most importantly, where they weren't. And he hadn't left his trousers on the bed. With his hand clutching the towel, he stalked through his apartment to confirm what he already knew.

She was gone.

The Princess's tote bag had been removed from where he had left it on the floor of the living area and in its place was a wedding dress. He skirted it as if it were a dangerous animal—which, to a man whose idea of hell was holy matrimony, it might as well have been. It looked as if she'd let the froth pool at her feet like champagne and simply stepped out of it. His imagination was suddenly a wild cascade of erotic images of toned limbs in silver heels and a waist he wanted to bracket with his hands.

None of which helped him with the fact that he had a princess on the loose in Paris and he needed to find her. Now. He marched back to his room, discarded the towel and dressed with the same ruthless efficiency he used to marshal his financial empire. The entire time he reassessed everything that he knew about the Princess. Reluctantly, he was forced to admit that he had written her off as nothing more than a spoilt princess with a rebellious streak. But while he accepted that he had been played, the game was not over and by the end she would realise that it was she who had underestimated the lengths he would go to secure his payment for her capture and containment.

He scanned his wardrobe and identified which items were missing: one pair of black superfine wool dress trousers, one white shirt and one thin black leather belt. Presumably the Princess was still wearing silver heels.

He pulled at his cuff sleeves, the snap of cotton familiar and satisfying. He reached for his cufflinks and threaded the fixed bar through the buttonhole, feeling his pulse settle with the familiar act and the air of respectability they lent him. He lifted the suit jacket that held his wallet from the back of the chair and stopped. The weight was off and he flung the jacket back on the seat and pinched the bridge of his nose.

Lykos couldn't believe it.

He, who had once been the most notorious pickpocket in Athens, had just had his wallet stolen.

By a princess.

CHAPTER THREE

MARIT LOOKED OUT of the back window of the taxi hurtling through Paris towards the Gare du Nord train station. She'd half-expected to see Lykos running out of the entrance of the swanky apartment building in nothing but a towel. But he hadn't.

Ignoring the strange pang of disappointment, she turned instead to riffle through the dark brown leather wallet she'd taken from Lykos's jacket pocket. The only reason she hadn't taken the car was because she didn't know how to drive, so she'd settled for throwing his car keys off the balcony, her only regret that she wouldn't be there to see the look on his face when he realised what she'd done.

The eyes of the taxi driver flickered over her through the rear-view mirror and she clenched her jaw. It was not as if she'd been spoilt for choice. She'd hardly have been able to make a quick getaway in the wedding dress. She'd rolled up the hems of the trousers and cinched the belt tightly around her waist beneath a shirt that definitely passed as oversized and had managed to appear almost stylish.

Marit counted eight hundred euros in cash, but no credit cards. Unusual, yet somehow fitting for a man she believed enjoyed being contrary for the sake of it. She looked into each little pocket. No photos, no receipts, nothing tucked away for safety. There was no sense of who he was. She pulled out a driver's licence and stared at the black and white image of Lykos Livas, frowning in all his brooding glory. How could she dislike someone so intensely, yet still feel acutely…acutely…*not* like the way any other man had ever made her feel?

She threw the wallet into the bag by her feet, catching sight of the bright red cover of her passport, which she needed to get into Italy. Unlike her brother and sister, the amount of freedom she'd enjoyed up until recently had meant that she'd been able to keep hold of it, rather than handing it over to close protection officers. Of course that would change when she took her sister's place in the royal family. Security details, every minute of her day planned to the second, public speaking, public events… Sweat started to gather at the back of her neck.

As the lights turned, allowing the taxi to move closer to the train station, her pulse picked up. The closer she came to her last bit of freedom, the more fearful she became that it would disappear. Images of a strong male hand wrapping around her bicep had her heart thrumming in her chest. Her breaths came quicker as she glanced at the sign for the Gare du Nord and she nearly cried when the taxi was caught in another stream of traffic. She glanced behind her again, in caser Lykos had somehow found her. No. She couldn't stay here. It was as if she could feel him snapping at her heels.

'Arrêtez-vous ici, s'il vous plait,' she said, and the driver pulled to the side of the road. She thrust twice the amount needed at the driver and launched herself from the cab. Pulling the tote over her shoulder, she jogged down the street towards the station. She checked

the time. She had just over fifteen minutes to buy her tickets and get on the next train to Milan if she hurried.

She wondered whether Lykos would tell Aleksander what had happened, or whether he'd try to find her before he had to.

I need you to keep her.

Just for the week.

I don't want her.

The words ran on a loop through Marit's mind. It would serve Lykos right if Aleksander found out and decided not to give him the shares. She had half a mind to let her brother know of her escape, if she didn't think it would lead directly to her capture.

Drawing a few curious glances, she entered the train station and found the departures board. Checking the train was on time, she rushed over to the ticket stall. She wasn't running away. She *would* go back, just… not yet.

Her heart turned over as she thought of just how much Freya loved what she did, how good she was at it. A better princess hadn't been born. Marit had argued with her over and over again, insisting that Freya didn't need to step down, but she wasn't blind. The press were cruel and a princess with fertility issues…one who was supposed to provide spare heirs for a ruler so new and untested as their brother… Reporters would tear her apart and the fallout would cause deep fissures in the confidence of the Svardian people in their royal family. The international implications didn't bear thinking about.

So, no. Marit was under no illusions as to where her future lay. It was just that before she did step into Freya's shoes she wanted some time to herself. To do some of the things she'd thought she'd have the time to do, to feel all that she'd wanted to feel, and to experience all that she possibly could before her life became one of dictates and strangers and public royal duties…and marriage and children she wasn't ready for.

Her fingers drummed a beat against the cold steel of the ticket office counter as she waited for the clerk to process the cash payment and checked her watch. She had five minutes to get to her train before it left.

Lykos looked up at the train station sign. Why? His only explicable reason was that it was where he would have come. But he felt it deep in his gut—the part of him he'd learned to trust when he was young and on the streets. She was here. The problem now was figuring out where she was going to.

As he took stock, he pulled at the cufflinks, setting the shirt smartly beneath his jacket, and he cursed the Princess *again*. The first time he'd cursed was when he'd caught sight of the small key fob he'd wasted precious minutes looking for, fragmented into microchips and black plastic on the road outside the apartment, that would take time and money to replace. And if Lykos hated anything it was unnecessary waste, he thought as he revised his earlier impression of Marit once again. Definitely spoilt and completely ignorant of the value of money or possessions.

As he entered the sprawling international train station, the sound of thousands of voices filled the air and Lykos began to feel the first stirrings of unease. A childhood habit rose from the mists of time to snake around him as he instinctively scanned the sea of people for targets—just like his father had taught him. And he saw them all. The wealthy businessman making a show of checking his expensive watch to the girl at the kiosk counter. The man rolling his eyes as his wife debated which magazine would be best for her trip. The mother in expensive clothes, telling off her teenage son while her daughter made faces at the boy behind her mother's back.

Lykos rolled his shoulders, trying to shake off the discomfort the instinctive act made him feel. As a seven-year-old, he'd have had three fat wallets within fifteen minutes and a hard smack across the cheek for leaving the easiest prey of all. The grey-haired lady with the walking frame, her bag hanging half open from the handle, picking through her open clasp wallet for change as if each penny was precious.

He glanced up at the departures board. London, Brussels, Belgium, Germany, Milan, the Netherlands. Of course, if it were him, he'd have been tempted to disappear into the underground and stay in Paris. But while he was sneaky, Marit was rebellious. And they were two very different things. Surely a young, rebellious woman wouldn't be able to resist the lure of London. He checked the time and the platform number. Ten minutes. Easy.

He passed the stall with the irritated mother and the lecherous businessman, and found his target. He stood directly in her line of sight.

'*Mademoiselle?*'

'*À mon âge?*' the elderly lady replied with a twinkle in her eyes, her hands shaking so that he worried for the contents of her purse.

Lykos nodded. '*Madam,*' he corrected with a small bow of his head. '*Je peux?*' he asked, tucking the fallen strap of her bag securely over the handle bar of her walking frame without her notice.

'*Mais oui. Merci.*'

The businessman scowled at him and the girl at the kiosk counter's eyes followed Lykos as he stalked off to the train to London, *after* buying the elderly lady's magazine.

Marit found her window seat on the quiet train, casting looks up and down the carriage, still convinced the enigmatic Greek would come stalking down the train to snatch her back up. The overhead announcement warned passengers they had one minute before departure.

Her heart pounding in her chest, Marit slid into the window seat, putting her bag on the seat between her and the aisle, hoping that it would deter a stranger from taking it. She held her breath as she heard the beeps sounding that the train doors were closing. Her eyes drifted shut and she prayed.

Please. Just give me this. Then I'll do what's needed, I promise. Just this.

Her heart lurched forward with the sudden jerk of the TGV, adrenaline coursing through her veins along with a sense of victory. She had a feeling that fooling Lykos Livas wasn't an everyday occurrence.

But now that the train was moving she allowed herself to think about her destination when she arrived in Milan. She reached into her bag for her music player, fitting the wireless pods into her ears and pressing play, letting the opening notes from one of her favourite songs slide over her, familiar and soothing.

She'd wanted to visit Sforzando for years, its reputation as the best blues bar in Italy unprecedented. Marit might have been given many freedoms over the years, but there were some her parents had still baulked at.

Don't be silly, Marit. A princess can't be seen in a blues club.

Piano lessons are fine, as long as you stick to classical pieces. But a guitar is out of the question.

A music degree, Marit? Really? Don't be so naïve.

Fresh blooms of hurt sprang from the remembered words. What her parents—and even her siblings—had failed to understand was that it wasn't just music, it wasn't just part of some rebellion. It was so much more than that. Music had been her escape. It was a way for her to express emotions and feelings that she was unable to put to words. It had been an outlet for her anger before she'd known it was anger, loss before she'd realised she'd felt loss, and an expression of yearning before she'd ever known what she was looking for.

She looked out of the window, unseeing of the bricks and wires twisting in the shadows as the train left the station to the sound of a deep, constant, rhythmic guitar strum that was hypnotic. She frowned when she felt a presence standing in the aisle on the other side of the seat where her bag was. More than a little disgruntled that the fellow passenger couldn't find any other seat to pick, she lifted her back and angled herself further away from the person, ignoring the way the man folded himself into the seat. Impossibly long legs looked almost comical pressed up against the back of the seat in front.

Just as her favourite singer proclaimed that she couldn't find her way home, a stillness settled in the air between her and the passenger, Marit's whole body filling with sudden tension as she slowly turned to find Lykos staring at her with a raised eyebrow.

Dammit!

She pulled the pod from her ear and he was momentarily distracted by the blush of anger forming on her cheeks, making those freckles even more golden.

'Hello, Princess,' said Lykos, leaning back against the seat, making a big show of getting comfortable, despite the way his pulse was racing from having to sprint to the train before it left. If he hadn't caught sight of the particular shade of blonde of Marit's hair from the corner of his eye as he took the escalators in the wrong direction he'd have completely missed her.

From the Princess's scowl, she clearly didn't realise how close she'd come to getting away with her plan, whatever that plan was. He shifted his shoulders, disliking the way that sweat stuck his shirt uncomfortably to his back, even as the youth in him delighted in the game, celebrated victory at having caught the Princess. It added a little flavour to the pounding of his heart in his chest.

'How did you find me?' she demanded.

'I'm that good.'

She narrowed her eyes. 'You got lucky.'

It was an accusation that had been levelled at him again and again over the years. At least one of them had been delivered in a Russian accent. But each and every one of them had been an underestimation of the determination and power driving him forward; of the lengths he would go to, to leave the dirt of the streets of Athens behind him. Had *left* behind him, he mentally corrected.

'Luck is what you make of it.' His father's words were out of his mouth before he could pull them back, leaving teeth marks on his tongue and burns deep in his heart. As if the verbal slip disproved his assertion that he was no longer the same street thief *scrabbling for scraps*. The sweat on his skin turned frigid and he wanted a shower to wash off the memories. Instead, he was leaving his apartment in Paris far behind him at a rate of knots.

'Why did you run?' he asked, rooting himself in the

present. 'We had a truce,' he accused, the gravel in his voice vibrating from the distaste of a broken agreement.

'Clearly, I have some…*free time*…before I am needed in Svardia. I thought I'd do a bit of travelling.'

Christé mou, she'd overheard his conversation with Aleksander. And must have heard what he'd said after.

I don't want her.

It might have been the absolute truth in that moment, but the reality was always more complex. And, no matter the reason, no woman, no *one*, ever wanted to hear those words. Justifiable guilt swirled in a conscience he would have professed not to have.

But, Lykos realised, instead of falling into tears or retreating, the girl beside him had taken his clothes, stolen his wallet, destroyed his means of transport and got herself on a train to Milan. He was almost impressed.

He glanced at her from the corner of his eye. Her head was turned towards the window, the waterfall of golden hair tucked behind her ear, revealing the pod and the gentle hum of music he couldn't quite make out. The curve of her cheek was plumper than those high cheekbones of the brunettes he usually acquainted himself with. It spoke of a softness that belied the fire within her and he appreciated the duality, the drive, even if it came at his expense. An expense that he couldn't afford. Kozlov needed to pay and Aleksander had the shares to help make it happen.

Lykos felt her shiver, as if Marit had somehow picked up on the sudden drop in temperature from his thoughts alone. He frowned, realising the closeness of the seats. 'Why did you not buy a first-class ticket?'

Catching her gaze in the reflection on the glass, he marshalled the jolt that continued to shock his body, until she broke the connection.

'I wanted to save the money,' she said with a shrug.

'What would a princess know about saving money?' Lykos scoffed, remembering in a heartbeat every single time he'd scrabbled in the street for pennies or, in desperation, used the 'skills' his father had taught him almost as soon as he could walk.

'Quite a lot, if she's never had free access to it herself.' She turned to look at him, her pupils flaring unconsciously as she registered how close they were; her body's response starting a chain reaction in his own, shorting out his ability to reply to her statement. 'What?' she asked of his silence. 'You think it's easy for a princess to go and get a summer job?' she demanded, clearly—and thankfully—misunderstanding the reason behind his lack of response. 'You ever wondered why royals don't have handbags? Because their wallets and keys are kept by security personnel. Why aren't I travelling first-class? Because the only money I have is the money I took from your wallet. I was saving the rest for...'

Like a bloodhound, he followed the trail of unspoken words. 'For what, Princess?'

'My name,' she growled, 'is Marit. And clothes, of course. What else would I spend your money on?'

He stared at her, trying to see though the lie she'd told him, but he recognised the stubborn glint gleaming back at him. What he didn't recognise was the sense of kinship that suddenly bloomed in that moment. Because he realised she was protecting herself. And that Lykos both respected and understood. Neither of which would matter, of course, if it stopped him from getting what he was owed from Aleksander.

He turned away from her steady gaze, giving a point to the Princess, just as he heard her stomach growl and he allowed a smirk to pull at his lips, covering the strange sensation from seconds earlier.

'You see,' he drawled, 'if we were in first-class lunch would have been served by—'

She shot out a hand and slapped him on the arm.

'That's assault,' he warned mockingly, his head dipping slightly, only to be hit by a gentle hint of salt and the sweet scent of pears.

'It's self-defence. I'm being kidnapped,' she replied, and the breathless way the words escaped her lips hitched his pulse, causing an alarm to scream in his head.

'Actually, you ran away, so it's probably more akin to retrieval,' he couldn't help but reply.

'Retrieval?'

'And theft. You stole my wallet, my clothes, and I haven't even started on the car.'

'Did you find the keys?' she asked suddenly, the urgency and concern across her features startling. It was on the tip of his tongue to ask why she would care, when it hit him that, why aside, she did actually care.

'Yes, all fine,' he replied, fascinated by the concern leaving her features.

'It would have served you right if they hadn't been,' she chided.

'Yes, it would have,' he agreed, wondering why on earth he'd just spared her feelings. 'I'm going to hunt down some breakfast,' he said, easing himself out of his seat and into the aisle. 'Princess—'

'Marit.'

'*Marit*. Don't. Go. Anywhere.'

Her name, spoken in his thick, luscious accent, had struck her so still he needn't have warned her not to leave. Her body remained motionless long after he'd left the carriage until, unable not to, her lungs exploded into action with a huge inhale. She still felt pinpricks across her skin from how close he'd been, the way her heart had lurched as he'd teased her, the way each and every breath took in that rich, savoury scent of his aftershave, and the way she'd had to fist her hands to stop herself reaching for him.

Breathy. She'd sounded breathy, even to her own ears.

I don't want her.

Shame curled her stomach. Was she doomed to repeat this cycle over and over and over again, wanting people who didn't want her? The memory of nine-year-old Freya's face, when at the age of five Marit had asked if there was something wrong with her that she wasn't allowed to go to lessons with Mummy and Daddy rose in her mind anew.

A belief that had become more and more certain as the years had gone on. She didn't know why it was, only that it was. Her parents were not outwardly loving in any real way, unless there were cameras present, but even then she just wasn't as important as Freya and Aleksander were. Or at least she hadn't been until now.

Now, she was needed but still not wanted.

Marit's mouth trembled until she pressed her teeth together hard enough to make it stop. She couldn't forget that. Whatever had come over her, she had to remember where she was and who he was. Lykos Livas was acting on her brother's behalf and only then because he needed Aleksander's shares. He was not here for her.

By the time Lykos returned to his seat, Marit was putting all her efforts into focusing on the music rather than the man beside her. But even then, while the right side of her brain homed in on the notes and composition

of the piece, the left side insisted on memorising everything about the Greek billionaire next to her.

Billionaire? Oh, absolutely. It wasn't the clearly expensive watch or the cut of his clothes that years as a
princess had enabled her to recognise as handmade, it
was his attitude: a careless irreverence that she'd not en-
countered before amongst the courtiers at the Svardian
palace or the international delegates, or even the students
at the Swiss university her parents had made her attend.

He put down her tray table and placed on it a steaming paper cup of coffee and a slightly greasy paper bag
and ignored her as studiously as she ignored him. She
stared at the items he had procured and felt strangely as
if she were being assessed as he consumed his pastry in
impossibly large, man-sized mouthfuls. She felt the dare
to refuse such simple food buzz against her skin as if the
force of his thoughts pressed against her. Lykos was a
man just as arrogantly comfortable at the coffee cart of
the TGV as he was in a five-star hotel, which was most
definitely at odds with the moneyed men and women
she'd met throughout her life.

And, with that, she realised that she'd never met anyone like Lykos Livas.

Everything in her wanted to rebel, to refuse the food
he'd bought simply from habit. But he clearly thought
her too pampered a princess to stoop to the greasy offering, and that she rebelled against more. She turned to
face him, reaching blindly for the flaky pastry inside,
tore off as big a chunk as she possibly could, tipped
her head back and fitted as much of it into her mouth
as she could. She kept her eyes on his so she saw just
how hard he was trying not to smile as he ate his own
piece of pastry.

'You look ridiculous,' he dismissed, but the way the

corner of his lips twisted hit her heart hard. Making him smile against his will? One of the best things about that day so far. Especially as she had the impression it didn't happen very often.

'It's really tasty,' she said with her mouth full, flakes of iced toasted almonds peppering her stolen shirt.

'Shut up and eat your breakfast.'

'It's three in the afternoon!'

'A croissant is *always* breakfast,' he replied imperiously, forcing her to choke back a laugh.

The next few hours were strange for Marit. It had started when he'd asked her about a castle.

'But you have one, yes?'

'Well, there *are* castles that belong to the royal family,' she'd tried to explain.

'Any for sale?'

'No, Lykos, none for sale,' she'd replied.

He'd seemed strangely disappointed and, after making a cryptic comment about always having wanted a castle, he'd simply leaned his head back against the headrest and settled. At one point his eyes had drifted shut.

She wasn't sure he was actually asleep, there was something alert about him—as if half of his mind was utterly aware of everything going on around him. Nevertheless, she took the time to study him. There was a small scar just beneath the corner of his mouth, glinting like a silvery line from the dark stubble, that marred his almost perfect jaw. His cupid's bow was so pronounced she wanted to press the pad of her thumb to the cleft above it. Lips carelessly sensual, thick and—she bit her bottom lip, mirroring her unconscious thoughts. His nose would have been straight as an arrow were it not for the slight kink near the bridge that made her think of fists and fights. His face whispered a history that seemed contrary to every wealthy person she'd ever known. He was a curiosity she needed to ignore, she decided as she skipped the next track on her playlist and looked out of the window at the Italian landscape.

'What's in Milan?'

She could pretend she hadn't heard him but that felt childish. She turned to find him looking at her as if waiting to navigate through her response for the truth and wondered what it would be like to just tell him, to give up this endless fight that she seemed to have been waging for years.

'There's a club I want to go to.' Because she was watching closely, she saw the glint of disappointment in his otherwise utterly impassive face. And it stung. 'Not that kind of club.'

This time his face blared mock innocence. 'What kind of club did you think I was—?'

'Not that kind of club either!' she scolded in a whisper, hating the way her cheeks pinked up at the sudden thought of Lykos in a…in a sex club. Her body started to tremble, low and strong, and for a moment she feared that Lykos could tell. As if he sensed her body's reaction because he went incredibly still, aside from the muscle at his jaw flexing as if he were bracing himself.

'What's in Milan, Marit?' he asked again, this time a strange force in his tone that she knew instinctively not to push.

'A blues club.'

This time, the look of surprise on Lykos's face looked genuine.

CHAPTER FOUR

LYKOS WONDERED WHEN he'd get a handle on Princess Marit of Svardia. At almost every turn, she did the opposite of what he was expecting. From the moment the train had pulled in to Milan and the closer and closer they got to this, apparently, world-renowned blues club, she hadn't stopped talking. Passion and enthusiasm lit her features as she named supposedly famous musicians that had played in the hallowed halls of Sforzando which she found 'inconceivable' that he'd never heard of. Long gone was the pallor he'd first seen across her features, or the frustrated fury from his apartment in Paris. Blues and jazz, it seemed, brought a bronze glow to her that vibrated from her like sound waves, brushing against him like the tide.

She was utterly lost in their conversation as they walked the streets of Milan, unaware of the young man who tripped over his feet at the sight of her, or the woman who barged her boyfriend with her shoulder for staring at Marit a little too long. Marit seemed completely unaware of the effect she was having—and Lykos knew that it was nothing to do with her title. In fact, from what he had gleaned, despite some rather painful and embarrassing encounters with the press as a young girl and teenager, all attention-seeking behaviour had seemed to stop after the skiing accident she'd had at fourteen. The resulting surgery had impacted her parents' diplomatic visit to Japan, Marit's mother returning to Svardia to take care of Marit while her father remained behind with his delegation.

Lykos had flicked through the press articles and photographs of Marit's mother descending the steps of a small jet, her face hollow with concern. She'd gone straight to the hospital, where more photographs caught her in intense discussions with doctors, appearing beside reports from the school friends on the same trip quoted as saying how scared they'd been and how reckless Marit had been.

Even now Lykos felt rising resentment at the childish behaviour of the young woman beside him. He would have given anything as a child to have his mother be with him when sick, instead of dropping him at an orphanage and not looking back even once.

Aleksander had briefed him on why he needed Marit to return to Svardia. He'd been sworn to secrecy over their sister's infertility issues that meant Marit needed to step up and into that role. And what had she done? Run away. And when Aleksander needed more time—the reason was honestly none of Lykos's business—she'd run away *again*. To a blues club.

With one ear he continued to listen to her expounding the virtues of different female singers in country blues and classic blues as he purposefully held onto his irritation. What he couldn't understand was why the knowledge of her spoilt selfishness was not enough of a deterrent to his body's reaction to her. Maybe he was coming down with something. A cold? The flu? It was inexplicable.

Lykos was acutely familiar with attraction and

arousal. He was a healthy, virile Greek. He enjoyed his sexual exploits as much, if not more, than the next man. But blondes weren't his type. Princesses weren't his type. And twenty-two-year-olds who had absolutely no idea what they were doing were Not. His. Type.

He was so busy telling himself that, he hadn't realised that she'd stopped walking and pulled himself up short to find her staring up at a building ten feet behind him. The look on her face whipped concern through him in a heartbeat.

'Marit?' He closed the distance between them in short strides, the distress marring her features making him want to pull her to him. Her eyes sparkled with a sheen of tears she hastily tried to blink away. Teeth pierced her bottom lip, as if to stop it trembling. She swallowed once and then shrugged her shoulder.

'It's okay. It was foolish to come here without…' Marit's words trailed off as she looked back up at an old building that he could now see had once been a large three-storey bar. Chipboard covered all but a few windows, the rest shards of jagged glass. A sign that read 'Sforzando' was missing a few letters, old posters curled and peeled down from the wall, months if not years of rain and pollution destroying images of musicians and set lists. It reminded him of an old *rebetiko* tavern he and Theron used to sneak into when they were teenagers, but this building was derelict. No music played here any more.

He turned back to see Marit taking in the desolation of the building she had stolen a wallet and crossed countries to reach, and even if she was the spoilt youngest daughter of a king it didn't make her sadness any less real or evident.

'Marit,' he said, stretching out his hand.

She shook her head and stepped back from his reach, looking up and down the street to mask her feelings. She opened her mouth to speak, but the words wouldn't come and he realised that she'd come to the end of her fight, the defeat in her eyes so much worse than her rebellion or anger.

He whistled to the cab he saw turning into the top of the street and when it pulled up beside them he ushered Marit into the white car. Throughout the journey his gaze flickered back and forth between Marit, the road ahead and the driver who, thankfully, seemed to have no idea who his royal passenger was.

Lykos checked his watch. It was six-thirty by the time the driver pulled up outside the grand entrance of L'Aranceto. The liveried doorman had a frown on his face until the moment he recognised who it was emerging from the taxi.

'Signor Livas,' he said, walking forward with renewed vigour. 'My apologies, we weren't expecting you.'

'Nothing to apologise for, Benito. It was a spur-of-the-moment decision,' Lykos replied, reassuring the man with a friendly hand on his shoulder. 'Hence no luggage. Nevertheless, discretion would be appreciated,' he whispered congenially. Lykos didn't think that either Aleksander or Marit would appreciate a resurgence of rumours about Svardia's youngest royal, especially not now.

Benito dipped his head. 'Of course.'

Lykos turned back to the cab and held his hand out to Marit, who must have been upset as she took it without question or complaint. Which, perversely, Lykos didn't like one bit. It seemed as if she were in shock, but why it had been the blues club rather than—say—kidnap, a failed wedding or an international chase, Lykos honestly couldn't fathom.

He guided her through the gold-framed doors that Benito held open and nodded to him as he moved through to the hotel bar, knowing that the doorman would attend to checking them into suitable accommodation.

Over the years Lykos had travelled the globe, the transient nature of his business suiting his needs and his temperament, but this was one of his favourite hotels. The suites all had a balcony, which was necessary for a man who never slept well at the best of times but it was much worse when he couldn't see the sky, and the staff here knew him and liked him. As evidenced by the smile he was greeted with from Oriana, the dark-haired beauty behind the bar who, despite being twenty years older, enjoyed their flirtatious banter as much as him.

'Lykos, it is very unkind of you to bring such a beautiful companion into my bar,' she chided, her English better than his Italian. Although a quirk of Lykos's intelligence had given him the ability to easily and quickly pick up foreign languages, he knew Oriana enjoyed the practice on a forgiving customer.

'If the situation wasn't so dire, I would never have betrayed you in such a way, *tesoro mio*.'

She flicked a white dishcloth at him that snapped satisfyingly through the quiet of the bar. 'Go sit down. I will bring you your drinks.'

'*Grazie mille,*' Lykos replied, a hand hovering at Marit's back, guiding her to a booth in the shadowed end of the bar.

Marit let him all but pour her into the seat at the round dark marble table and watched him with large eyes as he took his opposite her. He placed an elbow on the arm of his chair and leaned into his palm, rubbing the stubble on his chin as he watched her as openly as she watched him.

This time their connection wasn't one of challenge or judgement, rather it was a reassessment of sorts. So far, nothing in the last ten hours had been as he'd expected from the pampered Princess he'd read about in his file from Theron.

'You didn't order any drinks.'

'I didn't have to.'

'You're that good?' Marit asked with a raised eyebrow.

'No. Oriana is.'

Marit couldn't work him out. And she didn't like that. Although it was easier to focus on the enigmatic man in front of her than how she felt about Sforzando. She wished she could explain the longing she'd felt to visit the world-renowned blues club. The desire she'd had to see it before returning to Svardia so she could have a moment for herself to take back with her. to remember. to keep her going through the years of her duty.

The waitress placed two drinks down on the table between them. Lykos's was a dark amber swirl poured over a large ice cube in a short, square, heavy-looking glass, decorated with a twist of orange peel. Hers was a much lighter concoction, still orange, but served in a martini glass with a sprig of rosemary.

She felt Lykos's eyes remain on her the entire time the waitress was there, cutting through her natural instinct to rebel. That same yearning need she couldn't explain about Sforzando seemed to bleed onto Lykos. A yearning need for him to see her as she was and not as some spoilt runaway princess.

'How long do I have?' she asked. 'Before you return me to Svardia,' she clarified in response to the rise of his brow in silent enquiry.

'Five days.'

She bit her lip. 'Did he tell you why I'm needed back home?' she asked.

He nodded, his face half hidden in the shadows of the bar. But not well enough to hide the judgement, the distaste, at what he clearly saw was her running away. He didn't understand. She could—*would* never turn her back on her new future. Freya was hurting more than Marit could ever imagine for the loss of a future she had wanted with every fibre of her being. And if taking on her duties and role helped Freya in *any* way, Marit would do it. But she would also do it for Aleksander, and for the people of her country, who deserved peace and security and a stable monarchy leading them in uncertain times. She felt that beat as strongly in her heart as her siblings did. She'd just never been called on to prove it. Never been trusted to. So, no. Nothing would stop Marit from returning to Svardia and becoming second in line to the throne.

'I was always going to go back,' she said as he reached for his drink and took a sip. She bit her lip, imagining the burn of alcohol on her tongue, and glanced towards her own drink, waiting for the tremble in her fingers to stop before reaching for it. 'It's just…' The fight to prevent the truth from falling onto the table between them was real.

Just say it. He might hear you.

'There were things I wanted to do. Before I returned to Svardia to take up a royal position that was never meant for me.'

The frown was back, hanging low over his silvery gaze. 'Like what?'

Like, *everything*.

Marit's laugh was heartbreaking to her own ears. 'Like take a walk in the park without a mass of people following my every move.'

'You've never done that?'

'Everyone on the university campus knew who I was. And I was under strict instructions from my parents not to cause trouble.'

'Or what?' Lykos's tone was almost dangerous, his gaze intent, a focus that burned.

She shook her head immediately. 'Nothing like that,' she assured him, understanding the implication in his question. Her parents were never violent, but their disapproval had been almost physical. Descending further in their opinion had always hurt in a way she still couldn't understand. 'But in the end I didn't have time to. I barely scraped a pass for my degree and that took every second of studying there was.' It had been the last promise to her parents, before they'd let her be and do what it was she wanted. Go to university. Get a degree. And then she'd be free.

And less than eight months later everything had changed.

'So, you wanted to go to a blues club without anyone recognising you?' he asked, returning to the original subject of their conversation.

She nodded, blinking back the emotion that threatened to overwhelm her.

'But marriage? To that idiot, André?'

Marit looked at the table. 'It wasn't his finest hour. But he is a good friend. He understood.'

'Understood what?'

'My situation. My future. That my husband will be chosen by the King of Svardia. That he will be titled, as the legislation requires for the second in line to the Svardian throne. That,' she said, a silent sob cutting into her words, 'the first—and last—person I ever kiss will be a stranger.'

Marit hadn't meant to reveal so much. She was usually better at hiding her feelings, or at least plunging them deep beneath an act of rebellion. Why was it this man that called forth the truth from her without even seeming to ask for it?

She reached for her glass, taking a mouthful of the sweet citrus drink, and blamed the alcohol for the sudden rawness in her throat and the jolt to her heart. Lykos turned in his seat and—with the bend of a single finger on a half-raised arm—summoned the waitress. After murmuring something quietly in Italian, she handed over her pad and a pen and disappeared, by which time Marit had swallowed the hitch in her throat and was composed.

'Make a list,' Lykos ordered.

'Of what?' Marit asked, catching the pad and pen he slid across the table.

'Of all the things you want to do before you return to Svardia.'

And, just like that, he surprised her again.

As the early morning's rays pierced through the crack in the curtains, Lykos pinched the bridge of his nose, trying to ward off the migraine that had started shortly after she'd handed him the list she'd made last night.

He should have known better. Really, he should have at least set some parameters. The list had been both shocking and not, and he'd sent her to her suite to order herself room service just to put some space between them. Because last night, instead of seeing Marit as a spoilt runaway princess, or even the key to getting shares in Kozlov's company, he'd seen a young girl being forced into a life she did not want. And it had reminded him of the way his mother used to look at him. Distaste and discomfort had swirled in his gut, leaving him with a bad taste in his mouth even now.

I was always going to go back.

That Marit seemed willing was unfathomable to him, and Lykos wasn't sure that it made anything about the situation remotely okay. He could see what she'd been trying to do with André now. Could even admit that in her position he might have done something similar. He shook his head and cursed.

What was her brother playing at? She was clearly too young to be married off to some stranger and forced to produce heirs like a broodmare. He would never understand that life, their kind. The kind for whom money, tradition and status dictated a life path no one in their right mind would choose. And her future husband would have to be titled. That spoke of extreme snobbery at best, and whispered of eugenics at worst.

But Lykos had made a deal. Unlike his father or Kyros, when he gave his word he meant it. Even if Marit made him question it. From the moment he'd arrived in London, the sting of Kyros's betrayal burning hot and hard in his heart, Lykos had realised that neither his mentor nor his father were models for the man he wanted to be. So he'd sat in that hotel room and decided: remade himself to who he wanted to be. He would never allow himself to be in that situation again. The only person he could trust was himself. And his words, his acts and his reputation were the only things that could never be taken from him. Aleksander had asked him to keep her from Svardia for five days and he would.

Five days. After her quite spectacular disappearing act, Lykos had imagined he'd spend the entire week trying to catch sand. But since the music venue the fight had gone out of her. The bone-deep defeat had reminded him of his mother and he'd hated seeing the same look in Marit's eyes. So when she'd started talking of things she'd wanted to do before she returned to Svardia, the solution had been clear. He would help her fulfil her wishes, and hopefully that would occupy her enough that she wouldn't cause any more trouble.

Entering the living area, he looked through the French windows to see the sunrise pouring across a pale blue horizon above the Milan skyline as he thought about the list of things Marit had scribbled on the pad. She'd spent such a long time on it that he'd thought her list would fill the entire page. Instead, only seven lines had been filled.

Ice cream in the park.

He'd expected that; after all, she'd said as much in the bar last night.

Eat at a café on the pavement like normal people.

Equally expected and completely doable.

Twenty-four hours out of sight and contact from the world.

Too easy. At this point, Lykos was more than happy to lock her in her room for a day. But some of the others… He squinted at the paper as if it might bring on the headache.

Go to a concert.

A little trickier.

Dance until my feet hurt.

Not impossible.

A tattoo.

His pulse raced a little more. No way was he going to be responsible for returning Marit to Aleksander indelibly marked with ink.

And then there was the last item on the list.

A date.

He felt the vibrations from the slide of the French windows in the adjacent suite and watched Marit walk towards the balcony railing, her hair strands of gold gently rippled by the wind.

He should have left her alone, used the time instead to figure out how on earth he was going to fulfil this list. Maybe even catch up on some sleep, which had been even more elusive than usual. But it was as if there were a piece of string tied between them; where she went he would follow and he felt the tug of it now, low in his gut, undeniable and irrefutable. It was the promise, he told himself as he followed it out onto the balcony.

Marit's gaze stayed locked on the horizon, even though she must have heard the slide of the French windows.

'It's early,' he stated.

'Would you lounge in bed if you had five days of freedom?'

'Yes, actually.'

'Says the man who can do whatever he wants whenever he wants.' She turned to him then, frowning, as if she took in the shadows beneath his eyes. 'You have trouble sleeping.'

He nodded once, surprised that the gesture raised the corner of her lips into a half-smile.

'Your list—'

She raised a hand, cutting him off midsentence. 'I know, they're silly and—'

'We're doing them.' The words cast his promise in stone.

She looked up at him, the sun balancing delicately behind her head, its rays setting her hair on fire, none of which compared to the sparks of golden fire dancing with the slivers of jade in her eyes. She bit her lip as if to prevent just how much it meant to her from escaping, but it failed. He felt her joy, her thanks like a punch to the solar plexus, so powerful he needed a moment to catch his breath.

'But first,' he said, forcing himself not to cast his gaze across her body as he wished, 'clothes.'

She looked momentarily confused, as if she'd forgotten that she'd run from Paris in his shirt and trousers, and then her eyes crinkled with mischief. 'Okay, but Aleksander pays.'

Marit twisted her body in the mirror, surprised by the fit of the wide-legged cropped trousers the shop assistant had promised her would look 'dee-vine'. Marit smiled. She wasn't sure about divine, but the burnt orange heavy cotton did look good. Contrary to the plans she'd had to rack up horrifying bills against her brother's account, she couldn't bring herself to be that wasteful.

Marit might have been overlooked by her parents but she'd always had the greatest of respect for the position their family held and the faith and trust of the Svardian people. Their family's money was the people's money, which was why she'd taken her university degree seriously, even if it hadn't been her choice. Which was the same reason Marit couldn't run up a huge debt just for some clothes.

Something Lykos seemed to be strangely irritated by. She had the sneaking suspicion that it was precisely because he had expected her to, and that made her feel…uncomfortable. Lykos clearly thought she was a spoiled little princess. And while Marit couldn't deny that she had grown up around money—something she instinctively knew Lykos disliked and distrusted— she had never taken that for granted. In the last eight months, her work with the kids in the city youth orchestra had brought her in touch with children from all levels of household income, some of which broke her heart to witness in her country. Just the thought of it made her feel guilty for running off, first with André, then to Milan. To be here now, it just felt…selfish.

With that feeling a dull echo in her heart, she folded up the bare essentials the shop assistant and she had decided on to get her through the next five days, and was about to leave when she heard a tap on the dressing room wall.

'I hope you don't mind, but I was wondering if you might try this on?' said the assistant, a blush on her cheeks at the odd request. 'It's just that my little sister designed the dress. She's working her way through fashion school and I know that it would look incredible on you.' The words rushed out of the proud older sister, and Marit was helpless to refuse.

The moment she was handed the oyster-coloured silk she felt tingles buzz along her skin as if in warning of how precious this moment was. She hung the dress on the hook and, refusing to think too hard on it, slipped out of her clothes and into material that felt like cream against her skin. Gently puffed sleeves gathered at her wrists, framing the V-neck sheath that fitted close to her chest and torso, snugly wrapping around her waist to pour down from her hips to the floor like a waterfall. But it was the hundreds of lines of tiny cream-coloured sequins through the whole dress that made it so magical. They were spaced at different intervals, the closer collection of sequin lines gathering at the front, from where they fell around the V and down, drawing the eye, making Marit look taller and more sophisticated than she'd ever felt.

The lines made her think of music, of sound waves, and although she'd intended to politely refuse the dress, Marit knew that she'd never forgive herself if she didn't take it with her.

The shop assistant gasped when she caught sight of her in the dress—'so beautiful'—the words for the dress as much as Marit, and Marit could only agree.

'Do you want to show your handsome man waiting so patiently out there for you?' she asked.

Something turned in Marit's chest and, biting her lip, she shook her head.

'Ah. Yes, so much better for it to be a surprise,' she whispered conspiratorially.

Marit turned back to look at herself in the mirror without replying, wondering suddenly whether she would ever wear the dress. For some reason she didn't feel that it would be part of her life in Svardia—instinctively knowing that this dress belonged to the five days of freedom a girl called Marit had been given, rather than the Princess who would soon become second in line to the throne. It would be a crime for this dress never to be seen in public and Marit was about to tell the assistant she'd changed her mind, but the woman had already whisked the dress away to be wrapped up.

When she emerged from the dressing room in the small boutique she almost stopped dead in her tracks. Lykos's tall frame lounged in a leather armchair, one leg bent lazily over the other. His elbow was pressed into the arm of the chair, his chin propped up by his thumb and his temple speared by his fingers and, despite the fact that his eyes were closed, he exuded such an air of sensuality that the other customer in the shop had stopped to stare.

Marit's heart stuttered and she pressed her thighs together, trying to quash the pulse of heat that flashed outward across her entire body.

'Are you done?' Lykos asked Marit without opening his eyes.

The other customer squeaked and fled the shop in embarrassment.

'That was cruel,' Marit chided as she went to the counter to make the call to the Svardian embassy to arrange payment.

'She was staring,' he replied, once again with his eyes closed, making Marit wonder if he had a headache.

'You're handsome. It's not her fault.'

There was a pause before his eyes sprang open and their gazes locked. He looked as if he were about to say something when, thankfully, the embassy answered the phone.

CHAPTER FIVE

His phone buzzed in his trouser pocket but he ignored it, unable to take his eyes off Marit as she charmed the ice cream vendor into providing ice creams for what looked like an entire school bus of children. This was not out of the kindness of the vendor's heart. No. Somehow Lykos was footing the bill.

She turned to look at him directly then, the smile full of bright red lipstick that suited the summery outfit she'd bought from the boutique. Rather than heading straight for stores with famous designers, instead she'd found a little privately owned shop with brightly coloured clothes that reminded Lykos of the films he and Theron used to watch at the open-air screen by the beach in Piraeus.

The dress made Marit's waist look even smaller, cinched by a broad belt, with a skirt that spun out when she turned, the ballet pumps on her feet more comfortable than stylish, but pretty nonetheless. She walked straight to him, perhaps she too was following the invisible thread between them, making his breath catch in his throat in a rather unmanly way, and returned his wallet to the inside pocket of his jacket, the contact shockingly intimate.

'Don't worry, Aleksander will reimburse you.'

Lykos's response of a growl was more grouse than

bite, partly because he was trying to control his body's worryingly swift reaction to her touch.

'It is, after all, for the children.' She play-pouted and he rolled his eyes. Spinning away from him, she took up a slow walk down one of the paths in Parco Sempione. Lykos had found it on the internet last night while trying to figure out how to get through Marit's list in the short time that they had. The largest park in Milan boasted lakes and views of the Arch of Peace, as well as being conveniently situated near their hotel.

His eyes scanned the area, the large group of happy children slowly working their way towards a sugar high, teachers trying to wrangle the few stragglers. A couple passed them hand in hand, the dark-haired man making him think of Theron and causing him to wonder how his partner, Summer, was getting on with their new baby. As his attention focused on a young boy, Lykos mentally kicked himself for ignoring Theron's most recent invitation. The baby was cute, he could admit that. But that didn't mean he had to drop everything and rush to admire his friend's progeny. Especially given the baby's biological connection to Kyros Agyros.

He pressed pause on his thoughts and slowed as he saw the young boy move to stand a little too close to the trouser pocket of one of the teachers. And while he might not be overly familiar with children's clothing, he did know clean from dirty, new from old. And he knew a child thief when he saw one. After all, he had been one of the best.

Marit had stopped a few feet ahead and turned to follow the direction of Lykos's gaze. Not wanting to alert the boy, Lykos gave what looked like his full attention to Marit as he pulled his wallet from his pocket discreetly and swapped out his credit card and driver's licence.

Marit frowned, clearly realising something was up but thankfully kept her silence. Lykos replaced the wallet in his trouser pocket as he reached Marit and held out his arm to her.

Bemused, Marit took his offer, threading her hand through the crook of his elbow and together they carried on their walk, just like the happy couple they had passed. Lykos wondered how long it would take the boy to notice a much richer mark and, not a minute later, he felt the grab. The boy jolted into him, not too hard, the pressure just right—as if he'd been trying to get round Lykos but misjudged. He imagined the park offered the kid a fair bit of income during the summer months and wouldn't begrudge the loss of the leather wallet at all.

'What was that about?' Marit asked, leaning into his arm conspiratorially after the boy had run off.

'What was what about?' Lykos replied, catching the moment the kid checked the contents of his wallet and saw the boy's eyes grow wide.

'The thing with your cards and your wallet?'

Lykos turned to her, his face purposely blank, but she wasn't buying it, not for one second. Sighing, he pulled her back onto the path as they made their way towards the Arch. 'Do you see that kid?'

'The one running off?' she asked.

Lykos nodded. 'He just stole my wallet.'

'What?' Marit demanded, shocked. 'Should we call the police?'

Lykos laughed. 'No. He earned it. It was a good lift.' Once again he felt the tug of her confusion. 'If I hadn't expected it, I doubt I would have felt it. It takes years of practice to get that good. And, besides, it was only money. As you saw, I'd removed my cards and ID beforehand.'

'How much was in the wallet?'

Lykos frowned. 'Five, maybe six?'

'Hundred euros?' Marit asked, her voice a squeak.

Lykos shrugged. He had more money than he knew what to do with. What he didn't have—as Kozlov pointed out to anyone who would listen—was pedigree. Unlike Marit. In that moment he knew he had more in common with the kid who'd stolen his wallet than the Princess walking beside him.

'So you let him take a wallet containing six hundred euros?'

'Marit, I know this may be hard for someone like you to understand, but if the kid is stealing wallets he probably needs the money.' Irritation and years old resentment rose to colour his words in harsh tones. And the look of hurt that marred her pretty eyes slapped against his conscience.

She looked at her feet, then off into the distance where they had last seen the boy. Marit nodded absently and gently withdrew her arm from his, the sudden snap of cold where there had been heat making him feel it even more. He could feel the burn of the blush marking his cheekbones, as much for his guilt as for the shame in what he was about to admit. 'I used to be that kid,' he thrust from between his clenched teeth.

It was her, he realised. It wasn't shame about his humble, if somewhat illegal, upbringing. It was because he didn't want her to look at him like Kozlov. As if he was still that same dirty, streetwise, backtalking kid.

'My father taught me how to steal, how to thieve, as soon as I could walk. By seven years old, he would drop me at a shopping centre and give me a number. If I didn't come back with that amount of money, I'd have to walk home.'

He hadn't spoken to anyone of his past for years. The memories made his throat thicken, his voice gravelly.

The muscle at his jaw pulsed and he rolled his shoulders to loosen the tension cording his neck. He felt the furtive touch of her gaze against his cheek, there and gone just as quick, an encouragement to continue.

'My father was a bastard,' he said, simply and truthfully. There had been no redemption for Aeolus Livas. Three years after his mother had left him at the orphanage, Lykos had been caught by some wannabe gangsters Lykos and Theron had tried to rob. One of them, a friend of his father's, recognised him, let him off the hook for old times' sake with a drunken mumbled apology for Lykos's loss. That was how he'd been told about his father's death. As he'd later found out, he'd crossed the wrong guy and had been 'dealt with'. And Lykos had never spared him another thought. Aeolus had been a better drunk than thief, and a violent husband on a good day. 'But don't think I didn't use the skills he taught me. I stole from rich businessmen who wouldn't miss their money in order to buy food. To buy water.' He shut his mouth before more revealing words could pour forth. Thirst. That was what he'd remembered most. Not the pangs of hunger gnawing at his stomach, or the fisted grip fear had on his mind, refusing to let him sleep. Delirious thirst. That had been the worst.

'What about your mother?'

The bright sky fractured into the starburst of a headache and he winced. 'She did what she had to,' he replied, coming to the end of the park and hailing a taxi.

'*The only way I'll be safe*,' his mother had said as she'd left him on the steps of the orphanage, '*is if he can never use you against me again.*'

Marit was less shocked by the devastating description of his childhood than the way Lykos swayed as he got out of the taxi at the hotel.

'Lykos—'

'Migraine.'

Pain arced across his features as if even that word had come at a price. Closing the door to the taxi, she slid beneath his arm so that she was able to support him. He looked down at her as if unsettled by her presence, but his gaze was so unfocused she knew he was in no position to argue. Benito held open the door for them and helped Marit up to the suite with Lykos, sliding the room key over the pad for her as she took more of Lykos's weight than he would ever have been comfortable with.

Benito waved off her thanks and retreated back into the hotel as Marit made her way to the bedroom in a suite that was the mirror image of her own. She backed them onto the edge of the bed and when Lykos was safely sitting she went immediately to draw the curtains across the windows, where the early afternoon's sun stretched rays out towards them.

There was enough glow from the light of the living room that she could see Lykos's outline but not so much that it caused him more pain. He tugged at the buttons on the shirt as he kicked off his shoes, Marit clenching her jaw seeing the pain even this seemed to cause him. She'd never had a migraine, but the headaches she had during her period always left her shaken. And that was what Lykos looked. *Shaken.* His face had lost that natural bronze of his tan, a slight greyness beneath the sheen of sweat that looked cold against his forehead. She went to him, kneeling on the floor, pulling his hand gently back from where he was struggling with his cufflinks.

'Ridiculous,' he managed.

'It's okay,' she soothed, slipping the cufflink through the hole and placing it on the floor beside her as if her skin wasn't covered with a thousand pinpricks. She looked up to meet the silvery gaze that found focus on her face and forced herself not to react to the wildfire that burned outwards from her heart to her chest, her legs, her body. His eyes flickered across her as if sensing it, as if tracing the burn patterns he'd caused across her skin, before closing his eyes as if disgusted with himself. For the vulnerability she had seen in him or for the desire he had seen in her, Marit couldn't tell.

Biting back the sting of such obvious rejection, she reached for his other cuff and removed the silver link. As Lykos sat unmoving she inhaled and, making her breath so silent as to not provoke him, she raised onto her knees and reached for the buttons on his shirt. She saw the flare of the muscle at his jaw, as if he was forcing himself still. Or maybe he was simply warding off the migraine. In that moment Marit would have given half of Svardia to know. Because then it would mean she wasn't alone in this crazy thing. The thing that had taken over her pulse and her breathing, that trembled beneath her skin wanting to get out, wanting to bring something in. Wanting *him*.

She slipped the button from its hole, anchoring her bottom lip with her teeth at the sight of the dark swirls of hair, her fingers trembling a little as they moved to free the next button. And the next. She was halfway down his torso when he moved, his chest filling with air and expanding beneath her hands. He leaned side to side, wincing in pain as he lifted the bottom of the shirt from the belted waist of his trousers and exhaled in sufferance. But when his eyes opened, the slice of silver that caught her was molten and fierce. As if she'd woken a slumbering dragon. She paused, caught in an act of theft, having selfishly stolen this moment for herself, only able to breathe when he closed his eyes again. Resisting the urge to shake the tingles that sparked from where her palms had pressed against his body, she slowly slipped the last button from its hole. Swallowing, she turned her face away from the strip of nakedness that tempted her beyond anything she'd ever experienced.

Logically the next step would be his belt and trousers, and the thought burned her cheeks with red slashes. Fingers shaking, she went to reach for his belt and suddenly her hands were caught in a powerful vice. She looked up to find Lykos's eyes clear and full of intent.

'Go.'

She took a breath.

'Now.'

She didn't need to be told twice.

Lykos took stock before he opened his eyes. The pounding in his head was gone and, gently turning from side to side, the severe pain cording his neck with tension had dissipated to almost nothing. He checked the clock and marvelled that he'd slept through the night all the way to seven in the morning.

By now, Lykos knew the drill. Every few months, the sleeplessness he'd experienced ever since he was a child would catch up with him and he'd have an episode. If he'd been able to return Marit to Svardia she wouldn't have been witness to his weakness. Frustration as much as determination forced him to open his eyes.

Marit. Milan. Cufflinks. *Christé mou*, his belt.

Go. Now.

The look in her eyes as she'd fled the room. The look in her eyes *before* she'd fled the room.

Thank God he hadn't been so out of it last night that he'd reached for all the comfort she was offering, consciously or otherwise. And, just like that, the fantasy of crushing her to him, seeking comfort, an orgasm blowing the migraine from his body… He groaned as need shaped him, hardened him with an arousal that would never be satiated.

He couldn't touch her. She was a princess. She was an *innocent* princess he was charged with protecting. He'd given Aleksander his word and nothing, not even an increasingly urgent desire for her, would stop him from honouring that. Because if he didn't keep his word, all the money in the world wouldn't make him different to his father, or to Kyros. He'd be just like them. Men who betrayed their families, men who betrayed *themselves*. The thought alone was enough to douse the fire in him and force him to the en suite bathroom and beneath the powerful, frigid jets of water in the shower.

He emerged fifteen minutes later, dressed and about to go looking for Marit, when he heard voices out on the balcony. *His* balcony. He took in the strange angle of the pillow and the hotel quilt and realised that Marit must have slept on the sofa. That she'd stayed, even after his harsh order for her to leave… She'd stayed because of her concern for him. That realisation twisted something deep in his gut.

But, *Theé mou*, if he'd known she was within reach…

And, just like that, all the ice-cold shower's good work was undone in seconds. He bit back a curse. Even as a teenager he didn't think he'd been this driven by his hormones. Forcing his body back under control, he made his way out onto the balcony, squinting slightly at the early-morning sun with still-sensitive eyes.

Marit had turned towards the Milan cityscape but Benito greeted him with a small deferential bow, which Lykos immediately waved off.

'I brought Miss Marit some breakfast and coffee. There is fresh fruit, but if you would like something more—'

'*Grazie*, Benito. This is more than fine,' he said, standing by the table. Marit flashed Benito a radiant smile as he left, and returned her gaze to the horizon.

Lykos hovered. Why, he didn't quite know. He wasn't accustomed to hovering, but Marit had this effect on him and he didn't like it one bit.

'About last night—'

'There is nothing to say,' she replied, finally turning to look at him, squinting up into the morning sun.

Lykos opened his mouth.

'Coffee?' she asked. 'I'm sure it's absolutely the worst thing you should do after a migraine, but you don't strike me as a hot water and lemon kind of man.'

It was on his tongue to ask what kind of man she found him, but thankfully he had a few working brain cells left to stop him. Instead, while his grunted response was far from eloquent, it did the job. She poured him a steaming cup of heaven and retreated to her side of the table that she had magicked onto the balcony. Without his notice.

In the last twelve hours, Lykos had shown more vulnerabilities to this one woman than he had to anyone in a lifetime. Bad enough that she'd seen his episode, but that he'd been so out of it that she had slept in the next room and had a table brought through the suite onto the balcony without him stirring?

Unacceptable.

He opened his mouth to speak, but again she cut him off and he barely resisted the urge to growl.

Marit was struggling to meet Lykos's eye. She'd had a terrible night's sleep, which had nothing whatsoever to do with the sofa. No. She'd tossed and turned the entire night because of him. Because of this thing. It was as if a switch had been flipped and now she couldn't stop the…the…things.

Until at around four that morning she'd remembered what had happened before the migraine.

I know this may be hard for someone like you…

It wouldn't take a rocket scientist to pick up on all the little hints and subtleties at his dislike of her status. The way he said 'Princess', his surprise when she hadn't chosen the most expensive dress or train ticket, or the way he showed more deference to those with lower incomes. It had been strange at first for a billionaire, but what he'd said last night about his father, about growing up on the streets of Athens…

She passed him the cup of coffee she poured him and before she could stop herself she asked, 'How did you get from the streets of Athens to here?'

He stood beside the table looking down at her, holding the small white cup, and the look on his face would have been comical if it hadn't been full of a deep shock that made her wish a thousand times over to take it back. Her question was blunt, untimely and clearly in bad taste. But she hadn't been able to stop herself. She'd spent the entire night tossing and turning, thinking of him as a man and then as a small child, vulnerable to his father's demands…but what about his mother? And how had he ended up on the streets? The uncomfortable silence between them stretched several heartbeats, lasting much longer than she wanted to experience ever again.

'Why, Princess, you'd like to hear my rags-to-riches story?' he mocked. 'You don't believe such a thing can happen?' His questions were bitter and resentful, and utterly justified.

The shame she felt coursing through her from her crass question burned through her, mocking the heat for him she'd felt last night. 'Lykos, I'm sorry. I didn't mean it like that.'

'Then how did you mean it, Princess? Because from where I'm standing—'

'I want to know about you!' The words ripped from her throat, angry and raw. Something changed then. She saw the question reframed in his eyes, the context of last night filtering through to the morning.

'No, Marit. You don't want to know about me.'

Anger, thick and fast, boiled into her bloodstream. How many times had she been told what she did and didn't want? What she could and couldn't do. As if she had no sense of herself, her wants, her desires. Her parents or her siblings, the tutors at university leading her dissertation into an area 'safe' for a princess, safe enough to secure the basic grade she was barely going to scrape.

Her fingers began to itch as her pulse tripped into three-four time. She knew better by now than to fight how people saw her. And she could only imagine how Lykos saw her. Spoiled little princess with no idea of how the world worked. Marit wasn't *that* naïve. She knew there would always be parts of life and the world she would never experience, but that didn't mean she couldn't respect or empathise with those who had different experiences. It had been part of what she'd wanted to achieve with the youth orchestra project. Because one thing she did know was how it felt to not be able to speak of your emotions, feelings that were sometimes bigger than words, that were either impossible to say or would never be heard. But music? It had been a release for her. Through it she'd been able to channel that inexplicable sense of the chaos of her feelings. And she'd wanted so much to help children find that same way of expressing themselves.

Marit nodded, acknowledging Lykos's dismissal, rejection building from a very deep place within her. It was as if someone had whispered *prestissimo* to her body, the blood rushing through her veins as fast as possible. She left without another word, and he let her go.

She passed the sofa she had not slept a wink on, left his suite and swiped her card into hers. She closed the door behind her and resisted the urge to collapse back against it. Instead, she went to the suite's control panel and brought up the sound system settings. She linked her phone to the programme and picked a playlist, turning the volume loud enough to be heard, in all likelihood, above and below. Marit finally didn't care. Because it was also loud enough to drown out the voices that taunted and teased her heart into misery.

Lykos exhaled heavily when the music stopped blaring about three hours later. If he hadn't already recovered from his migraine, the noise from her suite would definitely have brought it on. Any hope he'd had of getting some work done had been obliterated as a classical piece of music swept into a jazzy froth that transitioned into a sassy bluesy number which morphed into a soulful folk song. On the surface, all the pieces were different and had absolutely nothing in common. But Lykos recognised something slithering through each piece, something that spoke of hurt and hope and need, that pulled at his conscience for being too harsh on Marit. That same something that spoke of a complexity he knew Marit had, but he didn't want to see.

He'd lashed out at her. Yes, her question had caught him by surprise and, yes, it had been blunt, but she hadn't deserved his scorn. Yesterday, she hadn't chosen the most expensive designer labels to fill her replacement wardrobe with, she'd chosen a small family-run boutique. She hadn't gorged on every single ice cream in the park yesterday, she'd had one and bought the rest for a group of schoolchildren. The list of things she wanted to do before she returned—it wasn't full of impossibly rich destinations and luxurious experiences—they were things that she would never get to do once she became second in line to the throne: once she became the female face of Svardian royalty. Once she became a wife, a mother.

Not that it mattered. She was, and always would be, a princess.

A princess he was stuck with for another four days.

His phone pinged again and this time he ignored it. Thinking back over her question, it was like an earworm, digging into his thoughts.

I want to know about you!

He felt the difference between Marit's curiosity and the way that business associates had started to look at him since Kozlov had unearthed the facts of his childhood and started spreading rumours. Hers wasn't the eager glee, poring over his poverty, abuse and betrayals as if they were a form of entertainment. But what Lykos couldn't account for was the urge to tell her about it.

Before he could change his mind, he left the suite and knocked on the door to Marit's. He spent so long imagining her response when she opened the door that it took him a moment to realise that she *wasn't* there.

Anger flashed through his entire body. The music, the volume—a ruse? She had run away again and he had fallen for it entirely. Her sweetness and innocence—it was all an act. Cursing, he returned to his suite, thankful

CHAPTER SIX

LYKOS BURST FROM the door at the side of the hotel onto the pavement, startling a dog walker and causing the little beast to howl disapprovingly. Inside, he felt…betrayal, the cold, hard, familiar twist of it turning in his gut. And stupid. He felt stupid. He was usually much more careful than this, better at seeing through people's lies. He'd had to be. But he'd been distracted by a pretty face and a princess's tantrum.

No. He'd been distracted because he thought he'd seen the truth in her eyes when she'd claimed to want to know about him. A *princess*. And now she'd run. He should have known better. His heart was pounding heavily in his chest, not from the run but from *her*.

He cursed loudly in Greek and fisted his hand. It caught Benito's attention and he came rushing over.

'Signor—'

'Have you seen her?' he asked, his gaze sweeping back and forth across the street.

'Miss Marit? Yes, she asked about a street café and I directed her to Carlotta's.'

'What?' Lykos asked, his brain trying to clear through the damp fog of his thoughts, unable to understand why Marit would have asked Benito about a café. Unless it was another misdirect, his cynical mind suggested.

'Carlotta's. It's by the park. I'll send you the directions I gave Miss Marit.'

Lykos started jogging in the direction Benito had gestured and, pulling his phone from his pocket when it pinged, he realised he had several missed calls and text messages. He frowned. No one texted him these days. He pulled down the top bar and saw that just beneath a work email were four text messages from a number he'd programmed into his phone two days ago.

Didn't want to bother you, but got a little hungry and thought I'd cross something off my list. Benito knows where I am if you want to join me, but no pressure.

PS This is Marit. I'm assuming you have my number.

PPS And clearly you could track my phone should you wish.

His jog slowed to a walk as he read Marit's first message, and he slowed to a stop as he read the next and the next. Each one threw his feelings into even more confusion until he felt vaguely nauseous. She hadn't run from him this time.

He looked up and saw tables and chairs spilling onto the open square beneath an awning that said 'Carlotta's' in bright blue against brilliant white. At one of the tables he saw her, a cascade of beautiful golden hair and a pair of hazel eyes staring at him. Eyes that morphed from pleased to hurt, before the shutters came down as a waiter brought her a bulbous glass of something bright orange. Her smile to the café's employee was glorious and generous and the poor boy looked as if he'd been struck by lightning. Lykos walked towards Marit's table, unable to take his eyes from her, sliding his phone in his pocket before taking the seat opposite her.

'You thought I'd run,' she accused, glancing towards him, unable to hide the hurt that marred her features.

His stomach twisted, but he wouldn't do her the dishonour of lying to her. 'Yes.'

She turned her head aside in the most gracious of cuts and a conscience he seemed to have grown only in the last two days jabbed and prodded again. He called the waiter over with a raise of his finger, his gaze still locked on Marit. He ordered a beer, not his usual drink but it was early in the day and for some reason he felt a nostalgic pull towards it.

'I don't think I've had a beer since I was with Theron in Piraeus over ten years ago,' he revealed. Nothing in him ever wanted to discuss his past. But with Marit? It was especially hard with her. It felt as if it would create an even greater divide between the Princess and the one-time pauper. But she had asked because she wanted to know and, instinctively, he felt it would be a peace offering that she'd understand. And maybe if they stopped fighting each other and kept that truce he would stop feeling this twisting frustration that had him by the gut. Maybe if he answered her question from that morning the desire he saw burning golden flecks in her hazel eyes would burn to dust.

'I met Theron about two years after my mother left me at the orphanage. I was nine and he was seven. His parents had been killed in an earthquake that devastated Athens and he was so wide-eyed and scared.' Lykos shook his head thinking about the vulnerable little boy his oldest friend had been back then. 'Of course he'd kill me for telling you that,' he said, allowing the bond of friendship to pull his lips into a small smile. A friendship they'd only just rekindled. He paused while the waiter placed the beer in front of him and stared at it a beat before reaching for the condensation-covered glass.

'We were the scourge of Athens,' he announced with pride, tipping his drink upward in a toast, a title thoroughly earned and utterly justified. 'No businessman's wallet was safe, no unsuspecting tourist's camera and phone protected. One time, we stole a whole tray of muffins from a coffee vendor. Theron tells me the old man has neither forgotten nor forgiven it,' he said with the huff of a laugh.

Marit's gaze was drawn by his words, her eyes sparkling as he told her more stories of the easy, gentle thievery he and Theron had used to get up to. No one ever left out of pocket too badly and no one ever hurt. He told her about lifting Kyros Agyros's wallet. How Theron's soft heart had made him insist they returned it to the billionaire businessman when he'd seen a picture of the man dancing with his wife.

'Kyros was…' Lykos shook his head, feeling that powerful force he'd first felt when he'd met the older man '…impressive. Rich. *Very* rich,' he said wryly. 'What he saw in two street kids, I'll never know. But he made us an offer. He paid for our education, trained us, taught us everything we could learn, with the condition that we went to work for him after finishing school and national service. And every Sunday he invited us for dinner at his house with his wife, Althaia.' His heart twisted with grief from her passing three years ago, despite not having seen her for over ten years.

Marit frowned, as if noticing the swift turn in his feelings. 'I'd never been foolish enough to look up to Kyros the way that Theron did—' *Liar*, his newly vocal conscience claimed. 'But I did respect him. Until he sent me looking for an Englishwoman. An Englishwoman with a little girl who had Kyros's eyes.'

And, just like that, the scales had fallen from his eyes. His mentor wasn't the kind, devoted married businessman, determined to help two kids from the streets, to treat them like the sons he'd never had. No, Kyros Agyros was just like everyone else: ready to use Lykos's debt to buy his silence.

'Oh.' There was a glimmer of understanding in Marit's eyes and he could see the pulse flicker at her throat, her soft heart beating with too much empathy.

'Kyros's wife was ill. She had multiple sclerosis. For Althaia it was a life sentence, and it made Kyros's betrayal so much worse.' Anger coloured his words with gravel and sand. 'I presume he sent me thinking I would be so grateful that I'd not say anything to Althaia.' Kyros's betrayal had cost Lykos everything: the family unit he'd never thought he'd have after his mother's abandonment disappearing in the blink of an eye.

'Instead of going back to Greece, I went straight to a small hotel in London.' It had been years since Lykos had allowed himself to think of those first few days. The blinding pain of being used and betrayed by the man he'd thought of as his *true* father. The shocking blow to his sense of self and everything he'd known had brought on a migraine so bad Lykos had almost called an ambulance. But when the aura of agony had receded, Lykos felt a clarity of thought he'd not experienced before.

'While I was there, I used the money I'd saved from the two years working for Kyros to play the stock markets.' For the first time, Lykos's sleeplessness had become a benefit. During the late-night hours he'd hunted the stock markets for quick hits and even quicker sales, surprised to find that the lessons he'd learned from his father—misdirection, disguise, speed and intense focus—had become a transferable skill. Kyros's act of betrayal had further forced a complete trust in himself and his own instincts.

But those skills were the only thing from his past that Lykos chose to take with him into the future. From that moment on, he promised he'd never trust anyone but himself. He'd chosen the tenets he would live by: his words, his acts and his reputation. His future was severed irrevocably from his past as a thief from the streets of Athens.

'Within a month I had doubled my savings,' he said, no trace of arrogance tainting the statement of fact, no hint of the negative bent of his thoughts. 'Within the first year my name was a whispered warning, and in five years I had majority shares in more companies than I could remember the names of.'

Over the years, more and more companies had required face-to-face meetings and, after his childhood on the streets, he had settled easily into a nomadic way of life in luxury hotels across Singapore, Zurich, New York, Hong Kong, Toronto, Sydney and here in Milan. Not once in all that time had anyone peered too closely at his past. Not once in all that time had anyone *wanted* to know.

Until Kozlov.

Until *Marit*.

'And that is how I got from the streets of Athens to here,' he said, finally taking a sip of his beer, the amber liquid tasting like memories and regret.

Marit didn't think Lykos had meant to reveal so much, but she'd been able to see through his words to the betrayal he had felt at the hands of his mentor. After a father who had given Lykos nothing but abuse and mistreatment, to be used by a man he'd thought was safety and hope personified…it must have been devastating for him. Yet he simply shrugged dismissively as if it hadn't cost him a thing.

'It's an incredible achievement,' she said sincerely.

He simply inclined his head as if acknowledging the truth of her observation while not taking the praise. Marit reached for her drink. The large slice of orange soaking in the midday sun made the drink look frivolous, not to mention the candy-striped straw and the little cocktail umbrella.

Lykos swallowed, put his beer back onto the thick white cotton covered table, leaned forward and nudged the paper umbrella before she could pick up the glass. 'You and your sweet tooth.' He tutted as if disappointed, the tease pulling at the corner of her mouth, anchoring her in the present and away from the shadowy images he had painted in her mind of a childhood that couldn't have been more different from her own.

He leaned back in his chair, his gaze holding her enthralled, forgetting her drink, forgetting their fight and once again that awareness twisted and turned deep within her. It smashed the defences she'd built last night and suddenly they were back in that darkened room, her breath caught in her lungs, his chest beneath her palms—

'What was growing up like for a princess?'

His question snapped her back into the present as if she were on a leash he held and because she was so distracted the truth fell from her lips.

'Lonely.'

They both blinked at her answer and she shook her head, trying to understand why this man seemed the only person to whom she said what she never wanted to say. Focusing on picking at an imaginary bit of fluff from her trouser leg, she had marshalled her features by the time she looked back up at him, her voice cool as she said, 'I'm sure you don't want to hear about the poor little Princess.'

He held her gaze and in it she heard her words to him earlier that day. *I want to know about you!*

She would have given anything to hear him say that. It made her cheeks pink and her heart turn. He was stubborn enough to keep on staring at her in silence until she answered his question, even if it took all afternoon.

'There are little girls all around the world who dream of being a princess,' she said.

'Not you?'

Marit shook her head and shrugged easily. 'How can you dream of what you already are?'

Only she wasn't. Not really. Freya was the real Princess. Loved by the people and her parents and, despite the sting of jealousy, loved by Marit most of all. The absence of her parents' attention—love—had always made her feel *invisible*. As if she didn't matter. As if her thoughts and feelings weren't important. But it had been Freya who came to her room when Marit had a nightmare. Freya who soothed her tears when she fell over. Freya who told Aleksander to stop being a beast for hiding her toys. Freya who helped get Marit out of the palace maze when one of their nannies got distracted. But even Freya hadn't quite been able to compensate for the lack of love Marit received from their parents.

'So, you are what you always wanted to be?' he asked, the doubt in his tone making it clear he too thought little of her being a princess.

'I wanted to be a musician,' she said, wanting to

pierce the arrogance of his response. 'But a royal cannot be such a thing.'

'Who decided that?'

Marit stifled the urge to make a pithy comment, to hide her hurt in a joke or a distraction, but Lykos had honoured her with the truth and she would not disrespect him in return. 'My parents. It wasn't up for debate,' she said, taking a sip of her Aperol Spritz, not tasting the sweet orange and herby bitterness of it at all.

'What were they like?' His silvery gaze glinted in the afternoon sun and she couldn't shake the sense that he was hunting her response for something that would explain who she was on a level she didn't want him to see.

'They were the King and Queen of Svardia.'

He levelled her with that gaze that demanded answers, demanded honesty.

'They were distracted and very busy. Always in meetings, or on trips to far-flung countries,' she said simply. 'Papa wasn't supposed to have ruled, but his brother died in an accident before he had heirs, so he was propelled into a position I don't think he wanted.' It was the first time she had said the words out loud and the first time she wondered for the space of a heartbeat if she might have something in common with the stern-jawed, dark-eyed man who was her father. That he had never been meant to rule had always made Marit wonder if that was somehow to blame for the way her parents immersed themselves so deeply into the role that they rarely looked up. 'But he certainly made sure that Aleksander and Freya knew their roles and their future responsibilities.'

'And you?'

'The only expectation for me was to stay out of trouble.' So simple, and yet so damaging too. At dinners, their parents tested and prepared her siblings. Even if Freya tried to bring her into the conversation, it never lasted long. Aleksander had watched with a kind of helpless fury which had only made things worse and, in the end, Marit had settled with trying to make the silent waiting staff react to little silly pranks unseen by her parents.

'Well, that worked out well.'

She held her hands up in mock surrender. 'It was absolutely not my fault that the son of the German ambassador ended up with cherry juice all down his front just seconds before the photographs.'

Lykos raised an eyebrow.

'He got handsy! And how on earth was I supposed to know that my skirt was tucked into my knickers on the red carpet on the New Year's Eve parade?'

Lykos choked on his beer. 'What about the suspension from boarding school?' he demanded when he'd recovered.

'Yes, okay. I'll admit to that, but—'

'And the skiing trip that cut your mother's trip short when you were fourteen?'

It was as if a knife sliced through the afternoon, silently knocking the air from her lungs. Marit hated that this one moment in her history still had such a debilitating effect on her. She tried to smile it off, but Lykos had seen, she could tell by the way he leant forward across the table, the way his eyes narrowed.

'What?'

'What?' she asked in response, as if she had any hope of covering it.

'Marit.' His voice was a warning.

'Ah, yes. The infamous skiing trip that ruined my parents' very important trip to Japan,' she said, her tone full of a humour that hurt. 'The one where my mother was photographed leaving the private plane chartered to return her home. Snapped on the steps of the hospital looking so very concerned as she spoke to the senior surgeon. And even caught in the act of shaking the hands of the nurses that had helped care for her daughter. The one,' Marit said, unable to conceal the years' old hurt from her voice, 'where my mother never actually came to see me. *That* skiing trip.'

Marit hated that she sounded like such a child. Hated that it made her want to cry. In front of this man who had endured so much worse. Did he know just how embarrassing it was to admit that her mother couldn't even be bothered to come and see her in the hospital? That Marit mattered so little to her.

She wished she could make him understand. But how could she explain the agony of the loneliness of her childhood? The anguish of feeling invisible in a palace full of people. As if she were screaming and no one heard her.

Lykos ground his teeth together to prevent the words from coming out of his mouth. Was he guilty of seeing her cynically, as 'the poor little Princess'? Absolutely. Could he understand why her parents couldn't conceive of her as a musician? Probably. He wasn't sure why it seemed unfathomable, but it did. But for her mother to cancel a trip, ensure that she was photographed arriving at her child's sickbed and not visit the child?

Lykos had been forced to grow up quickly and, although he'd never admit it to a living soul, he'd still never stopped wanting his mother. There was only one reason he had stayed away from her all this time and that was because it had been her request. But Marit's mother had been at the hospital and *not* seen her child. He just couldn't comprehend it.

'Were you unconscious when she visited?'

Marit looked up, blonde hair gently curling in the wind, eyes wide as if half afraid that closing them would release the tears he could see gathering. She risked it and only one fell, but Marit didn't seem to notice it as it slipped down her cheek. The sight of it tore at something deep in his chest.

'No. She left before I was out of surgery.' She shook her head and painted on a smile. 'Freya arrived so it was okay.'

'When did she arrive?'

'As soon as she could.'

'When?'

'Three hours after I'd woken up.'

Finally, as if she were too tired to fight any more, the mask dropped and he saw it. The hurt, the rejection—so different to his own yet so familiar. How had it taken him this long to recognise it in her? Was that why he reacted so strongly to her? He was normally infallible when it came to seeing what people wanted to hide; when had he become arrogant in his assumption that she was simply the spoiled runaway Princess?

Christé mou, he cursed. There was nothing spoiled about her.

The waiter came to enquire about their drinks and, checking his watch, Lykos asked Marit if she was ready to tick something off her list. The smile on her face and the brightness in her eyes was his reward and someone dropped a glass and Lykos didn't even notice.

They ordered lunch and Lykos moved the conversation to easier things, partly so he could take in and reframe all that he knew about her. She ordered a pizza and ate it with her hands, laughing more in the sunshine than he could have imagined. He had pasta, but he'd never be able to say what sort it was because the only thing he remembered of that afternoon was feeling lighter than he had done since he could remember.

While she was freshening up his phone rang and, absentmindedly, he answered.

'What are you up to, Livas?' The Russian accent coming through the phone's earpiece was thick and harsh in the Italian sunshine.

'Actually, I've decided to take a bit of a holiday.'

'You don't do holidays. But to find that you *do* blondes is interesting to me. Princess Marit, she's quite a beauty. Though what she's doing with a street thug like you, I've no idea.'

No one watching Lykos would think that he felt anything in response to the Russian's statement. But deep down he was as close to violence as he had ever been. His pulse rocketed from nought to sixty and he felt a cold sweat break out across his shoulders. 'She has nothing to do with you, Kozlov.'

'On the contrary, she is the sister of the man who owns a number of shares in my company and is therefore of *great* interest to me.'

'It's a rather large number of shares, from what I hear,' Lykos warned, reacting immediately to the implied threat to Marit.

His accent harsh and anger dripping from each word, Kozlov's response was a guttural growl. 'I've allowed you to chase the scraps I have cast aside because it amused me. But no more.'

The line went dead just as Marit appeared from the back of the restaurant.

Kozlov's threat circled in Lykos's mind and fury

burned incandescent within him. Swallowing the fiery heat of his rage, he marshalled his features with a ruthlessness honed over many years. While Marit was walking though the restaurant, completely unaware of the waiter's puppy-dog eyes, Lykos's mind processed options at the speed of light.

That Kozlov knew about Marit now was untenable, and the first chance he got he would call Aleksander to warn him. Kozlov might see the shareholder as a threat now that the Svardians had been linked to him, Lykos realised. A cold, hard fist gripped him. He would never put Marit in danger.

In the space of a heartbeat, Lykos was six years old, skinny, thin and utterly helpless against the sound of violence in the room next door. A tremor rose within him, cracking and fracturing the stone seal he'd placed on the memories of those nights. *The only way I'll be safe is if he can never use you against me again.* A cold sweat broke out across the back of his neck and as Marit approached, bringing sunshine and warmth with her back to the table, he still felt as if he had plunged his hands into an oil slick.

No. This time he would get it right. He would protect her.

She sat down and was about to say something, but she frowned, choosing something entirely different to ask instead. 'What's wrong?'

'We have to go.' The words ground out of him as he signalled to the waiter.

'Back to the hotel?'

'Yes. But only to pick up our things.'

'Why?' she asked, confusion clouding the precious shards he loved seeing in her eyes.

'We're going to London.'

CHAPTER SEVEN

MARIT GAZED OUT of the window of the car winding its way from a private airfield on the outskirts of London through city streets bathed in a teal-coloured dusk. She refused to look at the self-made Greek billionaire who had remained thin-lipped and grim with determination throughout their journey. Something had happened while she'd been freshening up in the bathroom and by the time she'd returned to the table the warm glow of an afternoon spent with someone she had come to admire, to find amusing, both of which had been more of a shock than the almost constant pull of awareness she felt to him, was gone. She thought they'd made a connection, shared an understanding that had made her feel…seen.

She almost laughed at herself for being so foolish. Before Lykos had come along, she'd made her peace with stepping into her sister's shoes. She'd even begun to hope that finally she might be able to prove herself worthy of her title, finally able to exceed the expectations her family had always lowered for her. In some way, André had been part of that peace. It wasn't love. They hadn't even kissed. But they'd both hoped their friendship would be enough to get them through their futures.

And then Lykos had barged into her hotel room and everything had changed.

Sharing ice cream in the park, having lunch together, sharing confidences... She had felt like a sunflower turning towards the sun, she had felt her soul sparkle when he'd teased her, when he'd been impressed by her. She'd found herself wanting to earn his admiration, his respect, his *affection*. It had shown her what had been and what would be missing from her life after she returned to Svardia. It had made her want to reach out to him, hold him to her for the short while they had.

Until he had whisked them from Milan to London. His withdrawal from her, the meaningful silence between them, felt horribly similar to how her parents had often been with her. But somehow this hurt more. She shivered at the thought and, without word or question, Lykos simply adjusted the temperature controls. With her gaze on the crowds of people flocking the central London streets, even at this time of the early evening, she unclenched her jaw. 'Why are we in London?'

Turning in the silence between them, she found his gaze locked on her. And because she was looking so intently herself, she saw it. The moment the lie formed in his mind.

'We're here for your date.'

She swallowed the wave of hurt that threatened to clog her throat with tears. 'My date?' she asked, her lips strangely numb.

'Yes. On your list. We're going on your date tonight.'

'How lovely,' she replied, while inside something curled in on itself, irrevocably wounded. For just a moment back in Milan, Marit had trusted him, found comfort with him, happiness even, and Lykos had lied to her, obliterating any sense of connection she'd felt.

She'd had it all wrong, she realised. He'd never seen her at all.

Lykos had called Aleksander while Marit had slept on the private jet. The King had offered the support of the security services, but Lykos had refused. More people meant more attention and more notice. Years ago, he'd learned that small meant quick, nimble and often invisible. As such, keeping it to him and Marit was actually the safer option. Aleksander had agreed, but his embassy was on alert and he gave Lykos a direct telephone number that would be changed the moment Marit was back on Svardian soil.

Lykos appreciated the reminder and it became a mental line in the sand. After he returned Marit to Svardia, everything would go back to normal. He'd have the shares to bring Kozlov down and be able to return to the nomadic lifestyle that he enjoyed: hotels in every city, a willing woman in every bar who'd appreciate a brief encounter as much as he did. No one to ask meaningful questions, no one to dig deeper than he wished. His future was as he liked it, on his terms and his terms only: alone and uncomplicated.

He looked out of the window, wondering why it felt a little hollow.

We're here for your date.

It had been the only reason he could think of to explain why they had left Milan and now Lykos was taking Marit on a date. Which was very complicated. He clenched his jaw as he called himself every single kind of fool. He could tell that Marit was upset by his withdrawal, but his intention to break the connection forming between them had been for her own good. And then he'd gone and told her he was taking her on a date.

The car pulled up outside the black iron railings that fronted the Regency terrace townhouse he'd bought after a year in London. He had wanted it on first sight. It was everything that he'd not been, everything that he'd not had growing up: money, history, permanence, sophistication. It wasn't quite a castle, but it wasn't far off.

Beside him, Marit was staring up at the townhouse with a frown.

'This is yours?'

'Yes,' he said, pride and satisfaction infusing his tone. 'You don't like it?'

'I do,' she said, peering through the car window, still taking in the perfect façade. 'It just doesn't feel like you.' With that she exited the car, closing the door behind her and leaving him feeling...confused.

He got out. 'What do you mean?' he called over the roof of the car, but she was through the gate and had followed the driver with their luggage to the front door.

Unlike his properties in Europe, this purchase had nothing to do with convenience. He'd had a large amount of work done restoring or recreating as much of the original fixtures and mouldings as possible because, while it was everything his childhood hadn't been, it was exactly what he wanted in his future. It was why he'd teased Theron with his desire to buy the Soames estate, which was as close to a castle as one could get. Lykos had always wanted that grandeur, something that would *endure*, a level of class that would protect him from the harm done to him in the past. At least that was how it had felt to him until Marit had taken one look and seen right through it.

When he reached her at the front door she turned to him, the security light turning her hair even more golden and her eyes glistening. 'It is perfect for the financial genius that stalks international stock exchanges,' she assured him.

He opened the door with the press of his thumb to the security pad, realising that her final observation didn't make him feel much better, and ushered her through to the hallway. He picked up their luggage and brought it across the threshold to find her standing there, hands held to her chest, something else clearly on her mind.

He put down their bags as her lips quivered into a reluctant smile. 'I've never been on a date before.'

Theé mou, she was too innocent even to be in his company. That he was taking her on her first date…she deserved so much better. She deserved—

'I'm glad it's you,' she said, looking up at him, the truth of her words shining in her eyes. 'Don't get me wrong,' she rushed to say. 'I know that this is because of my list, that this isn't real. Not really,' she said with a shrug of her shoulder that made him want to argue with her, to disagree wholeheartedly. 'But it's not and I think it would have been worse if it had been.'

'Why?' Curiosity meant the question sprang from his lips before he could call it back.

'Because…' She frowned, little lines marring her forehead as she sought the right words. 'Because if I had to return to Svardia and marry a man of my brother's choosing after feeling…more for someone else, I think that would have been a tragedy.'

It was as if she'd struck him with a knife and twisted, all the while smiling prettily as if nothing were horrifying about what she'd just said. She hadn't meant 'more', she'd meant love. And in that one sentence,

Lykos realised what it *really* meant for her to return to Svardia and marry a man appropriate for the second in line to the throne.

An hour later Marit stood before the mirror in the guest room and turned, watching the way the sequins flashed and flickered in beautiful lines running down the front of the dress like streams of water. As the only dress she had with her, there hadn't even been a choice, for which she was thankful as she might not have had the courage to wear it otherwise. Against the oyster-coloured silk, the cream sequins were only visible when they caught the light and were more breathtaking for it.

Marit looked at a reflection that she had never seen before. The dress clung to curves that were womanly, elegant and beautiful. She didn't feel like a child playing dress-up. She felt…like *her*. Like how she was supposed to be seen. The silk fell from low on her hips and rippled into fluted waves that looked nothing short of luxurious and the deep V at her breast was short of indecent but long past conservative.

She leaned into the mirror to put the last sweep of mascara to her eyelashes, and if she had to blink a little to press back the desire for this entire evening to be real then that was what she had to do. The little antique bronze clock on the table beside the large bed clicked over to seven, chiming prettily seven times, announcing the hour Lykos had told her the car would arrive to take them on their date.

But in her heart it rang for something else. This was her third night and she was just over halfway through the time she had left. Pressing a hand to her sternum to soothe her heart, she realised that it wasn't the return to Svardia that was feeding the sense of urgency in her breast. Actually, she was beginning to hope that she could show her parents, her siblings that she could do it, that she *could* be trusted in Freya's role.

But she was painfully aware of the experiences she would miss when she did. And her list—the seemingly simple experiences she'd given to Lykos to complete—to have those without the judgemental eyes of the press or public on her…they would have to be enough to leave her with memories in a future of confinement. Like tonight. A last freedom. With that determination steeling her backbone, she left the room ready to face whatever the evening held.

The town car pulled up outside what looked to Marit like another row of stunning English townhouses. Residential, she thought, wondering if they were to visit a friend of Lykos, which felt a little peculiar for a date, but who was she to know? Then she noticed two men in dark suits standing, as if to attention, either side of a door with such slick black gloss it looked as if it had been raining.

She looked across the dark interior of the town car to where Lykos was once again watching her, the hairs on the back of her neck riffled by the feel of his eyes on her.

'You look incredible,' he said again. He'd said it the first time she'd come down the stairs to find him waiting for her. She hadn't wanted to hear it, didn't want his false flattery, but there had been a tone in his voice, a subtle bass chord beneath an arcing tremble of treble notes, and she'd felt it. She'd wanted to believe him then, just as she did now. And, just like before, she nodded, before looking back to the strange place they'd come to.

Lykos exited the car and stood on the pavement as the driver opened her door. Placing one hand in the driver's and picking up her skirts in the other, she stepped out of the car and onto the pavement. She tried to ignore him, but her skin was scorched by Lykos's gaze and she felt it everywhere. The driver presented her to Lykos like a prize, something to be cherished, and when Lykos held his arm out for her to take she wondered if it would be so bad to just pretend. Just for tonight. That he was a devastatingly handsome man unable to keep his eyes from her because he wanted her just as much as she wanted him. She so desperately wanted him to want her, not because she was needed, not because she was a means to an end, like the shares, or the role she was about to step into, but for who she was.

Her breath caught in her lungs and came out in a sigh the moment she gave in to the fantasy and went to stand, arm tucked in his, beside him. He looked down at her, his face half hidden in the shadows of the fast-approaching night. 'Nervous?' he asked, concern rather than his usual tease striking a discordant note.

'Not with you,' she answered honestly, and the shadows cleared in his gaze for just a heartbeat before he turned to face their destination, pulling once at each cufflink before leading them to the door.

'Mr Livas,' said one of the men, a small but deferential bow accompanying his words, while the other man pushed open the door. 'Welcome to Victoriana, Princess Marit.'

Marit looked back over her shoulder at the man who had welcomed her by name. 'Did you call ahead?' she asked Lykos in a whisper.

He shook his head. 'The staff here are as well informed as they are discreet,' he explained as they were greeted by a woman wearing what looked like a costume from the English Victorian period. The hostess wore a waistcoat over a white shirt with some kind of old-fashioned cropped trousers, looking oddly stylish. Marit and Lykos were led down a dark hallway with wooden panels and a tartan carpet in dark browns and creams that made her feel cocooned until the hallway opened out into an inconceivably large room. Literally inconceivable as it was bigger on the inside than on the outside.

Unable to help herself, Marit spun in a circle, trying to take in her surroundings. A long bar made of green swirling marble ran the length of what she realised must have been at least two houses brought together. Behind it stood men and women also dressed in the same Victorian clothing, mixing brightly coloured cocktails. There were wooden plaques above doorways leading off the central area with gold cursive announcing 'The Library', 'The Billiard Room', 'The Orangery', as if the place was some old English country house.

Lykos, beside her, gestured for Marit to follow the hostess, who wove her way through tables that had discreet, gentle lighting to a doorway where Marit's feet faltered when she read the plaque above it. 'The Music Room'. Lykos drew to a stop behind her, the heat of his body blanketing her. Her heart pulsed with useless longing that she knew Lykos would never entertain and shook off the moment to follow the hostess into a room that took Marit's breath away.

A chandelier hung into the centre of a large room, with a fireplace that might have dominated the room entirely had it not been for the grand piano that stole all of her attention. She had vague impressions of dark panelled wood, bookcases and pampas grass. Dark greens, burgundies and gold, but it was the perfect sound of the clearly very well cared for musical instrument that sounded like silken threads filling the air in the room.

Threads that wound into her heart and pulled it into the sky.

The pianist seemed lost in his music and for just a moment Marit enjoyed the image of it, the fantasy of the Victorian music room. She turned to Lykos, knowing that he'd done this, that he'd tried to shape this evening around her and what she liked, and it meant so much more than he'd ever know. He might have withdrawn from her reach, but he had given her what he could. He had given her *this*.

He looked at her, his eyes skimming over her features as if he were mentally recording her reaction and, once satisfied, gestured for her to take a seat. There were a few other tables in the room, couples seated close together, gently whispered words that couldn't be heard but made a beautiful backdrop. Their presence made Marit feel more discreet as they become anonymous in the company of the room.

Marit took a seat at the small table where she could see the piano player best and tried to ignore the way she felt when Lykos sat, not opposite her but at an angle next to her. A drink was placed to her left and a different drink was placed beside Lykos by a waiter so discreet Marit barely saw him leave.

She stared at the tumbler, a white froth above a rich amber, topped with a twirl of orange peel and a bright glossy cherry.

'What is it?' she asked, looking up at Lykos.

'You'll love it,' he said with a confidence that sang to the blood rushing in her veins.

She reached for her drink when his voice stopped her.

'Marit…' He paused. Shook his head a little, clenching his jaw so that she could see the flex of muscle there. He took a deep breath. 'Marit, if you don't want to go back—'

'To Svardia?' she asked in shock.

'I will not make you. So if you want—'

Her fingers pressed against her lips to stop the tumble of words on the tip of her tongue because, for just a second, she feared she wasn't strong enough to refuse his offer. Her shock had stopped his words, the concern in his eyes so much, too much for Marit to bear. He reached for her but she shook her head, and his hand stopped inches from her elbow.

If he failed to return her to Svardia, there was no way her brother would give Lykos the shares he needed. He would give that up for her? She couldn't think about what that meant for her, for him. It was too much. As her heart began to settle and she forced herself to think through her feelings she smiled sadly, looking for the words that would explain.

'I might not have been raised to be second in line to the throne, but I *was* raised a Svardian princess. It won't be easy, and I'll never be as good as my sister is, but I *love* Svardia. I am proud of our country and I would be honoured to represent them. My brother will be a fantastic ruler and I… I would never do anything to jeopardise that.' The truth and conviction ran through her soul, and sentiment and love raised goosebumps across her skin. 'So, yes. I do want to go back. I will *always* go back, no matter what, because my family and my country need me and I would never dishonour them.'

For the first time since meeting her Lykos realised the truth of Marit's royalty. There was nothing young or naïve about what she'd said, or even about her in that moment. It was a duty that, while she might not realise, suited her even if it demanded such a great sacrifice. A blush that had nothing to do with desire but was all about self-fulfilment lit her features and it was more devastating to his protective armour than even her touch. Her eyes sparkled with righteousness and assurance and he lost his breath.

'But if I'd said yes, what would you have done? Without Aleksander's shares?'

He wished he'd never told her. The fact that Kozlov's name was even in his thoughts at this table with her was abhorrent to him. 'I would have found a way,' he said truthfully.

'But how long would it have taken?'

Any number of years would have been worth it if Marit had wanted her freedom. Instead, he said, 'This is hardly appropriate date conversation.'

She smiled and his unease grew rather than diminished. 'Really? And what *would* be?' Marit asked, taking a sip of her drink, and he watched as her eyes grew round with unexpected pleasure. 'Oh.' The exclamation fell from her lips, making him think wicked thoughts. With ruthless determination he turned his focus on her question, realising that his experience was less of the date variety and more of the companion variety.

She arched an eyebrow, as if coming to the same conclusion about his experience and was about to tease him on it when in a panic he threw out words that surprised them both. 'I'd like to hear you play.'

The teasing expression on her face morphed into shock in an instant, and he could have cursed himself to hell and back.

'What?' she asked, her gaze locked on his even though he was sure that more than half her attention was actually on the piano.

'You play, don't you?' he asked, not quite sure why he was pursuing this, other than the awareness that her reaction made him even more convinced that it was the right thing to do.

She shook her head, even as she said, 'Yes.'

'Then I'd like to hear it.'

She looked at the table, hiding from his gaze. He was beginning to think he'd got it all wrong, when she raised her eyes to meet his and they were full of a yearning so pure that this time he really did lose his breath. It was as if he'd been punched right in the chest and he found that he was bracing himself in his seat just to stay upright.

'Really?'

He could see it. The disbelief that he'd want to hear her play. And he wanted to curse her entire family for making this woman doubt such a simple thing.

'More than anything else in the world.'

Lykos watched as Marit made her way to the piano. The musician seemed happy enough to let her play and, after a brief conversation between them, seemed eager to hear her too.

Lykos wasn't blind to the way the young man's gaze raked over her and he was forced to cage the proprietorial beast raging in his chest. But for a moment he saw Marit as the younger man did. Yes, there was a lightness to her, a youth, that was effervescent but not—as he had once told himself—naïve. There was also an experience that was beyond even his knowledge, the weight of inherent duty adding something to Marit that made him wonder how she'd kept that sense of fun and joy he'd witnessed in the park with the children and in the café in Milan; even in the boutique the shop assistant had seemed genuinely to turn towards her as if they were sunflowers and Marit was the sun.

She took a seat at the piano and swept a light touch across the keys with one hand and a smile curved her lips as if she were welcoming an old friend. Of the other few couples in the room, no one had seemed to notice, so lost were they in each other, making Lykos feel as if it were just the two of them. An intimacy strange for its publicness.

Suddenly he was hit by a wave of nervousness. Not because he thought she would be terrible, but he could see how important this was to her. He wanted it to go well because she needed it to go well. He clenched his jaw and swallowed. No matter what, he'd tell her that she was wonderful.

And then she started to play.

But what he hadn't expected was for her to sing.

Marit's fingers flew over the piano keys almost luxuriously, a series of notes that pulled at him and threw him into a song that filled him with a sense of old America and yearning. It was not what he'd expected and it made him stop and sit up.

Her voice was sultry and gentle as she sang about being at the end of one's life, a woman with her mother's name, building a world in his mind where people were trapped by life and helpless to fight against it. She sang of a desire like lightning that burned houses and he was enraptured.

And he felt it. The moment that everyone in the room stopped to listen. The sound of her voice and the piano raised the hairs on the back of his neck and poured longing, sadness, futility into his soul and his breath caught in his lungs.

She sang about the loss of youth, years passing and

staying trapped and, even though she was conjuring images of rodeos and cowboys, he saw it—her future of missed opportunities and regret—and his heart turned for her, being stuck in a loveless marriage and wanting to be an angel that flew just as her voice spun into the room and beyond.

There were many times in his life that Lykos had felt trapped. He'd thrashed and raged against the cages of poverty and powerlessness. But what he saw in Marit was a woman who refused to let that trap be a cage, who instead welcomed it, embraced it, accepted it and allowed herself a freedom within it. How could he have ever thought her foolish or spoiled? How could he have ever dismissed her desire to become a musician as a petty whim when she *was* a musician down to her soul?

She was coming to the end of the song and he didn't want it to end. He could have listened to her for ever but, more than that, he knew if she stopped her song would come true. That this was her future. And he didn't want that for her. He wanted to take her away from it, to stop it from happening.

And as she drew her hands from the piano and placed them in her lap she turned to him and he saw it, the truth she had known from the very beginning and that he was only now understanding.

I will always go back, no matter what.

CHAPTER EIGHT

HER HEART WAS thundering in her chest. She'd never done that, never sung or performed in front of people before, and the moment of silence after she finished had her trembling on a precipice until the sincere clapping of the few people in the room broke into the quiet and drenched her in a happiness she'd never experienced before.

This was what she'd wanted for the young performers in the orchestra she worked with. That cresting shining wave, washing away all the nerves and all the fears of making a mistake or getting something wrong and basking in the light of being able to truly express themselves freely. Lykos had given her that. Something she'd feared she might never have. She wanted to tell him how much that meant to her, she wanted to thank him for bringing her dream to life.

And when she looked to him amongst the smiling faces in the room she found him sitting there, unmoving. For a moment she feared she'd done something wrong. But then she felt the sheer force of his gaze, the explosion of something between them that blocked out everything else. Her pulse pounded harder than it had done in the hotel room when she'd placed her palms on his chest. Heat flashed over her skin, making her feel cold and shivery and hot all at the same time.

And in that moment she realised for the first time that she wasn't alone in this feeling. That what she had seen was him fighting the same need, the same desire that swept over her like a tsunami. Its tide pulled at her feet as she made her way from the piano to their small table, threatening to push her this way and that. But it was his gaze that made her strong enough to make it, that filled her with a steely determination he must have seen in her eyes, because his gaze turned from speculative to assessing, even if he hid it behind the blink of an eye.

But it was too late. She had seen it. She had seen the extent of his need for her and she couldn't ignore or deny it any more. Plates of artfully catered food were placed on the table and she didn't break the connection of their gaze.

'You should eat.'

'I'm not hungry,' she declared. Not for food anyway. She didn't have to say it. The slight flare of his nostrils, the renewed determination in his eyes, the flex of the muscle at his jaw. Before, she would have seen rejection, a dismissive warning, but now she knew what they were—the evidence of how much he was fighting his reaction to her. Now, they were a red flag, encouraging and taunting.

She'd meant what she'd said. She would *always* return to Svardia to where she was needed, where she would finally prove herself. But she still had two days left and she couldn't stand the idea of living the rest of her life without knowing what it was like to feel his skin against hers. To know what it was like to kiss this powerful

Greek billionaire and have him break his own armour for them to be together just for one night.

'I want to go home.'

'To Svardia?' he asked, purposely misunderstanding her meaning.

She narrowed her gaze at him and Lykos was instantly on guard. She shook her head very slowly, her gaze locked with his, and he felt hypnotised. Everything in him was fighting this. She was a princess. She was young. She did not know what she was doing, and certainly knew less of what she was asking for.

Because she *was* asking. Her unspoken request was as sure as any siren's call. And although she wasn't full of confidence and sensual experience like his previous bedfellows, she was so much more devastating than any of them.

'No.'

'No, what?'

'Marit,' he growled, the warning there in the depth and rumble of his voice. 'This is not a game.'

'I didn't think it was.'

'Then hear me when I say, *absolutely not.*'

Her eyes glinted in the low lighting, their food untouched, their drinks discarded.

'Tell me I'm wrong.'

'About what?'

'Tell me that you don't feel it. The attraction between us.'

He cursed. 'Of course I do. But that doesn't mean I have to act on it.'

'But what if I want to?'

'Consent works both ways, Princess.'

She reared back as if struck. 'You are accusing me of forcing myself on you?'

'No!' His harsh word cut through the softer ambience of the room. 'But I am not agreeing to this.'

She looked up at him, her eyes glistening, and for just a moment he thought her lip trembled, until the shutters came down and she nodded. 'Okay.' The word fell between them like a surrender and when she looked back up at him a mask was in place and it cut him deeper than he'd expected.

'Lykos, thank you for an enjoyable evening,' she said, 'but I am quite tired. It must have been the flight from Milan. And I didn't sleep well last…' her words trailed off, leaving memories of his migraine, of the way she'd unbuttoned his shirt, of the heat of her palms against his body to fill the space between them '…last night. If you wouldn't mind, I really would like to return to your house so that I can rest.'

A stubborn part of him wanted to refuse her request. Because it was wrong. Because he hadn't done this right. Because she'd asked for a date, her first and perhaps only 'date' before she married a stranger, and he'd failed. He'd given her an evening that had ended in disappointment and hurt feelings and he didn't like it. But neither would he force her to stay. He had denied her once already—he couldn't do it again.

He nodded finally and stood from the table. He held his hand out to her more from habit than intent, and he couldn't fault her for refusing it as she swept from the room as regal as any queen. The car ride back to Knightsbridge was just as bad. A silence that nudged and jolted his conscience every time the car turned or stopped at a set of lights. She was so quiet he couldn't hear her breathe and it was only the whiteness of the knuckles on her fisted hands that showed any kind of emotion.

He wanted to explain. He wanted to comfort her. But what use were his words when he wouldn't act on them? Far better for her to think him an unfeeling bastard than to admit…what? That he feared touching her? That kissing her would be his downfall? Because, in truth, he wasn't sure that he'd be able to ever let her go? That it wasn't her that he was trying to protect, but himself?

He cursed out loud and she flinched, but before he could apologise they pulled up beside his home and, without waiting for the driver, Marit slipped from the car and out into the night. He took his time getting out of the car, in the hope that he could control himself before he did something drastic like reach for her and draw her to him. The thought put images into his mind that began to unravel his willpower.

She was waiting by the front door and he had to reach around her to place his thumb on the security pad of the house. The sound of the lock releasing cut into the night and Marit pushed at the door to escape him. She was halfway to the staircase by the time he closed the door behind him. He couldn't leave it like this. He couldn't let her go thinking… He cursed. He couldn't even imagine what she was thinking. He needed to let her go.

'Marit.'

The word erupted unbidden from his lips, stopping her dead in her tracks, but she refused to turn to look at him. He wanted to make sure she was okay, he needed to see that she was.

He closed the distance between them, his hungry gaze raking over the dress that clung to her skin. His eyes swept down her back as his hands wanted to do and snagged on the way the material clung to her hips, the curve of her backside, the tops of her thighs… His gaze flicked back up to shoulders that were stiff with tension and cut to hands that were fisted.

'Marit.' This time her name was a plea as he caught her wrist and turned her to him, instantly regretting it the moment he saw the tears gathered in her eyes.

He reached up to cup her jaw, his thumb gently grazing her cheekbone, sweeping up to snare the lone tear that had fallen as she'd closed her eyes to prevent him from seeing her pain. Angry words and hot demands he could deflect and reject, but the hurt, the pain he'd seen glittering there? It was the final blow to his defences and he knew in that moment that he would lay himself bare for her and still be there when she walked away from him.

Her eyelashes glistened with unshed tears as she prised them open to cast him with such a look that he felt turned to stone.

'What can I do?' he demanded, his voice ragged and full of gravel, bringing his other hand up to frame her face.

She speared her bottom lip with her teeth and, unable to help himself, his thumb dropped to her lips and gently prised it free from its ivory cage. She raised her eyes to his and placed her hand on his wrist at the side of her face to hold him to her when he might pull away.

'I know I can't ask for more, I know that is impossible, but please. Let me have what little I can.'

Lykos felt the whispered words against his skin, sinking deep into his body, his soul.

'You deserve more than *a little*, Marit, you deserve *everything*.'

'I don't want what you think I deserve. I want you.'

The simple words stripped a layer from the walls he'd

placed between himself and his princess. He searched her eyes, looking for doubt, looking for uncertainty, but all he saw was naked pleading and she should never have had to beg.

'No more,' he whispered to himself.

'What?'

'I will fight you no more,' he said, just before he lowered his head and swept his lips across hers.

The feel of his lips against hers swept all her concerns away: fear that he would reject her, that he didn't want her. It was too close to how everyone else treated her, but Lykos was different. This Lykos, his lips claiming hers, was everything. Marit knew what she was asking for, despite her practical innocence. But to enter a loveless marriage without ever knowing the intimate touch of affection would be a tragedy to someone who felt so much.

When Lykos touched her she felt *alive*. Alive in a way she'd only felt when she was playing the piano. It was as if she were the musical instrument that sang beneath his deft fingers, strings vibrating and trembling, a tone so pure, so true and clear, that it was a siren's call, weaving a spell that affected them both equally.

His tongue swept across her lips, teasing her until she opened for him and, *oh…*

As Lykos took possession of the kiss all rational thought stopped and Marit succumbed to pure sensation. His tongue danced with hers, pulling a crescendo from deep within her, rushing towards some seemingly impossible conclusion. His hands cradled her face and she leaned into the gentle cage, wanting to feel him against her skin everywhere. Her heart fluttered in her throat as if wanting to escape her body and fly to his.

Her hands slipped beneath his jacket to the breadth

of his shoulders, his skin hot beneath her palms through the soft cotton of his shirt. She clung to him, to the muscles rippling beneath her touch, and realised just how much he was holding himself back. And she didn't want him to hold back. She wanted him as Lykos. Unleashed, powerful, demanding and challenging. Everything that people around her thought she was unworthy of, or too delicate for.

She pushed his jacket from his shoulders, neither caring where it fell, and her hands swept down, over biceps and elbows to a waist corded with muscle, and pulled the shirt free of his belt. They'd done this before, the echo of déjà vu pulsing between them, making Lykos pull back from the kiss and study her once again.

Marit felt the loss keenly and almost followed him back as he leaned from the reach of her lips, but he soothed the loss by sweeping his hand from her cheek to rest it against the thunderous beating of her heart. The gentle pressure was reassuring and comforting in a way that was nothing to do with the sensual play between them and spoke of something deeper, something lasting, no matter how little time they had to share together.

'Latriea mou,' he whispered, the lyricism of his words building a rhythm in her soul that she'd never forget. He shook his head, his eyes raking over her as if disbelieving of what he saw and, for the first time, Marit didn't doubt that it was *her*. That he was cherishing, relishing and wondering purely at *her*. It was an intoxicating feeling, one she could quickly become addicted to if she were not careful.

'Are you sure that this is what you want, *agápi mou*?'

She nodded but, seeing the pleading look in his eyes, put her intent to words. 'Absolutely.'

'If you change your mind, if you want to stop for

any reason—' Marit was already shaking her head, but again he gave her a look that warned her, *wanted* her, to take this seriously. That he cared more for her needs than any discomfort of his own meant too much to her. She didn't know what to do with that, so she closed the distance between them and drew his bottom lip between her teeth and nipped him gently, quickly soothing the sting with a sweep of her tongue.

Shock and surprise were evident on his face for about two seconds before desire lit his eyes like fireworks and he plundered her mouth with his own. Marit lost her breath and her mind to the kiss. For what felt like hours she drowned in exquisite sensation. The way his tongue teased and taunted, his lips bringing moans of want and cries of need from her mouth, his hands leaving her face to mould a body that rose to his touch, as if she were a marionette and he held her strings—the connection between them invisible but too tangible not to be real. Marit felt as if she'd been living a half-life until his touch.

Frustration began to unspool within her, twisting and turning from her core, making her hot and unsettled. She wanted their clothes gone, she wanted him against her, her body's primal reaction to him instinctive and urgent. This time she drew the kiss to an end, shifting her thighs together and the heat of impatience stinging her cheeks. She didn't know how to ask for what she wanted. She *heard* it, a whole string quartet played in her mind of what she wanted Lykos to do to her, to do *with* her. But the words…

She felt his eyes rake over her assessingly and then at the same time they both said, 'Bedroom.'

Marit couldn't help the laugh that bubbled up, cutting through the frustration and building something softer, sweeter, but no less needy between them. As if he'd come to a decision, Lykos nodded to himself in that way of his and swept her up into his arms, marching them up the staircase of his townhouse towards the floor where she had got dressed earlier that evening. But instead of turning into the guest suite Lykos pressed forward and they entered his room, his footsteps slowing, his eyes only for her as he shifted his hold so that she could stand on her own two feet again, but still within the circle of his hold.

Once again, his hand rose to cup her jaw. His eyes flashed silver in the dark room. Two large sash windows displayed a magnificent London skyline, but Marit wouldn't look away for the world.

'*Kardiá mou*, Marit...' He seemed as unable as she was to be without touch or contact for long—as if they knew how little time they had to share and couldn't, wouldn't, waste a moment of it. 'I wish you could see what I see,' he said between the kisses he pressed to her lips, her throat, her collarbone, following the pattern his fingers traced across her skin.

Her hands clung to his waist, pulling him to her, relishing the feel of the power and length of him against her body and finally, when he leaned back, she had enough room to sneak her hands between them. Quick fingers made light work of the buttons on his shirt and she spread his shirt apart and slipped it from his shoulders, all the while unable to remove her gaze from his chest. Her palms itched to feel the swirls of dark hair covering the clearly defined muscles that spoke not of hours in the gym but pure raw masculinity and power.

She could feel the weight of his gaze as he watched her taking him in, the depth of his curiosity, but, drawn back to him by that invisible string, she pressed kisses to his chest and thought she heard him groan, felt it in her core. Downward her kisses went, but when she reached the snap on his trousers he gently pulled her away, turning her in his arms so that she faced the windows and a large standing mirror in the corner of the room.

'It's my turn,' he whispered as he kissed just beneath her ear, sending a shiver of sparks over her body and pebbling nipples already teased and needy. Her breath stuttered in her chest as he swept her hair over one shoulder, his fingers finding the barely visible zip at the back of the dress and slowly, ever so slowly, drew the tab downwards. In the mirror she could see that his eyes followed the path of the zip and his hands, relished the slight flush beneath the tan of his skin, the way his lips had parted slightly as if so utterly consumed by what he was seeing he'd given up all self-awareness. Marit took all that in and more.

The way her own eyes hungrily devoured him, the way her body responded to his, standing taller, prouder, empowered by his need. That his arousal and desire would feed her own was something she never could have expected or imagined. She bit her lip and in the mirror saw wantonness and need. She saw not the loss of innocence but the gain of something wondrous and her heart sank the moment she realised that she couldn't keep this, couldn't keep *him*.

Without a title, he would never have a place in her future and in that second she knew she would never have the chance to feel loved for ever. The only thing that kept her standing was the knowledge that she would take this moment with her, and it made her bold when she might not have been otherwise, made her determined when she might have conceded power. Lykos met her gaze in the mirror and she could feel the question hanging in the air, before she shrugged the dress from her shoulders and bared herself to him.

Lykos would have cursed if he'd been capable of speech. She had turned him to stone and it was a moment he would remember for the rest of his life. She watched him taking her in and it was the most erotic thing he'd ever experienced, hardening his erection to the point of near pain. Holding himself back became a physical thing, his jaw clenched, hands fisted to stop him from bruising her with his need. She met his gaze in the mirror before turning to him, a bare inch between them and she felt painfully out of his reach. Until she closed the distance and her chest pressed against his, her thighs, the juncture of them, meeting the hardened length of him through the trousers he still wore.

Then he noticed the hesitancy in her eyes and the bottom fell from his world.

'What is it, *agápi mou*?' he whispered, her cheek fitting into his palm as if she'd been made for him. She bit her lip and his thumb soothed it free again. She looked away as if unable to say what she wanted and he hated that. Hated that she feared his response. Didn't she know that he'd give her anything that she asked?

When she looked back up at him, determination, need and something very close to fury blazed in her eyes. She had morphed into a phoenix, traces of the defiant runaway Princess twisted into strength and power, and it was incredible.

'Make me yours so that no one can ever take that away.'

It was as if the leash holding him back had been cut and all the desire, all the need, all the *feelings* he'd held back for so long rushed to the forefront and overwhelmed him completely. He walked her backwards to the bed and she relished it, her eyes delighting in his power and his desire for her.

He kissed her and guided her back against the pillows of the bed, her body instinctively opening for him as he leaned on one hand and used the other to trace the curves of her body, her skin like satin beneath his palm, shivering and trembling with need as he smoothed his way over the curve of her waist, hip, sweeping around to the inside of her soft thighs, pulling the thong from her body, spreading her legs and delving into the blonde curls damp from her desire.

Her body arched as he parted her with his fingers and a moan of pleasure mixed with an intake of breath. He watched every minute of it, utterly undone by Marit's rapture. He lost himself in it for an infinity, the gold and jade shards in her eyes on fire, the pink flush of her cheeks and the hitch in her breath as she climbed closer and closer to her orgasm.

Her body undulated with the shift of his hands and tension corded her as he delved deeper into her with a finger, gently testing her muscles, readying her so as to make it as least painful as possible. In a heartbeat that tension rolled into a wave of ecstasy and he could have died then, the happiest he had ever been. Believed even that he might have found his life's purpose, and then she opened her eyes and pinned him with a gaze so hot that he felt branded to his very soul.

Her hand reached down to circle his forearm, the sight of her slender fingers wrapped around him pushing him towards the edge of feral.

'Lykos,' she said, his name a plea he could no longer deny. He leaned back from her only long enough to remove his trousers and underwear, casting them away with ruthless efficiency and returning to her, bracing on his forearms, his hands once again cradling her cheeks.

'I have been told that this will hurt. Not terribly—'

'Lykos,' Marit replied, her voice husky from her pleasure. 'I've had the birds and the bees talk,' she teased. But not too much, he could see what it meant, his concern for her. 'I want this. I want it to be with you.'

Her words did something to him that he wouldn't, couldn't look at now. Instead, he reached into the nightstand and removed a condom from the drawer, silently vowing to make this as pleasurable for Marit as possible. He rolled the latex over himself and settled between her legs, his erection pulsing with restrained need, and slowly, so incredibly slowly, he joined with her.

A pleasure so sublime it hurt his heart filled him as he filled her, never once taking his eyes from hers, never missing a single moment of her response to his intrusion. He felt the moment she experienced her pain, the tension and stiffness around him making him stop instantly while she adjusted to the new experience, saw the moment the shock left her eyes and was replaced by wonder. Shifting beneath him, moving at first for comfort and then an instinctive search for pleasure, more and more as her hips rolled beneath him. Every moment as wondrous for him as it was for her.

Finally turning to him, her eyes now full of questions. 'Is it always like this?' Her whispered words were full of awe.

He wouldn't lie to her. 'No,' he replied, his heart in his words. 'It is never like this, *agápi mou*.'

There was no misunderstanding, no confusion between them. He wouldn't allow it. She could see how much this meant to him, because he too had laid himself bare for her. It was an intimacy he had never allowed anyone. And when she reached up to cup his jaw he knew she could see the truth of it.

Slowly he began to move, Marit's body instinctively arching into his, her head falling back against the pillow, the golden strands of her hair fanning out like a halo. Again and again he pushed them to the brink and back, drenching her in pleasure and drowning in her cries until neither of them could take any more and, with one last thrust, Lykos launched them into a sea of ecstasy, leaving them to drift on currents that sent ripples through their bodies for long hours after.

The sound of Lykos's phone ringing woke them as the sun's early morning rays were filtering in through the sash windows of the room. Having only just closed his eyes after making love to Marit again, he groaned in frustration, eliciting a gentle laugh from the half-asleep Princess next to him.

'Aren't you going to answer it?'

'No, I'm going to hope that they get the message and go away,' he grumped into the pillow, muffling the words and sounding like the kind of carefree youth he had never been.

She turned her head and pierced him with shards of gold and green and tease and his heart turned. He'd never seen anyone so beautiful. And then the phone rang again, ruining the moment. Marit's gentle giggles turned into a laugh and Lykos snared the phone and barked, *'Nai?'* without taking his eyes from her once.

'Lykos? It's Theron. I need you to come to Greece. Right now.'

CHAPTER NINE

MARIT HAD NEVER seen Lykos like this. Angry? Yes. Frustrated? Aroused? Yes.

She bit her lip to stop herself from raising her fingers to her mouth in memory of last night, in *wonder* of what they had shared. A part of her knew that it would have been easier to resign herself to her future if she had not known, not experienced, just what it was that she would be denying herself.

Love.

No. She shook her head. She might have been innocent last night but she was not naïve. She wasn't in love with him and, as she looked at Lykos, she knew he would never feel that way about her. She cared for him a great deal—of course she did, she wouldn't have been able to give herself to him as she had done last night if she did not. But…love? No. Marit had spent her entire life looking for love, one way or another. The moment she had gone to Paris to marry, she had put such thoughts and such desire from her mind and heart for ever.

But when she saw the dark bruises beneath Lykos's eyes, the muscle flexed at his jaw, she knew that she would do anything to ease his fear if she could.

'Theron didn't say anything other than that he needed you in Greece?'

'*Óchi.*' He shook his head. 'He said he had to go. That Summer needed him. If something has happened to Katy, their little baby girl—'

Marit reached across the space between her seat and his, anchored by the seatbelt needed for the private jet's descent into Athens. That he didn't shake her off was sign enough to Marit that this man who, by all accounts, considered himself an island, untouchable and above the connections of the mere mortals around him was scared, *terrified*, for his friends.

Disembarking the plane happened in the blink of an eye, a sleek black town car waited for them on the runway, chauffeured by a suited man in dark glasses and a set jaw. Through the entire journey to their destination Lykos's knee bounced against one fisted hand, the other tightly wrapped in Marit's. She knew better than to assure a man with Lykos's life experience that it would all be okay. Instead, she became the silent support she instinctively knew he needed.

They pulled up to a house and the sight of other cars lining the grand estate did absolutely nothing to ease the tension racing through each of them—as if they were now connected on a level Marit didn't yet comprehend. The car stopped opposite the front door, Lykos only releasing Marit's hand to leave the confines of the car and vault up the steps to the door, where he paused as if bracing himself for what he might find. Marit slipped behind him, her hand on his back, and finally his fist fell on the door.

What happened next was so confusing it took Marit a moment to sort through it all.

A tall, dark-haired Greek with a broad smile opened the door to demand what had taken Lykos so long. Behind him was the sound of a party in full swing, the happiness and bright sunshine utterly at odds with the drama of Marit and Lykos's desperate journey here at dawn, fearing the worst.

Beside him was a small but utterly beautiful woman with a tiny baby held preciously in her arms. The woman seemed to realise what had happened much more quickly than her partner—which Marit guessed by the way that she reached out to slap his arm.

'Theron, I *told* you he would think the worst,' she scolded angrily in English.

'What? No, I just knew he wouldn't come otherwise,' Theron Thiakos said happily to his wife, until he finally caught sight of the expression on Lykos's face. 'Ach, *sygnómi*, Lykos.' Summer, from what Lykos had told Marit about Theron and his partner, looked between her partner and his friend and, cradling the baby with one hand, pulled Lykos into a firm hug with the other.

'Lykos, he's an unthinking beast. I'm so sorry,' she said.

'Does that mean you've come to your senses and will finally leave the *maláka* for me?' Lykos teased.

Marit could have had whiplash from the change in Lykos's tone. Summer seemed equally suspicious, but Theron was instantly put at ease. Neither was Marit fooled by the teasing, bold flirtation, having experienced the real thing the night before.

'That's my woman,' growled Theron.

'I am no one's woman, thank you very much,' Summer replied in English. 'Please ignore these brutes,' she said, playfully swatting them both on the arm—even though there was something softer when she looked at Lykos. She introduced herself and their little baby girl

Katy—short for Catherine—and brought them into the beautiful villa.

'Why the cloak and dagger?' Lykos asked in English for the benefit of Summer and Marit.

'We didn't think you'd come,' Summer explained.

They looked between Summer and her husband until Theron said, 'Kyros is here.'

A swift sharp nod preceded a clenched jaw. 'Of course. He is your father. I wouldn't have expected anything less.' The shoulder shrug should have dismissed their concerns but it only raised Marit's curiosity, until she linked the name with the father figure who had betrayed Lykos.

'Which is why I expected you to find an excuse not to come,' Theron clarified, cutting through Marit's thoughts.

'Fair,' Lykos admitted, seemingly good-naturedly.

'That's what I thought. See?' He turned to Summer. 'Told you.'

Summer bumped shoulders with her partner and turned back to Marit. 'Forgive me for staring, but you do look quite familiar. Have we met?'

It took ten minutes to talk Summer down from her panic at having a princess at their party and then another ten to assure her that they didn't have to follow any particular rules of etiquette. Marit, as if sensing the broiling mass of emotions swirling like petrol in his stomach, drew Summer and Theron into a conversation about Katy—which would give Lykos anywhere from five to twenty minutes to get himself under control.

He pulled at his cufflinks and flexed his hand, opening and closing it to restore circulation to his fingers. His pulse was still wildly out of control, not that anyone would know to look at him. He had found himself in a quiet corner of the estate, in the garden overlooking the Aegean Sea, a sight that had always calmed him in the past.

The rays of the midday sun beat down on his skin, familiar and welcoming. It was a ridiculous sentiment, but one he couldn't shake. A London sun could be painfully harsh or frustratingly weak. Hong Kong's was humid, damp, and for Lykos was too close to the skin. But here it was *home*.

But even such serene thoughts did nothing to diminish the pounding at his temple. It was too soon for another migraine, surely. He ran his palm over the stubble on his jaw, not having had time to shave when he'd come here thinking the worst.

Christé mou, he'd thought something had happened to Katy. Fear and frustration had pounded through him all the way here. And now that he knew Katy was fine, his pulse still raced. Concern still edged at his awareness and he could no longer ignore why.

In ten years he'd amassed a fortune that would have made his father weep and Kyros blink. He'd dominated financial markets, his name whispered in the wealthiest of circles. He had apartments all over the world, and a woman whenever he wanted…

But none of them had made him feel anything like what he had experienced last night with Marit. And she was the one woman he would never be allowed to keep. She was one thing that no amount of money, no amount of apparent respectability could attain. Marit must return to Svardia so that she could be married off to some titled noble, as Svardian legislation decreed. Lykos let out a bitter laugh. No matter how much money he'd made, or what he'd achieved in the time since he'd left Kyros, it *still* wasn't enough.

His gut churned as he remembered that in exchange for taking Marit home he would receive Aleksander's shares. The thought made him feel nauseous. As if the night he had spent with Marit had payment. He'd meant what he'd said in London. If she wanted to escape, if she wanted her freedom, he would do everything in his power to make it happen.

I will always go back.

Something about the way she'd said it had reminded him of his mother and it had cut deeper, and darker, than he could ever have imagined. In his mind's eye, he saw his mother's large glistening eyes, the feel of her palm against his cheek.

The only way I'll be safe is if he can never use you against me again. So don't look for me. Don't come for me.

And he couldn't shake the feeling that when Marit left his life, this time he would be even more alone.

A cold sweat at his nape turned icy with a fresh blast of salty air, anchoring him in the present. When he felt a presence behind him he could have sworn that somehow the past was repeating itself.

Kyros came to stand beside him, less than a foot between them and closer than they'd been in over ten years. A silent roar of rage built inside of Lykos, thrashing and snarling and wanting out, the hurt from too many things in his past colliding in this one moment, but he had too much control to do so. Instead, the world would have seen two old friends perhaps, in a shared moment.

'You've done incredibly well for yourself, Lykos.'

'Yes, I have. But if you think for one moment your acknowledgement of that fact means anything to me then you are sorely mistaken.' His pulse throbbed painfully in a throat that felt thick and sore.

'I did you a great disservice when I asked you—'

'*Sent me.*'

Kyros surrendered a sigh. '*Sent you,*' the old man confirmed, 'after Mariam.'

Lykos felt the weight of the blue-eyed gaze on his cheeks. Was Kyros taking in the changes that time had wrought, as Lykos had done in Norfolk a few months ago? He hadn't liked how shaken he'd been to see the larger-than-life vibrant man from his youth with wrinkles, shocking white hair and a sadness in his eyes that had been for more than the loss of Althaia, his wife.

'Lykos, I didn't know. I had no idea that Mariam had a child.'

'Why did you do it then? Why did you send me after her? What were you hoping to achieve? You had a wife, Agyros. She was sick and you had been with another woman.'

'What drew me to Mariam—and Mariam to me—is between us,' Kyros growled, the roar of an old tiger not yet done with the world. Inside, grief and hurt twisted in Lykos's heart. 'I told Althaia as soon as it had happened. But I shouldn't have done it and I certainly shouldn't have used you to track Mariam down. Lykos, even then, in a way I cannot explain, I loved both women. I thought that perhaps now you might finally understand how far we will go for the women we love…but perhaps not.'

Lykos's jaw ached from how tightly he had clenched it. Kyros's gaze burned into him and it took everything in his power not to react.

'That, however, is not what I wanted to say.'

'Oh, really? There's more?' Lykos cursed himself, knowing how childish he sounded, but he felt out of control, wild and frantic. *This was what happened when you let emotions in, he warned himself. This was what happened when you let Marit in.*

Kyros was frowning, as if finally sensing the unease within him. The old man went to place a hand on his shoulder. 'Lykos—'

Lykos shook him off before the touch could connect and it seemed Kyros decided to keep whatever he'd been about to say to himself.

Kyros's sigh seemed weary and weighted, even to Lykos's ears. 'No matter what has passed and what may come to pass in the future, if you allow it, I owe you an apology. I should never have asked you to do that. And I know that I let you down. I am sincerely sorry for that, Lykos.'

Lykos didn't know how to respond. He'd spent so many years being angry at this man, resenting him and hating him sometimes. But now that he'd received the Kyros's apology it didn't quite mean what he'd thought it would.

'It will take time, Lykos, but I promise you I'll show you that I mean what I say. Having my daughter in my life…it has changed so much. And it's reminded me of what I've missed. With you. But I understand if that's not what you want. Just…' Kyros seemed to run out of the energy that had driven him this far '…just keep it in mind.'

Kyros waited and after a beat longer than he'd probably expected, and less than Lykos had planned, he nodded, surrendering to a desire that he thought he'd buried a long time ago. A desire for family, for a home.

Marit watched Lykos with an older man who, she realised, was Kyros. She'd tried to look away, to give them the privacy they deserved, but she'd been too worried about Lykos. He'd brushed off Theron's trick easily enough, but Marit hadn't been fooled. From what Lykos had told her, being here would be incredibly difficult. Confronting Kyros? Inconceivable. Summer sat opposite her rocking Katy, unable to hide the glances she also sent in their direction.

'So, how long have you known Lykos?' Summer asked, making it sound like more than just polite conversation. The warmth in her was apparent, putting Marit at ease almost instantly. She reminded Marit a little of her sister Freya and the thought stung a little more than it should.

In the last few years they'd not spoken as often as they once had, with Marit unable to hide the resentment at the loss of Freya's attention as she took on her royal duties. At the time it had reminded her too much of her parents. But now, faced with the same position, Marit *understood*. She understood each member of her family a little more. Understood the purpose and the bone-deep willingness to serve their country, making it hurt to think how selfishly and childishly she'd behaved. It was as if somehow, being seen by Lykos, *feeling* seen by him had enabled her to see herself more clearly. She shook the thought off, trying to find her way back to answering Summer's question.

'It feels like a lifetime,' she answered, unsure how the other woman would react to the news that they'd only known each other a matter of days. But as she said the words she felt them as the truth. Only it was a different lifetime to the one that lay ahead of her, or even behind her, as if she had been allowed to slip into a parallel world before stepping up to do her duty.

'He is a complicated man,' Summer observed of Lykos.

'Do you think so?' Marit couldn't help but ask.

'You don't?' she asked with a smile.

As if drawn once again by that invisible thread, she felt the tug as he approached the table, the shadows in his eyes masked by the softness in his gaze as it focused on Katy and he pressed a kiss to the baby's cheek once he reached the table. Marit was surprised when his hand reached out to her shoulder and she couldn't have stopped herself from anchoring it there with her own. Summer's eyes took in the small gesture and smiled. Marit looked up at Lykos as he turned to her, the question in her eyes answered by his. They would talk later.

'Ah, there you are,' Theron said. 'I've been looking for you everywhere.'

'Really, Theron. You are old enough to go to the toilet by yourself these days,' Lykos teased.

'Well, it's just that I might need your help to hold—'

Marit coughed as air got caught in her throat and Summer cried her outrage, slapping her husband and drawing curious gazes from the guests.

'When will you two behave?' Summer demanded.

'Never,' they both replied, before breaking into wide genuine grins. For the first time since arriving, Marit felt something ease in her chest and she took in the powerful bond between the three. It was full of love, affection and trust and for a moment she allowed herself to feel a tendril of grief that she would never be able to be a part of that. No. Her future lay in Svardia with another man and another set of duties.

The rest of the afternoon passed in easy conversation and delicious food. Lykos spent a long while followed around by a group of children. One clung to his leg, one to his arm and another tried desperately to climb onto his back. Not surprised in the least, it warmed Marit's heart to see him so gentle and patient with them. She saw him whisper to a girl who looked about sixteen, who ran off eagerly to do his bidding, but Theron took the chair beside her and distracted her.

Eventually Lykos relaxed enough to exchange a civil conversation with Kyros—bringing so much happiness to Summer that Marit knew exactly why both men were trying so hard to fix something that had caused so much pain. Lykos might tease and taunt, might charm and flirt his way through his exchanges, but now that she had seen through the mask, seen the truth that he hid from the world, she would never be able to not see it.

The mask was a shadow, a mirage, protecting a man who had so much love to give but had never been allowed to. His father had abused it, his mother had refused it, Kyros had betrayed it and Theron had rejected it, *before* their reunion.

'What is it, *agápi mou*?'

'Mm?' Marit asked, leaning into the palm of his hand.

'What has you looking so sad?'

She couldn't tell him. Because the answer had surprised her so much it had stopped her tongue. Instead, she forced a smile to her lips and simply said that she was tired.

'I will make our goodbyes. But, before we do, I have something for you.'

His eyes twinkled irresistibly, their silver sparks drawing her gaze rather than what he held in his hand. Finally she looked down and when she realised what it was she gasped.

'A tattoo!' she cried.

'A *temporary* one,' he clarified, referring to the silver transfer in an ornate pattern.

The detail was beautiful and that he'd thought, even now, of the list she'd written back in Milan—a list that she'd never thought he'd take seriously—it meant so much to her. She put the temporary tattoo into her bag, realising that she would never use it. It would, instead, be locked away with her most prized possessions, as a reminder of the kindness she'd once been given by a Greek billionaire.

Within ten minutes Lykos had extricated them from the throng at Theron and Summer's party with Marit having had her cheeks pinched only a few times. Lykos fared worse, or at least seemed to. There was a lot of shouting in Greek and gestures that ranged from warm to aggressively affectionate. A handshake between him and Kyros was more than anyone had expected and it was clearly a sign of hope to so many.

'Are you really tired? Or were you just ready to leave?' he asked as they closed the door to Theron and Summer's gorgeous villa.

She bit her lip and turned to him.

'Thank you,' he mouthed exaggeratedly and pressed a swift kiss to her lips that seemed to take them both by surprise. Lykos cleared his throat and Marit turned away to hide her smile. 'Are you happy to walk?' he asked. When she nodded, he threw his jacket to the driver and dismissed him for the rest of the day.

They turned onto a street but Marit couldn't have described it, instead her attention was caught by the way Lykos removed his cufflinks, putting them in his pocket before rolling up his sleeves. She thought at first what had caught her attention was the sight of his powerful forearms, but after a while she realised what it was; she had never seen him so relaxed. Only with them gone did she realise how many times she'd seen him pull on his cufflinks as if in the habit of checking everything was 'just so'.

She tucked the thought away the moment Lykos took her hand in his and instead, with the constant awareness of how little time they had left, she chose to enjoy the moment, finding something peaceful in walking beside him. Even more when he let go of her hand and drew her beneath his arm, tucking her into his side as if they both wished that she could stay there.

A shuddering sigh vibrated through his body. 'He apologised.'

'Kyros?' she asked, though she was sure that was the answer.

Lykos nodded. 'I don't… I don't know what to do with it.'

She tried to imagine what it would be like to hear an apology from her parents and realised that she never would. Everything they had done was for Svardia and if Marit confronted them with the hurts of her childhood, Svardia would be their answer and she couldn't argue with that. It was sad that it had taken being *needed*, being given that responsibility, to finally understand what it was like to go against the heart's wishes for duty. But maybe her parents had gone against their own wishes too. Maybe Kyros had and only now was able to admit it.

'Perhaps,' Marit said, thinking of how much time she'd needed even to begin to feel some kind of peace with her hurts, 'you don't have to do anything with it yet. Maybe you need time just to feel it?'

He stopped and pulled her to stand before him. 'Can I kiss you?'

Love blazed in her heart for this man and she promised that even though they could never have a future, this would be what she took with her. 'For the next two days, you don't have to ask.' She pulled him to her and the kiss burned from sweet to almost indecent in a heartbeat.

'Perhaps we should find your apartment,' Marit teased.

'Soon. There's something I want to show you before we do.'

Curious, and a little excited, she searched the length of the cobbled street he'd brought her to. There were boutiques and coffee shops on either side of the street, but nothing that she could tell as being special. A knowing smile curved Lykos's lips as he pulled her towards a small wooden door she had missed completely.

Frowning, he drew her across the threshold and down a set of stairs. As they reached the bottom of the stairs, the dark underground room opened up and she saw a bar on one side and small tables opposite. The place was packed, the smell of wine and something sweet, and there were so many conversations going on that it made her feel deliciously anonymous rather than overwhelmed. But beneath it all she heard something that made her look towards the corner of the taverna where a man sat on a dais. A quick peal of notes rippled over the chatter and soon the audience quietened. Lykos watched her with a smile and she knew somehow that this was what he'd wanted her to see.

'What instrument is that? It sounds like a mandolin, but…lower in pitch?' she hedged.

'It is a bouzouki.'

Listening intently, she didn't realise that she'd pulled them through the mass of people, leading Lykos by the hand until she stood at the front, watching the man on the small dais, his foot resting on a block and a long-necked instrument in his lap, his fingers flying across the metal strings. Marit marvelled at the stillness of his body and the incredible flight of notes that poured into the air between them.

Lykos drew her against his chest as they listened, his arms enfolding her. He dipped his head to her ear and, keeping his voice low, told her how he and Theron used to sneak in here when they were teenagers. He explained that the music was called *rebetiko*. In words that raised goosebumps on her skin, he told her that it was the music of the underground, favoured by the country's *undesirables*. Many of the songs had been subject to censorship for a time because the lyrics spoke of alcohol, drugs, and were politically disruptive.

As Lykos spoke to her of the music's history the song morphed and the cycling chords drew foot taps from the crowd, growing loud enough to become the song's heartbeat. Claps soon joined in and somehow the music took on the weight of an orchestra, as if everyone present had a part to play in the production of the music. And, above it all, the trembling melody spun higher in a pitch that wound in her heart until she felt a burning against the backs of her eyes. She felt the rebelliousness of the song in her soul, the expression of frustration and fight similar to that of blues, but different. There was a yearning to *rebetiko* music that felt strangely just out of her grasp. As if she were so close to understanding it, to feeling it, but also knowing that it was something she would never be able to hold.

She began to sway in Lykos's arms just as some of the crowd pulled back from a man, arms outstretched and clicking his fingers in time with the claps and foot taps. His hat, looking like something from the thirties, was at a downward angle, his face partially hidden as he swayed from side to side, his footsteps surprisingly light for the circular steps he was making. There was a grace that reminded her of flamenco dancers, but heavier, grounded, deeper and so much part of the music that the dancer and musician became inseparable.

'Are your feet hurting yet?' Lykos whispered into her ear beneath the trill of the music she had half fallen in love with.

'What?' she asked, momentarily confused.

'Your list,' Lykos whispered in her ear as she wondered whether she and Lykos might have also become inseparable. 'You wanted to go to a concert. And this is the best one I've ever been to.'

'And dance until my feet hurt,' she remembered.

He looked down at her, and the words sat on her tongue, waiting for her to speak them. Waiting for her to tell him that she loved him. But she couldn't. She just couldn't be another person who claimed they loved him and walked away. So instead she kissed him with all the words that she couldn't say, she kissed him with such passion that the crowd around them began to laugh and whistle and, smiling into one last kiss, Lykos took her home.

CHAPTER TEN

LYKOS WOKE WITH a start. It was not a gentle way to do so. His pulse raced, his breath was rapid in his chest, as if someone had fired a starting gun and not told him that he was in the race. He looked to where Marit should have been in the bed beside him and saw that it was empty. Panic fired through him, even though he was sure she was still in the apartment, because he saw in an instant that this was how he would wake every morning for the rest of his life. Knowing that something was horribly wrong, because she would never be there next to him.

It was only when he caught sight of her on the balcony that looked out onto the azure blue of the Aegean that his breath slowed, even if his heart didn't. She was wearing one of his shirts—the blue cotton dwarfed her and billowed around her thighs in the early morning breeze. The blonde jagged twists of her hair fell around her shoulders, making him want to sweep them aside and press kisses to her shoulder blades. And then he realised why he was so disorientated.

He had slept. He had slept not only through Marit waking up, but he didn't remember anything after bringing her to the bedroom last night. But he never slept.

In all the years since he'd been on the streets he would pace his way through the night hours. He had never felt comfortable in a bed. As if he didn't trust the softness of it. Never stopped expecting it to bite him or be taken away. He racked his brain. He'd not had a drink yesterday at Theron's party, not with so many people around and not with Kyros.

I let you down. I am sincerely sorry for that.

Kyros's apology whispered into the morning. He still didn't know what to do with it. Those words had recalled a part of him he'd thought he'd buried so deep he'd never have to face it again. It made him feel unsettled and disorientated, but also in the midst of all of that was a core of stillness. A moment that made him felt *heard*, that made him felt *seen*.

And he began to understand what Marit had been trying to do by marrying the Frenchman. To avoid being tied to another person in her life who didn't see what she needed, what she loved, what she was so damn good at that he wanted the world to see it too. A new fresh pain sliced into his heart then. In doing her duty by returning to Svardia, Marit was knowingly sacrificing her soul's needs for her country and her family. A family that might never see her the way she needed. He wanted to rage against the injustice of it. He wanted to howl at the fact that, for the first time in his life, there was nothing he could do about it.

You're wrong. This isn't the first time.

Memories sucker punched him in the gut. His mother walking away, without even looking back, her last words to him written on his soul.

No! He would not let that happen. Not again. He would show Marit that she had a choice. That she could have the future she wanted away from Svardia, away from duty and people who were blind to just how incredible she was. She could have a future *with him*, if she would just take it and let the rest burn. Kozlov, the shares, the whole damn lot.

Determination filled his thoughts and actions as he launched out of bed, putting his quick mind to work on a plan that would not only fulfil the last item on her list still left to complete, but also show her that she had a choice.

Marit looked at the blindfold with a great deal of suspicion. Not because she didn't trust Lykos, but because she knew that her scepticism made it fun. And she wanted the rest of their time together to be that. Fun.

Last night Marit had come back from her shower to find Lykos deeply asleep. Yes, she'd missed his touch, the feel of him within her, the memory so powerful it made her ache with need but, knowing how difficult he found it, she couldn't begrudge him the rest. Instead, she'd used the time to just take him in. To learn the rhythm of his breath, the pulse of his heartbeat, the pitch of the sigh that sometimes escaped his lips. She'd spent half the night just looking at him. Imprinting everything she would need to take with her.

'Marit?'

'A blindfold?'

'We have one last thing to tick off your list. And this is the only way to do it properly.'

Tomorrow they would have to return to Svardia, but today he was making sure she had done everything she had wanted to do before she became the royal replacement for her sister. She reached for the blindfold in his hands, pulling him into a kiss she poured everything into.

Lykos groaned. '*Agápi mou*, if you do that we'll never leave the bedroom.'

'Would that be so terrible?'

'No. But, despite my very healthy and totally warranted ego, I promise you this will be better.'

Marit let out a shocked cry of indignation. 'Surely not! Wash your mouth out,' she replied, making him laugh and chasing away the last of the shadows in his eyes. He circled her then, capturing her within his embrace, and gently placed the blindfold over her eyes.

'Yes?' he asked before covering them completely. She placed her hand over his, bringing the blindfold against her eyes.

'Yes,' she replied, handing him her complete trust.

Marit could smell the sea and hear the thrust of the waves against...not sand, not a beach, but against a barrier. They must be in a port. As if in confirmation, she heard the deep bass of a ship's horn burst beneath shouted voices and gulls crying overhead. She smiled, the inkling of where Lykos was taking her growing by the second.

After a conversation between Lykos and someone, he led them forward, warning her to watch her step. She wobbled a little in his hold as the ground beneath her changed to what must have been a short platform and she was led carefully down some steps at the other end into what she knew was a boat by the way it swayed beneath her.

'Can I take the blindfold off now?' she asked with a smile so wide she couldn't contain it.

'Not yet, *agapoúla mou*. Your list was very clear. Twenty-four hours out of sight and contact with the world.'

You are my world. The thought threatened to rob her of her smile, of her joy, but she wouldn't let it. There would be time to mourn the loss of what she would never have, but not yet. She wouldn't waste their time like that. Instead, she nodded and allowed Lykos to lead her to a cushioned seat as a few more shouted exchanges were made and finally the boat beneath her was set free.

That was how it felt as the boat launched forward. As if once unleashed the boat danced on the water. There was something so musical about the way it swayed from one side to another. Still blindfolded, she held the edge of the seat, bracing herself against the rise and fall of the boat against the waves. She squealed in delight like a child on a rollercoaster when she was hit with the sea salt spray and, encouraged by the sound of Lykos's laughter, she screamed again, *sure* that he steered them against the edge of the oncoming waves just for her.

Eventually the water became smoother and Lykos tried to remove the blindfold. But she shook her head. Here, in the darkness, there was no light on the sands of time that slipped through her fingers, there was no sun to illuminate the short steps left on their path.

The boat's motor cut out and they drifted gently. Lykos's steps towards her raised an expectation beneath her skin, wanting his touch, reaching out for it. She sensed him kneel before her, felt him take her hands in his own.

'If you keep it on, you won't see what I can see, and it is truly beautiful.'

He cupped her cheek and she leaned into what had become her most favourite place in the entire world. She didn't doubt what he'd said, she imagined the view was nothing short of spectacular, but right there, leaning into his palm was better than hearing her favourite song.

'The sea is sparkling, Marit. Like silk strewn with diamonds being shaken by the gods.' His words were a feast for her senses and she was helpless to resist. She slipped the blindfold from her eyes and took in a sight that was everything he'd described and more. She stood, Lykos rising with her, and she turned in full circle, seeing nothing and no one other than nature's beauty and Lykos.

Twenty-four hours out of sight and contact from the world.

She had written it as an impossible task. Something inconceivable. She should have known that this man, *only* this man, could have made it come true. He came to stand behind her, encircling her with his arms.

They were on a yacht. Not massive or obscenely ostentatious but perfect for two people. The sail was down, but she imagined that it would be a slice of brilliant white against the soft blue sky when raised. Wood the colour of butter lined the small vessel, every detail simple but exquisite. Silver lines gleamed in the sunlight and myriad shades of blue surrounded them as far as she could see. No land, no people, nothing but them.

'This is… Lykos, it's more than I could ever have imagined.'

There was a pause. 'I know what you mean.'

Suddenly they were talking about something else. Something that she simply couldn't face.

'Marit—'

She turned and pressed a kiss against his lips, stopping the words she couldn't bear to hear. Her hands plunged into his hair, holding him to her when he would have pulled away. He let the kiss linger as long as she needed it, but the man was more stubborn than she had given him credit for. He held her in his arms, offering her the world she'd always wanted and now could never have.

'Don't do it,' he said. 'I'll give you whatever you need, take you wherever you want to go. I'll complete any list of things you like.'

Her eyes began to fill with tears she wouldn't dishonour him by wiping away.

'We'll run away. I'll find the most beautiful home for us and you'll fill it with music every day. You'll sing every day. We'll dance every day. And I'll—'

'Lykos, don't,' she said, shaking her head to stop his words. She couldn't trust herself not to give into what he was saying, what he was offering, because it was everything her heart wanted. And then she saw it. His jaw clenched and his eyes darkened the moment he felt her response as a rejection of him. 'No, Lykos—'

He turned from her and the pain she felt as he began to shut her out was devastating. 'Would I have ever been enough?' he asked, his gaze on the sea, pain glittering in his silvery eyes stealing the breath from her lungs.

'How could you ask that?'

'Are you going to tell me that the fact I grew up a child thief in an orphanage has nothing to do with why you won't be with me?'

'Lykos!' His words sliced little cuts into her heart, but she recognised them for what they were. A lifetime of hurt and rejection. 'Look at me,' she demanded, so he could see what was in her eyes, her heart. She waited and only when he turned towards her could she answer him. 'Everything you have done, everywhere you have been, it is a part of what makes you *you*. You shouldn't deny your past because it is the very thing that has driven you to achieve such incredible things. It's what makes you see the people most are blind to, makes you so generous with your time to those who deserve it, and what makes your heart so, so valuable, and you so amazing to me.'

It killed her to see the distrust in his eyes.

'Then tell me, if the legislation wasn't in place, would you marry me?'

Her heart stuttered at his question, stumbling over the thought that he might have wanted to marry her and the realisation that even then she couldn't. She felt tears gathering in her eyes, and he must have seen it because darkness swept into his eyes and she hated herself but she could never lie to him.

'No.'

'But you would have married André? And it's *not* because of where I came from?' His question was loud, angry and full of hurt and disbelief.

'No.'

'Then what is it?' he demanded.

'*Me!*' she couldn't help but yell back. 'It's me! I've changed, Lykos. Because when I ran away to marry André I was only thinking of myself. I was ignoring the fact that Aleksander didn't *want* me to make an advantageous marriage, he *needed* me to. The second in line to the throne must marry someone titled for the sake and security of the royal family and our country. Marrying André—marrying you—would be so selfish,' she said, shaking her head, her heart breaking over what she wanted with every fibre of her being, what she couldn't have. 'But if I am going to do this properly then I have to do it all, including marrying someone with a title.'

Lykos glared at her. 'And this has nothing to do with you trying to prove yourself worthy to a family that has never seen you, loved you, for who you truly are?' he accused.

It hurt how closely his question cut to the bone. She couldn't deny that there was a truth there, but it wasn't the sole reason behind her decision. In the last few days she had changed so much and it was because of Lykos. She had flourished in the freedom he had given her and, in that, found herself—even if it had cost her her heart.

'Tell me you don't love me,' he demanded, not waiting for an answer to his earlier question.

Every part of her ached to say that she did, burned to tell him how much she loved him. But she couldn't. 'Please,' she begged, 'don't make me another person in your life who tells you they love you before leaving you.'

He closed his eyes, his inhalation sharp and swift, speaking only of pain, the muscle flexing at his jaw, and her heart ached for him, for her, and for what they would never have.

'They don't deserve you.' Lykos's reply came strong and true, a slash of his hand through the air.

She cast her gaze to the floor, unable to stand the ferocity and truth in his gaze. 'That may be. But Svardia does.'

She looked up, letting him see how much this cost her, let it shine from her eyes. She poured out her hurt into the seascape and let the salt tears flow. Her sob caught in her chest and the first, 'Sorry,' came whispered on her breath, then another, then another, until all around them her apologies echoed until Lykos swept her into his arms and soothed the deep sorrow lying in her heart.

He brushed her hair from her damp face and pressed kisses to her heated skin, her forehead, her cheeks, beneath her ear, her lips, her lips again, and slowly her mouth opened to his, wanting him selfishly just one last time. She came to life beneath his touch, her hands reaching for the front of his shirt, fisting the cotton, the buttons straining. She feared that she wanted so much it would never be satiated. Until a want deeper, more primal rose within her. One that was urgent and hot and just as desperate, but the exact opposite. Now she needed to give.

Lykos felt the change in her ripple beneath her skin and taste different on her tongue. It felt like…power. She pulled him into a kiss that forced the sea to move differently beneath his feet, as if they were pushing against an impossible tide and for just this moment in time they might succeed.

Arousal swept him up in a storm, ignited by the passion twisting and unfolding in his arms, burning through the ache in his heart. There would be time to feel it later, long after he had returned Marit to Svardia. But he could not, *would* not, damage her by removing her from what she felt was her place in the world. He'd felt the strength of her decision, the way that it had settled about her shoulders. It wasn't because she felt she *had* to; it was what she needed to do for her sister, her family and her country.

He pulled back from her kiss, her hair a wild halo of gold, picking up the flecks of yellow starbursts in her eyes that looked like the feathers of a phoenix. Her lips were kiss-bruised, a flush riding high on her cheeks, her breath as ragged as his own. If this was their last day together then he would make sure that it was spectacular.

He lifted her in his arms, the squeak of surprise drawing a curve to his determined lips, delight unfurling within him as her legs instinctively wrapped around his waist and hooking at the ankles behind him. Finally, her lips were level with his and he took full advantage. He plundered her mouth for treasure, his tongue dancing with hers, teasing her, filling her, foretelling exactly what he wanted to do with her. She met him stroke for stroke, touch for touch, but when she pressed herself against his arousal he forced his grip to soften when everything in him wanted to hold tighter, to draw her to him and never let her go. But, like the phoenix she reminded him of so much, he would *have* to let her go. She had risen, changed, become the woman she was always meant to be, so tomorrow she would fly.

The thought momentarily rocked him, until she placed the softest of bites on his bottom lip. Arousal flared within him and he took her mouth in a kiss that was a sensual punishment for them both. She gasped into his mouth and it went straight to his erection, hardening him to near pain. Need became an almost feral thing, and he palmed the underside of her thighs, bringing her even closer against his body. The suite below deck felt as if it were miles away, but she deserved more than the rough comfort of cushions on wood.

As if sensing the internal debate within him, 'Here,' she pronounced and shifted in his hold, sliding luxuriously down the length of his body and tearing at his shirt, uncaring of the buttons that went flying across the deck. Her hands were hot and fast against his skin and just as desperate as his own that pulled at her top, drawing it swiftly over her head. Impatient, he flicked the clasp of her bra, drawing the straps from her shoulders and throwing it aside. Nipples pebbled, he palmed her breasts, drawing cries of pleasure from Marit. Pressing into his touch, her head fell back, exposing the long length of her neck to his open-mouth kisses. He luxuriated in the taste of her skin, traces of salt from the earlier sea spray, urging him on, the flicker of her pulse against his tongue driving him wild.

She pulled at his hips, her fingers finding the fastening on his trousers, his hands reaching for the same on hers. Frantically they pulled and pushed at clothes, laughing in their desperation until they were naked beneath the soft blue sky, the sun's rays on their skin nothing compared to the heat that drew them together in a kiss so passionate, so powerful Lykos was branded to the depths of his very soul. She had imprinted herself on him and he would never be the same again. He knew it then as deeply as he knew that he loved her. When she left she would take a part of his soul with her and he would never be whole again. The thought curled within him, folding in on itself, and he tucked it away, knowing he could never reveal that to her, knowing that to do so would cause her even more harm.

So, instead, he touched her, covering her with his palms, learning every single inch of her body, her chest, the swell of her abdomen, the dip of her hip and the curve of her backside, her skin hot and smooth and, between her legs, wet with need that only he could sate.

Lykos dropped to his knees before her, gently parting her legs and folds and, before she could say anything, swept his tongue across her clitoris, drawing a pleasure from her so pure she would have fallen had he not been holding her in place against his mouth.

The decadence of it stole her breath. Naked to the world, being pleasured by a man who knelt at her feet. He made her feel like a queen. The sweep of his tongue had her trembling, hot and needy. She felt both powerful and utterly weak at the same time as he hurled her towards an orgasm that nearly scared her with its intensity. One palm on the curve of her ass, the other on the inside of her thigh, she felt possessed, owned and branded by him.

She felt every single sweep of his tongue, every single

full-blooded heartbeat pulsing through her veins, every single spark that exploded in her heart. She luxuriated in an arousal that became something almost threateningly powerful, but it was a power she wielded. It was as if she were at the bow of a great ship, hurtling into mountainous waves knowing they could not hurt her. Knowing that she was protected by him and his love. As if that knowledge, that awareness, was all she had needed to push her over the edge of her orgasm, Marit shattered into a thousand pieces, assured that Lykos would catch every single one of them and hold her together until she could do it for herself.

When Marit came back to herself she was lying against the breadth of Lykos's chest, anchored by his legs and gazing lazily over the yacht's rails, his hands brushing over her arms. His chin was resting against the top of her head and she wanted so much to stay there it hurt.

They were on the cushioned seat and there were plates of delicious-looking food and a metal bucket containing a bottle of champagne dripping cool condensation onto the wooden deck beside them.

There were so many things she wanted to say in that moment. That she was sorry she couldn't be the person he deserved, he *needed*. That she would be yet another person to walk away from his love—it hurt her, changed her on a fundamental level. There were many ways that Lykos had impacted on who she was, but this was the most devastating.

She couldn't imagine him walking through life alone. She wanted more for him even if she couldn't have it for herself.

'So, who will you kidnap next?' she asked, forcing herself to have a conversation that made her stomach burn and her tongue ache.

He stilled beneath her, his fingers halfway between her shoulder and elbow, and she forced her body to relax, instead summoning the teasing tone she'd once relished so much between them. She twisted and looked up at him, having to shade her eyes from the sun, but his eyes burned just as bright and fierce and she steeled herself.

'That is not funny, *ángele mou.*'

'I know,' she said sadly, apology in her eyes. 'But—'

'Stop.'

'Lykos—'

'No. Marit, you made your decision. I cannot stand it, but I *understand* it and I respect it. You should do the same.'

Marit felt the sob rising in her chest, but she couldn't. She couldn't cry any more. They didn't have enough time.

'You deserve love, Lykos.'

'So do you.' His words were harsh, almost a bark. To anyone else they would be accusatory. To her, they were a stubborn declaration that his future was her future, even if they weren't together.

She climbed up his body, her lips needing his, her heart needing his touch and his love, even if just for these last few hours. As the sun rose and fell over the Aegean, the yacht swaying as gently as possible on the rise and fall of the waves, they talked, soothed, ate, drank and made love again and again until a dawn so beautiful it was talked about across the whole of Greece rose over the sea, heralding Marit's return to Svardia.

CHAPTER ELEVEN

THE JOURNEY FROM Greece to Svardia on Lykos's private jet was too short, as if time had sped up as the last grains of sand slipped through Marit's fingers. The wide arc of the sky as the small plane banked to land was as familiar to Marit as the turn in the winding drive leading to the palace front door, but it still felt strange. As if it was happening to someone else—a dream—and that her time in Europe had been the reality.

How, she wondered, was it possible that she had only been gone for five days? It felt more like five years. She twisted her hands in her lap, a nervous gesture she hadn't performed since Lykos had swept her up on the morning of her supposed wedding, thrown her over his shoulder and walked out of the hotel with her.

Looking back on it, it was a miracle that there had been no press to witness it. But, thinking it through logically, knowing Lykos the way she did now, she wouldn't have put it past him to make sure they were otherwise occupied at that exact moment. The cabin crew member announced their imminent arrival and Marit looked away, not seeing the beautiful sculptured gardens of the palace, the maze where she had once got lost, the large trees she had hidden in as a child.

Instead, she saw the sun glinting off a rippling sea,

she felt the heat of its rays on her skin, turning it pink through the day and slightly bronze as the sun set. She'd caught her reflection in the plane's bathroom mirror and wondered how it was that she appeared to look so healthy just as her heart shattered into a million pieces.

She'd not been able to look at Lykos the entire flight. She'd felt his gaze occasionally on her, but he'd not tried to break her silence, as if he'd known she needed it. Because if she opened her mouth, how could she *not* tell him to turn the plane around? Beg him to take her back to his yacht. To give her one more day, week, month, year. To give her for ever.

She'd meant what she'd said to him on the yacht. And even in the bar in the hotel in Milan. She would have always come back. And yes, there was a part of her that feared—as Lykos had accused—that she was trying too hard to prove herself, to her parents, to her siblings, to *herself* even, by doing what her family and country needed her to do. But for her sister, to whom she owed so much, her brother, who would be an excellent king, and her people, who were kind and generous, proud and determined... She could never let them down the way her parents had let her down. They deserved this from her and she would do it with all the broken pieces of her heart.

When the plane drew to a stop on the private runway in the palace grounds she released the safety belt, stood and smoothed out the crinkles in her trousers and swallowed a sad laugh before it got to her lips. The wrinkles were hardly going to be a surprise to anyone. She steeled herself. It would take time to overcome her reputation as the most disastrous princess in Europe. But she would.

She took a moment as Lykos talked to the crew unfolding the stairs onto Svardian soil. This was it. When she put her foot onto palace grounds it would be done. The decision irrevocable. She would be going straight to the office of her brother, the King. A timeline for the press announcement about Freya giving up her title and Marit becoming second in the line of succession to the throne would be decided. And if she knew her brother at all he would want her engaged to someone appropriate by the time the announcement was made.

Someone appropriate.

The phrase burned her throat as if the words dripped acid on her soul. Lykos was so much more than *appropriate* and she hated that she had made him feel less than that. But this was the moment she had to make peace with it. She would take the love she had for him, the love she had felt from him and make that enough. She breathed in deeply, hearing the tremble and mewl of the *rebetiko* music from the Greek tavern crying for her and Lykos and ached for a future she was actively choosing to walk away from.

Finally, this time when she felt his gaze on hers, she met it head-on, nodding once determinedly in that way she had borrowed from him. Her heart turned viciously as she walked up the narrow plane aisle and she passed him to take the steps down onto the tarmac to return to the palace.

Lykos waited in the corridor outside Aleksander's office, as far from Marit as he could be. She had slowly been distancing herself from him since they'd returned the yacht and boarded the plane. He'd felt it deep down and hated every second of it. But he wouldn't dishonour her or himself by asking her again. She'd told him that first day, when they were in Milan.

I will always go back.

She'd never once lied to him. But why did it feel so very much as if they were lying to themselves?

He cast a gaze at the garish baroque style that filled the entire Rilderdal Palace, everything in him revolting at the symbols of money, snobbery, emotional neglect and manipulation that it had all come to mean to him since knowing Marit.

Princess Marit.

He shook his head. The last person he'd thought he'd ever fall for. There she was on the other side of a hallway, less than two metres away, but as far from his reach as the moon. He clenched his jaw, straining at the reins that held him back: his promise to her to respect her decision. A door behind them creaked open and a small, plain-faced brunette caught Marit's eye with a sympathetic smile.

'Henna,' Marit said, meeting the woman with a warm embrace. 'Have you heard from Freya?' she asked, pulling back. 'I've been trying to reach her.'

'She's okay,' Henna replied. 'She's just out of contact at the moment.' When the dark-haired woman cast a glance in his direction he wondered how on earth Marit had failed to see the other woman's evasion. Then again, Marit only had thought for what lay beyond the door to her brother's office. The brunette nodded to him in deference and Lykos resisted the urge to laugh. If he hadn't, the sound would have been bitter and cynical and, once again, his soul lashed out at the self-imposed restraints.

'He will see you both now,' Henna announced, finally drawing Marit's gaze to his. Both as confused as the other, they passed Henna, who held the door open to them and closed it, leaving them alone with King Aleksander of Svardia.

He was leaning back against the front of his desk,

flicking through a manila folder that seemed to contain more than a few pages. He might have appeared distracted, but Lykos knew how devious Aleksander could be when he wanted—or didn't want—something. Refusing to make eye contact with his audience was definitely a power play by the King.

But Lykos was done with games and he had nothing left to lose. The shares he'd wanted to bring Kozlov down had completely lost all meaning. Let someone else deal with the bastard. Lykos was here for one reason only. To make sure that Marit was returned safely. After that? The only thing Lykos saw in his future was alcohol. A lot of it.

'Still unmarried?' It was the first thing that Aleksander said to his little sister after she'd run halfway around Europe just to find some kind of independence from this family, and it cut Lykos to realise just how little Aleksander knew his sister. *Saw* her.

'Yes, Your Majesty. I am still unwed.'

Aleksander narrowed his eyes as if something in her response didn't suit.

Lykos fisted his hands behind his back, but Aleksander's gaze briefly landed on him as if he'd seen the motion, before returning to Marit.

'And you are ready to take Freya's position within the family. Her duties and…her *obligations*.'

It was an outrage to hear him talk of marrying off his sister as a family duty or obligation. Lykos would have dragged her with him into the greatest of poverties knowing that her love was more valuable than any position, any status, any amount of money.

'Yes.'

There was nothing but pure conviction in the woman standing beside him. She was completely still even though she was taking a sledgehammer to what remained of his heart. He couldn't bear to stand here and watch this. But he would. For her. Because somehow he knew that while she couldn't look at him, couldn't touch him, she needed him here for this.

'André will keep his mouth shut?'

'Yes.' Lykos surprised the siblings by answering this time. He would make absolutely sure that nothing would taint Marit ever again.

Aleksander nodded in acknowledgement. 'I must say, Marit, even I hadn't thought of that loophole. I'm impressed. Marrying *before* you ascend to second in line to the throne could have really opened up the playing field.'

Lykos almost choked at her brother's tone. He knew Aleksander to be a lot of things, but this seemed particularly cruel.

'But never mind,' the King pressed on, 'I have found the perfect candidate to be your consort.'

'Yes, Your Majesty.'

Lykos raged in silence. Had she so little care about herself now that she didn't even want to know? To ask who it was her brother had found for her to marry? To have *children* with?

'But we are on a very short timeline, so the wedding will have to take place in three days' time. I am aware that this is *difficult*—'

This time Lykos actually scoffed. Out loud. This was her family? This was her future?

'But we have very few options available to us.'

'Of course. If I may be excused? There are things I need to attend to before the announcement.'

It was as if he weren't even there. As if he were being forced to watch this travesty take place and was utterly powerless and helpless to stop it because she'd asked him not to.

'If you mean your youth orchestra, then I've taken care of it.'

It was the only time during this farcical encounter that Marit showed any sign of reaction. She was shocked, Lykos could see, but she reined it in immediately.

'It will be included in your duties as second in line to the throne.'

'Thank you, Your Majesty. I would still like to speak to them personally about the change in my status if that is okay.'

There was a tic throbbing in Aleksander's jaw as if she had angered him somehow, not that Marit could have seen it as her eyes were cast somewhere over her brother's shoulder.

'Yes, you may leave.'

There was a moment, the space of a heartbeat when he thought that she might look at him, that she might meet his gaze for one last time. Her lips trembled for just a second, until she bit down on the bottom one as if to hold it in place, and turned away from him, from her brother, and left the room.

The moment she left he glared at Aleksander. 'You would do that to your own sister?' he demanded.

'Are you going to stop me?'

For a moment it sounded like a genuine question, before Lykos realised that it could only be the arrogance of a king.

'She asked me not to,' he growled, even though everything in him wanted to do exactly that. To stop the man.

Aleksander shrugged his shoulder and walked around the desk to resume his seat behind it. Lykos's gaze fell on the folder left open on the desk. A full colour photograph and the name of the man Marit would marry.

'I will have my lawyers draw up the papers for the transfer of shares. I've always hated having them. I detest that man.'

Lykos forced a nod, not trusting himself to speak and unable to take his burning gaze from the photograph, his eyes quickly taking in the man's title: Prince Henrik. Lykos didn't bother with where he was from, the kid looked young. And weak. He might have a title, he might be a prince and fit for Aleksander's purpose, but he was *not* right for Marit.

'If there is nothing else?' the King asked.

In the silence between them Aleksander levelled him with a glare that screamed disappointment and disapproval, but Lykos was too angry to care. He turned on his heel and stalked from the room. He slammed the door behind him, not caring that the sound crashed through the palace. Fury rose so swift, so harsh, so *much*, it erupted. Spinning, Lykos slammed his fist into the palace wall, denting the plaster and damaging his knuckles, and still it didn't help. Nothing would help. Not now.

Marit sank beneath the layers of quilts and throws on her bed and still it did nothing to ward off the cold that settled in shivers across her shoulders. Her body trembled as if in shock, even though she told herself over and over again that she was doing the right thing. In three days' time she would be married. It didn't matter to whom. It wouldn't be Lykos and that was all that did matter. And as lonely and sad as the thought made her, it was Lykos her heart ached for.

She wanted her sister. She needed Freya to tell her that she was making the right choice. But she couldn't.

If Freya knew what this was costing her, she wouldn't let her do it. Her sister had the biggest heart of anyone she knew and, no matter the consequences to herself, Freya would revoke her decision in a heartbeat. But it was time for Marit to become the Princess no one had ever expected her to be.

She reached for her phone and pressed the call icon beside her sister's name, knowing that, wherever she was, she wouldn't get the message probably until after Marit was married. She choked back the teary laugh that bubbled as she realised that, again, her sister wouldn't be there on her wedding day.

Please leave a message after the tone.

'Hi, Freya, it's me. I... I'm sorry that I ran. I'm sorry if you were worried. To be honest, I'm not sure where you are. Maybe *you're* running.' The thought made Marit smile a little. 'Should I be worried?' she half teased. Marit inhaled deeply. 'Thank you. I don't think I've ever really said that before. But thank you for being everything I needed growing up.' As Marit said the words she hadn't meant to, she realised how right they were. At every hurt, every pain she remembered, from excruciating dinner times, to night terrors, to hospital visits, Freya had been there. And, somewhere in the background, even Aleksander. It felt as if she had been searching for something her entire life that she would never get, and all along what she'd wanted had been right there in front of her.

'I know that I haven't been the easiest sister and that you've probably wanted to throttle me more times than not. And while things with Mama and Papa were difficult, you...you always made me feel loved. I might not have realised it at the time, but I do now. I have...' She broke off, trying to find the words. 'I *know* that now, the feeling of being loved. I know that, no matter what happens now or in the future, I will always have that. I didn't realise how rare that was, how much safety that love gave.'

Her voice broke on the last word, because it was absolutely the truth. She had been *seen* by him. *Loved* by him. And that had become an anchor for her. It had anchored her self-worth and sense of self and it was so strong and so deep that it had given her the strength she needed to do this.

'Please know that I do this because I want to. I do not and will never resent or place blame for the change in our succession. But I so wish you could be there. I'm not sure if you will get this in time, but my wedding day is in three days. And…if you can, I'd like that. Love you,' she finished quickly before the tears fell.

The next thing she did was pull up her messages, finding the name that she'd put into her phone back in Greece on the day of Theron and Summer's party.

She typed out a message in English.

Summer, please tell Theron that Lykos needs him urgently. This isn't a tease or payback. Please, just tell him?

Marit signed her name, hit send and then deleted Lykos's number from her contacts, deleted the sent messages to Summer and turned off her phone. The temptation to know how Lykos was would be too much for her. This was the only way that she could bear to go ahead with whatever marriage her brother had planned. Knowing that it was for the good of her family, her country… it was all that mattered.

Deep in the centre of the palace, Aleksander paced his room. Back and forth, back and forth. Things had not come about how he'd hoped. It infuriated him beyond belief, but it was not a decision he could make for them. Both Freya and Marit deserved so much more, which was why he'd put the plan into place in the first instance.

He stared out of the window, hoping that there was enough time for them to come to their senses. There was a knock on the door. He had needed to take his sister's lady-in-waiting into his confidence, not something he had enjoyed or wanted, but necessity had forced his hand. There were two people in the world he could trust and one of those was himself.

'They are waiting, Your Majesty.'

Aleksander nodded. 'Make the call.'

Henna's eyes flashed curiously, as if she wanted to admonish him. The thought was almost laughable. No one had dared try that for years. He simply stared at her until she managed to get herself under control. It took a remarkable amount of time to do, but he was a patient man and, besides, it gave him time to remember a little more about her family. And an idea seeded in his mind at that moment.

Just as she turned to go, he called her back. 'You have a sister, that is correct?' he asked, vaguely noticing the way her cheeks flushed. Curious.

'Yes, Your Majesty.'

'Single?'

'Yes, Your Majesty.'

'Your mother, she is a marchioness, is she not?'

This time her teeth clenched. Interesting. 'Yes, Your Majesty.'

'And your sister—?'

'Will inherit the title. Yes, Your Majesty.'

He raised a disapproving eyebrow and she responded in kind. *Fascinating.*

'I believe we are done here,' she stated.

'For now,' he warned, and she disappeared through the door.

CHAPTER TWELVE

LYKOS HAD REALISED the truth the moment he'd lain on his bed, staring out of the window at the moon rising over Paris, and in its silvery rays he'd seen Marit, her hair dancing on a breeze that he couldn't feel. She was the reason he'd been able to sleep. With her beside him, he'd not woken once and it had been the one and only time in his life he could remember that happening.

He'd not wanted to leave Svardia—to leave Marit—but he hadn't trusted himself to stay. So instead he'd come back to where it had all started. And he'd been confronted with Marit's wedding dress still crumpled in the middle of the living room floor as if she'd just stepped out of it.

He left it there, ignored it as he stripped off his clothes and took the longest shower he'd ever had, in the hope of washing whatever *this* was off him. Not even the dirt of the Athens streets had been so ingrained in his skin, in his psyche.

He let the water stream down around him until the tank ran cold and still he stayed beneath the spray, beating against his skin until it was numb.

But if you're numb, why does it still hurt?

It was a facile question to ask himself, when he knew the answer well enough.

Because I love her. I will always love her.

With that thought he slammed off the water, jerked back the shower door, leaving it rattling, and stalked into his room.

'*Theé mou*, Lykos, do you always walk around naked?'

'Only when there are unexpected guests,' Lykos replied without even looking up. Without even caring that Theron was there in his apartment. He couldn't even raise the energy to be shocked or surprised. 'I'll turn around if it will spare your blushes,' he threw over his shoulder as he reached the wardrobe and grabbed a pair of loose linen trousers and a long-sleeved white tee.

'Well, that's hardly better,' Theron said, standing in the bedroom doorway with his hands on his hips, his jacket flaring slightly behind the bracket of his arms. 'Now you look like some male catalogue model,' he accused, flicking his hand up and down.

Lykos simply glared at the man who was as close to him as a brother and left the room, forcing Theron to turn to make space for him to do so.

'How did you get in?' Lykos asked, mildly curious, as he walked barefoot to his alcohol cabinet, picked a glass and poured an unhealthy amount of whisky into it.

'I'm the head of an internationally renowned and respected security firm, Lykos. It would be worrying if I *couldn't* get in.'

Lykos paused for a beat, nodded in agreement and thew back the measure of whisky in the glass and poured himself another.

'Do I get one, or are you planning to drink the whole bottle yourself?'

'I was absolutely planning to drink the whole bottle myself and consider it an act of rudeness that you didn't bring your own,' Lykos declared as he ignored the wedding dress in the living area that Theron was staring suspiciously at and pulled back the French window to access the balcony.

He padded out onto the wooden decking, placed his glass on a chair and set about building the logs and fire-lighters in the firepit, wondering if he could put the dress on it in one go, or whether he'd have to cut it up. Suddenly the image of him sitting there with a pair of scissors, cutting a wedding dress into strips and feeding it into a fire seemed a little overly dramatic and he decided that he'd wait until Theron was gone.

The door slid open a little wider and Theron stepped out onto the decking and went to stand at the balcony, looking over the Paris skyline.

'Nice digs,' he commented.

Lykos barely spared him a grunt. Finally, he struck the match and threw it into the bottom of the triangle he'd built and stood back, watching the flames catch and twist and wished he hadn't because he instantly thought of Marit.

'Are you okay, Lykos?'

'Don't be such a girl. Of course I'm okay,' he growled. *'Liar.'*

Lykos wasn't sure whether it was Theron's voice he heard, or Marit's.

'Honestly, after the crap you pulled with me and Summer, you think you're going to get out of this so easy? No chance.' Theron placed a bottle of whisky that had most definitely *not* been in his alcohol cabinet on the side table and took a seat as if he was moving into the apartment.

'What do you want from me?' Lykos demanded.

'First I'd like to know why you're even here and not in Svardia getting your woman back.'

'Promise me never to say that again. You sound like some eighties neanderthal. She's *not* my woman, she's a goddamn princess and you will treat her with the respect she deserves.'

'Okay!' Theron said, raising his hands in surrender, the glass of whisky wedged between his little finger and thumb. But the tease in his tone didn't last for long and eventually Theron levelled him with a gaze that Lykos knew was very close to the line. He wouldn't accept anything but the truth now.

'Everything I've done, everything I've achieved, earned, worked for. Everything I have. It was all for nothing.'

'What on earth are you talking about?' Theron demanded as if Lykos was mad.

'I wasn't enough for her.' Shame cut through Lykos as he said the words. He stared at the ground between his feet, hating that he felt so much hurt, so much agony. Hating that Marit in any way reminded him of his mother. Hating the way he wasn't sure which woman he was talking about. Hating that it made him tear up. 'She walked away without a backward glance.'

They both had.

He clenched his jaw, hoping that somehow it would stop the press of wet heat against his eyes, that it would force down the swell of agony rising in his chest as he fought a sense of rejection and abandonment so acute that, if he'd been standing he would have fallen. Even now he was half afraid he might not get back up. His breath shuddered silently, the crackle and pop of the fire, the distant sounds of the Aegean on the Piraeus shoreline filled the silence for what felt like an eternity and somehow Lykos had known what Theron would ask.

'Did you ever look for her? Your mother?'

'She told me not to. She told me it was for her own protection. That Aeolus would use me to hurt her and keep hurting her. Tell me, Theron,' Lykos demanded, glaring up at his old friend, 'how could I have looked for her? How could I have, knowing, believing truly, that it would cause her physical harm?'

Lykos's gut twisted, not feeling as sure as he had once done as a teenager.

'And after we found out he'd died? I don't get it. You kept track of Summer's mother for years…but not your own.'

The words sliced, quick and clean, at his heart. Lykos shook his head. 'I…' Shame and grief and loss swirled like a noxious substance in his stomach. 'What if she didn't want me? What if she'd moved on and I was a re-minder of *him*? What if all I could ever be to her was pain?'

The empathy burning in Theron's eyes was almost enough to push him over the edge. He shook his head again. The friend closer to him than any brother could have been put a hand on his shoulder.

'Lykos, we all make mistakes. As children, when it is done by adults, it is inconceivable to us. Your mother thought what she was doing was right, of that I have no doubt. But if you want to find out, to track her down, then know that we'll be here for you. Summer, me. Even Kyros. You think you don't have a family, you think you're alone, but we're here. For you. So if you ever want to find her, say the word. It's done.'

Reeling with shock from Theron's words, his offer, Lykos realised that he'd never, not once, wondered if his mother had made the wrong decision. Perhaps because he'd had to be completely sure that she was right because emotionally that had been the only way he could make peace with the situation.

It was as if a giant fissure had cracked open in the ground beneath him.

'What?' demanded Theron, who must have picked up on it.

'My mother was trying to do the right thing.'

'Of course,' Theron replied as if it were obvious, and then, his eyes narrowing in understanding, 'like Marit,' he concluded.

But Lykos had to dispute it. 'Theron... She is a *princess*. I am little more than a street thief with a bank account.'

Theron was silent for a long time. Long enough to draw Lykos's gaze.

'Is that what you think? *Skatá*, Lykos. I saw the way she looked at you.'

'It doesn't matter.'

'Do you love her?'

'With every single beat of my heart and breath I have left on this earth.' The sincerity of his words spoke to the depth of their souls as if it were a prayer and a promise. For a shocking second Lykos felt a hot damp heat against his eyelids and fisted his hands until it went away. He used the anger. Fed off it to push the sorrow back down where it belonged. He wrestled with the idea that she might have made a mistake, thought through the logic and tested it against what he knew of her and her situation.

'She is sacrificing herself and they don't even see it. Her family, they are supposed to protect her. They are supposed to put her first. I swear, Theron, if she marries this guy, it will kill her. Slowly, bit by bit and day by day, it will ruin everything that is pure and perfect about her.'

Words choked in his throat and he threw back another mouthful of whisky to ease the tightness.

'You want me to dig up some dirt on him?' Theron offered.

'And, what, we blackmail them? They're kings, Theron. *Actual* royalty.'

'And maybe you're letting that mess with your head.'

'What do you mean?' Lykos growled in warning.

'You were the greatest pickpocket in Athens, Lykos, or are you so ashamed of your past that you forget who you were? Who you *are*,' he stressed, staring Lykos dead in the eye with a determination and fire that Lykos felt in his soul. 'You say that it will kill her, marrying this guy? Then stop it. Do what you have to do to save her. She might want to do what is right, Lykos, but if you say it's wrong I believe you and I will support you one hundred per cent.'

'And I do what, kidnap her on her wedding day, *again*?'

'For real this time? Absolutely. So, what do you say?'

'I say,' Lykos said, standing from the chair, 'that the Pickpocket of Piraeus is going to attempt his greatest act of thievery yet. I'm going to steal a princess.'

Marit stood in the stone corridor of the Svardian family chapel. It had been there for as long as there had been a palace. She smoothed a palm over the large solid blocks of stone that made up the walls of the small church. Cold to the touch, Marit found it fitting somehow. Beyond dark wooden doors, her brother, the priest and her groom waited. The agreement between the two families had been made, Marit not really aware of the specifics. Her brother's machinations had long since stopped surprising her. Her greatest regret was simply that her sister wasn't there.

Her parents were still on their year-long sabbatical, protocol thankfully meaning that they were out of contact to all their children for the first three hundred and sixty-five days of the new monarch's rule. Marit didn't mind so much about the parents who had been little better than absent for most of her life, but she missed Freya terribly.

She wasn't quite sure where Freya was. She could have sworn that she'd heard one of the staff talk about her return to the palace, but Marit hadn't been able to find her and she wasn't answering her calls. Her absence had stung at first, until she remembered that her sister wasn't the source of her hurt and it had lessened the ache in her chest. Instead, Marit had drawn on the love she'd felt from Lykos to fill the void in her heart, realising that in the end, whether she spoke to Freya or not, she would marry Prince Henrik and do her duty by her country.

She ran a slightly damp hand down the front of her dress, smoothing imaginary wrinkles from the silk. It was a pretty dress this time and, while it might not be what she would have chosen for herself—an image of the stunning dress she'd worn to Victoriana flashing in her mind's eye—at least it fitted.

Footsteps clacked on the stone flooring, coming towards her, and for an insane moment she hoped that it was Lykos, come to whisk her away. Her heart pounded in her chest and her cheeks flushed with anticipation, her hopes crashing to the ground when she caught sight of Henna coming around the corner.

'Your Highness?' she said, rushing towards Marit in concern.

'I'm…fine, thank you, Henna. I don't suppose you've seen Freya?'

Henna's eyes clouded and she shook her head, her lips a thin grim line.

Marit nodded, telling herself that it was okay. That it didn't hurt.

'Are you…sure that this is what you want?' Henna asked. 'You need to know that you have a choice here, Marit. You don't have to marry Henrik.'

Marit was taken by her tone—the sincerity and assurance in it was powerful and strong. But the thing was, she knew that she didn't have to. Yes, Marit wished things were different, but her sister was stepping down and her family and her country needed her. She dug deep within herself and found the strength she needed.

'It's okay. I'm ready.'

A simple piano version of Pachelbel's 'Canon in D' played as Marit took her first steps down the aisle. She wore a simple veil, short across her shoulders, falling lower at the back, and through the cream gauze the chapel took on an ethereal quality. Her brother stood behind a man who looked familiar only in that she had seen photographs of the Prince. He seemed…young. With each step she took in not the man she was to marry but the ways in which he wasn't Lykos. He wasn't dark-haired like Lykos, he wasn't as tall or broad as Lykos, his jaw wasn't as strong, his eyes didn't spark silver shards that she could stare at for hours.

She mentally shook herself, knowing that it was cruel to be comparing Henrik to a man he never had a hope of matching. This was different, Marit told herself. This would only ever be… Her footsteps faltered and her gaze flickered to her brother's. There was something there, something in Aleksander's eyes, that she hadn't seen before. Worry? Concern? Regret?

All thoughts, however, were wiped from her mind as the wooden doors behind her burst open and clattered furiously against the stone walls. Shock sliced through her, causing her—and everyone else in the chapel—to turn.

Framed in the now open doorway, Lykos looked like an avenging angel. He filled the space, sunlight streaming in behind him, casting him in shadow, and the lock of hair fallen across his forehead seemed almost purposely disrespectful somehow. Lykos cast a look over her shoulder, but Marit only had eyes for him and her heart soared, even as her mind blanked.

He stalked down the aisle, the first step apparently enough to prompt the priest to ask what was going on. Marit half expected her brother to step forward, but he didn't. She knew that she should move, should stop Lykos, should step from his path, but the sheer determination simmering in his eyes had struck her still. He had but one intent, a single focus so sure, and she knew— *knew* that he would not be stopped.

Within a heartbeat he had closed the short distance she'd travelled up the aisle and had stepped indecently close. Their ragged breaths billowed the gossamer-thin veil between them. Her hungry gaze consumed the sight of him. Her heart was pounding so hard in her chest she was surprised it didn't echo around the small chapel like the whispers of the men behind her. She wanted to weep and sigh and reach for him and push him away all at once. She followed his gaze to where it had been caught, flickering between her eyes and her mouth, finally homing in on her lips as if he wanted nothing more than to feast upon them.

'Forgive me?'

His words were so unexpected it took her a moment to register them. 'For what?' she asked, just as a smile curved wickedly at his lips.

'For this,' he said. It was all the warning he gave her as he grasped her wrist, bent slightly, leaned into her and hauled her over his shoulder as he straightened.

'Lykos!' she screamed.

Her cry cut sacrilegiously through the serenity of the chapel, met by a chorus of shocked gasps from the groom and the priest.

Lykos shifted Marit on his shoulder, one hand securing her in place, the other pointing at Aleksander, his heart finally settling now that he had his hands on her. He angled himself towards a tableau he would have found amusing had it not been so tragic.

'This is done,' he announced to Aleksander. 'She will not be your puppet any more.'

Aleksander nodded. Lykos was surprised to see what could have been satisfaction in the King's eyes.

'She deserves your words, *Your Majesty*,' he growled. Marit needed to hear it. Needed to know that her family weren't using her and that they wouldn't come after her. There would be time for them to discuss it properly, but for now she had to know that she had a *true* choice. Only then would she be free.

'Yes. She can go now.'

A relief so vast and so sure swept through Lykos in an instant and he had to force his lungs to work as if for the very first time.

'And Kozlov?' the King demanded.

It wasn't even a contest. He would choose Marit. Every. Single. Time.

'He's your problem now. I'll transfer my shares to you

so that you have the majority. I am sure you will find a suitable way to dispense with him.'

'I will,' the King confirmed, before raising a hand to stop Lykos from turning when he would have. 'She needed someone who would fight for her,' Aleksander said, his tone as much a warning as an explanation. In that moment, Lykos understood a different interpretation of events than how he had seen them only moments before.

He could only hope that Marit's brother deserved that interpretation.

'*Entáxei*, we are done,' Lykos announced as he stalked from the chapel, making his way past Henna. He was about to thank her, as he would not have been able to return to the palace without her help, but she waved him off before he could form the words, glancing back to the chapel where her King was watching her every move. Lykos would have wished her luck, but wondered whether Aleksander might need it more.

He walked out into the sunshine as male voices behind him were raised in what sounded like a nauseating outburst. Words like *outrageous*, *unbelievable*, *disrespectful* filled the air in a deeply whiney tone until a very commanding, 'Enough!' stopped the flow. Lykos was happy to leave Aleksander to it. The man had made his bed, he needed now to lie in it.

'Lykos—'

'Not yet,' he interrupted. He might have won the battle but not the war. He needed to focus on what came next, and he couldn't do that with his hand on the curve of Marit's backside, holding her to him and destroying concentration.

He approached his convertible and pressed the key fob so kindly replaced by the dealership. The locks clicked satisfyingly as he came to the passenger side door, pulled it open and poured her into it. There was less tulle this time, the affair much sleeker than it had been ten days ago, but he still wasn't happy with her dress. She looked, once again, as if she were playing dress-up, but this time it came off as old, staid, serious. All the things that she was *not*.

Marit fumed up at him from the seat of the car as he shut the door on her, but simmering beneath the glare was heat. Heat and something he didn't quite yet dare to hope for. Lykos rounded the car, half expecting her to flick the locks, but she didn't. He couldn't tell whether that was a good or bad sign.

He opened the door and slid behind the wheel, his hands wrapping around it to stop himself from reaching for her, from dragging her to him in a kiss that would never end. There were things that needed to be said.

'Lykos—'

'Not *yet*,' he said again, unsure that he could trust himself to say what he needed to if she distracted him. 'I need you to know that, no matter what, you can go. You can go anywhere. You don't have to choose me. You don't have to feel obliged or indebted. Your life is your own now. I know what you were doing. Aleksander and Freya know too. And clearly it meant a lot to them, for you to be willing to make a sacrifice of yourself.'

'Ly—'

He pinched the bridge of his nose and squinted his eyes shut. 'Marit, so help me, if you don't let me say this, I never will.' He practically felt the way her lips closed, imagining them pressed together between her teeth. 'The thing is,' he pressed on, 'they are your family. And they will support you, no matter what, just the way that you and Aleksander will support Freya. But you cannot expect them to see you, if you erase yourself in such a way. And I promise you, Marit. Marriage to that puffed-up Prince would have made you invisible.

'*Make* them see you by showing them who you are. By honouring yourself and them with choices that come from your heart,' he said, thumping his chest—which might have been a little dramatic but, dammit, that was how she made him feel. After all, he'd just kicked open the door of a church and walked off with a princess bride. 'And if that choice is not me, Marit, then,' he said, breath shuddering in his lungs, 'I will stand by that.'

The car was filled with silence for much longer than Lykos liked.

'Is that it?'

'What?' he asked, turning to face her.

'That's your big declaration, is it? Pick me? Choose me?'

'Well…yes,' he answered, a little stuck for words.

'I didn't hear anything about love in there. Not once,' she huffed—and his heart rose up in his throat at the sight of the tease in her eyes. Not that she wasn't right. He'd been so worried about making sure she knew that she didn't have to stay, he hadn't told her why she should.

'*Prinkípissa mou*, you are the key to my heart and everything that lies within it. It was closed, locked away until you snuck past defences that no one has *ever* breached. I might have been a criminal in my youth, but you are the real thief. You have stolen my heart for ever and I don't even want it back.

'Because I *see* you. The talented, crazy-hearted, beautiful, fiery, fun woman that you are. Because I see the incredible partner, the amazing wife and perfect mother you will be some day. And because I love you. With every single beat of my heart and breath in my lungs, I love you.'

Marit's eyes glistened, the shards of jade and gold glowing with a love that Lykos had to pinch himself to believe. Her lips had formed an O and a gentle sigh fell from them and warmed his heart.

'Lykos…'

He waited, but she remained silent. 'What is it?'

'Well, I had thought you might interrupt me, so I was giving you time.'

He glared at her, but it was such a mockery of anger, Marit knew that he enjoyed her tease as much as she did.

She reached for his hands, loosening their iron grip on the steering wheel and taking them in her own. She reached up to cup his jaw in her palm and her heart soared when he leaned into the affectionate touch.

'Thank you,' she said at first, because she did need to say it. 'I am sorry that I would have done you such a disservice in the name of duty.' He shook his head as if to ward off her apology. 'I…' She paused, finally allowing herself to believe that this was real. That he had freed her from a duty she was *never* supposed to have borne. 'But what about Freya?'

'I believe that your brother has plans for her that will make things right.'

'Really?' Marit looked up, so very hopeful.

'Absolutely.'

With his confidence so assured, Marit's heart soared. 'I love you, Lykos. More than I ever thought possible. I didn't know that this was what it felt like, to be loved and to love. I didn't trust in it before but now I do,' she said, her heart trembling in her chest. 'You make me feel so special, so wanted and so loved, all I can hope to do

is show you how much that means to me, each day for
the rest of our lives.'

He turned the key in the ignition. 'We need to leave.
Now.'

'What's the rush?'

'I need to get you out of that damn dress, because
there's no way I'm proposing to you while you're wearing a wedding dress meant for another man,' he growled
and floored the gas pedal. Her laughter pealed out of the
open window as the Aston swept from the palace with a
spray of gravel on the driveway as they began the first
day of the rest of their lives together.

EPILOGUE

LYKOS SAT WITH his face turned to the sun, legs stretched out before him and his heart filled with love as he listened to the sounds of his children laughing and the delicate notes of the bouzouki being massacred. The high-pitched trill came to a sudden stop and a curse was uttered, low and angry.

'The children, Marit,' he called, eyes still closed, knowing that his voice would carry to her.

'That's Princess to you,' she yelled back grumpily.

He smiled as he heard a sigh, before the instrument was put down on the floor of the music room that led straight out onto the long garden, at the bottom of which ran a shallow stream the children adored. Her footsteps sounded closer and closer, her presence raising goosebumps across his skin even after ten years of marriage. He held his arm out to catch her as she passed, hands wrapping around her waist and hauling her into his lap, where his wife did a truly terrible job of trying to escape.

'You know I could run if I wanted to?' she said as his eyes finally opened to see her beauty.

'I know that you can do whatever you turn your heart to,' he said, knowing the words touched her by the way her eyes flared gold. 'Just perhaps not the bouzouki.'

She slapped at his arm and he pulled her closer and pressed kisses against her neck that went from playful to passionate the instant Marit groaned and shifted in his lap. He stilled, not because he didn't want to, but because the children would return soon, eagerly anticipating the arrival of Katy, Theron and Summer. Pressing his forehead to Marit's, he cupped her cheek and loved the way she leaned into his palm, appreciating how she instantly understood why he slowed his affection.

'*Agápi mou*, you just need patience.'

'It was never one of my strong points. But then you came along and then I learned—'

Marit's laughter burned bright as he went to kiss the tease from her lips and the passion that burned between them was still as bright as it had been when they had met. The day he'd kidnapped her for the second time, he had whisked her away on his private jet and flown them back to Paris, where he'd divested her of another wedding dress not meant for either of them and later, naked and satiated, he had proposed.

Of course, he'd then had to propose again properly and in the grandest way possible—in part because he'd discovered how Theron intended to surprise Summer and the drive to best him was irrefutable, but mainly because Marit deserved it. She deserved a man who would proclaim his love for her to the world. So each year he found new, devious, attention-grabbing ways to remind Marit that she was the most loved. He'd been doing rather well and even Theron was on the verge of admitting defeat, until Marit had bested them both with a gesture so grand and so impossible it was unbeatable.

As Marit gentled her kiss, she snuggled into his chest and they lay there in the sun, outstretched on a lounger until the sun passed behind the turret and they were momentarily cast in shade.

About a year after they'd married, Marit finally extracted why it was that Lykos had always wanted a castle. He'd never told a living soul, but it had started when his mother had told him stories while his father slept off his hangover. Stories of castles and maidens and an English thief called Robin Hood, the son of an Earl, who'd lost his lands and title when fighting in the Crusades and returned to England appalled by the poverty he'd found there. He'd robbed from the rich to give to the poor and Lykos had known that his mother had told him this story to make him feel better about doing his father's bidding. As a child, he'd decided that one day he would live in a castle and never have to steal another thing.

And his wish had come true. The last thing he'd stolen had been Marit's heart and he would never need anything again. Not even the castle Marit had made their home in. Lykos marvelled at how he felt more love now for Marit than he ever had. While she'd returned to university to study music and then later music therapy, he continued to work, but much less intensely. Marit had learned to play every instrument she could find and they had enough musical equipment to outfit an orchestra. Marit's youth project had been a roaring success even before Aleksander had kept his promise to support it.

His wife had an insatiable curiosity about almost everything and when she'd asked him to teach her how to steal wallets he'd laughed, but she'd been insistent. Aleksander still had not forgiven him for that, making him give his word not to corrupt any other heirs to the Svardian throne.

His phone alerted him to a message from his mother, letting him know that she was set to arrive as planned in the next two days. Finding her had been the easy part. It hadn't taken Theron long to track her down. But it had been a difficult process. His mother had lost many years to alcohol and other addictions and had refused to meet with Lykos.

It had hurt more than he thought he could stand when he'd felt that sense of rejection from his mother—and if Marit hadn't been with him he wasn't sure he'd have survived it. In the end, Kyros had paid a visit to her and had convinced her to let them help her with rehabilitation. For the next few years, she had allowed Kyros and sometimes Theron to meet with her, tell her about the son she had abandoned, and it became clear the guilt and shame she felt over that had been a large contributing factor to her addictions. Patience, time, therapy had slowly begun to ease her feelings and eventually she and Lykos had been able to begin a painfully slow process of getting to know each other again.

But Lykos would never forget what Theron and Kyros had done for him. They had given him the chance to have a relationship with his mother. One late night after the others had gone to bed, on a visit to the Soames estate in Norfolk, England, he and Summer had stayed up, determined to finish the bottle of Limniona, Theron's favourite wine, and he had confessed how much he felt he owed them.

'Love isn't a debt to repay, Lykos.' She'd said it with a hand on his arm and stone-cold clarity in her eyes, before she'd hiccupped and he'd sent her to bed with a laugh. He'd never forgotten her words and instead showered everyone close to him with as much love as possible from that day on.

The doorbell rang, bringing screams of hysterical joy from his two daughters at the bottom of the garden, their little bodies streaking past as they ran to open the door to Theron, Summer and Katy. Lykos went to shift Marit, but she held him in place.

'They've got it, husband.'

'They will terrorise our guests before I can even get a word in,' Lykos warned, well knowing how enthusiastic their daughters could be.

'I know. But there's something I wanted to tell you first.'

'What is it, *agápe mou*? Have you found another instrument you want to learn? Another wedding dress you want to wear? Another list you'd like me to fulfil?'

'Not quite,' she said, biting her lip in that way that always drove him wild. He wasn't concerned in the slightest, because he knew his wife and her rapid heartbeat meant she was excited. Though what she had to be excited about, he... His mind shorted.

'No. Really?' he demanded, launching upward, forcing Marit to cling to his shoulders just to stay upright. 'Are you sure?' he asked, his heart wanting to explode from pure joy. She nodded, sending her crumpled blonde curls into disarray, and he stood up, bringing her with him, and swept her round in a circle.

'We're pregnant again,' Marit whispered and Lykos's heart soared.

Theron, Summer, Katy and their children came to stand at the door to the garden.

'Another one?' Theron demanded.

'Yes,' replied Lykos smugly.

'Seriously?'

Theron spent the rest of the afternoon muttering the word *Rabbits*, and one of the most perfect days Lykos could remember settled into a warm, summery haze of friendship and love as he recalled how it had all started with the Princess who stole the pickpocket's wallet.

* * * * *

A DIAMOND FOR MY FORBIDDEN BRIDE

JACKIE ASHENDEN

MILLS & BOON

CHAPTER ONE

Olivia

A MAN WAS leaning in the doorway that led to the upper floors of the Silvera mansion and, even though his face was in shadow, his head was turned in my direction and I could tell he was watching me.

I could feel the pressure of his gaze like ghostly fingers trailing down my spine.

A shiver whispered across my skin.

I couldn't make out his features, since he was leaning just out of the light, but I could see already that he was tall and broad-shouldered and powerful.

Unease coiled inside me.

Security had been tight for Domingo Silvera's funeral and it was even tighter here in Madrid, at the Silvera mansion, for his wake.

But, given Domingo's fame, how could it not be? He'd been the CEO of Silver Incorporated, one of Europe's biggest companies, with shares in tech, R&D, manufacturing, finance—you name it, Silver Inc probably had a stake in it. It was a behemoth, making more than a few governments give it a sideways look.

Domingo's father, Diego, who'd inherited the family traits of ruthlessness and arrogance from the ancient line of Spanish aristocrats they were descended from, had started the company nearly a hundred years earlier, and since then it had grown and prospered. Yet it hadn't been until Domingo had taken over that it had flourished to become the massive company it was today.

Many people had come this evening and the ornate marbled ballroom of the mansion was full of politicians, business people, heads of state, the rich and the famous…all here to pay their respects to one of Europe's most powerful men.

Even Domingo's rivals and enemies, of which there were many, were here.

Perhaps that man in the doorway was one of them. An enemy come to gloat over the corpse of a dead foe. What else could explain the aura of menace I'd felt emanating from him?

Normally I'd never let something as basic as unease get to me, but I still shivered yet again, and found myself shifting closer to my fiancé, Constantine Silvera. He was Domingo's son, heir to all Domingo's power, and was now newly crowned CEO of Silver Inc.

I didn't need his protection, but he was tall and powerfully built, and radiated a certain reassurance that in the moment some part of me craved.

Constantine was cold, arrogant, ferociously intelligent, a wolf when it came to business and frightened people just as his father had. All those aristocratic traits had been distilled in him and he used them to his advantage. Ruthlessly.

He was also the possessor of the famous Silvera beauty—black hair, black eyes and the kind of profile that would have looked good on a coin. He'd been named for an emperor and an emperor he was. One that didn't bother with the velvet glove. There was only the iron fist.

So, yes, I should have felt safe with him in a mansion surrounded by the tightest security on the planet.

I was the CEO of Wintergreen Fine Diamonds, my family's old and illustrious jewel company, and had a fairly powerful security team of my own, all of whom were present tonight.

Yet I didn't feel reassured.

Constantine was probably deciding when the appropriate time was to give his speech, thanking everyone for coming and so on. If he noticed my uneasiness, he gave no sign, his cold, black eyes surveying the guests dispassionately.

Usually nothing could get past the façade of cool competence and poise that I'd cultivated over the years. I'd had to. Being a female CEO of a very traditional company required a certain strength and I didn't like anything to undermine it.

Things such as the shadowy presence of a stranger.

Constantine would be appalled if he knew. He saw my icy calm as strong, and strength was a quality he admired, as he so often told me.

Though, ours wasn't a love match.

My own father had died eighteen months earlier, leaving behind him a legacy of terrible financial mismanagement that could have resulted in Wintergreen going bankrupt. It had come as a terrible shock, since I'd always seen him as the consummate businessman. So had the board, and they'd been very clear that they didn't want me at the helm. It had been a…testing time. Then the past had come calling unexpectedly in the shape of Constantine Silvera.

I knew him from years ago, when I was a child and our families would holiday on the same Caribbean island. While there had been…difficulties back then, that was all water under the bridge now.

He'd said he'd heard about Wintergreen's financial issues and that he'd like to help. He'd been prepared to help me, to pay my father's debts and get the company solvent again as long as he took over management of it until the company was on its feet again. Oh, yes, and in return all he'd required was my hand in marriage. He needed heirs, it was time and he'd always appreciated the Wintergreen genes.

Initially I'd been suspicious of his offer. The board already thought I was unsuitable to take over Wintergreen, since they were all traditionalists who didn't like a woman managing the company. Having Constantine take over management for a time would make me look weak, as would marrying him.

Then again, if I wanted the company to survive, accepting Constantine's offer had been the best way forward. Also, there was another plus: children.

Wintergreen was a family company, and if I wanted it to remain so I would need heirs, just as Constantine would. My father had always said that I could be CEO of Wintergreen or be a mother but I couldn't be both, and that when I had children I would have to step down.

He had generally been right about most things when it had come to running Wintergreen but, given his financial mismanagement, I'd begun to question a few things.

I didn't see why I should have to have to step down from being CEO, for example. I wanted a child, I wanted to be head of Wintergreen and Constantine could definitely give me that.

I'd been told by my doctor that I had a limited window in which to get pregnant, and if I wanted children I had to start now, so it was that in the end that swayed me.

Also, there were worse things than having children with a physically perfect specimen of manhood who also just happened to be one of the most powerful men in Europe. His family history, of course, left a lot to be desired, which might not have made him the best choice to be the father of my children, but I could make it work. The child would have me, after all.

So I hadn't refused, I'd accepted, and here I was— his fiancée.

'Something the matter, Olivia?' Constantine's deep, cold voice tinged with the soft, musical Spanish accent he hadn't quite been able to get rid of jolted me. 'You seem disturbed.'

So, it seemed he *had* noticed my discomfort after all. How irritating.

I was excellent at projecting the kind of cool strength required of a CEO, but the fact that Constantine had noticed my discomfort meant my usual veneer was slipping.

I didn't like that. He wasn't a man who invited deep confidences—not that I'd have felt comfortable sharing them with him even if he had been—and had given me nothing but chilly courtesy for the past three months of our engagement.

I didn't trust him. He was pure predator, just like his father had been, and if there was one thing I'd learned in the last eighteen months in the boardroom it was that showing weakness of any kind in front of a man like him was a mistake.

'I'm fine,' I said coolly, trying not to glance at the dark figure in the doorway yet again. 'Only wondering when you were going to start the speeches.'

'In a minute.'

I looked up at him. He sounded distracted, which was

unusual. Normally he was all razor-sharp focus, like a shark sniffing blood in the water. When he had a target or a goal, he pursued it relentlessly.

Now, though, with his black eyes sweeping over the crowds like a searchlight, it seemed the target wasn't his speech but something else.

Strange. Was he looking for someone? Perhaps it was Jenny, his stepsister, who'd promised to be there for the funeral yet hadn't turned up so far. Or perhaps he'd sensed the guy in the doorway too.

Whatever, he didn't seem to be bothered by it the way I was. Then again, Constantine had always seemed impervious to any feeling whatsoever. He was like a glacier—cold, glittering and perfect.

I'd known Constantine since I'd been seven years old, but we'd never been close, despite him only being a few years older than me. He'd been cold even then, more interested in his studies and doing whatever Domingo asked him to than playing games with Valentin and I...

Valentin.

An old, worn grief twisted inside me, a grief I thought I'd left behind a long time ago; the edges were somehow still sharp even after all these years.

How ridiculous. I shouldn't be thinking of him.

I forced my gaze away from the man I was going to marry, the man who was the mirror image of the boy I'd once loved with all of my poor, silly teenaged heart.

The boy who'd died in a car accident fifteen years ago.

He and Constantine were identical twins, and many people had been unable to tell them apart, but never me. I'd always known who was who.

How can you marry him? When all you'll ever see is everything he's not? Everything you lost...

I ignored the thought. Really, I should stop listening to the ghost of my fifteen-year-old, overly dramatic self. I'd buried that weepy, hysterical child after Valentin had died and I'd moved on. I was nothing like her now and I didn't want to be.

Abruptly, Constantine stopping searching and nodded to one of his aides, who immediately called for everyone's attention.

The buzz of conversation died and I shoved away the echo of a long-ago grief, composing myself, turning myself back into the diamond heiress and Constantine Silvera's cool and poised fiancée.

'Friends,' Constantine began, the ice in his voice searing all the warmth from the word. 'Thank you all for coming. We are here today to celebrate the life of Domingo Silvera, my father—'

'That sounds like my cue.' The words were deep, gravelly, cutting through Constantine's speech like a hot knife through frozen butter.

A shocked silence fell as everyone in the room turned and looked in the direction of the voice.

It had come from the man in the doorway.

A premonition gripped me, wrapping around my throat and twisting hard.

I had no idea where it had come from or why, but I suddenly knew without a doubt that something terrible was about to happen.

I opened my mouth to warn Constantine but, just at that moment, the man shoved himself away from the door frame and stepped out into the ballroom.

A ripple of sound passed around the room, a kind of gasp and sigh combined, and an abrupt, scorching heat swept over me.

That man… I knew him.

He strolled into the room with the powerful, predatory grace of a panther, his hands thrust casually in his pockets.

He was as tall as Constantine and as broad. He had the same strongly carved, fiercely beautiful face. The same straight nose, high cheekbones and hard, carved mouth. The same coal-black hair, black brows and deeply set black eyes.

Constantine's mirror image.

Yet there were some slight differences. This man's hair was slightly longer, grazing the collar of his white shirt, which he wore open with no tie, unlike Constantine. He didn't have Constantine's air of icy control, either. No, this man had the opposite.

He burned like a flame.

As suddenly as the heat had swept over me, it vanished, leaving behind it the freeze of a deep, echoing shock.

I'd only ever met one other man who burned like that, and he hadn't been a man, but a boy. And that boy was dead. He'd died long ago and I'd mourned him with everything in me.

Valentin Silvera, Constantine's twin.

My poise vanished. My fingers were blocks of ice, and so were my feet, and I could feel the same shock that gripped me wash through the assembled crowd. They were all staring at Constantine Silvera's duplicate, strolling calmly through their midst as if they weren't even there.

The man didn't look at the crowd. He looked only at Constantine, who didn't move or speak, as if he'd been turned to stone.

'Hello, little brother,' the man said in perfect, unaccented English. 'Long time, no see.'

The entire ballroom was utterly silent.

If I hadn't heard him speak, I'd have been certain I'd gone deaf.

'"Why are you here?" I hear you ask,' the man went on, even though no one had asked. No one had said a word. 'That's a good question and I'm glad you mentioned it.' He smiled, easily and friendly, but for the flames that leapt high in his eyes. 'I bet you'd forgotten, hadn't you, that I'm your elder by five minutes? Which of course makes me the oldest son.' He had a panther's smile, predatory and white. 'And, since I am, I'm going to claim the company, Constantine. Because you are not a fit man to run it.'

His smile widened and then his black gaze settled on me, burning far more fiercely than I remembered. Instead of the warm, comforting glow of a hearth fire, this was the wild heat of a forest blaze. 'Oh, yes, and that pretty fiancée of yours? You're not a fit man for her either, so she'll be mine too. Then again, she always was, remember?'

No, he couldn't be here.

He was dead. It had been a tragedy. A terrible tragedy. And I'd cried endless, dramatic tears at his funeral while Constantine had stood by the grave side, his face so pale it had looked as though it was carved from ice. And Domingo had been beside him, dominating the proceedings, a powerful, terrifying figure betraying no expression whatsoever. As if he hadn't just lost a son.

The silence in the room was deafening, not that I'd have heard anything anyway, over the blood roaring in my ears.

He wasn't dead, he was here, large as life and radiating an aura of menace that the boy I remembered had never had.

A hundred times as gorgeous too.

The heart I'd thought I'd buried all those years ago suddenly shuddered to life in my chest, like an old machine starting up. It was beating so hard it felt as if it was going to break all my ribs.

Desperately, I curled my fingers into my palms, my nails digging in, trying to find my poise, my usual strength.

'What?' Valentin asked sardonically. 'Got nothing to say, Con? Don't worry, I'm sure you'll think of plenty tomorrow. Especially when my lawyers contact you.' His smile flickered like a flame. 'So, how would you like to play this? In full view of everyone? Or would you prefer to discuss this in private? Either is fine with me, though I have to tell you now, I do like an audience.'

I couldn't take my eyes off him. I couldn't breathe.

What was he doing here? What had happened to him? How was he alive? His body had been identified in the burned-out wreck of a car on the outskirts of Madrid. An accident, the police had determined.

There had been rumours he'd been trying to escape from Domingo, about whom rumours of violence had swirled, though everyone knew him to be a perfectly charming if arrogant kind of man. Rumours that perhaps it hadn't been entirely an accident.

And yet…he was here, right in front of me.

He hadn't been in that car, had he?

'You're dead.' Constantine's voice was a dark, icy wind, as if somehow saying the words would make Valentin's presence less real. 'You died fifteen years ago.'

Valentin's sardonic smile remained. 'Apparently reports of my death have been greatly exaggerated. As you can see.'

People were whispering, shock echoing and rebounding through the room.

I dug my nails harder into my palms, the cold seeping through me, unable to keep from staring at him, cataloguing all the changes the years had made.

He wasn't the same. I could see that now.

There had been a warmth to the boy I'd known and a calm patience I'd found so reassuring and steadying. My father had had no patience with my 'girlish tantrums', as he'd termed them, but Valentin had never minded.

We'd met on a secret beach on that Caribbean island and had become friends. And, as we'd grown older, we'd become something more.

He'd always had time for me. He'd always been kind too, and funny. He hadn't seemed to care that I was only a girl.

But there was no trace of the boy in the man standing there with his hands in the pockets of his black trousers, his expression amused. He appeared casual and yet every line of him blazed with intensity.

He wasn't a flame now; he was a furnace.

The whispering grew louder.

'Silence,' Constantine ordered, that wind becoming a low, howling gale.

The whispering stopped.

The tension that had gathered in the room the moment Valentin had appeared pulled so tight it was nearly unbearable.

I forced my gaze away from Valentin to look at my fiancé instead, because I had the oddest feeling that Constantine wasn't so much shocked at his brother's appearance as he was angry.

Incandescently angry.

I wanted to say something, to stop whatever was

going to happen next, because I knew it would be terrible; I just knew it. But I felt paralysed by shock, my throat too thick to force words through.

'You look perturbed,' Valentin observed casually, strolling closer to his brother. 'Understandable, what with me coming back like Lazarus, on top of managing this farce of a funeral. Well, don't worry, I won't take up too much more of your valuable time. I'll just take what's mine and then be on my way.' That intense black gaze of his flicked back to me and he held out a peremptory hand in my direction. 'Come, Olivia.'

I stared at him, my head full of memories.

Memories of the last time I'd seen him, on the small hidden beach, the one that no one else had known about; the one that had been our special place. It had been night, the black sky above scattered with jewel-bright stars, and he'd kissed me for the first time.

He'd whispered in the dark that one day, when we were both old enough and free of our families, we'd get married and be together for ever.

I'd never wanted anything so badly.

We'd lain in the sand, still warm from the day's heat, talking about how our life together would look and what we'd do. Marry, have a family, be free.

I'd loved him so much.

Then the next day he hadn't come down to the beach as he'd promised and it wasn't until later that I'd heard he and Constantine had been sent back to Madrid.

I'd never got to say goodbye. I'd been upset about it, but not worried. Because he'd had my mobile number and we could have texted each other and called.

Except he hadn't called. And he hadn't texted. And he hadn't emailed.

I'd never heard from him again.

Six months later, he was dead.

I'd only been fifteen and full of the desperate, dramatic emotions that often fill teenage girls. He'd been my first love, my first heartbreak.

But I was a woman now, not a child, and I'd left all of that behind me. I was stronger, harder and colder, as I'd needed to be to manage my company. So I had no idea why I was suddenly full of emotion, full of a blistering rage that left me shaking.

Because how dared he?

How dared he have left me without saying goodbye? Without a text, a call or even an email? How dared he break my heart like that, knowing how much I'd loved him? How dared he tell me he loved me, only to leave?

And, more than anything else, how dared he pretend to die?

I opened my mouth to tell him where he could stick his, 'Come, Olivia'.

Then all the lights went out and the ballroom was plunged into darkness.

For an instant, there was only silence.

Then the entire place erupted into chaos, people shouting and screaming.

I stayed where I was, rage and shock still coiling through me, making it difficult to think. Someone called my name, but I couldn't tell who it was or in what direction it had come from. Then I felt someone grab my hand, their grip large, warm and strong.

Constantine.

Strange that I should feel better with his hand holding mine, since I'd never needed reassurance from him before. Nevertheless, I did now, so I held tightly to him as he gently pulled me along through the blackness.

Light was coming through a doorway, his tall, broad

figure momentarily blocking it out as he approached it. Behind me, I could still hear people shouting in confusion and the sound of smashing glass.

My heart was still beating far too fast, though my fear was receding.

What on earth had happened? Had there been a power failure or something? Yet, even as I thought it, I knew the idea was ludicrous.

The lights had gone out with perfect timing, just before Constantine had been about to take charge. Which meant it was no power failure.

Valentin had engineered it, I was sure, but why? To what end?

Constantine drew me through the doorway and I stood for a second, blinking as my eyes adjusted to the light. And, as they did, he turned around.

And my heart dropped all the way down into my uncomfortably high stilettos.

Because it wasn't Constantine.

It was Valentin.

CHAPTER TWO

Valentin

FINALLY. FINALLY, AFTER ALL those months of planning, Olivia Wintergreen was mine.

But then, she always had been.

Her clear, light-grey eyes had widened and I had been able to see the shock rippling over her pale, delicately featured face.

She'd assumed it was Constantine who'd taken her hand so naturally she'd be surprised to find it was me instead.

Her hand was cold, her fingers icy, and I remembered how she'd get cold after a swim in the sea, and I would take them in mine to warm them up. Once, I'd kissed the tips of her fingers and she'd laughed because it had tickled. She'd always had the most beautiful smile.

Except she wasn't smiling now.

Not that I expected her to.

I'd let her think I was dead—I'd let everyone think I was dead—for the past fifteen years and so I hadn't exactly anticipated being welcomed with open arms.

She certainly wouldn't be happy when I got her back to my villa in the Maldives. But I'd deal with that later.

Once she was there and safe, she'd have all the time in the world to yell at me.

First, though, I had to get her away from Constantine.

I'd planned this meticulously, right down to the very second I'd had my men cut the power, then I'd moved, crossing the space between us so it was my hand she'd grabbed in the darkness.

Me, leading her to safety.

I didn't have time for explanations, not with Constantine's security. I had to get her out of the mansion and with the least fuss possible before the confusion brought about by the power cut wore off and Constantine realised what had happened.

Yet even though I knew time was of the essence, for a second all I could do was stare at her, noting how changed she was.

She'd been fifteen the last time I'd seen her, all long, slender limbs and waist-length straight silver-blonde hair. A wildcat, yet with the sweetest smile I'd ever seen. My friend once, before she'd grown into something more.

She'd been so beautiful. The only thing I'd had in the hell of my childhood that had been mine.

Until Constantine had taken her from me.

Satisfaction was a cooling balm to the rage that had ignited inside me that moment six months ago when, during my daily press briefing, one of my staff had informed me that Constantine was now engaged to Olivia Wintergreen.

Well, he wouldn't be engaged to her much longer.

Just as he'd no longer be inheriting Silver Incorporated.

He might have had a couple of years' grace at being CEO if he hadn't involved Olivia. But he had. And now he would have to deal with the consequences.

The fury I'd glimpsed in Olivia's eyes just before I'd had the power killed leapt again, and she tried to jerk her hand away.

I tightened my grip. I didn't want her running, not before I had a chance to secure her. I'd been forced to give her up all those years ago and I wasn't going to let her be taken from me a second time.

'For God's sake, Valentin, what are you doing?' she demanded, those diamond-bright eyes of hers flashing. 'Let me go!'

Perhaps if I'd been kinder and more reassuring, gentler, things might have gone differently. But I wasn't. Because the boy who'd once had all those qualities was dead. He'd died in that car accident all those years ago.

And someone else had taken his place.

I wasn't Valentin Silvera any longer and I hadn't been for fifteen years.

I'd left him behind in the wreckage of that burned-out car, along with some of my DNA, in an effort to finally escape that bastard Domingo once and for all.

Now I was just Val, CEO of a company that had its roots in the shadier of Europe's crime networks, but was now straighter than an arrow, dealing with all kinds of security from tech to personnel to equipment.

And I wasn't kind or gentle or reassuring any longer.

I smiled at Olivia, my bright little star. 'Oh, sweetheart, I'm not letting you go. I'm not letting you go ever.'

Another woman might have been scared, but fear had never ruled Olivia before, and it didn't now.

Temper glittered in her eyes, her pale cheeks flushing pink.

Standing at Constantine's side, she'd been tall and slender as a lily, dressed in a plain yet expensively tailored dress of sombre black wool, as was fitting for a funeral. The colour hadn't suited her, making her look even paler and more washed-out than she actually was, yet her expression had been diamond-hard.

She seemed so different from the young girl I remembered. She'd been such a passionate little thing back then, a ray of sunshine in the darkness of my childhood. I'd been drawn to her, unable to help myself, at first fascinated by that passion and then, as I'd got to know her, by the sweet smile that she saved for me alone, the one that reminded me of a summer dawn.

There were no smiles now, but I could still see her passion in her anger, lighting her up from the inside like someone had put a candle inside her and lit the wick.

'You're insane.' Her chin lifted with all the defiance and authority of an empress giving the order for war. 'Let me go before Constantine calls his security team.'

'He can try.' I tightened my grip and held her fast, noting that her fingers no longer felt so cold. 'But I've had my men infiltrating his staff for the past six months so, unfortunately for him, it is no longer "his" security team.'

Her gaze flickered. Was that fear I saw there? I didn't want her to be afraid, but if she was it couldn't be helped. There wasn't time to allay any fears, not when they'd involve more than a few complicated explanations.

Besides, she should already know that the very last thing I'd do was hurt her.

'I see.' There was no fear in her voice, only a cold, flat tone that made her sound like Constantine. 'What do you want with me, then?'

Her long, pale blonde hair had been coiled in a chignon at the back of her head and locked in place by what looked like a million hairpins and several bottles of hairspray. I was half-convinced that if I touched her hair it would feel as hard as the diamonds her company sold.

I didn't have time for this conversation, not right now, yet I found myself answering all the same. 'You really have to ask that question? What do you think I want with you? You're marrying my brother, and I can't have that.'

'So, what? Instead of sending me an email, or maybe even picking up the phone, you decided to infiltrate Constantine's security and disrupt your father's funeral with some bizarre kidnapping scheme?'

I laughed. 'Well, when you put it like that, it does sound a trifle...bizarre. But I have my reasons. Besides, if I had sent an email, would you have called off your engagement?'

'No, of course not.' Impatiently, she tugged at her hand again, trying to get free. 'Let me go, damn you.' It wasn't a plea. It was an order.

Sadly for her, I had no time for orders.

Even if I had sent her an email, Constantine would never have let her go. He was too much like Domingo, which was why I had no choice except to take not only the company but Olivia as well.

Domingo Silvera destroyed people, and so did Constantine.

I would not allow him to destroy her. This was about keeping her safe from him and I would go to any lengths to ensure that.

So I didn't let her go. Instead, I pulled her in closer to me, watching her face with its delicate, precise features.

She'd lost the openness she'd once given me, the emotional honesty that had been so precious. Her expression held nothing but icy calm, and there was a hard quality to her, a toughness that hadn't been there before that belied her delicate build and pretty china-shepherdess face.

What had happened to her in the years since we'd last seen each other? I'd always hoped she'd forget me, that once the news of my death got out she'd put me behind her and move on with her life.

Except I'd known the instant she'd seen me come into the ballroom that my hopes had been in vain.

She'd gone dead white, frozen in shock like everyone else in the room, and for a brief second I'd regretted being so public with my plan.

But secrecy wouldn't have worked and would have given Constantine some measure of cover if he'd retaliated. Plus, the world needed to know I was back in order for me remove him as CEO of Silver Inc. So why not make a public gesture of it? And what better timing than at that bastard's funeral?

Olivia would get over the shock and, indeed, it looked as if she already had, her hard expression betraying absolutely nothing, not even a trace of the fury I'd seen before.

I could feel the resistance in her arm, but I didn't relent, bringing her in closer.

Where had that fury gone? Was it still there? Did it mean she still felt something for me after all these years? Perhaps she didn't. It had been a long time and we'd only been teenagers, after all.

Or perhaps she'd been angry because I was taking her away from Constantine. Did she love him? My research indicated that she didn't; I thought they hadn't slept together, but had she let him touch her after all?

I could feel my own jealous rage rise at the thought, and I let it, since anger had always been a useful fuel for me.

Domingo had once told me that emotions were vulnerabilities and they had no place in his world; that I needed to free myself of them, because only then could I become the great man I was destined to be.

But he'd been wrong. He'd always been wrong.

Anger was power. Anger was fuel. And I burned it without compunction.

'Valentin,' she said coldly. 'I have my own security team. They're all military trained and, if you don't let me go right this second, they will end you.'

'Call them. They can try to end me, but I've died before and, as you can see, it didn't take.'

'If you don't—'

'You're not going anywhere except with me,' I said. 'So you might as well come willingly.'

'I will never come willingly, not with you.'

I shrugged. 'Then you will come unwillingly. The former will be easier for both of us; the latter will be inconvenient, but nothing more than that.'

Despite her icy expression, her breathing was fast and the pulse at the base of her throat was frantic. Again, though, she wasn't afraid; I could see that clearly. No; what she was, was furious.

Ah, that brought back memories…

I pulled her in even closer. So close I could hear her breath catch. Her perfume was faint and subtle, sophisticated. That was new; she hadn't worn perfume back when she was fifteen. Yet beneath that perfume I could smell something ineffably sweet, like honeysuckle. Her…

I remembered lying on warm sand beneath a star-studded sky, my own heart beating hard as I brushed my mouth over hers. Her lips had been soft, as velvety as rose petals, and she'd given the most delicious little sigh, as if she'd been waiting all her life for my kiss.

Now her eyes darkened as she stared up at me, like

quartz filled with thunderclouds. Was she remembering that same moment? That same night? Did she remember that kiss as I did?

She looked delicate. As though she were made of spun glass.

A feeling tightened in my chest that wasn't anger, for a change, yet I didn't know what else it could be. And, though I wasn't gentle any more, I said, 'I won't harm you, little star. But you will come with me. I'm afraid you have no choice in the matter.'

For a second I thought she might give in, melt against me the way she had when we'd been young, giving me her trust and her surrender.

But she didn't.

Instead, she shook herself, giving me a look of the most complete disdain. 'I think not.'

And the feeling inside me twisted again, turning into something else.

Anticipation.

That girl she'd once been hadn't gone, it seemed. Under that diamond-hard veneer, little Olivia Wintergreen was still a wildcat.

Good. I liked a strong woman. And a strong woman who challenged me? Even better.

How had Constantine handled this new version of her? Had he tested that stubbornness? Had he broken through her diamond walls? Or did the pair of them freeze each other out?

Suddenly I was desperate to know, and know everything about their relationship. She would tell me. I'd make her. And then I'd make sure she never thought of him again.

Olivia opened her mouth, no doubt to tell me she'd

scream again, but time was running out and I'd already lingered too long.

Before she could get a word out, I lifted her up and tossed her over my shoulder.

For a second she lay still, draped over me, her body warm as I turned in the direction of the front door. I thought I might get out without her creating a fuss.

Then she went stiff. 'Valentin! What the hell are you doing? Put me down!'

I smiled. There she was, the wild Olivia I remembered. 'What do you think?' I put an arm around her thighs to keep her steady and to stop her from kicking, which she probably would. 'I already told you that you were coming with me.'

'Don't you dare!' A fist thumped hard against my back. 'My security are armed!'

'Not any more, little star,' I said. 'My team have already secured their weapons. But feel free to scream on your way out.'

Then, gripping her tightly, I strode out of Constantine's mansion, Olivia Wintergreen screaming a furious blue streak all the way.

CHAPTER THREE

Olivia

THE MOST DELIGHTFUL warm breeze washed over me. It was gentle and brought with it the smell of salt and the heavy, sweet scent of tropical flowers.

I stretched, not wanting to open my eyes, because the bed I was lying in was so comfortable and the breeze felt good brushing over my bare skin…

Wait…

My *bare* skin? Since when had I slept in anything but pyjamas?

My eyes popped open, an unfamiliar ceiling above me.

Rafters in a honey-gold wood criss-crossed the big vaulted, empty space, a white fan turning lazily above the bed. Strange, silky-looking patterns of light rippled over the exposed ceiling, almost as if it was the reflection of the sun shining on water…

I stared at the patterns, not taking it in.

My brain felt sluggish, my head vaguely achy and my mouth dry, as if I'd had an emotional overload at some point, a crying jag, which couldn't be right. Not when I liked to stay in control at all times. Had I somehow forgotten myself at Domingo's funeral and wake?

I hadn't been grieving him, not when I hadn't liked him in the first place.

The wake... The shadow in the doorway...

My breath caught as memory came sliding in slowly like the tide.

Valentin.

A flush of violent heat went through me as the memories came flooding back. Valentin's sensational appearance... Constantine's fury... My own intense shock. And then the lights had gone out and someone had taken my hand in theirs, warm and reassuring. Except it hadn't been Constantine's hand, as I'd assumed, and I could still feel the shock as the tall man had turned round and I'd found Valentin's black gaze burning into mine.

'I'm never letting you go...'

The memories came flooding in even faster. He'd picked me up and slung me over his shoulder as if I weighed nothing, ignoring my shouts of rage and my fists hammering his strong back. He'd carried me out, tossed me into a car that had been waiting in the driveway and then, before I'd known what was happening, I was being driven away. He hadn't come with me and, not twenty minutes later, I'd found myself at private airfield being ushered into a sleek jet by two burly security staff.

Furious, I'd tried to argue with them—demanding an explanation, demanding to know where I was being taken, demanding to speak to Valentin—but all I'd got back was silence. I'd tried threats next, but that hadn't worked, either.

Valentin had arrived a few minutes later and proceeded directly past where I was sitting, heading to the work space at the back of the plane. He hadn't even looked at me.

Then we'd been in the air and, when I'd finally been

able to unbuckle my seatbelt, I'd tried to confront him, only to be prevented from getting anywhere near him by the same stony-faced bodyguards.

I think at that point I might have shouted. I'd definitely called him every name under the sun and then some.

Then, left with nothing else to do, all my fury expended, I'd gone back to my seat and had promptly fallen asleep, exhausted.

Now I sat bolt-upright, looking round wildly at the four-poster hung with gauzy white curtains that had been drawn back.

I was sitting in the middle of the vast mattress of that four-poster bed, a white sheet wrapped around me. The room was big, the walls panelled in that same honey-golden wood, the floors the same colour, and directly opposite me were huge sliding glass doors. The doors had been pulled back to admit a wonderful breeze and I saw immediately that in fact, the pattern on the ceiling *was* the reflection of the sunlight on water.

Through the doors was the ocean. A deep, intense turquoise-blue ocean.

A lagoon with a reef lay just beyond.

A wooden deck lay outside the doors and I could see stairs leading down from it, presumably straight into that beautiful water.

I didn't move, staring at the tropical sea a stone's throw from the bed, my heartbeat loud in my ears, along with the sound of water lapping gently against wood.

All I could see was Valentin's black eyes and all I could feel was his hand enveloping mine, the heat of his skin burning me, and his body as he'd drawn me in close, hard and hot. Not the body of a teenage boy any longer, but of a man. A broad-shouldered, powerful man.

He'd smelled so good, like cinnamon and cedar: warm and spicy and delicious...

'Feel free to scream on your way out...'

And just like that the rage of the night before returned. There was no trace of my cool, calm façade now. It had been crushed by the weight of the fury that washed through me.

Fury at being taken here against my will.

Fury at someone who was supposed to be dead, someone I'd loved and mourned, who was clearly not dead and had somehow duped everyone into thinking he was.

Fury at myself for being so weak and allowing all of that to happen.

And, just as I was fulminating about that, another thought struck me.

I looked down, pulling up the sheet wrapped around me.

Yes, as I'd suspected: I wasn't wearing the black dress I'd put on for the funeral. I'd been put into a delicate nightgown of white silk instead.

I was supposed to be focused and driven and in command of my emotions. I wasn't supposed to let them command me.

My father had always been very clear about that. He'd wanted a son to inherit his company but, as my mother had been unable to have any more children after me, he hadn't been able to have one. So he'd done his best to mould me into his idea of the perfect CEO, despite my being female. And the perfect CEO was ambitious and cold and above all strong.

I wanted to be all those things. I didn't want to be like my trophy-wife mother, fluttering around ineffectually, all weepy and emotional, doing everything my father told her in a futile effort to make up for the sin of not producing a son. He had been a difficult man, and my mother had never stood up to him. She'd let him walk all over her, and one thing I'd sworn to myself was that I'd never let any man do that to me. I'd never stay with a man who treated me that way. I'd never be her.

So, I wasn't. I cultivated my ambition and kept my emotions locked away in a box. I was strong and in control.

But in that moment I forgot every single lesson my father had drilled into me as fury gripped me, hot and bright and intense. I launched myself off the bed, clutching the sheet around me.

I was going to find Valentin Silvera and then I was going to wring his neck.

With my bare hands.

And then movement caught my eye from the deck outside beyond the big, glass sliding doors.

A man was coming up the stairs from the ocean.

He was still wet, the sheen of water on his bare, deeply tanned skin glistening in the sun highlighting the width of powerful shoulders, the planes of a broad chest, the carved corrugations of his rock-hard stomach and the length of his strong thighs.

Water dripped from his night-black hair and, as he reached the deck, he shoved one long-fingered hand through it, pushing it back from his face.

I froze in the middle of the bedroom, my fury forgotten for an instant.

He was stunningly beautiful.

He was also very, very naked.

Blood rushed into my cheeks.

It was, of course, Valentin.

'Good morning, little star,' he said as if he wasn't

entirely naked, his voice deep, rich and much warmer than Constantine's had ever been. 'I see you're awake.'

My cheeks were burning, shivers of heat whispering over my skin. I wanted to look away from him and yet at the same time I wanted to keep staring, mesmerised at the sight of all that masculine glory.

He'd always been tall back when we were children, and in the water of that hidden beach I'd given him co-vert glances. At thirteen I'd been strangely compelled and at the same time oddly flustered by how muscular his body was.

He'd been beautiful then, and he was beautiful now, and I was very conscious that I was not thirteen any longer.

I'd steered clear of men altogether after Valentin had supposedly died, and since I'd taken over the company they'd steered clear of me. I'd been told I was too in-timidating, which had been pleasing, and not something I wanted to change.

I'd never met anyone I'd wanted to change for, any-way. And I still hadn't.

Except this feeling now…wanting to look at him, touch him, see if his skin was as velvety and hot as it looked, glistening and brown in the heat of a tropical sun… It was unfamiliar sexual attraction and I didn't like it.

Part of the reason I'd decided to marry Constantine was because, though I admired his cold beauty, I didn't feel any need to touch it. I wasn't attracted to him, no matter that he looked like Valentin, which was exactly what I'd wanted.

Having children together would require some amount of touching, but I deliberately hadn't thought about that aspect of it. It was the child I'd get at the end that mattered to me. I didn't think about sex, full-stop.

'Something the matter?' Valentin drawled, straightening up to his full height, his beautiful mouth curving in a wicked smile that sent yet more prickles of heat scattering all over my skin. 'Or did you see something you liked?'

My fury returned no matter how hard I tried to ignore it, doubling at my reaction to his nakedness.

It shouldn't bother me. I should have been over him years ago. I'd cried for him so many times and then, on the first anniversary of his death, my father had told me to snap out of it; that he was gone and all the crying in the world wouldn't bring him back. I should divert my energies into my school work, because didn't I want to go to university? Didn't I want to take over the company?

So, I'd told myself to stop being so stupid. Valentin was gone, and he'd dumped me anyway, so why was I crying for a boy who'd made me all those empty promises and then never spoke to me again?

My father had been right—crying was weak and pointless and it wouldn't bring Valentin back—so I'd stopped and had never cried over him again.

'I want answers.' I ignored his comment as I clutched my sheet around me. 'And you will give them to me. Now.'

'Oh, I will, will I?' His smile was all flame, hot and wicked, flickering around his mouth. 'And what will you give me if I do? I can think of several things already.'

'I'm not giving you anything,' I snapped, struggling despite myself to keep my gaze firmly on his face. 'You owe me, Valentin. A few answers is the very least you can give me.'

'I owe you, hmm?'

I took a step towards him, unable to help myself, my fury raging at the leash I was trying to keep on it. 'You kidnapped me, you bastard. And then undressed me.'

'Yes, so I did. Sorry about that.' He did not sound the slightest bit sorry. 'You'd fallen asleep, so I carried you off the plane then had a staff member put you in that nightgown, because who wants to be in the same clothes for fifteen hours straight? And, as for the kidnapping, well…it was the quickest and easiest way to get you out of Madrid.'

None of that mollified me in any way.

'I didn't want to leave Madrid.' I took another step. 'Where am I? What am I doing here? Why did you bring me here? And what happened to you?' The words spilled out of me heedlessly and I had to lock my jaw to stop myself from saying any more.

From telling him how you cried for him and how he broke your heart.

No, God, no. I never wanted him to know that. I'd spent years armouring myself against that kind of pain and I would never again willingly open myself up the way I had back when I was fifteen.

I was Olivia Wintergreen, CEO of Wintergreen Fine Diamonds. My father had always told me that in order to manage the company you had to be a diamond. You had to be hard, bright and sharp. Flawless in every way.

And so a diamond I'd become.

Valentin said nothing for a long moment, his hot gaze roaming over me, his expression giving absolutely nothing away.

Then, before I could move or make a sound, he strode towards me, still dripping wet and scattering water drop-

lets. Two steps and he was in front of me, his hot gaze
on mine.

'Did you miss me, Livvy?' He reached out, his fingertips brushing my cheekbone, his touch bypassing all
my armour, scorching right down to the centre of my
soul. 'It's been such a long time. Too long.'

He was so close, the spicy scent of his skin half-
drowned by the fresh salt of the ocean he'd just been
swimming in, and I was instantly transported back to
that night on the hidden beach.

It had been one of those warm, tropical nights when
the air had been heavy with the smell of flowers and yet
cool enough to be pleasant. We'd just been swimming,
even though my father had forbidden me to go swimming in the sea at night. He wouldn't have been happy
with me being with Valentin, either—if he'd known.

I'd loved Val so much. I hadn't wanted to be with
anyone else.

Our skin had been damp from our swim and we'd
lain in the sand together. My whole body had felt alive
with awareness of him so close to me. And then he'd
raised himself up on one elbow and looked down at me,
reached out and brushed his fingertips across my cheek,
as he'd done just now…

I'd trembled, wanting him to kiss me so badly.

And he had. Lowering his head, his mouth on mine
so unexpectedly soft, and warm…

I shoved the memories away. Hard.

'What's going on, Valentin?' I demanded, forcing the
husky sound from my voice. 'Why am I here? I have to
get back to Madrid.'

'You're not going back to Madrid.' He didn't smile
this time, his hand dropping away. 'You're not marrying him, Olivia. I forbid it.'

'What do you mean, you forbid it?' I stared at him in outrage as he turned away, going back out onto the deck to grab the white towel from the sun-lounger.

'You heard me.' He dried himself off with brisk strokes, then casually draped the towel around his neck, gripping the ends in his large, long-fingered hands, still making no effort whatsoever to hide his nakedness. 'You can't marry him. I won't let you.'

'You…won't *let* me?' For a minute all I could do was blink in astonishment at his arrogance, his sheer audacity. 'As I recall, no one died and made you king.'

Amusement glittered in his eyes. 'There's still time.'

There was an edge to him I could see. An edge that hadn't been there before, or maybe I'd just never noticed, but one thing was for sure: that edge was razor-sharp.

I took a breath. This wasn't the boy I'd known. This was someone different, a harder man, a man infinitely more dangerous than the boy had ever been.

He's fascinating…

The thought crossed my mind and instantly I pushed it away. No, I definitely wasn't going there. No matter that my heart was a guarded fortress these days and men were of no interest to me at all; he'd kidnapped me and dragged me halfway across the world without asking, and all because he didn't want me to marry his brother.

He was mad and there was nothing fascinating about that.

'I'm going to the police,' I said coldly. 'And when I tell them—'

'You're not a prisoner, Olivia,' Valentin interrupted. 'You may leave whenever you want.'

'But you just said—'

'Admittedly you'll have to fly yourself home, since

I only have one pilot and he's not here. But you're welcome to try it.'

The fury inside me leapt again and I moved, striding past him, still clutching my sheet, stepping onto the deck outside the bedroom and into the dense tropical heat.

The deck seemed to wrap around the entire house so I kept on walking, determined to figure out where I was and how I could get away.

I was right about the deck, it did wrap around the entire house, which was built over the clear, turquoise-blue water. A tiny island, a jewel-bright stud of green with crystalline white sand surrounding it, lay behind the house. The deck led onto a jetty that stretched from the island right into the deeper waters of the lagoon.

But there was nothing tied up at the end of the jetty. No boats. No planes. And there was nothing in the sea, just endless blue water, the sun striking sparks from the surface, the scented air warm and humid.

I was breathing hard, sweating in the heat, an anger I couldn't fight burning in my chest like a hot coal.

He'd lied. I *was* a prisoner. There was no way off this tiny island and he knew it.

I turned back to the house, though 'house' was too simple a word for the sprawling, luxury villa built over the water that looked like it was hanging suspended over the lagoon.

It had been a long time since I'd been to the tropics. I didn't like the sun or the heat, or the sand that seemed to get everywhere; not these days. I burned easily and I loathed having to constantly put on sunscreen and wear a hat to stop from getting sunburned.

I didn't want to be here.

I wanted to be back in Madrid. Or, no, what I actually wanted was to be back in London, in the gracious old home in Hampstead where my mother still lived. Back where everything was familiar and I was in control of things.

A thought flashed through my head.

What about Wintergreen? What about the debts? What about the board? What would they do when they discovered I'd been kidnapped by Valentin?

And Constantine? What about him?

My stomach lurched. Constantine... He'd known Valentin and I had been more than friends when we were teenagers, but he'd never mentioned it to me, not once. He'd never even spoken his brother's name. Would he come searching for me? Or would he think I'd gone with Valentin willingly? And, if he did, would he still want to marry me?

You'd better hope so otherwise you can say goodbye to Wintergreen.

The hot coal in the centre of my chest burned hotter, brighter. Those debts needed paying and the board had been looking for a way to get rid of me ever since Dad had died. They didn't like the fact that I was a woman and they liked the changes I wanted to institute even less. This would give them the perfect excuse to let me go.

Damn Valentin. Damn him to hell.

I had to get back. I *had* to. I'd worked too hard to get where I was, to prove I could manage the family company better than any son, and I couldn't let that slip through my fingers just because of some idiot man.

I strode back along the deck, the wood smooth and warm beneath my bare feet, the sheet still wrapped around me fluttering in the warm breeze.

Valentin had come out to stand on the deck outside the bedroom.

Mercifully he'd pulled on some clothes—a simple white T-shirt and worn jeans—and now he stood there, impossibly tall, impossibly gorgeous, his hands in his pockets, watching me.

His posture was casual, but the smile on his face was the fierce, predator's smile he'd been wearing when he'd appeared at the wake.

A panther who'd captured his prey and was now contemplating exactly the best way to eat it.

Except I wasn't prey.

'There, you see?' he said as I strode back to him. 'You can go wherever you want.'

But I didn't stop.

It felt as if I'd always had this anger burning inside me, an anger I'd had to swallow for the last fifteen years in order to prove myself worthy enough to manage Wintergreen, even though I'd had the misfortune of being born female.

'They'll never respect you if come over too emotional,' Dad had used to tell me about the board when he'd finally had to accept that, if he wanted the family company to remain in family hands, he was going to have to leave it to me. 'If you want them on your side, you have to be confident. You have to be cold.

'Be a diamond,' he'd gone on. 'Diamonds are beautiful, but they're also hard and sharp. They're created under pressure, so they're strong. And that's how you will be too.'

And so that was how I was.

But it turned out that, right now, I was not a diamond. Instead of being hard and sharp and cold, I was seething with frustrated fury. At Valentin for upending my carefully ordered life and putting my company at risk. Not to mention tumbling me back into all the emotional chaos I thought I'd put behind me.

I raised my hand and slapped him hard across the face.

CHAPTER FOUR

Valentin

SHE WAS MAGNIFICENT striding towards me, her hair tossed by the breeze and trailing out behind her like a veil, the sheet moulding to her curves and outlining perfect round breasts, the swell of her hips and slender thighs...

She was perfection, a vengeful goddess with her silver eyes flashing and her cheeks glowing pink.

There was no sign of her hard veneer, not now. No, there was nothing but the white-hot passion that had always lived inside her, that used to make her burn like a star.

And she was burning now.

Desire gripped me, intense and hungry. I'd always used to wonder what she'd be like as a woman, and I'd thought I'd get to see her become that woman too, if it hadn't been for Constantine. Now here she was in all her glory...

I wanted her. And, since I denied myself nothing, I would have her.

However, since she was clearly going to slap me, perhaps I'd wait to broach the topic.

Sure enough, her hand came up and for a split second I debated grabbing her wrist before she could land a blow. But, if slapping me helped her feel better about the situation, then I'd let her.

Violence was certainly a choice but there were other, far more pleasant ways to get rid of excess emotion. Perhaps I could show her that once she realised hitting me wouldn't change anything.

So I didn't move and I didn't flinch as her blow landed. I'd had worse, much, *much* worse, though she wasn't to know that.

The crack of her palm against my cheekbone resounded in the humid air and it stung—she was surprisingly strong. I smiled. Pain could make pleasure that much more acute and I wasn't averse to it.

'Feel better?' I asked mildly.

She was breathing very fast, her pretty eyes darkened with fury. Then the anger began to recede and a look of shock crossed her face.

'Oh, my God,' she whispered as if to herself. 'What are you doing to me?'

But I didn't want that fire inside her dying, didn't want that diamond veneer back in place, and as she started to back away I reached out and grabbed her wrist, pulling her closer to me. 'I didn't do anything,' I said. 'You did that all by yourself. And it was magnificent. You can even do it again, if you like. I don't mind. I enjoyed it.'

Her eyes were wide as they stared into mine and I could feel the tension between us grow then pull taut. Her skin was still pink and flushed, making her irises look darker, like charcoal instead of quicksilver, and the sun in her hair turned it into a deeper gold.

The sweet scent of her surrounded me, mingling with the salt to remind me of that secret Caribbean beach, situated between our respective holiday estates, where we used to meet. Of swimming, lying in the sand and talking about everything and nothing. Of driftwood fires and toasted marshmallows and arguments and apologies.

Of friendship that had grown slowly over time into something more…

She'd only been fifteen, and there had just been a kiss between us, but she'd had my heart even then. Just as she still had it.

And she's not fifteen now.

Her wrist in my hand felt delicate and fragile, my fingers mapping the beat of her pulse. Her skin was warm and I could hear her breath catch.

For a second, I thought she might lean forward and press those petal-soft lips against mine.

I could almost taste her kiss…

She ripped her wrist from my grip and took a couple of steps back, shaking her head. Then she turned around, her back to me, her spine stiff and ramrod-straight, looking out over the endless blue of the Indian Ocean.

I could feel the blood pumping hot in my veins, the sound of my own heartbeat loud in my head. I'd been certain for a moment there that she was going to soften for me, kiss me, let out that passion I knew lived inside her. But apparently not.

It made me want to close the distance between us very badly, to pull her into my arms, shatter that hard veneer of hers and discover the sweetness of her kiss once again. To tug away the sheet and bear her pale skin. Then pull her down onto that sun-lounger and have her right here beneath the sun.

I could. Even though she'd pulled away from me, I'd seen the flicker of desire in her eyes. It hadn't been all anger. She wanted me, I knew it; and, if I kissed her, she'd melt against me the way she'd done all those years ago.

Is that really how you want it to happen?

I stared at the tense line of her shoulders. Her whole posture was tight.

No, I'd never denied myself anything I wanted. Nothing at all. And that included all the forbidden emotions my father had despised: anger, love, lust, guilt, hate, grief...

But nothing was forbidden to me now. Anger in particular I enjoyed, because it gave everything such spice. Particularly sex.

Angry sex with Olivia would be incredible; I knew that. But something stopped me from closing that distance, from taking her the way I wanted to. I hated boundaries, hated rules. I loathed being restrained. Yet I stayed where I was, struggling with the unfamiliar urge to hold back.

I wasn't sure why, since I'd never held back before, but some long-forgotten instinct told me it was too soon to take her to bed.

I had a plan and I needed to stick to it. I was to get her here and keep her here until I'd neutralised Constantine as a threat. Then I'd rebuild the relationship we'd once had, make her fall in love with me once again and marry me.

So she'd be mine, and only mine, for ever.

I could certainly manipulate her into bed. It wouldn't be the first time I'd manipulated someone to get what I wanted, after all; that was exactly how I'd built my business. But it wouldn't be quite as satisfying as her climbing into my bed because she wanted me. Because she was desperate for me.

Desperate for me the way she had been all those years ago.

You were desperate too, don't forget.

Oh, yes, I was. I'd had all kinds of plans for how we could be together, away from my father and out of his reach for ever. Away from the beatings, the lessons and the tests. Away from his attempts to turn Constantine and me into his mirror image.

Cold. Hard. And above all, strong.

I had never passed his tests. Never learned his lessons. I'd never followed his rules and he'd punished me for it. Repeatedly.

Constantine, on the other hand, had done whatever Domingo had asked him to do. He had been Domingo's ideal son, learning all the lessons Domingo beat into us, becoming cold and hard, becoming Domingo himself.

So much so that when Domingo had told me I had to give Olivia up and I'd refused, continuing to meet her in secret, Constantine had told him exactly what I was doing.

My brother used to spy on us down on our hidden beach and she'd met him a couple of times. Once or twice I'd suspected he wanted Olivia for himself, but he was too cold a fish for her, and she'd preferred me. Then he'd told Domingo that I was still meeting with her and I knew then it wasn't her he wanted.

It was Domingo he'd thrown his lot in with.

And whose fault was that?

It was mine, of course. I'd failed to protect him from Domingo's manipulations and, in the end, he'd turned against me. He'd become Domingo, and I took full responsibility. That was why it was up to me to save the company and all the people in it from him, and to save Olivia too.

No one else knew that Domingo had been a psychopath, and that Constantine had become just like him.

No one except me.

So, no, I wouldn't manipulate her. That was something Domingo would have done, and I'd never stoop to that. But patience I was good at, patience I could do, and so I'd wait for her to come to me.

'I have a few tasks I need to complete,' I said to her slender back. 'And they're likely to take most of the day. However, we'll meet tonight for dinner and I'll answer your questions then.'

She didn't turn. 'And my company? What about that? What about my fiancé?'

Fiancé? No. He is not *her fiancé any longer.*

The thought of my brother brought my anger back to the boil and I let it bubble there for a moment, giving it some time.

Then I killed the heat, just because I could.

'You are free to explore the villa and the island,' I replied. 'Nothing is off-limits. There is clothing you can change into in the bedroom and I'll have a laptop brought to you in case you wish to work.'

Her head turned sharply at that, giving me her exquisite profile. 'Work?'

'Well, you did ask about your company. It's…at a delicate stage, I understand.' And it was. I'd seen all the financials, since I had my ways of finding out information, especially information other people didn't want known.

Olivia glanced at me over her shoulder, her expression utterly unreadable. 'What makes you say that?'

I debated revealing the full extent of my knowledge of her and everything she'd done since she'd been eighteen years old. Would it help my cause? Or would she find it creepy? Probably the latter.

Then again, I made no apology for it. Someone had to protect her and, while Domingo had been alive, that someone was always going to be me.

'Oh, I know all about you, little star,' I said gently. 'Everything. From how your father left Wintergreen on the brink of collapse due to some terrible investments, to how much Constantine is going to pay to prop it up. I know all about the degrees you worked so hard to earn and how you came top of your class in all of them. I know that you have few friends and that you've never once had a boyfriend. And I know that you're lonely and that, while Constantine will save your company, he'll kill all of your passion stone-dead.'

She went very still, as if she'd been frozen. An ice statue of a woman.

'I've been watching you,' I went on. 'Since you were eighteen years old. You needed protection and the only person who could give that was me.'

She said nothing for a long moment before turning around fully to face me.

I'd always been able to read her expressions; she'd never hidden how she felt from me. But now... I had no idea what she was thinking.

'Protect me?' She raised one imperious brow. 'Protect me from what?'

I'd hooked her; I could see that. She wanted to know more.

Which was my cue to leave.

'If you want to know, meet me tonight for dinner.' I smiled. 'I told you I'd answer your questions then and I meant it.'

I didn't wait for her to reply; I just turned around and went back inside.

Before I gave all my secrets away.

CHAPTER FIVE

Olivia

IMMEDIATELY I TRIED to find a way off the island.

I didn't bother to dress, striding down the deck to the island itself still wrapped in my sheet.

There were a couple of staff members I tried to talk to, but they either didn't speak English or didn't want anything to do with me, because they shook their heads and walked away before I could get a word out.

It was frustrating.

The island itself was small and covered with palms and some kind of dense, scrubby trees that made exploring off the pretty white shell paths that wound along the shore next to impossible. Not that I wanted to go charging around in the undergrowth wrapped only in a sheet and a nightgown anyway.

What was very clear, though, was that there were no handy boat sheds hiding boats I could climb into and use to sail away. In the end I had to accept that I was trapped on the island, with no way off it, and wandering around in a sheet wasn't going to get me anywhere, nor was being inarticulately furious about it.

Eventually, I went back to the villa in search of clothes. In the bedroom there was a wide built-in wardrobe with sliding mirrored doors, and inside were a lot of built-in drawers and shelves. There were rails too, with the prettiest dresses and skirts and long shirts hanging up, all floaty and light and made for wafting about in.

I preferred sharp business suits and tailoring, armour that helped the board of Wintergreen remember who I was—not a mere woman, but Wintergreen's CEO, and a better leader than my father ever had been.

Except there were no sharps suits and tailoring in this wardrobe, only pretty, floaty things that reminded me far too much of my mother, who was always pretty and feminine because that was how my father had liked her to be.

She'd done whatever he'd wanted, constantly trying to make up for having had me instead of the son he'd always longed for, and then for not being able to have any more children.

She'd blamed herself for that and had always been apologising to him for it. She'd loved him. That had been the problem. And, because she'd loved him, she'd stayed with him, even though he hadn't respected her and hadn't even seemed to like her.

I've never been able to understand why she'd stayed.

Love, that was the problem. Love turned you into a door mat and I didn't want anything to do with it.

I had no choice about the clothes, though. If I didn't want to trail around wearing a sheet all day, I was going to have to wear something hanging on those rails.

First, though, I had a shower in the huge white-tiled *en suite* bathroom, with a bath standing in the middle of the room directly in front of a huge window that looked out over the pristine lagoon.

There was something about the views of the lagoon and the reef, the clear, brilliant turquoise of the water and whiteness of the sand, that tugged at my soul. It reminded me of places I didn't want to remember and feelings I thought I'd buried.

It was disturbing, so I ignored them as I showered and then walked back into the bedroom, going over to the wardrobe to choose something to wear. There appeared to be no underwear, which was annoying, since I'd been wearing mine for a while now and I wanted something clean. There were only bikinis, so I put on a pretty lavender one with string ties at the hip. It wasn't something I'd ever choose to wear myself, but, if I thought about it as a bra and a pair of knickers, then that was okay.

Briefly, I wondered why Valentin had a wardrobe full of women's clothing then decided it was probably better not to wonder. Whatever the reason, I didn't want to know.

There was a lovely light-blue dress that I grabbed to wear over the top of the bikini with a V-necked empire line and long, floaty silk skirts, and it seemed to fit well. It wasn't my thing at all, and the feeling of the silk brushing over my bare skin made me uncomfortably aware of my own virtual nakedness beneath it, but there wasn't anything else to wear. And at least it was cool.

Dressed, I went to explore the villa.

It was large and sprawling, panelled in that honey-gold wood, with simple furniture upholstered in white linen. Folk art sculptures had been placed on low tables and there were simple yet effective abstracts on the walls.

Everything about it was low key, mainly because the view of the lagoon—which could be seen from every room—was so spectacular nothing could compete with it.

The only sound was the ocean lapping against the

supports of the villa, the sounds of sea birds and, every so often, the drone of a far-off boat or plane.

It was beautiful. Peaceful. And a part of me wanted to lie down on one of the long, low couches with a book and curl up to read. Or throw off the silky dress and dive into the warm, inviting water.

But I couldn't. This wasn't a holiday. I'd been kidnapped and brought here by Valentin and I needed to figure out what was going on back home and how I could possibly fix it.

I couldn't afford the Wintergreen board to think of me as a damsel in distress, which meant getting in touch with my management team to let them know where I was and try to instigate some kind of damage control.

I also needed to get in touch with Constantine and let him know I was okay.

In the main living area, on a low table, a phone and a laptop had been laid out and, since it was clear they were for my use, I went to them immediately.

I couldn't get hold of Constantine so I left him a voicemail. Then I called Rachel, my PA, and the first thing she said was, 'Why are you calling me when you're supposed to be on holiday?'

'Holiday?' I echoed, staring out through the big glass doors at the view of the lagoon. 'What holiday?'

'You took leave, remember? I've been telling you that for ages, and just last week you took a month's leave.'

I hadn't taken a month's leave. In fact, there was no way I would have, not with the company being at such a delicate stage, so why on earth did Rachel think that?

'Are you sure?' I asked. 'I don't recall…'

'Mr Silvera called a couple of days ago while you were in Madrid. He said he was planning to whisk you away for a special holiday.'

'Mr Silvera called you,' I repeated blankly, a sudden suspicion nagging at me.

'Yes. He sounded quite pleased about it.' Rachel gave a little sigh. 'So, come on, spill. Where did he take you? He said he wanted to surprise you.'

I gritted my teeth, the suspicion nagging even more insistently. 'Tell me, Rachel. Has anything...happened in the world recently? No kidnappings or abductions?'

'Kidnappings?' Rachel sounded surprised. 'I mean, probably somewhere. But there haven't been any in the news recently. Why?'

Mr Silvera had called my PA about a surprise holiday. And there had been no reports of kidnappings...

Constantine wouldn't take me away on a surprise holiday. He didn't do surprises in any shape or form, still less holidays. And as for the lack of reports of kidnappings...

Apparently, Constantine hadn't reported my abrupt abduction by the twin brother famously back from the dead. Why not?

'Thanks, Rachel,' I said shortly and disconnected the call, my heart beating fast.

I opened the laptop and turned it on, bringing up a web browser and doing a quick search of all the news websites.

There was nothing there about the return of Valentin Silvera. Nothing about how Olivia Wintergreen had been kidnapped from the wake for her late father-in-law-to-be. Nothing about any security incident at Constantine's Madrid mansion.

My heart thumped harder as I closed the laptop and stared at it.

It was Valentin who'd called Rachel, wasn't it? Valentin who'd pretended to be his brother, telling Rachel

I was going on leave. And then, for some inexplicable reason, Constantine had somehow managed to keep his brother's sudden reappearance and my kidnapping out of the media.

Why? What were his intentions? Did he not want to find me? Did he not care? What on earth was going on?

I picked up the phone and rang my home number.

My mother picked up. 'Oh,' she said when she heard my voice, 'it's you. How is your holiday?'

So Valentin had called her too, pretending to be Constantine, letting her know that he was taking me away for a surprise holiday.

Perhaps I should have been grateful that he'd contacted people to let them know what was happening, but I wasn't.

The bastard had planned this down to the nth degree, hadn't he?

'I know everything about you, little star... Everything.'

My mother was blithely unaware of my distraction, even being the one to disconnect the call so I could get back to 'being with my fiancé'. He was a special man, she told me. I had to remember to pay him lots of attention.

But then, that was my mother. As long as the men were being paid lots of attention, everything was great.

After I'd finished speaking to her, I sat on the comfortable couch, staring out over the lagoon, Valentin's words ringing in my head.

My palm stung as I remembered the crack of it across his cheek.

I'd been so angry. And beneath it, there had also been a healthy dose of confusion and shock. I'd been tumbled right back into the emotional chaos of that year when I'd fallen in love. When I'd been kissed then betrayed, and then suffered the most heart-breaking loss.

I'd been rebelling against Dad that year. He'd forbidden me from spending time with 'those Silvera boys', but I'd ignored him, sneaking off to the secret beach anyway, pouring out my anger to Valentin at his constant nit-picking at what he'd termed my 'ridiculous female tantrums', telling Val that I never wanted to run that stupid company, that he couldn't tell me what to do. I wanted to do what *I* wanted, not what he wanted.

But he had been right, my father. I *had* only been fifteen. And, after I'd lost Valentin, all the light had gone out of the world. It had become a darker, colder place, and so I'd become a darker, colder person.

I'd put aside my grief, my silly broken heart and my childish dreams. And I'd let the pressure turn me into a diamond, because nothing could touch a diamond.

Yet somehow, Valentin's shock return had touched me all the same. And the feelings I thought I'd excised from my heart had all returned with him.

I didn't want to feel that way again. It had never been part of my plan. What I wanted was to run the company, shake up all those stuffy traditionalists who thought me being a woman was a disadvantage and prove my father wrong.

He hadn't needed a son. He'd only needed me.

And it was a good thing that I was a woman, since marrying Constantine would pay off the debts my father had run up. The trade-off was having him take over for a year or two, just until the company got back on its feet again. It wasn't ideal, having a man taking over running the place for me, but that had been his price for his financial help, and I was prepared to pay it. He was also going to give me children and I wanted that as well.

IVF had been a possibility, but the process was time-consuming and gruelling physically, and if I had a man on call then why not use him?

Really, marrying Constantine had been the perfect solution to my problems.

Until Valentin had come along and upended my entire life.

My palm kept on stinging and I could still see the flames in his black eyes and his edgy predator's smile. He'd let me hit him. He hadn't flinched. In fact, he'd even told me to hit him again. And then he'd wrapped his fingers around my wrist and pulled me close, so that all I could see were those black flames; all I was aware of was the intense heat of his body, his warm, spicy scent and the sensual shape of his mouth.

I'd remembered then our first kiss. How warm that mouth had been and how surprisingly soft. How it had felt on mine, sending shivers all over my skin.

That kiss had been magical.

That kiss had changed my life.

You want to kiss him again.

My fingers closed into a fist and I dug my nails savagely into my palm to get rid of that stinging sensation.

No, there would be no more kisses with Valentin. I'd said goodbye to the boy he'd once been and wasn't interested in the man he now was.

He'd kidnapped me and brought me halfway around the world, and it was clear he was intending to keep me here to 'protect me', whatever that meant.

And the only thing I was interested in was the answers he'd give me, because that was what I was going to get from him tonight at dinner. He *would* tell me everything. And then I'd force him to take me home.

By any means necessary.

CHAPTER SIX

Valentin

THAT NIGHT, I MADE sure everything was perfect.

I had my staff arrange for a table covered with a white tablecloth to be placed on the end of the jetty. There was silver cutlery, the finest porcelain and the most delicate crystal glasses. Hurricane lamps were lit and placed at strategic points along the jetty, as well as around the table itself. The light was flickering and subtle, enough so we could see to eat, but not enough to obscure the stars.

I wanted there to be stars.

I'd also given the few house staff on the island the next two weeks off with double pay, as long as they went back to their homes on the other islands.

I wanted no interruptions. I wanted to be alone with Olivia for the next week, or even two, which hopefully would be plenty of time to bring her round to my way of thinking.

I'd spent most of the day catching up with my staff back in Europe, keeping tabs on Constantine and his re-action to my intention to remove him from his company, not to mention stealing away his bride-to-be.

My lawyers informed me that no one could get hold

of him, that he'd disappeared, which was odd. Then, when I couldn't find any mention of my triumphant return from the dead on the web, I realised that somehow he'd managed to keep what had happened out of the media. Indeed, when I finally heard from my mole in Silver Inc, I learned that Constantine had given very specific instructions that no one was to talk about me or what had happened at Domingo's wake on pain of instant dismissal.

There was no mention of Olivia anywhere.

I was amused, mainly because I'd predicted that this would be Constantine's reaction. He wouldn't want anyone to know his twin was back from the dead, not until he'd figured out how to keep control of Silver Inc and block me from claiming it.

He was nothing if not relentless at holding on to what he wanted. He would hate that I had taken Olivia too, and no doubt he was already planning how to get her back.

I had a couple of security launches patrolling the seas around my island, though, plus a few insiders with the authorities on Male, the Maldives' biggest island. If Constantine tried to come for me here, I'd know about it within minutes.

However, it had already been twenty-four hours and he hadn't made a move; I couldn't deny I was curious as to why. Olivia wasn't the only person I'd watched. I'd watched Constantine too, and I knew that he felt nothing for her personally. He didn't feel anything for anyone. But she was important to him nonetheless, and I suspected that was simply because he'd been intending to make her his.

However, now I'd stolen her back, I was sure he wouldn't let that stand.

I sure as hell wouldn't have.

I left warnings with my security team to stay sharp and then, as the day slid into evening and the last of my staff set out dinner on the end of the jetty, I went down to supervise.

All Olivia's favourite foods were present and accounted for, as was her favourite drink as an adult—expensive French champagne. I wanted to show her that I still remembered what food she liked, and that I hadn't forgotten what we'd once been to each other.

Once all was ready, and my staff safely dispatched to their homes, I pulled out a chair and sat.

And waited for Olivia.

I hadn't specified a particular time for dinner, but she'd be able to see me, since the end of the jetty was visible from most rooms of the villa.

I wondered if she'd keep me waiting and was curious to see if she would. I would, if I were her, particularly if I was feeling petty.

Yet I hadn't been sitting there long before I watched her tall, slender figure coming down the jetty towards me.

A typical tropical sunset was staining the blue of the sky with reds and golds and pinks. The heat of the day had faded, leaving the air warm and pleasant and still.

A perfect evening.

Yet the woman coming towards me was more perfect still.

Her hair was loose and floating free down her back in a silver-gold fall, the sunset tingeing it pink and red, as it did her pale skin. She must have investigated the wardrobe in the bedroom, the one I'd stocked with pretty things for her to wear, because she had on one of my favourites—a dress of pale blue silk that clung to and flowed with the shape of her figure as she walked. The silk was so fine it was transparent and, rather disappointingly, she must also have found one of the bikinis and decided to wear that in lieu of underwear.

Well, eventually she wouldn't bother with a bikini. I'd make sure of that.

I stood as she came closer, because a gentleman should always stand when a lady approaches. Not that I was in any way a gentleman, but it was important to observe the niceties. Especially at so delicate a stage in the proceedings.

I didn't wait for her to say anything; I went over to her chair, placed opposite me at the table, and pulled it out for her. 'Good evening, little star. Won't you sit down?'

Her expression was cool and detached, yet I could see the glitter in her eyes.

She might act like one of the diamonds her company sold all she liked, but we both knew she wasn't one, not with that white fire burning away inside her.

I left her with no choice but to sit, which I knew must have annoyed her, but she only gave me a cool glance and said nothing as she came over to the chair and sat down.

I pushed her chair in, indulging myself by pausing a moment to look down at her and breathe in her sweet scent. I very much wanted to sweep aside her hair, expose the nape of her neck and bend to kiss it, but I restrained myself.

Now was not the right time.

Once she was settled, I went to the ice bucket, grabbed the champagne and popped the cork before pouring us each a glass.

Or at least, I tried to.

Olivia put her hand over the top of her glass and

stared up at me, her gaze challenging. 'No wine. I want answers, Valentin. And you said you'd give them to me.'

Oh, so she was going to play it like that, was she? Interesting.

I had to admit, as much as I loved her fiery passion, a part of me was also beginning to find this new cool and imperious Olivia rather fascinating too.

In fact, both aspects of her were exciting, and I wanted to find out more.

'I said I'd give them to you over dinner,' I said mildly. 'And we haven't eaten yet.'

'I don't want dinner. I'm not hungry. Plus, I never agreed to that.'

Of course she was hungry. My staff had told me she hadn't eaten all day.

But, if she wanted a fight, I'd give her one.

I smiled, took her hand off the glass and poured champagne into it anyway—she didn't have to drink it. Then I placed the bottle back into the ice-bucket and sat down. 'You are hungry. You haven't eaten a single thing since we left Spain.'

'There is no "we", Valentin. Stop talking as if you didn't kidnap me from Domingo's wake.'

I ignored that. 'No one's forcing you to eat and no one's forcing you to drink that glass of champagne, either. If you don't want to for pettiness' sake, then I'm certainly not going to deprive you. Nothing wrong with a bit of pettiness.'

Her expression became even colder. 'I'm not being petty.'

'Are you not? Isn't that why you're refusing to eat any of the food my staff prepared for you?'

I could see the delicate line of her jaw harden in that stubborn way she had. Once, on our little beach, I'd tried to teach her the best way to start a fire. I'd just read a book on it and knew all about it. She'd refused to listen, telling me she already knew how do to it, and had insisted that her way was best even after I'd pointed out the many reasons she was wrong. She had been stubborn and wouldn't back down, and in the end we'd lit two fires at opposite ends of the beach.

She'd been right, though. Her way had been the best and the quickest.

'I'm not playing any more games with you, Valentin,' she said flatly. 'Tell me what you want and what you're going to do with me.'

'Well, I would.' I picked up my champagne and took a sip. 'But, you see, now you owe me.'

Her fair brows snapped together. 'What?'

'You slapped me, Livvy. And, granted, it didn't hurt, but still. You raised a hand to me, which means now you owe me.'

She didn't look away. 'If you're expecting an apology, you won't get it. You thoroughly deserved it. In fact, you're lucky I didn't wring your neck.'

Something intense and fierce sparked deep inside me, something that thoroughly enjoyed the uncompromising look she was giving me. Something that was finding this hard edge of hers extremely exciting and wanted to see more of it.

Had she always been like this? Certainly when we were children she'd sometimes hold a grudge for days and refuse to speak to me. Though it was true that, even when she was angry with me, she'd still come to the beach every day, even if it was only to sit on the sand and angrily throw shells into the sea. She'd known how much it meant to me to see her and she'd come anyway.

I nodded. 'I'm not apologising for bringing you here, either. So, no apologies all round.'

I knew it would infuriate her and, sure enough, I could see her temper flicker into life, glittering behind her diamond-hard veneer.

Except…she didn't look much like a diamond now.

She looked soft and pink in that pretty silk dress, with the breeze toying gently with the ends of her hair. It was only her expression that was hard.

Perhaps tonight I'd try and shatter that veneer of hers. Perhaps tonight I'd let that fire out.

'Wonderful,' she said coldly. 'Now we've cleared that up, you can tell me what on earth you think I owe you.'

There were many things I could have said, because there were many things I wanted, and mostly from her. But all I said was, 'A sip of that champagne. Just one. It's delicious, I promise you.'

She eyed me. 'Oh, for God's sake. You never give up, do you?'

I shrugged. 'No.'

She snorted, but picked up the glass and took a sip.

I watched her. It was a very good bottle—vintage. Her favourite. She kept her expression detached as she took a sip, but then she took another, which pleased me.

I let her see that too. 'I'm glad you like it.' I sat back in my chair. 'And now for some of those answers you wanted.'

She narrowed her gaze, but didn't put her glass back down.

'It wasn't a kidnapping,' I went on. 'It was a rescue. I had to get you away from Constantine as quickly as I could.'

'Why? What makes you think that—?'

'Because Domingo Silvera was a psychopath and,

while Constantine didn't start out as one, I'm pretty sure he's one now.'

She blinked, a ripple of emotion crossing her face, though what it was I couldn't tell, since it vanished the next second. 'A psychopath? What are you talking about?'

Perhaps it was surprise. If so, I didn't blame her. Domingo preferred to keep his…tendencies veiled. People were afraid of him, and there had been certain rumours about him, but no one knew the truth.

When I was a boy, I'd used to dream that someone would realise what a monster he was and have the police come to take him away. But that had never happened. Domingo had known how to be normal, how to charm. He'd had the looks and forceful personality that could combine into a relentless charisma that blinded everyone he met. He could appear on the surface a handsome, successful, charming man, while underneath he was the devil himself.

'Constantine's father—' I could never admit to him having been mine too, because 'father' assumed a certain relationship that we'd definitely never had '—was an abusive monster and Constantine models himself on him.'

Olivia's delicate features betrayed nothing, but she'd gone a tad pale. 'That's not true. I mean, Domingo wasn't an easy man, but—'

'I won't go into the details,' I interrupted, because she didn't need to hear them. 'Suffice to say that, when I heard of your engagement, I had to take action.'

'But—'

'Domingo forbade me to see you, did you know that? But I did anyway. And eventually he found out.'

No need to tell her about Constantine's betrayal,

either. That was between him and me. 'He was very angry.' I ignored the ice that coiled in my stomach at the memory. 'I decided I'd had enough by that stage, so I managed to escape. I was given a ride in a car from a stranger, but it was a wet night and he was driving too fast, and we crashed. I managed to get out, but he didn't. He was killed. Some of my DNA was found at the scene and it was assumed his body was mine. And I decided to stay dead, because if Domingo had ever discovered I was still alive he'd have followed me to the ends of the earth.'

This time, Olivia said nothing.

I still remembered that night: the skid of tyres and the smell of petrol; the sound of breaking glass and tearing metal. I'd managed to drag myself out of the car just before it had exploded and realised, in a sudden burst of relief, that if I played it right I could finally be free...

'That's why I died,' I said. 'I had to get away from Domingo. But I was afraid of what he might do to you, since he told me he'd hurt you if I disobeyed him. That's why I've been watching you all these years. I needed to protect you from him.' I took a sip of wine, my mouth oddly dry. 'And now I have to protect you from Constantine too.'

Olivia continued to stare at me, emotions flickering over her face so fast, I couldn't read them. Then abruptly she looked down at the table top and took a sip of her wine.

'I don't know anything about Domingo,' she said after a moment. 'Though, I've never felt...easy around him. And what you had to do... I'm sorry about that.' She looked up at me, her gaze again very direct. 'But you're wrong about Constantine. He's not like that.'

I just looked back at her. 'That's what everyone said about Domingo.'

'You've been gone for fifteen years, Valentin. But I've known Constantine very well for six months. I'm his fiancée. He's *not* what you think he is.'

'You're assuming,' I pointed out, 'That I haven't been watching him the same way I've been watching you. There's a reason I'm going to have him removed as CEO of Silver Inc. I'm sure he'll think it's because I want the company, but I don't. I have my own money, as you can see. No, I have to protect his employees from him somehow.'

But she didn't back down. 'That's ridiculous. Have you any evidence that he's…what? A psychopath? A cruel monster? He's cold, yes, and driven. And he's a ruthless businessman. But he's never hurt me. He's never even been rude.'

It was true that I didn't have hard evidence that Constantine was exactly like Domingo. I'd never found any rumours that he'd been physically violent or manipulative the way Domingo had been.

But he was cruel and callous and ruthless. Detached and cold and utterly without empathy. His staff were afraid of him, or so my mole had told me, and that was likely due to him holding something over their heads. It had been Domingo's favourite method of maintaining obedience, even though it had never worked on me, and I was sure Constantine employed it too.

'Yes,' I said. 'That's what he wants you to think. He's exactly like Domingo, though. And, while I haven't spent the past fifteen years with him, I grew up with him and I know exactly what goes on in his head.' *You did. Once.* I ignored the thought and smiled. 'I'm his twin, after all.'

But Olivia was shaking her head. 'You're wrong. And, apart from anything else, this is ridiculous. Keeping me here is ridiculous. What are you going to do with me? You can't keep me here for ever.'

'I don't need to keep you here for ever.' I held her gaze and let her see the force of my will. 'All I need to do is keep you here long enough for you to fall in love with me. And then you'll marry me instead. Like you always wanted to.'

CHAPTER SEVEN

Olivia

VALENTIN'S BLACK EYES glittered in the light from the candles in the hurricane lamps. There was nothing but fierce certainty in his hard, carved features.

Maybe it's not Constantine you should be afraid of. Maybe it's him.

But I wasn't afraid of Constantine, and I certainly wasn't afraid of Valentin. I was angry, yes, but not afraid.

The air was warm and soft and smelled of flowers, the light from all those pretty candles dancing over the wood of the jetty and casting a lovely glow. The only sound was of the waves lapping against the jetty supports.

The table and the silver service, the crystal glass full of champagne, the tropical setting…it was all so beautiful.

And so was the man sitting across from me in jeans and bare feet, lounging at his ease, his champagne glass held loosely in his long fingers. His black hair was tousled and the white of his T-shirt made his olive skin look darker, all smooth and velvety. It highlighted the darkness of his eyes and, even though they were so black they were like space, I could see the lights in them, flames burning.

Domingo was a monster and Valentin had been forbidden to see me. Domingo had threatened to hurt me. Valentin had faked his own death to escape him. I could hardly believe it. Or, no; maybe I could believe it.

I'd never liked Domingo. He had been charming but there'd been something about him, a kind of clinical detachment that had always made me uneasy.

But Valentin was wrong about Constantine. Yes, Constantine was cold, but he'd never made me uneasy in the way Domingo had. And he'd never been cruel, never hurt me in any way. And then there was Jenny, his stepsister, who worshipped the ground he walked on. Jenny, who was always so smiley and happy and cheerful. She'd never be that loyal to a monster.

But as for what Valentin had said, about keeping me here and me falling in love with him and him marrying me instead…

Something tugged deep inside me. A longing I thought I'd got rid of years ago.

But no. Marrying Valentin? What a preposterous thought. The passionate boy he'd once been had grown up, though he was obviously still passionate. But he was also arrogant, egotistical to a fault and it was clear that he'd never even heard of the word 'no'.

He was a difficult man, just like my father had been, and if there was one thing I didn't want in my life it was another difficult man.

And Constantine is easy…?

Well, no, he wasn't. But I didn't feel anything for him, I didn't have a history with him, and that made all the difference.

'You can't be serious,' I said coolly. 'Are you actually insane? What a preposterous suggestion.'

His teeth were white in the flickering light. 'Perhaps.

You don't grow up in the house of a psychopath without some scars, I suppose. But does it matter that it's preposterous? For the first time in fifteen years, we're alone, Livvy. And there's no one to stop us from being together if we want to be, not this time.'

From out of nowhere, an electric thrill shot straight down my spine, going all the way to the heart of the girl I'd once been. That ferocious girl, who'd argued and fought and played and laughed with him on that secret beach. That passionate girl who'd loved him with all of her soul.

And I'd loved being that girl. Because being with him had made me feel more like myself than anyone else ever had. I hadn't been silly or dramatic or overly emotional when I'd been with him. I'd been able to be angry without having someone tell me that I was turning everything into a big drama. I'd been able to laugh myself hoarse without being told to calm down. He accepted me and my emotions without question, and I'd loved that.

But there had been a weakness in that girl, in the end. A flaw in her supposedly strong façade. And it was the same flaw my mother had: our heart.

I'd loved a man who'd hurt me and so, no matter how much I'd loved being that girl, I'd never be her again. She'd been a child and I'd buried her when Valentin had supposedly died. I was in no hurry to resurrect her.

My instinct was to tell him he was mistaken, get to my feet and leave, but he wasn't wrong about the fact that I hadn't eaten all day. And, yes, maybe refusing to eat had been petty of me. It had certainly been a mistake. Because it was coming back to haunt me now, my stomach rumbling at the sight and smell of the delicious food that had been laid on the table.

An array of salads, fish and shellfish that had no

doubt been caught in the lagoon. Newly baked bread with a thick pat of butter. It all looked so fresh and tasty, and it was everything I particularly liked to eat.

Had he known? Had he done that on purpose? Oh, but of course he'd known, and of course he'd done it on purpose. He'd just said he wanted me to fall in love with him, and I suppose this was the start of his seduction.

Which meant that, naturally, I couldn't eat any of it.

Valentin put his wine down and leaned forward, his elbows on the table. 'There's dessert too.' His eyes danced, full of the wickedness and delight I'd always found so irresistible. 'I have marshmallows. We can build a fire on the beach and toast them.'

Instantly I was back on that beach again, arguing with him about the best way to build a driftwood fire. He'd been as stubborn as me and insistent that his way was the right way. We'd been twelve. I'd told him he was a dumb boy who knew nothing. He'd told me I was a stupid girl who knew even less. Then he'd kicked sand in my direction while I'd thrown a stick at him. Then we'd gone off to opposite ends of the beach and lit fires to prove each other wrong.

Valentin's rages had never lasted long. They'd been intense while they lasted but, like a hurricane, they'd blown themselves out quickly. I'd held on to mine much longer, unwilling to let them go.

But that day on the beach Val had eventually come across to look at my fire and he'd smiled suddenly; it had been like the dawn breaking. 'That's amazing, Livvy,' he'd said, as if he hadn't called me a stupid girl and kicked sand at me not minutes before. 'I couldn't even get a flame.'

Once his anger had gone, he hadn't cared about being

right. And that day we'd sat beside the fire I'd success-
fully lit and toasted marshmallows together.

'You can build the fire,' Valentin murmured. 'You're
good at building fires, as I recall.'

The thing that had tugged in my chest tugged again.
Painfully. Something that felt like yearning.

But I shoved it away. Hard.

I wasn't going there. I wasn't. I couldn't. Not again.

I took a breath and met his gaze, feeling myself as
consumed by it as I always had been. 'I'm not lighting
fires with you, Valentin. And thank you for the meal. I'm
sure it's lovely, and I appreciate the effort, but I'm not sitting out here and reminiscing with you about old times.'

I gripped the glass of champagne and raised it, swallowing the whole of it down, because it was delicious and
I needed it; and because, even after all this time, I still
found it difficult to walk away from him. 'But I'm not
the same person I was back then. That girl you knew…
She's gone. I'm not falling in love with you, and I'm certainly not marrying you, understand?'

I got to my feet, the champagne glittering in my
bloodstream, and reached for a roll. 'I'll take this for
my dinner. But that's all. Thank you for the wine.'

Valentin didn't move. 'So you're running away now?'

'Hardly.' I turned and stepped away from the table.

'You ran from everyone else, but you never ran from
me. Don't you remember?' His voice was quiet, yet I
heard.

I stopped a few steps away from the table and, even
though I hated myself for stopping, something inside
wouldn't let me take another step.

'You didn't want me at your beach, remember?' he
went on in the same quiet voice. 'I could tell. You were
sitting there, enjoying the silence, and then suddenly

this rowdy boy appeared. You wanted to leave, and you hated me for disturbing your special place, but for some reason you stayed.'

I remembered. I had been ten and my parents had had a fight, filling the house with my father's cold fury and my mother's weepy apologies.

I'd hated it when they fought, when my father was so cruel and my mother just took it. It had made me angry with her, made me want to yell at her to fight back. But I knew that would only make it worse, so I'd run away to the beach I'd discovered a couple of days earlier. It had been next to our villa, small, quiet and hidden by trees and cliffs, and no one had known about it. No one but me.

Valentin was right, though. I'd been enjoying the silence until this black-eyed, older boy had appeared. I'd hated him instantly for disturbing me, for finding my special beach and ruining it with his presence. And I'd been on the point of getting up and leaving when something magical had happened.

Unlike me, the boy hadn't been annoyed to find someone else there. No, his face had lit up, as if my being there had been the best thing that had ever happened to him. And his smile had been incandescent. He'd looked at me as if I were magic. As if I were incredible. As if I wasn't the constant reminder of my mother's failure to give her husband a son and treated accordingly by both my parents. My father had always been coldly impatient with me, my mother constantly anxious that I would do something to offend him.

'Don't go,' he'd said, as if sensing I was about to leave. 'Please stay.'

Even then I'd been able to see he was like a bonfire, intense and burning, holding me mesmerised. My father had been cold, my mother soft and floaty and ineffectual, but this boy had been…intense. And I had been drawn to his intensity like a moth to a flame.

No. I'd never run from him.

So why are you walking away now?

'Are you afraid of me?' Valentin's voice was low and deep, winding around me like a velvet rope. 'Did I scare you with all that talk of monsters and psychopaths?'

My heart was beating far too fast, and I didn't want him to come near me. Something might happen if he did. Something I wasn't sure I'd to be able to come back from.

So? Keep walking.

But I didn't.

Instead, I gave him a mocking look. 'Afraid? Of you? Seriously?'

He ignored my tone. 'Well, you have no guarantee I'm not as mad as Domingo. And I can't say for certain I'm not. But, no, perhaps it's not me you're afraid of. Perhaps it's yourself.'

I shouldn't have turned round then. I should have kept right on walking. Yet once again I stayed where I was.

The breeze lifted the silken skirts of my dress, the silk brushing against my skin making me very aware that all I wore beneath it was that tiny bikini.

'I think not,' I said icily, desperately trying to keep my cool.

Valentin didn't move, still lounging in his chair, yet the flames in his eyes leapt high. He was so fierce, so intense. So bright. He was the brightest thing I'd ever seen, and he still was.

'Aren't you, though? Isn't that why you're walking away?' He put down his wine and shoved his chair back, getting to his feet in one smooth, powerful movement.

'If I got close to you now, what would you do? Run away?' He came towards me unhurriedly, as if he had all the time in the world. 'Or stand your ground the way you used to?'

Something was bubbling up inside me, the fury I thought I'd put on a leash earlier that day. Fury at the impossible choice he'd given me, because walking away now would reveal far too much. Yet standing my ground was exactly what he wanted me to do.

It was all his talk of the past, of course. Somehow, he'd used that to reach inside me, bypassing my diamond armour and touching the soul of the girl I'd once been.

He'd manipulated me and I'd let him.

My father had always hated open, uncontrolled anger. It was a sign of weak character, he'd said. And, because I wasn't weak I'd never got angry. I'd only gone cold.

But I wasn't cold now. That fury was welling up inside me and I couldn't control it. Fury at him for reminding me of who I'd once been, for taking those old yearnings and desires and making me want them again. For putting me in this impossible position, where I could be a coward, like my mother doing whatever my father told her.

And, most of all, fury at myself for allowing myself to let him do this to me.

He was still coming towards me and the edge of the jetty was near.

So I didn't wait. I had to do something.

I took two steps, gave him a hard shove and pushed him off the edge into the sea.

CHAPTER EIGHT

Valentin

I KNEW WHAT she was going to do. If nothing else, those long summers on our beach had taught me that when Olivia was going to push me, shove me or throw something at me, she'd dart a glance round at her surroundings, as if to check no one was watching.

To be fair, I had been expecting another slap in the face, not a hard shove into the ocean—though, given how close the edge of the jetty was, I certainly should have predicted it. Especially when this wasn't the first time she'd pushed me into the sea.

She used to do it quite regularly, as if she couldn't help herself. I'd be innocently exploring some rock pools on our beach and out would come her arm, giving me a push. It was a game we'd played and, since it had made her laugh, and I'd loved making her laugh, I'd let her push me far more than was necessary.

She hadn't even minded when I'd pulled her in too. In fact, she'd laughed the last time I'd done it.

She wasn't laughing now, though, as I grabbed her just before I went over, a reflex I couldn't stop. But then, perhaps I wouldn't have stopped even if I could have. I wanted her to remember what we'd had together, all those bright days on the beach, playing and laughing together.

Domingo had policed the contact Constantine and I had had with other people. We hadn't been allowed friends or acquaintances. But he'd relaxed his guard on our Caribbean holidays and so I'd been able to slip away to the beach.

Olivia had been my first and only friend and, despite all the years that had passed and all the things I'd done to get where I was now, she was still the only one.

She'd always be the only one.

The only one for me.

So I pulled her in with me and she shrieked in outrage as we fell into the sea, the water as warm as a bath. Her skirts wrapped around my legs and her hair was everywhere, and there was a moment where she was obviously struggling to orient herself.

I was an excellent swimmer, so I held her in my arms as I found my feet on the sandy ocean floor, taking care to make sure she didn't swallow any water as we surfaced.

She was furious, yet her hands clutched onto my shoulders, as if holding on for dear life. Her eyes were brilliant in the flickering light from the candles in the hurricane lamps, sea water like jewels on her skin. Her hair streamed over her shoulders, the ends floating in long, silky skeins on the surface.

She was so beautiful, she stopped my heart.

Then she hit me hard on the shoulder. 'You pulled me in. That was so unfair!'

She sounded just like she had all those years ago, when I'd won whatever game we'd been playing, often accusing me of being unfair or cheating. And sometimes I had been.

But her fury had been just as mesmerising to me as her laughter, so I did what I'd wanted to do so many times on that beach long ago.

I bent and covered her mouth with mine.

I remembered our first kiss. It had been mine too, since naturally enough, if Domingo had forbidden Constantine and me friends, he'd always forbidden us girl-friends. I'd never held a girl before, never kissed one either, and it had been so very, very sweet.

I could still taste that sweetness. It was still there. But we weren't fifteen and seventeen any longer, and a very real, very adult heat leapt between us now.

It was electric.

Women had long since beaten a path to my bed and I'd lost count of those I'd taken. After all, sex was one of life's pleasures and I'd never denied myself.

But Olivia had always been different, and kissing her was as different from kissing all those other women as night was from day.

She tasted of champagne and sea salt, of sex and desire, and I wanted her now, right now. I was tired of waiting and I wanted it all.

She went rigid in my arms, her whole body taut and, even though it was the last thing on earth I wanted, I forced myself to let her go.

I'd given her a taste. If she wanted more, she knew where to get it.

Olivia stared at me, her brilliant grey eyes full of fury. But I could see the desire there too, burning hot. She looked as though she wasn't sure whether to kiss me or strangle me.

I didn't look away and I said nothing. I let her make the choice.

Then suddenly she lunged forward, her arms winding

around my neck, her hot, slender body arching against me as her mouth found mine.

Triumph filled me just before all thought shattered. Triumph that she'd made her choice and her choice was me. And then there was only her in my arms. Her, after so many years of watching her from the shadows, wanting her but trying not to. Dreaming of her and losing her every morning when I woke up.

But not now. Now she was here and she wasn't a dream. She was reality and she was finally where she'd always belonged: in my arms.

I could taste the fire inside her now, and I dug my fingers into the wet silk of her hair, pulling her head back so I could kiss her deeper, harder, chase that taste. Her mouth was so hot and she was trying to kiss me back, her tongue touching mine, at first tentatively, and then with more confidence, more passion.

She kissed like a virgin, which only sharpened the edge of my hunger. I'd suspected Constantine hadn't taken her to bed and this confirmed it.

She was mine. Every part of her was mine. And something inside me regretted all the women I'd taken to my bed over the years...regretted that she was not my first, my only. That I wasn't all hers the way she would be mine.

But there was nothing I could do about that now.

I might have had many other women physically, but my heart was pure. My heart had always been hers.

I kissed her with savagery, with demand and, because she was Olivia, she kissed me back the same way, her arms tight around my neck, her slender curves pressed hard to the entire length of my body.

The sea washed around us, swirling the silk of her dress around my legs, making me aware of all the clothes between us and how I didn't want them to be there. I wanted nothing between us, just her bare skin and the heat of her mouth. The tight clasp of her sex around me as I pushed inside her and made her mine.

I tore my mouth from hers and began to kiss my way down the slender column of her throat, tasting the salt water and sweetness of her skin.

Her head dropped back, the sound of her breathing ragged in the night air.

I fastened my mouth over her pulse, tasting the frantic beat of it with my tongue, and she shuddered, a soft moan escaping her.

Yes, I wanted more of that sound. More of her, a slave to this heat between us. I wanted to make her cry for me, beg for me; I wanted her as desperate as she'd made me.

I pulled hard at the neckline of her dress, silk tearing to reveal the lavender bikini top she wore beneath it. The last of the summer sunset had disappeared, her skin now glowing like mother-of-pearl in the starlight, and I wanted to see it. I wanted to see all of it.

I jerked the strap of her bikini top down, uncovering one round breast, and she gasped as I slid my palm around it, cupping her.

Dios, she was perfect. As perfect as I'd imagined. Her skin was silky-smooth and hot, her rosy-pink nipple hard and ready for my mouth.

I dipped my head, hungry for more of a taste, tracing the curve of her breast with my tongue and then circling that hard little peak.

'Val…' Her voice was husky and thick in the night, her fingers digging into my shoulders. 'Oh… Val…'

I teased her, then drew her nipple into my mouth, sucking hard, and she cried out.

It was the sweetest sound I'd ever heard. Just as she was the sweetest thing I'd ever tasted.

I gripped her hips, fitting her more closely against me. My heart was racing and the ache in my groin was insistent. I was harder than I'd ever been in my entire life.

But I didn't want her here in the water. I wanted her somewhere I could lay her out and tear those clothes away completely, have her naked under the stars. Somewhere more comfortable, where I could feast on her at my leisure.

Of course, the perfect place wasn't that far away.

I tore my mouth from her breast and lifted her, urging her to wrap her legs around my waist, because I didn't want to lose contact with her. She didn't hesitate, her arms looping around my neck, those delectable breasts soft and hot pressed to my chest.

She found my mouth, kissing me desperately as I turned towards the beach and began wading through the water. I let her explore, since I knew what she was doing.

She didn't want me to stop, because if I stopped this now she'd start to think. It would come back to her where she was and who I was and what we were doing. And that diamond-hard veneer of hers would come back down. The white-star heat of her would get locked away.

Well. Luckily for us both, I wasn't going to let that happen.

I waded out of the water and onto the little beach, the jetty stretching out beside us. The sand was still warm from the day, glowing white under the stars.

I let Olivia go and then I pushed her down onto the sand on her back, spreading her thighs with my hands so I could kneel between them.

Then I ripped the silk dress from her body.

She trembled but didn't stop me, her eyes wide as

they stared up into mine. I could see starlight reflected in them and the white heat blazing at the heart of her.

I leaned down, kissing her hard and deep, because I didn't want that sharp brain of hers thinking; I didn't want her having second thoughts.

This was where we needed to be for our first time together—on a beach, on the sand, at night.

So I kept on kissing her as I pulled away her bikini and she was finally where she always should have been.

Naked, beneath me.

CHAPTER NINE

Olivia

I COULDN'T BREATHE. I couldn't think. My heart felt as if it was going to beat its way out of my chest.

My skin was hot and far too tight, and I wanted to cast it off and crawl out of it like a butterfly from a cocoon. So I felt nothing but relief when Valentin tore off my dress and then the bikini beneath it.

The sand beneath me was soft and warm, but that was nothing compared to the heat of the man who knelt between my thighs. He gripped his soaking-wet T-shirt and tore it up and over his head in one smooth, powerful movement. And all I could do was stare at him as he flung it away.

From his wide shoulders, the water glistened along every hard, carved muscle of his torso. I'd seen it already, of course, but this was different. Now I could touch him, now I could run my hands over all the expanse of tanned skin and see if it felt as velvety and as smooth as it looked.

Dimly, something in the back of my head shouted a warning—that I was forgetting myself. That I shouldn't let this happen. That this was a step I couldn't come back from—but I ignored it.

As soon as he'd pulled me after him into the sea, I knew my fate had been sealed. Because his strong hands gripped me, and the warm water of the ocean closed around me, and I was back on that hidden beach again. Laughing at him as I pushed him into the water. Squealing as he splashed me, then shrieking as he pulled me in too.

My heart would burst as I surfaced to find him bobbing in the water next to me, his black hair hanging over his forehead, his dark eyes full of wickedness and the sheer joy of being alive.

'Stand on my shoulders,' he'd say, holding out his arms. 'I'll throw you.'

So I had, feeling the power in those strong shoulders even then, even back when he was seventeen. Then he'd gripped my ankles and crouched down in the water before surging back up, releasing me to leap high into the sky, as high as I could get before splashing back down.

I'd felt as if I were flying.

I felt as if I were flying now.

There was no need for armour, no need for the icy control I cultivated. There was only him and the desire I could no longer fight.

I sat up, desperate to touch him, reaching out for his wet skin, feeling heat and hard muscle. I shook with desire, with desperation, because I'd never touched a man's bare torso like this, and I couldn't believe how hungry it made me.

I'd never felt such desire for a man. I'd never felt desire at all for anyone, not even Constantine.

He looked like Valentin, but people had always been wrong in thinking that they were identical. They weren't. Constantine hadn't thrown me into the sky. Constantine hadn't argued with me about the best way to build a fire.

Constantine hadn't held me in the darkness and kissed me and told me he loved me.

'Ah, little star,' Valentin whispered, taking my hands away from his body and kissing my fingertips the way he'd used to do. 'No touching. Not yet.'

'I don't care,' I whispered back. 'Let me.'

'No.' And, before I could protest further, he pressed me back down, taking my wrists in one strong hand and pinning them to the sand above my head. He stared down at me, his expression fierce, blazing with intensity as he reached down with his free hand to undo his jeans.

The warning in my head sounded again, but I didn't listen.

I didn't want to.

I knew what he was going to do and I couldn't think of anything I wanted more, because it was perfect like this. On the beach, in the dark, under the stars.

'Estrella,' he murmured, the Spanish lilting and musical, and then something else, something I didn't understand.

I began to tremble as his hand settled on my bare stomach, his gaze on mine, and then he stroked me and every one of my senses came alive. His fingers were hot, a brand on my damp skin, and the ache between my legs suddenly felt like more than I could bear.

Every inch of my body wanted his touch, his hands, his mouth, his tongue. And I couldn't stop myself from arching up, from offering myself to him.

'Please,' I moaned.

'You want me, Livvy?' His hand slid down, his fingers grazing the curls between my thighs and making me shiver all over. 'Tell me. Say it.'

I shouldn't do what he said, yet I didn't even think of disobeying him. 'Yes, I want you. I want you now, please.'

'My name, little star.' His voice deepened, became a growl. 'Say my name.'

'Valentin…' I sighed, his name escaping like a prayer. 'I want you, Val.'

His hand moved, sliding down further, touching me where I was most sensitive, where I ached and ached and ached.

I shuddered as his fingertips struck sparks of pleasure along every nerve-ending I had, stroking through the folds of my sex, gently exploring me. A gasp escaped me and I shut my eyes as pleasure bloomed.

But then he said, 'No, don't close your eyes. Look at me, Livvy. Look only at me.'

So I did, staring upwards into his beautiful face. Because he was beautiful; he always had been. And, despite what I'd told myself all these years, I'd missed him so much. When I'd heard he'd died, a part of me had been ripped away.

He wasn't gone any more, though. He was here. He was right here with me, his gaze on mine, all velvet darkness, but not wholly black. Not completely. I'd never realised till now, but there were stars in his eyes, light glittering deep in all that shadow. I couldn't look away.

His fingers shifted, sliding inside me, and I groaned as the pleasure spread out, engulfing me like the sea. Then he took his hand away and put his mouth there instead and I burst into flames like a bonfire.

He explored me with his tongue, licking insistently, his hands holding my hips to the sand as I writhed in an agony of pleasure. I reached down and buried my fingers in his damp black hair, crying out his name as he continued to taste me with a single-minded relentlessness that had me losing my grip on reality.

There was nothing but the fire of his touch and the

black sky above me; the heat of his mouth and the pleasure that threatened to consume me. He pushed me to the brink with that magic tongue of his and then, when he pushed it inside me, he sent me over the edge and I cried out as the orgasm crashed over me, ecstasy glittering in my bloodstream like the stars above, making me shake, gasp and tremble.

Then he rose above me as I lay there panting in the sand and got rid of his sodden jeans and underwear. Naked, he looked like a god…a sea god…all wet skin, sleek seal-dark hair and glittering black eyes. His body looked as if it was carved from rock, taut and hard, and so hot that when he covered me I felt as if I'd been burned.

I reached to touch him, still trembling from that orgasm, but he shook his head, pinning my wrists again, holding me down. The expression on his face was so intense it took my breath away…so fierce. As if I were a prize he'd fought long and hard for which now he could finally claim. Finally, I was his.

It was thrilling to be looked at like that, because I'd been the irritating girl-child with all her various flaws. Reluctantly given a company I didn't deserve when, really, both my parents would much rather have had a boy.

But I'd never been a disappointment to Val. Not even that first day we met, when he'd appeared on the beach and his eyes had lit up.

'Don't go. Please stay.'

My heart throbbed, a raw, heavy emotion gathering in my chest.

'Val,' I whispered, not even sure what I wanted to say to him, only that I felt something huge, something without a name, and it scared me. And it was because of him.

He said nothing, just watched me as I felt the heat of

his bare skin shifting against me as he nudged between my thighs. His gaze burned, full of a raw heat that made my mouth go dry, and then I felt the head of his sex push against me, then into me.

I was so wet, there was no resistance and no pain. Only the intense sensation of my body stretching to accommodate his, clasping him tightly as if he was something I couldn't bear to let go.

I gasped aloud because, even though it didn't hurt, it was still a shock…and he was big. Were all men this big? I could hardly breathe for the pressure.

My fingertips dug into his powerful shoulders and I gasped again as he sank deeper, his free hand sliding under me, lifting me, tilting me so he could go even deeper.

'Yes, Olivia…' he growled, his voice rough and guttural, black eyes blazing down at me in triumph. 'You're mine now. You're *all* mine.'

Then he bent and kissed me hard and deep, conquering me, mastering me so completely that all I could do was surrender.

But maybe that was always what I'd meant to do with Val. I'd always meant to surrender to him.

Then every thought in my head fractured and broke apart as he began to move, at first slow and easy, and then faster, harder. He was relentless and powerful and I tried to move with him, arching and straining against the hold he had on my wrists.

But he didn't let me go, making me take whatever he gave until the sheer ecstasy of it consumed me whole.

I lost myself in the ferocity of his kiss. In the slide of him inside me, the exquisite friction of it driving me on past pleasure and into something deeper and more intense. Something that was made up of his kiss, his touch and the scent of salt and cinnamon. The heat of his body and the rough sound of his voice.

The beat of his heart and the way he said my name.

And then, at the end the sheer rush of pleasure that exploded inside me, he launched me off his shoulders and into the sky. Making me fly, the way he always had.

CHAPTER TEN

Valentin

I HEARD OLIVIA scream my name and felt her body convulse, her sex tightening around mine as the orgasm took her. And I let go of the leash I had on myself, moving inside her hard and deep, tasting her sweet mouth, covering myself in her passion, letting myself burn.

I couldn't make it last, though. I'd wanted her too much and for too long, and the scent and feel of her, the sound of her husky voice pleading for me, just about made me lose my mind.

The orgasm came for me far too quickly, an intense rush of pleasure that shot up my spine and exploded in my brain like a firework. Then my head was full of stars and, looking down into her eyes, they were all I could see…all those stars glittering in her eyes.

For long moments we stared at each other and I was conscious of every little thing about her: the glow of perspiration on her forehead; the pout of her kiss-swollen lips; the damp strands of hair stuck to her forehead; the deep flush in her cheeks; the frantic beat of her pulse at her throat.

Finally, she was mine.

And I wasn't letting her go.

A deep, intense satisfaction filled me, and I shifted, deciding that it was time we swapped the beach for somewhere more comfortable. She made a soft sound as I withdrew from her that sent a rush of yet more heat through me, but I restrained myself, settling for picking her up in my arms and carrying her down into the sea to wash the sand from us both.

She lay quietly against my chest, the warmth of her naked body making me hard again, staring up at me as if she'd never seen me before in her life.

I didn't say anything and neither did she, the silence settling around us as the warm seawater got rid of the sand.

'We shouldn't have done that,' she said at last, her voice slightly hoarse.

It might have annoyed me if I'd thought she meant it, but I knew she didn't. Because of course we should have done that. It was *exactly* what we should have done. It had been perfect—everything I'd dreamed about and more.

I glanced down at her. Her eyes had darkened and I could see that she wanted some confirmation from me, though why I wasn't sure. No; perhaps I did know why.

She was afraid. Afraid of the intensity between us. It made me aware yet again of how she'd changed, of how cool and hard she'd become. She'd always embraced her passions as a girl, yet from my observations of her now, and over the past few years as I'd watched her, it was clear that she didn't embrace them now.

Why? What had happened to make her so afraid? Was it her father? Managing that company she helmed?

Oliver Wintergreen had never wanted a girl, or so she'd told me once. He'd only wanted a boy, and so her mother had always tried to make her more acceptable to him, while her father had got impatient with what he saw as her 'girlish tantrums and drama'.

I'd never understood how they couldn't see what they had in her. She felt things very deeply and had a strong sense of justice and fairness. She also had a ridiculous sense of humour, and was fearless, yet had the most compassionate heart. She was perfect in every way, and I'd thought them as mad as Domingo in their own way, and just as blind.

'Why not?' I let the water lap up around her, my gaze dropping to her breasts, fascinated by how the cool touch of the sea made her nipples go hard.

'So many reasons.' She made no move to cover herself, her body relaxed and warm against mine. 'We didn't use a condom, either.'

A chill stole through me. I'd never forgotten protection, not once, since the thought of children was appalling to me. After all, who wanted to pass down the defective Silvera genes? Certainly I didn't.

'I'll call the doctor.' I kept my tone very casual. 'We'll handle it.'

The dazed look on her face began to dissipate and I could feel her body start to stiffen in my arms. 'What do you mean, "we'll handle it"?'

'I mean the morning-after pill. Children can't be part of this, Olivia.'

She stared up at me a moment and I could see it happen. I could see the softness leaching out of her, the hard veneer coming back down like a security screen in a bank. 'And what if...?'

But I didn't want to continue with this particular subject, so I made her break off in a gasp, sliding my hand up to cup one round breast, her skin slippery from the water. I teased her nipple gently with my thumb, feeling it get even harder beneath my touch.

'And what if…what?' I asked lazily, circling her nipple and squeezing her lightly.

She trembled in my arms. 'Don't…do that.'

'Why not? You like it.'

And I could see that she did, her head falling back against my shoulder, hunger darkening in her eyes. 'We need to…talk.'

'You don't want to talk, little star.' I pinched her nipple and she jerked, a groan escaping her. 'You want me to keep doing this.'

'I…don't…' Yet even as she said it her back arched and she pressed herself into my hand.

'We'll have time to talk later.' I dropped my head, brushing my mouth over hers, feeling her lips open beneath mine. 'Plenty of time…'

She had no response to that other than to kiss me harder, which soon brought our little chat to a close.

I carried her out of the water and took her back into the villa. Then I ran some warm water into the big white bath in the bathroom and washed us both clean. I teased her in the bath, tantalised her, stroked every inch of her body; and only when she was gasping, trembling and begging did I lift her out, dry her off and take her back to my bed.

I made love to her again, this time taking things slowly, exploring every inch of her so that all she was thinking of when I finally pushed inside her was me and the pleasure I was giving her.

After we'd both recovered she was ravenous, because of course she'd had nothing to eat all day, so we wandered back down the jetty to the table. The food wasn't any the worse for wear, and I insisted she sit in my lap so I could feed her little morsels of whatever she fancied.

Or at least, I tried to insist. She was adamant that wasn't happening, so I'd decided not to force the issue, as the last couple of times I'd forced it, it hadn't ended well for me.

A good choice, as it turned out, when five minutes later she changed her mind and sat regally in my lap as if I were her favourite chair.

It satisfied something deep in me to take care of her like this, as it had all those years ago when I'd managed to toast the perfect marshmallow for her, handing it to her with ceremony. The pleasure of watching her eat it had been…indescribable.

I'd never had anything of my own to take care of before. Constantine and I hadn't been allowed pets. Nothing we might form emotional attachments to. We'd only had each other, and even then Domingo hadn't liked it.

He had driven a wedge between us, and I had let it happen, because I hadn't wanted Constantine to follow my lead. I was his older brother, if only by a few minutes, and I was supposed to protect him, so protect him I had. His safety had depended on him being Domingo's favourite and that was what I'd made sure he was. By making myself Domingo's target.

Except you failed, didn't you?

But I didn't want to think about that right now, what with Olivia in my arms, so I pushed the thought away.

'Have you really been watching me all this time?' Olivia asked, lying back against my shoulder, her hair, dry now, spilling over my arm in a long, straight fall. I was only wearing a pair of jeans, so it felt like silk against my bare skin.

She was in one of those floaty dresses I'd bought especially for her, though it was more a long, filmy tunic in blue and lavender silk than a dress. It was just as transparent as all the others, which meant I could see her beautiful body through the fabric.

She didn't seem to mind this time. In fact, lying like this in my arms, well pleasured and now fed, she was nothing but passion and sensuality, her hard veneer gone.

She was magical like this.

'Not initially, no.' I wound a lock of her hair around my finger, watching the candlelight gloss it gold. 'After the car accident, it took me some time to get my resources together.'

She glanced up at me. 'What happened, Val?'

What to tell her?

Perhaps the truth?

Yes, but what truth?

I'd never cared what other people thought of me. Why would a lion concern himself with the opinions of sheep? Especially back then, in those early days after the accident, when I'd had to do what I could to survive.

But isn't that what you've always done? Whatever you have to?

There had been no other choice. My childhood had been a battleground that had left few survivors and I'd always made sure that my brother would be one of them.

'What happened?' I echoed. 'Well, like I told you, there was only one way to escape Domingo and that was to let everyone assume I was dead. So that's what I did. I managed to get into Italy and found some under-the-table work for a time. Then I...' How to put it? Would she accept that I'd fallen in with a mentor who was part of a crime network? And that I'd become one of them because I'd had nowhere else to go and no way to earn a living? Would she judge the company I'd built after taking over that crime network and turned it legitimate?

Would she judge *me*?

Dios, why did the thought of her judgement matter?

'You what?' she prompted.

I stared back at her, letting her see a bit of the truth in my eyes. 'If you're thinking mine is a plucky David Copperfield story, then you should think again.'

'I wasn't thinking that.'

Uneasiness shifted inside me. I didn't want to tell her, which was ridiculous.

She sat up in my lap all of a sudden, the silk of her tunic sliding over my skin as she faced me. Her pretty eyes were only inches away and I could see that there were still tiny grains of sand in her hairline. I liked her like this, all tumbled and ruffled, less poised and perfect.

'I think you did whatever you could to survive,' she said, lifting my own thoughts straight out of my head. 'You're a ruthless man, Val. I can see that now. And whatever you had to do, it probably wasn't easy.' She paused a moment, searching my face. 'You don't have to tell me if you don't want to.'

I didn't like that she could see so much of me, that she could read me so easily. No one else could. Then again, no one knew me the way she did.

She knew the boy. She doesn't know the man.

I stared into her grey eyes. 'I fell in with a man who ran a major crime empire in the south of Italy. Mafia connections, that kind of thing. I helped him run it and then, when he was killed in a car bomb, I took it over.'

Again, a flicker of some emotion I didn't recognise passed over her face, a shadow that made her eyes darken.

'Oh, don't worry.' I couldn't hide the edge in my

voice. 'I took it all legitimate years ago. You're not soiling yourself with some evil crime lord.'

If she found the sharp note in the words an issue, she didn't show it. She only frowned. 'It doesn't matter to me what you did. I'm just sorry that you had to do it.'

I let go of her curl, lifted my hand and wound all my fingers in her hair, not liking the strange, heavy feeling of regret that sat on my chest like a stone; wanting to feel softness against my skin instead.

'I needed money and power if I wanted to protect you and that was the quickest way to get both.' I closed my hand in a fist and said both to her and to myself, 'And I don't regret it.'

CHAPTER ELEVEN

Olivia

HE DID REGRET IT. I could see it in his eyes. Whatever he'd done to get that money and that power, he hadn't wanted to do it.

My heart tightened. All the anger I'd felt towards him earlier seemed to have vanished, lost in the passion that had consumed us on the beach. Now what I felt was a hard tug of sympathy, and a growing curiosity about the life he'd led after he'd 'died'.

It hadn't been an easy one, that seemed obvious, and it had pretty much crushed the boy he'd once been. The kind, loving boy who'd once been so good to me.

Yet, had that boy been entirely stripped away? Certainly, I could see traces of him in the food he'd had made for me and the French champagne in the ice-bucket. In the way he'd gently washed me in the bath, and in the way he was holding me now.

Protectiveness had always been in his nature.

It made it difficult to tell whether all of that—the dinner, the drinks, the talk of the past—had been manipulation or whether it had been him genuinely being kind.

I didn't know. Perhaps I needed to stop thinking about that boy and start concentrating on the man.

A ruthless, charming man. Manipulative, yes, yet also driven; I could see that. However, while he seemed quite happy to talk about our past, his was a different story.

And you don't want to push him on it.

No, I didn't, not now.

We had something of a détente and, while I hadn't meant to lie here comfortably in his arms, naked but for a silky tunic, I was strangely okay with it.

I hadn't wanted to initially, finding the thought of sitting in his lap a little too much like being his plaything for comfort. But he hadn't insisted, and somehow I'd found myself changing my mind. It seemed silly not to be physically close to him after what had happened on the beach, and if I wanted it, then why not?

It was my choice and that didn't make me a doormat. Besides, as I'd told myself as he'd picked me up out of the sea and washed me carefully in the bath, what was between us was merely physical. Just pleasure, nothing more.

It didn't mean anything was going to change.

I was still engaged to Constantine, and I still fully intended to find my way back to him. Val was wrong about him, I was certain, and those debts needed paying.

I also still wanted an heir, and it was clear what Val's thoughts were on the subject. His response to the lack of a condom had been unequivocal. He did not want children.

But he'd given me the most unbelievable pleasure, and, as I knew a marriage to Constantine wouldn't give me that, why shouldn't I take this while I could?

I'd worked hard for my father for years, so why shouldn't I have something for myself for a change? Constantine might take issue with it, but if he did it wouldn't be because he wanted me in particular. I wasn't special to him. I was just a vessel. He hadn't even told the press that I'd been kidnapped, after all.

But I wasn't just a vessel to Val. And he wanted *me*, so why resist?

A night, I told myself. I'd let myself have a night where I was his and he was mine and we could have the passion we'd never had as children. Where kisses could become more and our games wouldn't be about pushing each other into the sea, but touching each other in bed.

I was allowed this. I was finally allowed to be with the boy I'd once loved and then lost.

'What happened to you after you left the beach?' I kept my voice very casual. It had been so many years ago that that particular pain had long since scabbed over. 'I found out you and Constantine had gone back to Madrid and I thought you'd contact me. But you didn't. I didn't hear anything.'

Valentin's eyes glittered strangely in the light and I saw something dark cross his face. I could also feel his body tense beneath me. This wasn't something he wanted to talk about, was it?

'Well,' he said softly. 'That's quite the story. Are you sure you want to hear it?'

A chill whispered over my skin. It was going to be something awful, wasn't it? Something to do with his father, Domingo, the psychopath.

I stared into Valentin's eyes, the chill settling deeper into my soul. I hadn't fully taken on board what he'd said about his father before, but that soft note in his voice and that glitter in his eyes…

What had his childhood *really* been like?

I'd never thought about it as a kid, not in any depth. We'd complained to each other about our parents, of course, but that was what kids did. All parents were mean and unfair. But Domingo…

'Tell me,' I said, staring into those mesmerising eyes. 'I want to know.'

'Don't say I didn't warn you.' Valentin didn't let my hair go, rubbing a lock of it between his thumb and fore-finger. 'Domingo didn't want me seeing you, as you already know. But naturally I ignored him, because I always ignored him. He wouldn't have found out that I was still meeting with you if Constantine hadn't told him.'

A shock went through me. 'Constantine told him?'

Valentin lifted a shoulder. 'Oh, yes. He was such a good little soldier.'

'But…he's your brother.' I didn't want to believe Constantine could have done something like that, yet deep down I knew that of course he would have. He was such a stickler for rules.

'I tried to protect him by drawing Domingo's attention as much as possible so he would leave Constantine alone,' Valentin said. 'I…didn't know Domingo had been manipulating him behind my back and turning him against me. Not until he told Domingo about us.' Something in his handsome face shifted. 'That's when I knew I'd failed. That Domingo had got to him.'

Shock rippled through me. 'What do you mean, you failed? Why?'

'You have to understand,' Valentin said, his attention on the lock of my hair. 'Psychopaths don't need a reason to do what they do. They manipulate to get what they want for their own amusement. Because they like it. And I can't blame Constantine for choosing Domingo over me. We weren't allowed friends. Not even pets. Domingo didn't want us to form any emotional attachments to anything or anyone except him, and he didn't like it that Constantine and I were close. And I had no time for Constantine. I was too obsessed with you.'

His gaze came back to mine. 'Seeing you, meeting you, was like coming across an oasis in the desert, or a spot of colour in a black-and-white world. You were special, Olivia.'

I couldn't take it in. No friends? No pets? No emotional attachments? No wonder Constantine was so cold and so detached.

'I should have spent more time with Constantine,' Val went on, 'but I didn't, and that's my failure. Perhaps, if I had, he wouldn't have turned into Domingo. Anyway, that's all water under the bridge now. He found out I was still seeing you and told Domingo, and we were shipped back to Spain the next day. Then he took away my phone and my computer and he locked me in a room in the basement of our house in Madrid. I wasn't allowed to see anyone or speak to anyone.'

I didn't know what to say. He hadn't been able to contact me even if he'd wanted to and it wasn't because he hadn't cared. It was because his father had taken him prisoner.

The sympathy I'd felt earlier tugged harder. Two boys' lives had been thoroughly blighted by the one person who was supposed to have protected them. Who'd abused and manipulated them instead, not to mention ruining the relationship between them, because that was obvious to me too.

'That's awful,' I said. Such a meaningless and trite statement. Yet what else could I say? It *was* awful.

Val's mouth curved in a bitter smile. 'Yes, it is, isn't it? Domingo was quite subtle. He knew a beating wouldn't do anything, since I didn't care about pain. But he knew how to hurt me in other ways.' That bitter smile deepened. 'He told me he'd keep me there for as long as it took for me to learn how to obey.'

A cold feeling began to wrap itself around my heart. 'So…how long did he keep you there for?'

Val's expression didn't flicker. 'Six months.'

The cold feeling pulled tight, making it difficult to breathe.

Six months. He'd been kept a prisoner for six months.

I'd cried and cried when I'd never heard from him. And then I'd got angry. I'd hated him for a time, thinking he'd lied when he'd told me he loved me. That everything about our relationship had been a lie. He didn't love me, and he didn't care about me. And all I was was just a silly teenage girl who'd fallen for a handsome boy who'd lied to her for fun.

But he hadn't lied.

He'd been a prisoner.

'Val…' My heart felt strangely tight. 'I…'

'I don't need your pity, little star.' His voice was so mild. 'Domingo wanted to teach me a lesson and so he did. I could have promised to obey him, and he might have let me out, but I was still trying to protect Constantine.'

My heart tightened even further. 'You remained a prisoner for six months to protect your brother? After he told on you? On us?'

'Yes.' There was a bitter humour in his eyes. 'It wasn't his fault he turned out the way he did. I should have been there for him, and I wasn't.'

'Oh, Val.'

'I'd probably still be there if someone hadn't slipped me the key to the door and I was able to get out. Do you know, there were no windows? And once a week Domingo would take me outside to show me everything I was missing.' Val's gaze turned distant. 'He hated that I wouldn't give in. It made him so furious. He left me there three weeks once. I thought I was going to go mad...'

Horror gripped me, along with an aching pity that, no matter how hard I tried not to feel it, threaded through me all the same. Because behind his smile I could see that the boy had started to die even before that accident. He'd been so full of life, burning bright... What must being trapped in a room for six months have done to him? Not being able to see the sun, or the stars. The moon... Not being able to feel the air on his face or hear the sound of the sea...

And you hating him because he didn't text you.

He frowned suddenly, his gaze sharpening. 'Don't, Livvy. Whatever you're thinking, don't.'

But he'd given me some honesty and so I had to give him some in return.

'I was very angry with you after you left,' I said. 'For not saying goodbye. And then you didn't contact me. I didn't get a text or an email or a call. I thought... I thought you'd forgotten me.'

He opened his mouth, but I laid a finger across his lips. 'Then you died. And I was angry about that. I was angry with you for a very long time.'

His mouth moved again, but I pressed my finger slightly harder, feeling the softness of his lips against my skin. The only thing about him that was soft. 'I'm sorry I didn't know the truth. I'm sorry that I never asked you what Domingo was really like or...or what kind of life you had.' And I was so sorry. More than he'd ever guess. 'I probably should have picked it up or...'

He pulled my finger away, holding on to my hand. 'No, you don't need to be sorry. You were only fifteen and you had your own issues to deal with. You weren't to know what Domingo was like. And I didn't tell you, not the extent of it.'

'But I—'

'I didn't want you to know. I didn't want you to worry. Because there was nothing you could have done.' He gathered my fingers in his and kissed the tips of them the way he'd used to. 'Domingo had too much power, and you were only a kid, and so was I.' He let out a breath, an emotion I couldn't quite read flickering over his face. 'I wish I could have done more, but it's too late for that now.'

Was that regret? I couldn't be sure. Whatever it was, my heart ached for him and what he'd had to put up with. What he'd had to endure, he and Constantine both.

Domingo made my father look like father of the year.

'Anyway,' Valentin went on, brushing his mouth over my fingertips again. 'Enough about me. What about you? What happened to turn my Livvy into such a formidable CEO?'

Formidable. Yes, I was. Because that was what I'd wanted to be. That's where I'd put my effort. I'd become a diamond that wouldn't shatter, crack or get scratched. I was impervious.

Are you, though? Sitting naked in his lap in a silly dress, allowing him to kiss your fingers like you're a princess? You know what the next step is.

No, of course that wouldn't be the next step. There was a vast gap between choosing to sit in a man's lap and staying in a loveless marriage while putting up with all kinds of emotional cruelty.

'Well, after you died, I needed something to fill my time.' My voice sounded cool even though I hadn't meant it to. 'And I know that back then I always said I didn't want to run Wintergreen, but I changed my mind. So I studied hard at school and then went to university. And, when I asked Dad to take me on, he didn't refuse.'

Valentin's black eyes watched me with his usual intense focus. 'Is that what this is?'

'This?' I frowned. 'What do you mean?'

He touched my cheek, his fingers feathering over my skin before falling down to my shoulder and brushing gently along it. 'This tension. This…toughness. You're all bright and shiny and hard, like a diamond.'

I should have been pleased that he'd noticed. Pleased that he'd accurately guessed what I'd become. But for some reason it didn't feel like he was complimenting me.

'You say that like it's a bad thing.' I forced away the shiver at his touch. 'Hardness is always admired in men, but it's never admired in women.'

'That's true. And, to be clear, I don't think it's an inherently bad thing. You need a certain hardness when it comes to business. But when it doesn't come naturally to someone, they over-compensate. They become hard all the way through. All their passion is leached away, which is a pity, because good business needs passion too.'

A thread of annoyance wound through me. 'I'm not over-compensating, if that's what you're suggesting.'

A smile flickered around his mouth and it wasn't the same bitter one I'd seen before. This was more rueful, and somehow a hundred times more attractive. 'Actually, I was suggesting that.' He touched my cheek again, his fingertips tracing the line of my jaw. 'You never used to be like this, not so hard and bright and shiny. Why? What's the purpose of it? It's brittle, and I don't think you like it. I think it's hard work for you.' His smile deepened. 'You're much more yourself when you're slapping my face and pushing me off the jetty into the sea.'

The annoyance was starting to become anger now, and I could feel myself freezing over, trying to shut it out. Trying to detach myself from the emotion.

How he always managed to get under my guard, I didn't know, but it wasn't what I wanted. Not while I was naked and lying in his arms.

'Yes, well, I shouldn't have done any of those things,' I said coolly. 'And you're not wrong about me being a diamond. Diamonds are created under pressure, and they're impervious. Which is the best way to be when it comes to managing my company.'

I shifted in his lap, deciding I needed to get off him. It had been nice while it lasted, but I wasn't a pet. I wasn't going to stay there.

But his hands dropped suddenly to my hips, gripping me, preventing me from moving. 'Why?' he demanded. 'Who told you that?'

'My father. And he wasn't wrong.'

'Yes, well, your father is dead.' Valentin wasn't smiling now and there was something fierce glittering in his eyes. 'And he can't see you here. There's only me and I don't care how impervious you are. You don't need to guard yourself with me.'

'Don't I?' I shot back before I could stop myself. 'When you're manipulating me at every step, with my favourite foods and wine, and talking about the past? Reminding me every minute of that girl I used to be? You told me yourself that you're going to make me fall in love with you, and that's exactly what you're trying to do, isn't it?'

His expression hardened, his grip not easing one iota. 'Yes.'

It was clear he did not like having to admit that, yet he had, and it made my anger at him ease a fraction. But only a fraction.

'Well, then,' I said. 'I shouldn't need to explain why relaxing my guard with you will never be an option.'

A muscle flicked in his jaw, and he was silent a long moment. Then he said, 'There's a reason I call you "little star". Did you know that? It's because that's what you are. You're not a diamond, Olivia Wintergreen. You're a star. And stars are made to burn.'

And you're still burning all these years later. Burning for him.

No, I wasn't. I'd killed that fire stone-dead and it would never burn again.

'Let me go,' I said, pushing at his chest.

His fingers tightened a moment, his gaze getting hot. 'Are you sure?'

And I could feel it again, the wild chemistry that seemed to have got even more intense now we'd slept together building between us. The hunger gathering inside me despite all the barriers I'd tried to put between myself and it.

Because, no, I wasn't sure.

There was a part of me that didn't want him to let me go. That wanted him to hold me tight and keep me close. The part of me that wanted to know more about the man he'd become—a difficult, dangerous, challenging yet fascinating man.

The part of me that wanted to burn.

But I wasn't going to. He was too tempting, and already I'd forgotten myself enough to surrender to him on the sand. To let him wash me, feed me and hold me in his lap as if I were a child.

I'd had my night of pleasure and it was over now.

'Yes,' I said flatly. 'I'm sure.'

Something flickered in his night-black gaze and for a second I thought he wouldn't do it. But then his fingers released me and I slid off his lap.

'What changed?' he asked, an edge to his voice. 'What did you do with my Livvy?'

'I'm not your Livvy, Valentin.' I turned back towards the villa. 'And nothing's changed. It was nice to reconnect, but I have a company to run and a fiancé to get back to.'

'What? Did you think I was joking?' His voice was low and somehow menacing. 'Did you think that sex was all I wanted? That we could sleep together, have dinner and then I'd fly you back home tomorrow?'

I stopped dead, a shudder going through me.

Yes, of course I'd thought that. Perhaps not consciously, but I'd assumed…

He's not that boy, remember? And he's dangerous.

But I wasn't that girl, either, and perhaps I, too, was dangerous.

I turned around, the silk of my tunic brushing over my skin, making me very aware all of a sudden of how I was naked beneath it.

Val had risen to his feet, the rueful, beautiful smile vanishing as if it had never been there. His handsome face had gone hard, a razor's edge in his black eyes. He still burned—he'd never been cold like Constantine—but this fire was fierce and it was hungry. Like it had been back in the ballroom of the Silvera mansion.

I'd never been more aware that this was the man he was now. That the past fifteen years of his life had clearly been a furnace, tempering him. He was not a man who could be crossed. It was clear he did not like the word 'no'.

'Then I'll damn well learn to fly and take the plane,' I said, throwing down the gauntlet, because I wasn't a woman who liked hearing the word no. 'I'm not your prisoner, Val. And I won't be told what to do—not by you, not by anyone.'

'You're not marrying him. I won't let you.'

'Really? And how are you going to stop me?' I lifted a brow. 'Or are you going to lock me in, the way your father did to you?'

'He's *not* my father,' Valentin spat all of a sudden. 'And I don't need to lock you in.' He began to come towards me, striding down the jetty with all that predatory grace; all bright, fierce beauty. Lucifer, the light bringer.

Perhaps I should have run. But I hadn't run earlier, and I wasn't going to do that now. Besides, he wasn't going to hurt me. He was only going to intimidate me into doing what he wanted and, well, he could try.

So I stood my ground, lifting my chin. Letting him see he couldn't cow me or frighten me into doing his bidding.

He stopped, barely inches away, surrounding me with the seductive heat of his body and scent of cinnamon and salt. Reminding me that he was all man, and that I was all woman, and that I wanted him. No matter what I told myself about distance, I wanted him.

He said nothing, reaching out and taking the front of my silk tunic between his hands and jerking it apart. The silk tore soundlessly, the halves falling open, leaving me naked.

Heat and desire burned hot in his eyes as his gaze raked over me, and I didn't flinch from it. I let him look. Because it came to me that I had a power I hadn't fully understood until now. A uniquely feminine power that I'd always underestimated and dismissed.

The power of sex.

He wanted me. But he couldn't have me unless I let him.

He reached for me.

'Don't touch me.' I held his gaze, letting him see that I wasn't going to give in; giving him a taste of his own medicine.

His hands stopped where they were, halfway to reaching for my hips. Fury lit in his eyes as I saw him battle with his better self.

'What is this?' he growled. 'A test?'

'No. It's an ultimatum. If you want me again, you have to promise to let me go. And then you'll fly me back to London so I can marry Constantine.'

He cursed under his breath, something harsh in Spanish. 'You should know that I do not take kindly to ultimatums.'

'Too bad, because that's what you're getting.'

His eye gleamed like a furnace. 'It never worked for Domingo. Why would it work for you?'

'Because I am not Domingo.' I reached out and placed my palm against his rock-hard chest, tempting fate. Tempting him. 'Enjoy your cold bed.'

Then I turned on my heel and walked back naked to the villa.

CHAPTER TWELVE

Valentin

I SAT ON the jetty all night, gritting my teeth and seething. Fighting my rage.

Towards dawn, I flung myself into the sea to get rid of the heat burning ferociously inside me and then stalked back to the villa.

I went to my bedroom. The bed sheets were still rumpled from making love to Olivia. I could still smell her on the air, sweetness and feminine musk. It made me even harder than I already was, which didn't help my temper.

I dumped my clothes and then went into the shower, turned it to cold and stood under the water, letting it fall like needles of ice on my hot skin.

She'd been so very beautiful standing there on the jetty the night before, unflinching as I'd torn the silk of her tunic apart. She'd stood her ground, naked and proud, like a goddess made of starlight.

Telling me, no. Telling me that, if I wanted her, I'd have to let her go.

No one told me to do anything. No one. Not since Domingo.

How could I let her go, anyway? Let her go and marry another man? A man I'd done my best to protect.

My brother. My twin.

I'd wanted to ignore her, to grab her, to show her how easily her will could be broken with just the touch of my hand. I could have had her on the jetty, gasping and begging for me. I could have had her warm and wet and willing. I could have made her forget all about that stupid ultimatum of hers.

But I couldn't stop thinking about what she'd flung at me—about how she couldn't let down her guard with me—because I'd been manipulating her ever since we'd got here. And I hadn't been able to take that last step. A boundary had sprung up inside me and I hadn't realised I had it.

She'd said not to touch her, and I couldn't. Just as I couldn't ignore what she'd said about using her favourite foods and those memories of our childhood to manipulate her.

I hadn't thought about it at the time. I'd just done what I'd had to do to get what I wanted. And, yes, looking at it like that, I *had* manipulated her. I'd wanted her to remember what we'd had as children, what we'd been to each other... Yet, as she kept saying to me, she wasn't that child any longer. And neither was I.

So, I couldn't touch her. And I couldn't use food, memories or even sex to make her change her mind.

Fundamentally, I couldn't ignore her choice, because wasn't that what Domingo had taken from me? Hadn't that been my whole childhood?

Yet wasn't that what you were doing all along? Making your own choices anyway just to spite him? To show him he couldn't beat you, that he couldn't win?

No, it had had never been about winning. It had

been about protecting Constantine. That had always been the goal.

Yes, and you failed.

I pushed the thought away, not wanting to dwell on it. This wasn't about Domingo and Constantine, anyway. This was about Olivia. And, no matter what she said, no matter what ultimatums she'd flung at me, I still wasn't going to let her go back to Madrid to marry my psychopathic brother, and that was final.

After my shower, I stalked down the wide wooden hallway and into the room I used as an office. Like the rest of the villa, it had large windows and big sliding glass doors that led out onto the deck that surrounded the house.

The island and the villa I'd built was my favourite place to be. There was nothing shut-in about it, nothing hemmed in. Everywhere there were views of the ocean, and all you needed to do to get out was to slide back one of those big glass doors.

It was a hangover of being shut in that basement room for months. I still didn't like being confined and, once I'd had money, I'd spent it on wide vistas and freedom.

The room had bookshelves lining the walls, full of books in a wide array of different subjects and genres, and anything else that took my interest. A large, smooth white stone. An intricate shell. A piece of driftwood in an interesting shape. A piece of coral, bleached white, that had washed up on the beach.

I liked that I could put whatever I wanted on the shelves. I liked that I could do whatever I wanted with the villa. After a childhood such as mine, where everything had been tightly controlled, being able to make such small choices was a luxury I still enjoyed, no matter how many years had gone by.

A large wooden desk with clean lines stood near one of the windows, a wafer-thin computer screen sitting on top of it. I went over to the desk and sat down, turning on my computer.

I wanted to check in with my lawyers, as well as catch up on the media to see what progress—if any—had been made with my brother. I hadn't had any alerts overnight, which meant he hadn't made any move, which I thought was odd.

Surely, he wouldn't just let me walk away with Olivia? Especially when she seemed so keen to get back to him. Domingo wouldn't have permitted it, that was for sure.

I leaned back in my chair, scrolling through the day's news, most of my brain occupied with what my next move was going to be. I had to stop Olivia being so suspicious of me, get her to trust me somehow, and that meant changing my methods.

I couldn't let her leave, but perhaps I could let her lead our interactions. That wouldn't be manipulating her, not if she took the initiative. Perhaps she could tell me more about her company and her plans for it. I already knew a lot about it, but not all. And, if sex was out, fine. I didn't need it that badly. Maybe it would give me the chance to learn more about Olivia the woman rather than Olivia the girl.

After all, she hadn't seemed to dislike my company. I'd told her about Domingo, about what had happened all those years ago, and she'd told me how angry she'd been with me for not contacting her. Which I completely understood.

Your fault, though. You could have given in.

I sneered at the thought. Given in? To Domingo? And let him turn his sights on Constantine? Never.

Constantine had sat outside the basement door even

though he'd been forbidden to go near it, breaking the rules for me so he could slip notes underneath it. Notes asking me why I wouldn't just give in, because Papa wouldn't let me out until I did. Papa would keep me there for ever.

There'd been no apology from him, though. No apology for condemning me to months in a windowless room with no sky, glimpse of the stars or a laughing girl to keep me company.

No apology, even though I'd been making myself the target of Domingo's attentions for years for *him*.

I hadn't been angry about it. Because that had been the moment I'd understood that he wasn't my twin any more. He wasn't even my brother. He was Domingo's son in every way, and that was why there'd been no apology. He didn't care about me. He didn't care about Olivia. And why would he? Psychopaths had no empathy.

Anger collected inside me along with a bitter grief that still hurt even after all these years. Fury at Domingo and what he'd done to Constantine, what he'd done to us both and the bond that used to exist between us. The bond he'd broken, leaving me with no choice but to take from Constantine his company and his power so he wouldn't hurt anyone the way Domingo had.

Fury at myself for failing him.

I growled and reached out abruptly, sweeping the offending computer monitor off the desk and onto the floor. It cracked satisfyingly, but I was still furious. Domingo was dead; I couldn't take my rage out on him, but I had to get rid of it somehow. Yet the only options here were exercise or sex. And, since sex was clearly off the table, exercise it would have to be.

The gym was down the other end of the villa and after

I'd changed into my workout gear I got on the treadmill and put myself through a punishing run.

Olivia wouldn't like me keeping her here, but letting her leave wasn't an option. I had to protect her. I'd failed my brother, but I wouldn't fail her.

She could deny me her body, but that was fine. I could outlast her. We'd soon see who was more resolute. I'd been beaten, starved and isolated. I'd been locked in a windowless room for six months because I'd refused to surrender. I'd died and built an empire from nothing at all on the strength of my will alone.

Domingo himself hadn't been able to win against me and neither would she.

And where will that get you?

The thought came out of nowhere, whispering through my brain like a snake in the grass. I ran harder, trying to leave it behind, because it was a stupid question.

What would it get me? It would get me her. In the end, she would be mine.

And did resisting Domingo ever get you what you wanted? Even once?

I growled again, gritting my teeth as I hit the incline button, tilting the treadmill up to its maximum and running even harder.

Of course it had worked with Domingo. He'd done exactly what I'd wanted him to, which was turn his attention on me. My rebellions had kept him busy while he'd left Constantine alone. Constantine had been the good boy, doing everything Domingo had said, while I'd made sure I was the bad one. The one who disobeyed, the one he tried to punish.

But I never gave in. Not once.

You died. You lost everything. Your brother became

Domingo and you broke Olivia's heart. How is that winning?

I gave a guttural roar, slapping the stop button and standing on the treadmill, panting, sweat streaming down my body. Because, as much as I didn't want that thought in my head, it wound its way through my brain all the same.

It was true. That last burst of defiance hadn't worked as well as it should have. It had ended up with me 'dying', and it had ended up hurting Olivia.

She'd thought I didn't care about her; that I hadn't called her because I'd forgotten about her.

She didn't matter as much as your need to win against Domingo.

I tried to shove that thought away, going over to the gym door that led to the deck and stepping outside. Stripping off my sweaty clothes, I dove head-first into the water straight from the deck, letting the sea wash away the sweat.

But I couldn't get that thought out of my head.

What if I'd given in and agreed to never see her again? He would have left her alone because she'd never interested him. She was only a tool he'd used to get to me.

Perhaps if I'd done what he'd asked, perhaps if I'd made that promise, I could have found some way to get a message to her without Domingo finding out, to let her know what had happened. Then, when I'd finally grown up and Domingo had no power over me any longer, I could have come for her.

Perhaps if I'd done that we could have been married now.

And she might not have turned herself into that hard, cold diamond. She might have waited for you. But you failed her, like you failed your brother.

Something hot twisted in my chest, but I shoved it away. I couldn't go down that route; there was no point. The past was fixed. I couldn't change it. But I could certainly make things better for the future, so I would.

Surfacing, I turned in the direction of the villa and swam slowly back to the steps that led back up to the deck, turning an idea over in my head.

Compromise had always been difficult for me, but I had to give Olivia something. A gesture of good faith. A counter-offer. Something that would get us what we both wanted but would still ensure she didn't marry Constantine. Because, his psychopathic tendencies aside, she didn't really want him.

But she did want me. And I had everything he did, plus something else: the ability to give her pleasure. After all, it hadn't been his name she'd called out under the stars last night, and it hadn't been him she'd been thinking of.

It was me. All me.

Once I was out of the water, I grabbed a towel, dried myself and got changed. Then I strode down the wide hallway again to the guest bedroom Olivia was in.

The door was closed and, even though I was tempted to just walk in, I didn't. I raised a hand and knocked. Politely. Like a gentleman. Because if I was going to win her I needed to at least stop paying lip service to the idea and actually start acting like one.

'Come in,' Olivia called.

I pushed the door open and strode in.

And stopped dead in the middle of the room.

Olivia was sunbathing on the lounger on the deck just outside her room.

And she was naked.

CHAPTER THIRTEEN

Olivia

NAKED SUNBATHING WAS a calculated gamble. But, if Valentin could climb out of the ocean stark naked and wander about in front of me, I could certainly lie on the sun-lounger without any clothes on in front of him.

And I'd had to do something. I couldn't sit in my room, twiddling my thumbs all day. I'd had to act.

This morning I'd already been in touch with Rachel, making enquiries as to flights from the Maldives. She was surprised that I wanted to come home so soon but hadn't questioned it.

I couldn't let anyone know the real situation, because that was my only advantage. If the board didn't know I'd been kidnapped by Constantine's twin brother, if they still thought I was on some Caribbean holiday with Constantine himself, then at least I wouldn't look weak. I wouldn't look like some damn trophy wife two brothers were fighting over.

Which is what you are.

Not for much longer. Not if I could help it.

I had to get back to Madrid, and quickly, and I'd use every weapon in my arsenal to do so, including my new-found feminine power: sex.

It was the kind of tactic my mother had often used, prettying herself up for Dad with a nice dress, salon hair and expert make-up. Sometimes it had worked and sometimes it hadn't, and I'd never known why she'd bothered. Why she hadn't just up and left him, because I certainly would have.

Using such tactics myself felt like a step in the wrong direction, but Val was so strong-willed. So stubborn. Yet I knew he had one weakness: me.

I'd heard him come striding down the hallway and it had been a matter of moments to pull off the bikini I'd been wearing in preparation for a swim and lie down on the lounger, my heart beating fast.

I had to make him want me more than he wanted to keep me prisoner. Show him what he could have if he gave me what I wanted.

But you're using the same tactics against him that Domingo used.

The thought sat uneasily in my head, memories of what he'd told me last night replaying themselves over and over. Of him locked in that room. Of him wanting to draw his father's attention to save his brother. Of the anger inside him whenever he talked about it that he probably thought he'd hidden. But he couldn't hide it from me. I could see the flames in his eyes.

No wonder he'd always burned so brightly. He was a furnace of rage.

A part of me wanted to help him, while another part wanted to get away from him as quickly as possible. Because I knew what happened to women who stayed with difficult men. Their lives became miserable.

My mother's being a case in point. She'd stayed true to a man who'd married her because she'd been young and beautiful. A man who hadn't respected her, who hadn't even seemed to love her. Who'd blamed her for something that hadn't even been her fault.

So, if I stayed with Val, what would happen to me?

He'd burn you both alive...

My thoughts fractured as I heard his step and I threw one arm over my eyes, even though the sun umbrella was providing me with shade. I didn't want to see him just yet, not until my armour was in place.

His footsteps came to a complete stop.

Good. He'd obviously seen me.

I kept my arm over my eyes, my heart racing despite all my efforts to still it.

The room was silent, but I could sense his presence. He was watching me. I could feel the pressure of his gaze sending hot shivers all over my bare skin.

I'd never realised before how erotic it was to lie there naked while a man looked at every part of me. Wanting me. And he wanted me; I knew he did.

I didn't move. Every sense I had was trained on him, so very conscious of my nakedness and the ache between my thighs, a growing neediness that was difficult to ignore.

'Nice to see you enjoying the sun.' The deep, rough sound of his voice came from very near. 'I hope you've got some sunscreen on.'

He must be standing right beside my lounger.

I kept my arm where it was, my heart pounding, my mouth dry. Then I gave a stretch, arching my back as if I'd been sleepy and was trying to wake up.

'I do,' I murmured. 'But it's probably worn off now.' I paused. 'You could put some on me, if you like.'

He laughed, the sound genuine and deeply sensual, making me want to say something else to get him to do it again. 'For an inexperienced virgin, you certainly know how to play the seduction game. I'm impressed, Livvy.' I heard him move and then I could smell his aftershave—cinnamon and masculine musk. Delicious.

The squab on the lounger tilted slightly as I felt him sit on the end of it.

Why was he here? Was this a concession? Had I won? *You don't want to win; not this game.*

Maybe not. But I was tired of him holding all the cards. I wanted some of my own.

I shifted my arm at last.

Val was sitting on the end of the lounger, the bottle of sunscreen in one hand. He was in a black T-shirt today, and worn jeans, and he looked just as delicious as he had the day before. His expression was hungry and he made no effort to hide the desire in his gaze as he swept it down my body, lingering on my breasts and then further down between my legs.

Abruptly, my mouth was as dry as that sandy beach, and it came to me that this little plan had the potential to backfire. I hadn't realised that in tempting him I could just as easily end up tempting myself.

He lifted the bottle and squeezed some sunscreen into his hand. 'Turn over, little star. Let me put some of this on your back.' One black brow lifted. 'Unless you'd like me to start with your front?'

I should tell him not to touch me, to leave—or, better yet, make him watch me as I put sunscreen on myself. But everything in me was aching for his touch and I couldn't resist it. And why not, when I enjoyed him touching me?

After all, it wasn't as if I was going to let him do anything more.

I said nothing, rolling over onto my front.

He shifted and I felt him ease aside my hair so it fell

over my shoulder, the strands silky and soft against my skin. He moved closer on the edge of the lounger, the denim of his jeans brushing against my bare hip. The heat of his body was so very near, the familiar warm scent of him making me dizzy.

Are you sure lying here naked was a good idea?

It had been at the time. Now, I wasn't so sure. All I could think about was why I'd thought surrendering to him had been so very bad. It hadn't been last night; no, it had been…good. *So* good. Perhaps I didn't need to get back to Constantine so quickly. He didn't seem to be looking for me, after all, and a couple more days with Val surely wouldn't hurt…

And then what? You might not want to leave. You might want to stay here for ever and marry him, the way he told you that you would. You'll end up giving him everything he wants, become his perfect trophy wife the way your mother was…

No. No, I was *not* going to let that happen. I was stronger than that and certainly stronger than my mother. She hadn't been a diamond. She'd been nothing but marshmallow melting in my father's hand.

I was different. I wouldn't allow myself to be any man's toy or trophy, and especially not for the sake of a little hot sex.

The only things I needed from a man were Constantine's money and his genetic material, and that was all. Anything else, I'd get myself.

Cool liquid trickled down my spine and then Val's hands were on me, warm and strong and gentle, moving with long, sensual strokes as he massaged in the sunscreen.

Oh, he was so good at that. My whole body clenched tight with desire, both relaxing and thrilling at the same time, which didn't make any sense, yet was obviously happening. I wanted to melt into the lounger, or turn over and arch my back, encourage him to touch my hardening nipples and then go lower to touch other more sensitive, more desperate parts of me.

But, no, I had to stay strong.

'So,' he murmured, his voice like liquid honey. 'What's so very important about marrying Constantine?'

I had my head pillowed on my forearm, trying to pay attention to what he was saying and not the caress of his stroking hands. 'Dad made some…unfortunate business decisions in the last years of his life and it left the company in a financial hole. So when Constantine offered his help, I accepted.'

'He offered?'

'Yes. He'd heard we were in difficulty and came to me with a proposal.'

'Marriage was part of the proposal?'

There didn't seem to be any reason not to tell him.

'Yes.'

'How very medieval of him.' Val massaged my shoulders deliciously, then stroked down the length of my spine. 'I didn't think he was the marrying type.'

I stared into the darkness behind my closed lids, remembering how he'd come to me. And even though I'd prepared myself the shock of seeing him again after all those years had still stolen my breath away. He'd come into my office and for a second all I'd been able to think was, *Val. It's Val.* And then reality had asserted itself and, quite unexpectedly, I'd almost burst into tears.

'He thought it would be beneficial for both of us,' I said, forcing the memory away. 'He said it was time he settled down and got married. Produced some heirs.'

Val's hands paused. Then I felt more cool liquid on

my hot skin as he began to smooth it lower over the curve of one buttock.

I shivered, fighting the urge to lift my hips and press into his hand.

'Ah.' His voice was utterly neutral. 'Was that a condition of his financial help?'

'Yes.'

Val stroked over my rear, cupping me gently. His fingers curled between my thighs just a little, the tips grazing lightly over my most sensitive flesh.

I bit my lip, struggling not to tremble in reaction.

'And I assume he won't just pay the debts?' Val went on, as if he wasn't playing havoc with my senses. 'He'll want some kind of financial control over the company for a time?'

Why was he asking me these questions? If he'd been watching me all this time, he must have some idea already of what Constantine had offered.

'Do you genuinely not know?' I tried to keep the huskiness from my voice. 'Or are you just trying to manipulate me again?'

He gave a low laugh. 'And you're not doing the same thing? Flaunting all this delicious nakedness at me?'

Strangely, that made me want to smile. He was teasing, yet it didn't feel as if it was at my expense this time, but his own. 'Perhaps,' I said. 'Is it working?'

'I couldn't possibly say.'

I felt him draw a small pattern at the small of my back and allowed myself the smile. Yes, it was working.

'Anyway,' he went on. 'Maybe I did know that's why Constantine was marrying you. I'd still like to know the details, though.'

I relaxed a little. 'He said he'd manage Wintergreen

until the company was solvent. To instil confidence in my leadership, et cetera.'

Val had moved on to massaging sunscreen into my thighs and the backs of my knees, and his touch felt so good, I relaxed a little further.

'He'll never give it back to you,' Val said casually, as if it wasn't *my* company he was talking about. 'You know that, don't you?'

Ah, right. So we were back to Constantine being a psychopath, were we?

'No, I don't know that. Why would he keep it? He's got no reason to.'

'He'll want to retain something to hold over your head.' Val's hands moved down my calves, making me want to moan in pleasure. 'It was one of Domingo's favourite tactics and, like I told you, Constantine has become him.'

I didn't believe that for a second, but it was interesting that Val believed it so wholeheartedly.

'Why do you insist on thinking that?' I asked, biting back a sigh of contentment. 'Constantine is many things, but he's not Domingo.'

Val's stroking hands paused. 'He's charmed you already, I see.'

'Charm?' I didn't hold back my scorn. 'Constantine? Have you met him?'

There was a silence. Then Val said, 'Turn over for me, little star.'

I stayed where I was. 'Tell me why you're so wedded to this psychopath idea and I might.'

Another silence.

'He slipped me notes under the door.' Val sounded oddly muted. 'They were all, *"Why don't you do what Papa says?" "Give in and he'll let you out".* There was no apology for betraying me. There was no empathy there at all. And you know what they say about psychopaths.'

I heard it then, the note of pain and fury. But I couldn't tell whether it was directed at Constantine, his father or at himself.

'Well?' he asked. 'Will you turn over for me?'

Not an order this time, but a request. And why not? He'd given me a choice and, while his stroking hands might be a manipulation, it was one I'd engineered myself. And that we were both enjoying, apparently.

Besides, I liked his hands on me. It felt as if all my bones had melted.

I turned, keeping my eyes closed against the bright light, and I heard his soft intake of breath. It made me smile, even though I knew I shouldn't. 'It's still working, then?'

'You're enjoying this, aren't you? Minx. And, yes, it's still working.' The husky note of amusement lingered in his sexy voice. 'So he wants heirs, you said? Nothing wrong with being a wife and mother, but you must want more than that for yourself. You're ambitious and driven; I can see that. And I'd love to hear about your company and what your plans are for it.'

Despite myself, I couldn't help feeling a warm glow of pleasure at the genuine interest in his voice. Then cool liquid slid between my breasts and I shuddered as a different kind of pleasure, a more sensual kind, joined it.

'I want to make sure all the diamonds we sell and use in our jewellery are from ethical sources,' I said, because again there was no reason not to tell him and this was a pet project of mine. 'Because at the moment they're not.'

'Well, I approve whole-heartedly of that. Why isn't that the case already?'

'Because the board are dragging their feet. They're concerned about the bottom line.' And they were suspicious of me introducing new ideas that weren't in step with theirs. As if insisting people's lives were more important than money was a new idea.

'Sounds about right.' He stroked down over my chest, massaging in the sunscreen, his fingers curving around my breasts, his touch sensual yet not wholly sexual. 'And I'm not sure having Constantine in charge will help you with that.'

I bit my lip, giving up the fight to keep myself separate from the pleasure of his touch, relaxing entirely into it as his hands moved on, caressing my hips and down over my stomach.

'So, let me propose a counter-offer. You could marry me instead.' His fingers gently massaged the sensitive skin above my pubic bone, but no further. Not touching me where I so badly wanted him to. 'Marry me, and in return I'll pay Wintergreen's debts. I won't oversee your management. It's clear you have the skills to do it, and anyway the debts were your father's, not yours. You shouldn't have to pay for his mistakes.'

I stilled beneath his hands, oddly taken off-guard by his insight. Was that why I'd felt uncomfortable with Constantine's offer? Because I had, though I could never really pinpoint why. But maybe it was simply that, in insisting on having financial oversight, he'd made me feel as if those debts were mine. As if I was responsible for the company's mismanagement, not Dad.

Val's fingers were on my thighs now, massaging in firm, sure strokes. 'I will give you freedom, Livvy,' he went on. 'I'll never tie you down or limit you. I'll take care of you when you want it. And I'll certainly give you as much pleasure as you can handle. I'll always satisfy you. I'll never leave you hungry.'

My brain struggled to process what he was saying, everything in me having melted completely into the sun-lounger.

It sounded good, I had to admit. Marry him instead, have Wintergreen's debts paid, be in control of the company. Have my freedom, though why he thought freedom was his to give was anyone's guess. But…he hadn't mentioned children.

He gave me one last stroke and then I felt him move away.

I took my forearm from my eyes, blinking against the sudden, painfully bright light.

Val stood next to the lounger, looking down at me, and I could see the hunger blazing in his eyes. His whole body radiated tension; he was holding himself back, but only barely.

You've done that to him. You've brought him to the edge.

'Well?' he demanded, suddenly fierce. 'What do you say?'

'What about an heir?' I asked, my voice thick and sleepy sounding. 'Constantine promised me that too.'

For the first time since he'd brought me here, I saw uncertainty ripple over his features. 'Children? Really?'

'Yes. Wintergreen is a family company and I need a family to pass it on to.'

All the warmth and desire in his eyes drained away, his expression shutting down hard. 'No,' he said flatly. 'No. I won't give you that.'

Something in my stomach lurched, even though I knew I should have expected it. After that night in the sea, I knew how he felt about the issue of kids.

But Wintergreen was important to me. Passing it on to my children was important to me. I'd hoped that by having Constantine I could bypass the issue of IVF, but if Val wasn't prepared to give me a child, then what else could I do?

'I'll have to give myself a child, then, won't I?' I said, holding his gaze. 'I assume that won't be a problem?'

He stared at me a long moment, emotions I didn't understand flickering in his black eyes, a muscle leaping in his strong jaw.

Then he carefully put down the bottle of sunscreen and, without a word, turned on his heel and walked out.

CHAPTER FOURTEEN

Valentin

A CHILD. SHE REALLY wanted a child.

I sat in my office, trying to work yet finding myself staring sightlessly at the computer screen once again.

I hadn't expected her to be so certain about it, though on reflection maybe I should have. As I'd already discovered, she was driven and ambitious, and Wintergreen was important to her. She'd worked hard to get where she was now and, as she'd told me, it was a family company and she needed a child to pass it on to, as her father had passed it on to her.

All of that was very logical.

The thought of children was…difficult. My genes were tainted through and through, and as for being a father…impossible. I couldn't be any kind of parent, not when I didn't know the first thing about being a good father. After all, it wasn't as if I'd had any good role models.

Still, I shouldn't have had a problem with her 'giving' herself a child, which I assumed meant IVF. Except I did have a problem. The moment she'd mentioned it, something inside me had twisted hard in denial. Almost as if I'd wanted her to have *my* child which, naturally, I didn't.

I shouldn't have walked out on her, though. I should have agreed and then put the sunscreen away and done what I'd been wanting to do ever since I'd seen her lying naked on the sun-lounger: celebrated our agreement by making her scream with pleasure.

But I hadn't.

I swivelled my chair round to look out of the window, where a glorious sunset was happening outside. However, I didn't see the colours. All I could see was her grey eyes, full of heat from my touch and yet equally full of steel.

She'd grown formidable, my Olivia. And we were at an impasse.

The same kind of impasse you had with Domingo.

A strange dread sat in my gut, along with a hot thread of anger.

This wasn't how I'd thought it would go. I'd thought that eventually, once she'd got over her anger at me for my supposed death, she'd remember what we had and fall into my arms. I'd thought a week, tops.

A week hadn't passed yet, but nothing was proceeding as I'd planned, and I was now in uncharted territory.

Did you really think it would be that easy?

The dread grew stronger. I didn't want to compromise, I didn't want to give in. My will had had to be diamond-hard in order to combat Domingo's, and I found it was difficult when anyone went against it.

But she's a diamond too. And one of you has to make the first move.

It was true. I'd seduced the girl, but it was the woman who was in charge. And all the qualities I'd seen in her all those years ago—the courage, strength and stubbornness—had crystallised and hardened into that veneer.

She wasn't ripping off that veneer for me, though.

Every time I thought I was getting close to her, down it would come.

I stared at the sunset flaming in the sky, my thoughts ticking over.

How could I get beneath it? How could I reach the heart of her?

Why do you want to so badly?

Because I loved her, of course. Why else? And I wanted her to love me. But until she lowered her guard that wasn't going to happen. I wanted her passion *and* her heart, yet I wasn't quite sure how to get them.

As I'd already thought, she didn't trust me. And letting her take the initiative today had only resulted in yet another business proposition. But I didn't want a business proposition, I realised. I didn't want her to marry me because I was going to pay her debts and give her a child.

I wanted her to marry me because she loved me, and that had *always* been my goal.

Which meant I needed to get serious about this.

The key to her love was her trust and, in order to get that, I would have to make the first move. I would have to show myself worthy.

But I couldn't be rash about it. I needed some time to think.

In the end, I gave us both a couple of days' break, letting the idea sit in the back of my head as I busied myself with other things. My brother, in other words.

I'd had no luck getting any kind of response from his lawyers and now he'd apparently gone to ground completely. It was frustrating, but it wasn't as if I didn't have anything else to do.

Lately, I'd been toying with the idea of venture capital. I liked new ideas, I found them exciting, and I had plenty of money to invest, and it seemed like an excellent new field to branch out into.

So, I occupied myself with that as well as keeping an eye on the media. There was still no mention of my reappearance, which meant Constantine had well and truly suppressed it, and I was curious about that. What was he doing?

I'd expected him to come after Olivia, if not immediately, then at least within a day or two, but he hadn't. No one seemed to know where he was.

You should find him. You should talk to him. Remember the way he looked at you at Domingo's wake?

Oh, I remembered. He hadn't been shocked that I was alive and well; no, he'd been furious. Almost as if he'd already known that I wasn't dead.

Perhaps he'd known all this time, in which case…

Why didn't he come for you?

An emotion I didn't recognise shifted in my chest, but I ignored it. I didn't want to go there. Despite all my efforts, Domingo had turned Constantine so completely against me that he'd betrayed Olivia and me without a second's regret. So, of course he wouldn't come for me. Of course he'd only be furious.

That wasn't his fault, though. He'd been a child, Domingo far too powerful, and I hadn't protected him well enough.

My gut twisted, but I shoved the thoughts away, directing my attention to the financial spreadsheet I had on my computer screen instead.

It was afternoon, and it had been two days since I'd walked out on Olivia.

I hadn't seen her since then, deliberately keeping my distance as I worked through various plans to prove myself worthy of her.

I had options, of course, but none of them were good ones, since they mostly consisted of influencing her in ways she'd no doubt find problematic and not trustworthy in the least.

I was in the process of turning over yet another one, while I fiddled with my spreadsheet, when suddenly the door to my study opened and Olivia came striding in.

She was wearing another of those long, floaty dresses—not that she had a lot of choice, since those dresses were the only clothing in the wardrobe—in dark blue this time with a deep V-neck and long, loose sleeves.

The colour made her skin look like crystal, gave her grey eyes a blue glow and set off her long blonde hair to perfection.

My entire body tightened at the sight of her, desire licking up inside me. It had only been two days, but that had been a long time without her, and my fingers itched to tear that dress off, no matter how lovely it was, and take her right on the floor.

She stopped in front of my desk, folding her arms and lifting her chin.

'Nice to see you, Livvy.' I tried to control the sudden leap of my heart at the sight of her. 'To what do I owe the pleasure?'

'Have you finished sulking, Val?' She gave me an imperious look. 'I'm tired of waiting for an answer. If you're not going to marry me, then where is my plane?'

Delight surged inside me, because I'd missed her. And, *Dios*, how I loved it when she was commanding. It provided me with such a delicious target.

I leaned back in my chair and said lazily, 'Considering you didn't ask for a plane, it's probably still in its hangar.'

Her eyes narrowed. 'I told you I'm not—'

'I missed you,' I interrupted, the truth coming out of me before I could stop it.

She blinked, the imperious look fading, her expression softening. 'You could have come to me at any time. You were the one who walked away, remember?'

And abruptly I was tired of this. Tired of the games. Tired of the fighting. Tired of making plans that didn't work. They weren't getting me what I wanted, and I was done with them.

'Tell me what I need to do, Olivia,' I said honestly. 'Tell me what I need to do to get you to trust me.'

Surprise rippled over her lovely face. 'You want me to trust you?'

I gritted my teeth, not liking that this should come as such a big surprise to her. 'Yes. That's what I said.'

She gave me a long, measuring look. 'Well, not kidnapping me would have been a good start.'

'We've been through that,' I said impatiently.

Tiny sparks leapt in her gaze. And then she was striding up to my desk, slapping her hands down on the top of it and leaning forward, the look on her face blazing now.

'I don't think you understand, Valentin,' she said, abruptly fierce. 'You picked me up and tossed me over your shoulder. You *kidnapped* me. Then you said you weren't sorry about it. And that was *after* letting me believe you were dead for *fifteen years*!' Colour stained her delicate cheekbones and I could see, all of a sudden, the decades-old pain she was hiding. 'You broke my heart. How can you expect me to trust you after all of that?'

There was a wrenching sensation in my chest, as if there had been an arrow in my heart and she'd just jerked it free. And now I was bleeding, inexplicable pain radiating through me.

You knew what she felt for you. And you hurt her. Everything you've done has hurt her.

'I was trying to save you; don't you see?' My voice had roughened. 'Domingo was still alive, and I was afraid he'd so something to you if I—'

'You think you're the hero of this story, don't you?' she interrupted. 'And I'm just your damsel in distress. You have to save me, and you have to save Constantine, and I don't think for one minute it's about either of us. Because, if it had been, you wouldn't have pulled that ridiculously dramatic stunt with the lights and public announcement.'

She leaned forward a little more. 'You wouldn't have cast me in the role of the helpless victim you need to protect at all costs, taking away my choice by taking me away by force, and then using all my memories of you, the love I once had for you, to make me stay.'

She was breathing very fast now, her eyes glittering. 'You wouldn't have treated me like…like some weak little woman, like your pet or a plaything. And, yes, you could have sent me a damn email. You could have called me. You could have asked me to meet you to talk and we could have gone from there.' She pushed herself away abruptly. 'But you didn't do any of that.'

All the pleasure I'd felt at seeing her had drained away, leaving behind that pain and a hot, defensive anger, both of them demanding an outlet. Demanding I tell her that she was wrong, that she was wrong about all of it. I hadn't treated her like that, and I'd never seen her as some weak little woman, and especially not as a victim.

But you did. You saw her as still that fifteen-year-old girl with no power.

I didn't want to admit she was right. I didn't want to

accept that what I'd done hadn't been in her best interests but in mine. Yet the way she'd said it, and the look in her eyes, the pain I could see lurking in the depths…

Your fault.

'I'm sorry,' I said at last, forcing it out. 'I'm sorry for how I treated you. That was the…wrong thing to do.'

But she was having none of it.

'Are you sorry?' she demanded. 'Or would you do it all over again in a heartbeat?'

I gripped the arms of my chair and shoved it back, sending it skittering along the floor as I got to my feet, full of frustrated, directionless rage I didn't understand and didn't know what to do with. 'What more do you want from me, Olivia? Yes, it was wrong, and I'm sorry. What else do you want me to say?'

'I don't want you to say anything. What I want…' She stopped suddenly and took a breath. 'I'm not your victim, Val. But I'm not your enemy, either. I'm not Domingo and you don't have to fight me.'

Tension gripped me. 'I don't think that.'

'Don't you? Aren't you seeing me as him right now? Him trying to force something from you?'

'No, of course not.' I felt a muscle jump at the side of my jaw. 'No.'

But she only looked at me. 'I'm not trying to prove you wrong. That's not what this is about. You wanted to know what you have to do to get me to trust you—but how I can trust you while I'm still a prisoner on your island?'

CHAPTER FIFTEEN

Olivia

HE STAYED WHERE he was. He wasn't smiling any more, all that lazy charm gone. Now he was angry and defensive, with flames in his eyes.

He was dressed casually again today, jeans and a dark blue T-shirt that deepened his olive-skinned tan and made his eyes and hair look even blacker. The familiar scent of his aftershave wound around me…

I'd missed him these past two days. He was so beautiful, he made me ache.

I'd come in here all set to demand things from him, demand he stop sulking like a little boy and talk to me. Then he'd taken all the wind out of my sails by asking what he needed to do to gain my trust.

At first, I'd thought it was another ploy, but no. He'd been genuine; I'd seen it in his eyes.

So I'd told him and, as soon as I had, all my hurt and anger had come pouring out. Hurt and anger that had been building ever since he'd walked away from me two days ago. Hurt that he'd walked away in the first place. Anger that I'd been prepared to agree to his offer and yet, for all his insistence, he hadn't.

I'd spent the last two days trying to understand why

he'd had such a reaction to my IVF suggestion, and it still didn't make any sense. Because why should he care?

And now he'd completely upended things by talking about trust.

'Why are we talking about this anyway?' I asked when he remained silent. 'You obviously didn't like my answer. So I don't know why my trust should be so important to you now.'

He stood behind his desk, his hands in fists. 'Because I… I want your love, Olivia.' That muscle in his jaw flicked again. 'I told you that. I want us to have what we had all those years ago.'

At first, I didn't understand that either, because why should one teenage relationship be so important to him? Then slowly, as I recognised the intensity that seemed to radiate from every cell of his being, I knew.

He and Constantine had been starved of attention and care by someone who should have given them both. They had been starved of gentleness and kindness—that was why Constantine was so cold and Val so manipulative. Both of them were protecting themselves the only way they knew how. They'd been starved of starved of attention, and most of all they'd been starved of love.

That was what Val wanted, what he was so desperate for. He was an endless pit of need trying to regain that one moment in his life when he'd been loved.

By me.

My eyes prickled, a surge of compassion and sympathy for him swamping me. It hadn't been his fault he'd been so scarred—and he was. I could see it. There were deep fault lines that ran through his soul and had twisted his thinking. His upbringing and the past fifteen years had turned him into a dangerous man, but underneath that he was still that little boy.

A little boy who found pretty shells and driftwood for his study.

A little boy desperate to be loved.

My heart ached for that boy. And it was also aching for the man.

'But we can't have that.' My own sorrow at the knowledge cut deep. 'We can't ever have that again. We were children. And we loved each other as children do.'

He was breathing very fast, staring at me as if I was his one hope of salvation. 'Then you can leave.' His voice was nothing but deep gravel. 'I'll get you a plane and you can leave. Whenever you want.'

'What?' I blinked in shock. 'Do you mean that?'

'Yes.'

'And what about Constantine?' I couldn't help asking. 'You'll let me marry him if I want to?'

'Yes.'

I searched his face, my heartbeat thudding in my ears, looking for signs that this was another game for him, another way to get me to do what he wanted. Yet... I couldn't see anything in his beautiful features but determination.

He meant it. He would let me go.

The ache behind my breastbone felt abruptly even more painful.

'Why?' I asked huskily. 'After everything you did to get me here?'

His knuckles were white as he held his fists clenched at his sides. 'I don't want you to go. In fact, leaving is the last thing in the world I want you to do. But...if it meant you finally trusting me...then, yes, I'd let you go.' A muscle flicked in his jaw. 'And then I'd send you an email, asking if you wanted to meet me for coffee.'

My throat closed, a surge of some powerful emotion sweeping through me, and I was trembling, though I wasn't sure why. 'Val…'

'You're not a just thing to me, Olivia,' he said with sudden ferocity. 'You were *never* just a thing. It's true that I wanted the girl you once were, but I want the woman you are now even more.'

I could see the truth in his eyes. He wasn't hiding it, but then he'd never hidden it from me.

His thinking and his motivations might be skewed, but his emotions had always been true.

'What if I don't want to go?' I asked him. 'What if I stayed?'

He didn't hesitate. 'Then we'd have some more dinners. Spend time getting to know one another again. You could swim in the sea, read books, relax in the sun. And, when you were ready, we could discuss our future and whether that would be together.'

I was still shaking. He'd given me something, hadn't he? He'd surrendered something, and now I wanted to do the same.

'My mother was a trophy wife,' I said. 'Dad wanted a son, and she couldn't give him one. He treated her… badly. He didn't respect her; was cruel to her and she just…put up with it. She stayed and I'll never understand why. But one thing I do know is that I won't. I won't put up with being treated the way he treated her, like a thing, like a toy he'd got bored of playing with.'

I swallowed and lifted my chin. 'He treated me like that too until I told him that, if he wanted the family company to stay in the family, he'd have to leave it to me. He respected strength, and so strong is what I always tried to be.'

'Until I took that strength away from you,' Val said with unexpected insight, his black gaze pinned to mine. 'Oh, little star…' He moved then, coming around the side of his desk. But he didn't approach me, standing in front of it instead. 'I gave you no choice. I took you prisoner. I used your own emotions against you…' There was a bleak look in his eyes. 'Did I make you doubt yourself too?'

I wasn't sure how he knew that but…there had been an underlying uneasiness in me that I'd let him do all of this to me. That I hadn't fought hard enough, hadn't stood up to him enough, hadn't challenged him when I should have. That I'd been somehow…weak.

I didn't need to say it, though, because I could see he'd read my expression well enough.

Val muttered a curse under his breath in Spanish. 'You aren't to blame,' he said roughly. 'It was my doing, my responsibility.'

'But I let you—'

'You didn't let me do anything. You slapped me across the face then you pushed me into the sea. You made me work for every concession. You fought me every step of the way.'

I took a breath, not wanting to tell him this, but there seemed little point in not voicing this last doubt. 'I was going to let Constantine pay my debts. I was going to let him take over my company.'

Val took what looked like a helpless step forward before stopping himself, the look on his face blazing. 'First of all, Constantine came to you. And you agreed to his terms because you care about your company and want to save it. You also want heirs, so why not get them from him too? That's not weakness, that's playing the hand your father dealt you which, by the way, wasn't your fault, either.'

That last doubt was one I hadn't even realised was there. That my father's debts were on purpose, one last test for the daughter he'd never really respected.

'Val…' I murmured, suddenly feeling vulnerable.

'Your father was a fool if he couldn't see what he had in you.' Val's voice was full of certainty. 'Strength. Bravery. Passion. You're driven and you're smarter than anyone else I know. But you're not a diamond, Olivia. You're a star, remember? And stars burn.'

I met his gaze at last. Saw the need there, the sheer intensity of it.

He was a star too, wasn't he? A sun, full of rage and love and despair and hope. A difficult, conflicted man, but a man who not only had the ability to take, but the ability to give too. And he wanted to, that was obvious.

So why not let him?

'What do you want, Val?' I asked, knowing that I wasn't going to walk away, not now, not after this.

His dark eyes glittered. 'You. Only you.'

'Then I'll stay.' My breathing had accelerated, my heart beating fast. 'And we'll do all those things you said. On one condition.'

'Anything.' His expression was stripped down, nothing but hunger in it. 'Anything at all, you can have it.'

I took a shaky breath, aware of my own growing need. 'I don't see why sex should be off the table. And so, I'd… I'd like to give you pleasure.'

Surprise flickered over his face, but there was no smile of triumph or satisfaction, only a flare of sexual heat. 'Because you want to? Or because you feel you should?'

He wanted my trust, but trust was a two-way street. And I wanted his too.

So it was me who closed the distance between us, until I was standing right in front of him, and then I reached out to brush his cheek with my fingertips, his skin warm and slightly roughened by his whiskers.

'Because I want to,' I murmured. 'Because you're special to me.'

It felt risky to say it, but I couldn't not. After all, even after all he'd done, it was true.

He stared down at me a moment, his expression impenetrable, then he took my hand from his cheek in a gentle grip and he kissed each one of my fingertips, his mouth warm and velvety. 'Well,' he murmured with a ghost of his old charm. 'Who am I to argue with a lady?'

My heart clenched at the way he kissed my fingers, but I only said, keeping things light, 'Indeed you shouldn't.'

The tension around his mouth eased slightly as he let go of my hand, not so much a smile as an easing of tension. Then he leaned back against the desk. 'Surprise me then, little star.'

So, I did.

My palms were damp as I pulled off the silky dress, my heartbeat loud in my head. I wore nothing underneath it, because I'd been secretly hoping it would end this way between us.

His gaze flared as I let the silk go and it raked down my naked body, lingering in all his favourite places and making me shiver.

'Well?' I asked. 'Are you?'

His attention came back to my face, his smile gone now. 'Surprised? Yes. Yes, I am. You are perfection, Olivia Wintergreen.'

My breathing was fast but I made no attempt to control it and I didn't look away. I let him see the hunger inside me. I let him see the fire as it licked up higher. I let him see it consume me. Because, yes, I burned.

And I wanted him to watch.

I took the last step that separated us, getting close to him, watching the fire catch alight inside him too. 'Don't move,' I whispered.

And he didn't. He stayed exactly where he was, statue-still.

I put a hand to the buttons of his jeans, touching him through the denim, feeling the long, hard shape of him. The breath hissed between his teeth as I mapped him with my fingertips, the flames in his eyes leaping higher. Every part of him was tense, but he didn't move.

He was giving me this by doing what I said. He was giving me his trust. An aching, shifting kind of emotion washed through me then, powerful and familiar, deep and resolute.

His father had controlled and abused him, left him emotionally isolated with only his brother for company. A brother he'd tried to protect, who'd then betrayed him. He'd been shut in a windowless room for six months and, when he'd finally managed to escape, he'd had to fake his own death just to make sure his father would never find him.

He wasn't scarred on the outside, but he was on the inside.

But he was perfection too and I wanted him to know that.

So I concentrated on what I was doing, tracing him through the fabric of his jeans, stroking him, giving him as much pleasure as he'd given me.

I lifted my hands to his jeans, my fingers now shaking as I undid them. He didn't move, but I could hear his breathing in the silence of the room. It was ragged and short.

I had no idea what I was doing, since I'd never done this to a man before, but somehow that didn't matter. I could see what I was doing to him; he didn't hide it, so I just kept going.

He stayed still as I pulled open his jeans and when I touched him. When I drew him out and held him in my hands. His skin was smooth and hot, and he was so hard.

I leaned forward and traced him with my tongue, tasting him, salt and musk, and he made a soft growling sound that thrilled me right down to the bone.

I took him into my mouth, learning the feel and shape of him, and he made another of those delicious masculine sounds, half-groan, half-growl. His hands were in my hair, not pulling or directing me in any way, just massaging my skull gently before drawing his fingers through the strands, taking a sensual delight in them against his skin.

I glanced up at him, wanting to watch his face as I explored him, using his expressions as my guide, and he didn't look away. He let me see the effect I had on him.

'Livvy...' The words were rough and hot. 'Livvy, you are perfect... Ah, a goddess...'

I loved the husky note in his voice, loved how he hid nothing from me. So I gave him more, gave him hotter and deeper, and he watched me, our gazes connecting, losing ourselves in the fire we were generating between us and being consumed by it.

He growled my name in the end, and pulled my hair, but it didn't hurt, and I liked it. Tasting him had made me even hungrier for him, but I didn't need him to return the favour.

Yet it seemed he had his own ideas about that, because afterwards he helped me to my feet then gripped me, turning round and setting me on top of his desk.

Then he kissed me, long, deep and hard, his hands on my body, stroking me.

I trembled, every part of me alive to his touch. 'You don't have to,' I murmured against his mouth. 'It's not a favour you have to return.'

'I know I don't need to.' His lips brushed over mine. 'But I want to.'

So I let him and, when he found some protection in the top drawer of his desk and dealt with it, sliding inside me at last, all I felt was relief.

I wound my legs around his lean waist and put my arms around his neck, clinging on to him as he moved, a hard, driving rhythm that had me gasping against his mouth. He took me hard and fierce, and it didn't take long before the pleasure inside me burst apart and there were cascading stars everywhere.

'Val,' I whispered against his neck as I shuddered in his arms. 'Oh, Val…'

And, whether I'd said it just for the joy of saying his name, or whether it was a prayer, a request for more or something else, I didn't know.

But it felt as if something had shifted inside me, something momentous.

As if all the barriers had gone and the two halves of my soul had finally become one.

Because of him.

CHAPTER SIXTEEN

Valentin

WE DECIDED TO give ourselves a week.

A week of nothing but long, leisurely dinners on the end of the jetty and lazing about on sun-loungers, diving into the sea when we got too hot. I organised a couple of trips in my yacht, sightseeing around the islands and having picnic lunches on pristine, white sandy beaches.

We talked a lot, catching up on the changes in each other's lives and what we'd been doing for the past fifteen years. I gave her the brutal truth about some of the darker moments in my past, while she confided in me the doubt she had that the Wintergreen board would ever accept her.

It wasn't all plain sailing. We had a minor argument when I tried to insist on no sex, since our chemistry was a powerful force and I couldn't trust myself not to take advantage of it every chance I got. But then she said I was perfectly welcome to use it against her, if she could also use it against me.

Naturally enough, that was an argument that ended in bed, both of us using each other to our mutual satisfaction. And after that, since it was clearly pointless for me to insist otherwise, she'd joined me in my bed every night and we'd explored each other in other ways.

And as the days passed a strange feeling grew in me…something unfamiliar that I couldn't quite describe. Until one day I was watching her swim, her body tanned golden by the sun, and she came up out of the water, naked and dripping wet, and she smiled at me as if I was the best thing she'd seen all day.

And then I realised what the feeling was. Happiness.

It wasn't all sunbathing and sex, of course. We had to deal with Constantine. Olivia had tried contacting him to talk to him, but he remained stubbornly off-grid, so I tried too.

It was frustrating, especially in combination with my continued lack of progress with his lawyers. The will was clear, though. I was the eldest, and therefore everything came to me, which would make removing him as CEO easy.

However, his lawyers continued to stone-wall my efforts to take control. It was true that my former deceased status represented some legal challenges, but I was determined. The company would be mine and Constantine removed for his own good and that of his staff.

Since Constantine wouldn't answer his phone, and my staff was coming up against a lot of dead ends—apparently no one knew where he'd gone—I had to settle for leaving a message on his voicemail, informing him that he was no longer engaged. Olivia and I had decided in one of our talks that, while we weren't quite at marriage yet, she definitely didn't want to remain engaged to him.

We'd discussed what alternatives she could use to help pay Wintergreen's debts that wouldn't involve her giving up her power and, while I had offered some no-strings financial help, I also made it clear she didn't have to take it.

Even though a part of me was desperate to find a way to make her. Yes, my ability to compromise and not take control all the time was still a work in progress.

Then, just as a week had passed, I was supervising deliveries of certain items from the seaplane on the jetty when my phone vibrated.

Staff were carrying bags and boxes from the plane, and I waved them in the direction of the villa as I pulled my phone out of my pocket. I didn't bother looking at the screen to see who it was, hitting the 'answer' button automatically.

'Valentin,' a deep, cold voice said.

My entire body tightened, a pulse of adrenaline going through me.

Constantine.

'Con,' I said, keeping it casual. 'Thought you'd disappeared off the face of the earth.'

'No.'

'Clearly not. I thought you'd forgotten all about me. And not one word about my arrival back from the dead, either. It's almost as if you want to keep that from the media.' I stared over the endless blue of the ocean. 'Oh, and by the way, your lawyers can't stall things for ever. My case is water-tight.'

There was a deep, chilly silence that I found myself listening to intently.

He'd never used to be that silent. Once, he'd been talkative like me. We'd used to tell each other stories when things got bad, about how we'd escape Domingo and what we'd do when we were finally free. Be pirates together, or soldiers. Or cowboys in America.

'The company is mine.' His voice was like ice, reminding me so much of Domingo that I could feel all my muscles tense.

You never wanted that for him. You failed him.

The tight feeling wound around my heart and I found myself rubbing at my chest before I could stop it. Yes, I knew that. I had. As had Domingo. Domingo had failed us both.

'You know why I'm taking it.' I kept my voice as hard as his. 'It's in the best interests of your company and your staff.'

He ignored me. 'But, if you want Olivia, you can have her.'

'Really?' I struggled to hide my shock. It sounded as if she hadn't meant anything to him at all, which I didn't understand. 'Just like that? You're not even going to make a cursory protest?'

'It was never Olivia that mattered.'

It felt as if I'd been punched in the gut. 'What?'

'I didn't want her.' He sounded as detached as he ever had. 'I never did. What I wanted was my brother. But he made a different choice. So I had to take action.'

The shock deepened inside me and then widened, a freezing lake of it. He wanted…me? But that didn't make any sense. He already had me. And what choice did he mean? I'd never had any choices except the one I'd made to protect him.

'What are you talking about?' I growled. 'What choice? Everything I did back then was for you, you know that.'

'No, it wasn't.' For the first time I could hear a thread of heat beneath the ice in his voice. 'You chose your-self every single time. You chose that ridiculous feud with Papa.'

'Ridiculous feud?' I echoed in disbelief. 'That man was a—'

'If you'd only obeyed the rules, our lives would have been easier. But you didn't. You made it worse.'

A flash of rage went through me. 'The rules? You think I cared one iota about the rules? You put her life in danger. Domingo told me that, if he caught me seeing her again, he'd do something to hurt her.'

'I did nothing of the sort,' Constantine said icily. 'You were the one who put her in danger, Valentin. It was *your* choice to keep seeing her. If you'd really wanted to protect her, you would have done what our father asked and left her alone.'

He's right.

Well, he was. I knew that already and I'd owned it. Yet ice spiralled through my veins all the same.

I tried to ignore it, gripping tightly to my rage instead. 'I *meant* to disobey him. I was trying to draw his attention away from you, you fool.'

'Yes, that's it exactly.' He sounded frozen, like a glacier. 'You didn't want to let him win. You wanted to prove a point.'

You didn't care about Constantine and you didn't care about her. All that mattered was being stronger than him.

No, that was ridiculous. To have taken all Domingo's manipulative attempts to bring me in line…to have taken all his beatings and his emotional abuse simply to prove I was stronger? What kind of idiot did Constantine take me for?

'You can think that if you like,' I gritted out between my teeth. 'But I was doing all of that for you. I was trying to protect you.'

'I didn't need protecting. And, if you hadn't made things worse, neither would Olivia.'

You've turned him into a victim, the way you turned her into one.

Denial burned like acid inside me. 'So what is this? Are you defending him? After everything he did to us?'

I shouldn't have cared. This had all happened a decade and a half ago, and I knew he hadn't been able to help himself, that Domingo had turned him against me. Nevertheless, a small part of my anger was for him and his betrayal. We'd had no one but each other when we'd been growing up. Domingo had isolated us from everyone, so we had been each other's friends and confidantes. We'd been supposed to stick together no matter what, to look out for each other, because that was what brothers did.

He was my twin, my other half, and even though I knew it hadn't been his fault in the end he'd betrayed me.

'No,' Constantine said as if none of this touched him in any way. 'I'm merely stating facts.'

'So I was just supposed to sit back and watch him beat you to death? Is that what—?'

'I did not call you to talk about what happened fifteen years ago,' he interrupted icily. 'I called to tell you that you are welcome to marry Olivia. I do not care.'

Then he disconnected the call.

For a second I stood there, holding my phone in my hand, hot fury searing me from the inside out.

How dared he? How dared he tell me everything I'd done had been for myself? He was wrong. I'd done it for him, for my little brother. Every single thing.

Is he wrong, though? You liked fighting Domingo. You liked standing up to him. And all the choices you made

*were because you didn't want to give Domingo the sat-
isfaction of knowing he'd beaten you.*

No, that was wrong. That was the *opposite* of what
I'd been trying to do.

All those beatings I'd endured, all those punishments.
The systematic stripping away of all the things I liked to
do, with no friends, no pets. No going outside to climb
trees or swim in the huge pool that no one ever used.
No games with my brother...

Constantine thought all of that had been so I could
win?

It hadn't been a competition; didn't he understand
that? It had been a fight to the death. It had been me, constantly trying to make sure that Constantine survived.

My brother had always been the kinder of the two us.
The more generous, the more giving. He was the one
who'd once carefully manoeuvred a bumble bee that had
blundered its way inside into a glass and taken it outside
rather than kill it. Who'd been inconsolable when we'd
discovered a dead kitten under the trees in the garden
behind the mansion. And who'd tried unsuccessfully
to nurse a sparrow chick that had fallen out of its nest
back to health.

His softer emotions had made him an easier target
and, since I'd been the one who'd always stood up to
Domingo, I had become his shield. Because I hadn't
cared about the bee or the kitten or the chick. I'd felt
sorry for them, but I hadn't cried the way Constantine
had. Domingo had called me the stronger one, and he'd
been right, which had made it my duty to protect my
little brother.

So I had, and in the end I'd failed. But that was my
issue to make right and, even though it was too late for

Constantine, it wasn't too late to limit his influence and the damage someone like him could do.

Or is that just you turning yourself into the hero once again?

I growled under my breath. No, that was ridiculous. Perhaps I had done that with Olivia, but not with him. I might have failed him, but I couldn't save him. I could only save the company and the people in it.

Shoving my phone back into my pocket, I dismissed thoughts of my brother and got back to doing something more pleasant.

Being with Olivia.

CHAPTER SEVENTEEN

Olivia

I'D HAD THE most wonderful week. Spending time with Val had been a revelation. It had almost been like those days back on our secret beach, when there'd been only us, only each other.

Except this time it was better, because we were adults now, and our connection was based on reality instead of dreams. And we did have a connection; I could feel it. I could see it in his eyes whenever he looked at me, whenever he touched me, whenever he cupped my face between his large, warm palms and kissed me.

It was a different sort of connection, deeper, more intense. Initially I hadn't liked him taking care of me, because I felt like a plaything or pet, but I gradually saw how much pleasure he took from it. It made him happy to look after my needs. He'd always been protective and care-giving—it was part of his nature—and the pleasure he so obviously got out of it made me happy too. And soon I didn't feel like his plaything but his treasure.

I wasn't sure what would happen when our week of being together came to an end, but I was sure I didn't want to marry Constantine. And maybe, despite my own protests to myself, I'd never wanted to marry him, regardless of those debts.

I discussed the debts with Val and considered other options. Val had offered to lend me some money, because he couldn't help himself and, while I was appreciative, I refused. I wanted to find my own way out of the situation, options that didn't rely on a man's help for a start.

First, though, I needed to contact Constantine to break off our engagement. However, he hadn't responded to my texts or the voicemail messages I'd left on his phone. I didn't know what was happening with him and I couldn't deny I was worried. I didn't love him, but I'd still been engaged to him for three months, and the fact that he seemed to have dropped off the face of the earth was a concern.

But there was still nothing in the media about his disappearance, and certainly shares in Silver Inc were still flying high, which presumably meant no one else was concerned about him. He was still managing his company, though for how long was anyone's guess.

Val hadn't mentioned his takeover intentions again, but I presumed that was also still going ahead. I'd already told him I didn't like the idea of him removing his brother as CEO, but he seemed firmly wedded to it for reasons I didn't understand. It was a conversation I needed to have with him at some point, but I had other things on my mind.

Over the past couple of days, I'd been pursuing further my idea for sourcing only ethical diamonds. Dad had always paid lip service to the ethical part, but I didn't want lip service. And closer investigation seemed to indicate that the board had been...obscuring a few things when it came to sourcing our gems.

In fact, there were a few things about the board that

were suspect. Things that might have had something to do with Dad's financial mismanagement, and that was just downright unacceptable.

Perhaps it was time for a new broom to sweep away the remains of a past that clearly wasn't working. And perhaps it was time for me to be that broom. For too long I'd been trying to do things Dad's way simply so I could prove I could do them better. But maybe I needed to change my approach. Maybe I needed to do things *my* way, not his, and not worry about whether it was too female.

Concern for all employees of Wintergreen and those that supplied us with our precious resources wasn't merely a female thing. It was a human thing. And, just because a few old men didn't like the idea of spending a bit extra to make sure no one was exploited, that didn't mean I couldn't change things.

I was passionate about the business and I'd been reining in that passion for far too long because I hadn't wanted to seem too feminine and upset the board. But Val was right. There was a place for passion in business, and I was going to show them that once and for all. Women were dangerous and those old men had better watch out.

I couldn't wait to share my ideas with him.

I was sitting in the living area, the big glass doors pushed back to let in the cool breeze from the sea, when the sound of the seaplane leaving caught my attention.

I'd idly watched a procession of people carrying all sorts of items, moving along the jetty to the villa and back again, supervised by Val.

I wasn't sure what they were—probably more food, since our supplies were on the low side—but I soon lost interest as my attention caught on Val's tall figure, striding along the jetty as the plane took off behind him, every line of him radiating fury.

I saved the document I was working on and pushed my laptop shut, getting to my feet as Val strode from the jetty to the deck, coming towards the big glass doors. He wore a casual white shirt today instead of a T-shirt, the sleeves rolled up to reveal tanned, powerful forearms. I particularly liked that look on him. It was sexy.

He came through the glass doors and into the room, his anger swirling around him like a hurricane, his eyes full of black fire.

I frowned, concern tightening inside me, and I went over to him, placing my hands on his chest to calm him. 'What's wrong?'

He looked down at me, his expression hard, his jaw tight. 'Apparently, Constantine hasn't dropped off the surface of the earth. I just had a call from him.'

Everything in me went taut. 'Oh? What did he say?'

Val's hands dropped to my hips and he gripped me hard all of a sudden. 'Take off your clothes.' His voice was rough, his eyes glittering. 'I need to let off some steam.'

He was an intensely physical man, I'd discovered, and he'd use either sex or physical exertion to get rid of excess emotion, but I had a feeling that sex wouldn't calm him down this time. Not if it involved his brother.

And this wasn't just anger. This was more.

'Not yet.' I kept my voice cool to counter his heat. 'Tell me what he said, Val. You're upset.'

A muscle leapt in his jaw, his shoulders taut. His expression twisted and I could tell that he wanted to deny it, but he didn't. Instead, his hands dropped and he took a couple of steps back then turned sharply away. He strode over to the big glass doors then stopped, shoving a hand through his black hair.

'He told me I can have you,' he said after a moment. 'But he'll fight me for the company.'

I didn't care if Constantine wanted to let me go. After all, I didn't want him. But I wasn't sure why Val was so angry about it. Was it really just about the company?

'Well, okay,' I said, trying to sound measured. 'You must have known he wouldn't give up the company. And as for me—'

'You don't understand.' Val turned around sharply, the expression on his face blazing with fury. 'He blames me for it. He blames me for *everything*.'

I stared at him, bewildered. 'Blames you for what?'

He dropped his hand from his hair, then turned away again, pacing the length of the room before turning and pacing back again. Anger and frustration poured off him, making my chest ache.

I didn't like seeing him like this. No, I didn't just not like it. I hated it. I wanted to help him, but I didn't know what to do.

'Talk to me, Val.'

'What is there to say?' His black eyes burned, the ghost of his long-lost Spanish accent beginning to colour his words. 'All my life I protected him. He was the one most at risk from Domingo. He had a soft heart, he felt things deeply and that made him an easy target. I was the oldest. I was the strongest. Everything I did was to keep him safe.'

His voice deepened, became rougher, and there was something bleak in his expression. 'It wasn't the beatings that were the worst part, even though they hurt. The worst part was the isolation. He took…everything away. As soon as it looked to him as if you were taking pleasure out of something, he would take it. We couldn't run and play outside, no swimming in the pool or climbing trees. We weren't allowed friends. No dogs, no cats. Constantine had a plastic soldier that one of the housekeepers had given him and he loved it. He played with it a lot and I told him… I told him that it was a bad idea to get attached to it. But he didn't listen. Then one day Domingo caught him with it and told him to melt it down in the fire.'

He bared his teeth in a facsimile of a smile. 'Constantine was inconsolable and I couldn't stand it. So, I grabbed the solider and ran outside with it, and I threw I it on the roof where Domingo couldn't get it. He beat me half to death that night, but he forgot about that soldier. And that's when I knew what I had to do. I had to keep disobeying him so he'd leave Constantine alone.'

He'd told me some of this over the course of the past week, but not the details. Not about the soldier. Not about Constantine and his soft heart. And I'd been right to think that the scars inside him ran deep. I could see them right now in his eyes.

He was furious, burning up inside with rage.

I wanted to go to him, put my hands on him again, but he was back to pacing, and I didn't want to do anything that might make it worse, so I stayed where I was. 'And you did get his attention,' I said levelly. 'You did keep your brother safe.'

'No, I didn't,' Val growled with a certain amount of savagery. 'I didn't keep him safe, not in the end. I failed him. And Con said I made Domingo worse, that things might not have got as bad as they were if I'd only done what I was told and followed his rules.'

He spat out a harsh curse in Spanish.

'How could I do that, though? Was I supposed to

lie down and take it like my mother did?' He stopped, staring out to sea. 'Domingo killed her, I think. In the end, at least. She went for a walk in the mountains and just…never came back. They found a body eventually, at the bottom of a cliff, but I don't believe she fell. I will never believe she fell.'

My heart squeezed, a cold horror winding through me at the thought of two small boys losing the one person who could have protected them or shielded them…

It didn't bear thinking about.

I took a step towards him, wanting to put my arms around him, but stopped. Would he welcome that? I wasn't sure.

He wasn't looking at me but out over the sea, the strangest expression on his face. 'She did whatever he said. She lived her life in fear. And she told me I had to do what he said too, because that was what would keep Con and me safe.'

A muscle flicked in his jaw. 'But it didn't keep her safe, did it?' He turned his head all of a sudden, his gaze colliding with mine, the burning heat in it tearing the breath from my lungs. 'Only I did that. Only I saved him. And you want to know why I think he's every inch Domingo now? Because he told Domingo about our secret beach. About our secret meetings. He put you in danger and he wasn't even sorry about it.'

I heard the note of pain beneath the anger. He'd always been very up-front about his failure with Constantine, and I could see why he believed it. Yet some of it didn't ring true.

He could see me, and I was fine; nothing had happened to me. Plus, all of this had happened fifteen years ago, and Val wasn't a grudge-keeper. He wouldn't be this angry simply because his brother had told on him back when they were teenagers.

No, this went deeper, cut closer to his soul. Something had hurt him, and hurt him terribly. What was it?

This time I went to him without hesitation, coming to stand in front of him. 'Val, tell me. Why are you so angry? Is it just about that?'

'I protected him. That's why I took all the punishments Domingo dealt out. It was so he didn't have to. And I know I failed him. I knew it the moment he went to Domingo about you and me, because he'd never have betrayed me like that if Domingo hadn't got to him. But...' His black eyes glittered. 'I was prepared for him to blame me for not saving him. I wasn't prepared for him telling me I made it worse. That it was all about winning for me. About point scoring. About not giving Domingo the satisfaction of besting me.'

His voice was full of anger, but underneath that anger I heard the doubt.

He wasn't angry because he knew his brother was wrong. He was angry because he was afraid his brother might be right, wasn't he?

'I can't speak for Constantine,' I said. 'He never spoke a word about you or Domingo, or his childhood. But... why are you so intent on getting the company? What are you going to do with it? You don't need to protect Constantine any more and Domingo's dead. What are you trying to prove?'

Val's eyes flashed. 'So, you agree with him, do you? You think this is just about point-scoring too?'

'No, I don't think that. And stop putting words into my mouth.' I kept my cool and stepped closer to him, hoping my presence would help, because now his defence mechanisms were kicking in and they were looking for a target. 'I'm not the enemy, remember? I'm only trying to get to the truth. Who are you angry at—Domingo or Constantine? Or is it more that you're afraid that Constantine was right about you?'

Val lifted his hands and he grabbed me by the upper arms, not hard, but firmly enough to make me gasp. As if the pressure of his hold could make me see. His mouth twisted in a smile so bitter, it hurt to look at. 'Perhaps he was right. Perhaps it was all just me wanting to prove to my *father*'—he spat the word like it was poison—'that I was everything he thought I was. That I was strong, that I could take everything he threw at me. That I was worthy.' A sneer twisted his mouth. 'Perhaps it was never about protecting Constantine at all, but only about me wanting a psychopath to care.'

I could hear the desperation. That same desperation was in his eyes too.

He was afraid that it was true. That it was *all* true. He'd wanted someone to notice him; he'd wanted someone to care. He'd wanted someone to love him and the only person in his life he could have got that from was his father.

His psychopathic father.

You could give it to him. You could give him everything he needs.

As soon as that thought crossed my mind, I felt something break open inside me, the shell of an egg cracking, a pane of hard diamond shattering, allowing what was inside to come flooding out. An aching, burning, blazing, wondrous thing. Powerful and raw, the white-hot heart of a star...

Everything I'd been keeping inside me for so long. Everything that had been there all this time. Everything

I'd known the moment he'd walked into that ballroom in Madrid.

I loved him. I'd always loved him. I'd loved him then and I loved him now and I'd love him for ever. And he needed it. He needed me.

I reached up, took his face between his hands and pulled his mouth down on mine.

CHAPTER EIGHTEEN

Valentin

THE FURY ATE me alive, burning up like a fire inside me. But Olivia's mouth was cool, and suddenly cool was all I wanted.

Cool, to douse all this heat.

I didn't move, taking a moment to get myself in hand, to concentrate on her mouth and the soft touch of her fingers on my face.

Our kisses over the past week had been passionate and intense, but this was different. She didn't open her mouth this time, and she didn't press close to me; she simply cupped my face in her palms and kissed me delicately and without demand. As if the pleasure was all in my lips on hers and she'd be satisfied with that and nothing more.

I was impatient, though, and as suddenly as I wanted cool I wanted heat instead, and fire, channelling my own pointless fury into sex, which was the most pleasurable way to channel the emotions I didn't want.

I didn't want this fury. I didn't want Olivia looking at me as if she knew exactly what I was thinking, which she didn't.

She'd never had to deal with Domingo.

She didn't know what it was like to want the attention of a psychopath. To enjoy it. To like matching wits with him, to like standing up to him. To be pleased to see respect and approval in his eyes.

To know that all this time you'd been telling yourself lies about how you were trying to protect your own brother, about how you were the hero, when all along you were so desperate for your father's approval, you didn't care what you had to do to get it.

And you still don't care. You don't care that you took her away by force. You don't care that you're going to take Constantine's company from him like you took away his toy soldier. You dress it all up by telling yourself you're protecting them, but you're not. You're not the hero. You're the villain.

I reached for Olivia, jerking her close, trying to drown that thought in the sweet taste of her mouth. Drown all the terrible doubts that pulled inside me. The fear that, yes, I had made it worse for Constantine with my constant rebellions and defiance. And, yes, my choice to disobey Domingo had put Olivia in harm's way.

And maybe even something I'd done had led to my mother's death…

What if it did? You hurt people and you don't care about them. You only care about yourself.

Her hands were stroking me, my racing thoughts fracturing beneath her fingers, and abruptly I was desperate.

I needed to get rid of the voice in my head; I needed her and the pleasure she gave me to strip it away.

My hands tightened on her hips and I walked her back to the couch. Then I pushed her down onto it, raking up the thin silk of her dress.

She welcomed me as she always did, her legs wrapping around my hips, the damp heat between her thighs pressing against my fly. 'Slow down,' she whispered in my ear, her hands gently stroking. 'There's no rush.'

But I didn't want slow. I didn't want gentle. I wanted oblivion.

I shifted onto my knees between her spread legs and reached down, tearing the fabric of her dress completely apart. She was naked beneath it as during the past week she hadn't bothered with a bikini.

Her body was beautiful, her pale skin lightly tanned after a few days of swimming naked in the sun. She was perfect, so perfect. I reached down to undo my fly, but she sat up, her hands covering mine. Her eyes were full of heat and something else, something I couldn't read. It looked like tenderness or sympathy, or maybe even pity, and I didn't like it.

'Don't look at me like that.' I growled. 'Just lie down.'

'Don't look at you like what?' Her hands had found their way under the hem of my shirt, her cool fingers stroking my stomach. But the look in her eyes wasn't cool. It blazed with increasing intensity. There was no trace of her veneer, no trace of the diamond armour she wore.

But she wasn't purely the girl I remembered from years ago, either. She was more. She was strength and vulnerability and passion all at once.

She was a star. A pure, glorious star. 'Don't look at you like I love you?'

It shouldn't have been a shock to hear those words. It should have been something expected, because wasn't that the whole point of this mission? To get her to love me the way she had when she was fifteen?

She'd said those words to me once before, as we'd lain under the stars on our beach. And I'd said them back. I'd never had anyone love me or tell me so before, not even

Constantine, because why would he? He'd had no idea what those words meant, and neither had I. Not until her.

So this moment should have been triumphant; it should have been a win.

Yet it wasn't triumph that settled in my gut, but ice.

You kidnapped her. You manipulated her to get what you want. Everything you do is about what you want. And now you have it. You have everything.

The words filled my head, I couldn't stop them.

This was what I'd wanted all this time, yet…the only reason she'd said it was because I'd brought her here and forced her to deal with me. So…was it even real? If I'd sent her that email instead, met her for coffee like I'd told her that day in my office, would she have loved me then? Without me kidnapping her and manipulating her with our past? When it had just been me?

Of course she wouldn't. Why would she want some- one like you?

Her eyes were so clear, so beautiful. 'Because it's true, Val. I love you. I don't think I ever stopped lov- ing you.'

The cold spread inside me, deepening.

Psychopaths have no empathy. They don't care about anyone but themselves. You're the villain, remember? It's not Constantine who's exactly like him. It's you.

The cold became ice.

I pushed myself away from her, my heart freezing solid.

'Val?'

I got off the couch and took a couple of steps away from it, turning my back on her, trying to get myself together.

'Val?' Soft arms wound around me, her warmth against my back. 'I'm sorry. Should I not have said that?'

I stared at the blue sky and the blue sea. It was beautiful, so warm, and yet all I could feel was the darkness inside me. The darkness that had always been there, that I'd done anything and everything to deny.

But I couldn't escape it and I never would.

Constantine wasn't the psychopath.

The psychopath was me.

CHAPTER NINETEEN

Olivia

THE EXPRESSION ON Val's face was like ice. I'd never seen him so cold. He looked almost exactly like Constantine.

I'd only wanted to give him what he needed, the love he was so obviously craving, because if ever a man needed love it was this one. But he'd acted as if I'd stabbed him and I didn't know why.

I wasn't going to take it back, though. I could pretend I hadn't said it, retreat behind my armour, change the subject or walk away, but... I couldn't do any of those things.

He was too important.

'It's true, you know,' I said. 'I love you. And I'm not sorry I said it.'

He moved out of my embrace, pacing a few feet away. 'You shouldn't.' There was frost in his voice. He sounded just like his brother now, complete with that sexy accent. 'Because I don't think you quite understand what you're dealing with.'

I quelled the urge to go to him again and wrap my arms around him. 'What do you mean?'

His black eyes glittered strangely. 'Psychopaths don't

care about other people. They have no empathy. Other people's feelings don't matter to them in the slightest.'

'Domingo's dead. He's got nothing to—'

'Is he dead?' Val smiled all of a sudden, and it was a terrible smile. 'Or is he still here? Is he standing right in front of you?'

I blinked, my mouth going dry. 'Oh, Val, no. That's not—'

'I liked it. Did you know that?' He said it almost conversationally. 'I liked fighting with him. I liked challenging him. I enjoyed it. I liked the attention.' He kept on smiling that bitter smile. 'I wasn't kind like Constantine. I didn't cry about dead kittens and didn't care about that bird. I just wanted to win.' He met my gaze. 'Like he did.'

'No.' I made the word hard, flat with denial, because I knew what he was going to say next. 'You're not like him. You're not.'

'Aren't I? Domingo knew how to charm, to get people to think he was just a normal man. He knew how to manipulate them to get what he wanted. And he took what he wanted without thought. Doesn't that sound familiar to you?'

He did. He did think that. He thought he was the same.

My heart kicked, aching for him. Because it wasn't true. It had *never* been true. He was flawed, yes, and he was scarred too, but Valentin Silvera wasn't his father. And it wasn't true that he didn't care. He *did* care. He cared too much.

'No,' I said again. 'You're *not* him. You're *nothing* like him.'

'You really don't think so? And don't take the fact that I didn't hurt you as a sign. Because he didn't use physical force against people, not for the most part. Even with us, he didn't beat us often. He used our emotions against us; that was his favourite method.' Val's gaze went straight through me. 'The way I used yours.'

I moved closer to him, wanting him to understand. 'You're angry. You're angry at what he did to you, that's all. And anger doesn't come from nowhere. If you didn't care then, yes, I might be worried, but that's not the case. You do care. You care deeply and you're furious about it.'

But it was clear he wasn't listening.

'Did I care about you, though, Olivia? Did I even care for Constantine? I planned to take his company from him, and do you think I ever thought for one moment about how he might feel? And you? What about you? I didn't care when I threw you over my shoulder. I didn't even think about you. I was only thinking about myself.'

Bitter fury coloured his words. 'You told me I'd cast myself as the hero of the piece, and you're right. I did. I told myself I was making up for my failure by taking Constantine's company, that it was for his own good. And that I was saving you from him too.' He shook his head. 'But what if it isn't? What if all I'm doing is taking what I want because I want it? Because I can? Because it's fun.'

His expression was so bleak, my heart squeezed tight with pain. 'I'm not the hero, Olivia. I'm the villain.'

I looked at him, looked deep into his eyes, and beneath that bitterness I saw the pain. I could see, too, why he thought those things about himself. Maybe, a couple of weeks ago, I would even have agreed with him.

But I didn't agree now. Yes, his methods had been selfish and manipulative, but he'd listened to me when I'd called him on them. He'd apologised and been genuine about it. He'd asked me what I wanted, and what he could do to earn my trust, and then he'd gone about doing it.

But, more than anything else, this whole time he'd uncovered some of my own demons and helped lay them to rest. He'd helped me realise that I didn't have to be so hard and so cold. That I didn't have to hold myself back, that passion was allowed.

'You're not a villain.' I put every ounce of belief in my voice. 'And you didn't do any of that for fun. I think you did it because you're still angry at your father and you're trying to get back at him.'

'But how do you know I'm not using that to manipulate you right how?' He smiled and this time there was nothing bitter about it. It was all charm. 'How can you ever know if anything I do is real or genuine?'

I just looked at him. 'Like you're manipulating me right now? Trying to scare me away? No, Val. I know when you're genuine. Because I know you. And I trust you.'

Pain flickered over his face and I saw that change in his eyes, the shift. 'Except you can't, little star. You can't ever trust me. How can you, when I don't even trust myself?'

I had some premonition then, a certainty that gripped me. 'Don't,' I began.

But he didn't let me finish. 'You need to leave, Olivia,' he said gently. 'You should go back to Madrid. Tell Constantine you've changed your mind. Marry him.'

Of course he'd push me away.

Of course he'd want me to leave.

A bone-deep ache settled down inside me. 'You really want me to do that? You really want me to leave you?'

His expression had hardened. 'You can't stay. I won't let you. I'll only break your heart again, and you know it.'

I lifted my chin. 'Maybe, but isn't that my choice to make?'

'So, what? You'll stay with a man who doesn't even know what love is, let alone how to express it?'

The ache settled deeper inside me, because I could see that he truly believed that. And that I hadn't had long enough to teach him to believe otherwise. He didn't trust me, and he didn't trust himself, and I didn't know what to do.

He was a difficult man, scarred by his terrible childhood. But his instinct had always been to protect, no matter what he told himself about his battles with his father. He'd wanted to protect his brother; that was certain. And he'd wanted to protect me too. Those feelings had been genuine.

His heart was true.

'So that's it?' I demanded, suddenly furious myself. 'After everything we've been through, you just give up?' I strode over to him, giving him a taste of the passion and fire that lived inside me. 'It's because it's easier, isn't it? Easier to believe you're just like Domingo than it is to accept that I might love you. That I might want to be with you, to marry you instead. And I do, Val. You asked me a while ago what it was that I wanted, and I know now. It's you. I want you.'

Val stared at me, his eyes black flames. 'You don't know what you're talking about, Olivia. Your feelings... They're not real.'

But I didn't back down. 'Don't you dare tell me about my feelings, Valentin Silvera.'

'So if I'd come to you cap in hand in Madrid? Asked you out for coffee? What would you have done? You'd have turned around and walked away. The only reason you think you love me now is because I forced you to come here with me.'

I came closer, standing right in front of him, looking up into his eyes, trying to see where he was coming from him, trying to read him, and…he was afraid, wasn't he? He was afraid to take what I was giving him, because he didn't trust me.

I trusted him, but he didn't trust me.

And maybe he never would.

Maybe he'd never be able to give me that, never lower his defences enough to let me in. Maybe he was too scarred, too broken.

Maybe I'd end up just like my mother, staying with a man who didn't love her. Convincing herself that one day she'd change his mind and yet knowing it was never going to happen. Because she wasn't enough for him, just as I'd never been enough for him.

I could feel pain setting in, my heart fracturing along the same lines as it had years before, because the only option I had was doing the same thing she had: spending my life with a man who would never give me what I truly wanted.

His heart.

Except, that's not quite true, is it?

I blinked. Wasn't it, though? Love, as he'd said, wasn't something he knew anything about.

But I did. And so…why was I afraid? Wasn't my heart big enough for both of us? Wasn't I strong enough to deal with him? And why did I think I'd end up like my mother? Because I wouldn't. I would always challenge him, stand up to him. I'd never let him walk all over me. And that wasn't even what I'd been afraid of all this time—I knew that now.

It was love that had scared me. Love had broken me at

fifteen and I hadn't wanted ever to go near it again. But I was different now, stronger. And, strangely, I wasn't afraid. There was only that white-hot heart of the star burning inside my chest. A fire that would never go out, that would burn hot and powerful.

Love was that fire, and it wasn't a weakness or a flaw. It was a strength. A power.

I stared at Val, let my love for him blaze in my eyes so he would know what it looked like, so he would recognise it.

'You're wrong,' I said. 'You haven't forced me to love you. You only uncovered what was already there. I loved you then, Valentin Silvera, and I love you now. And, if you think I'm walking away from you, you can think again.' I paused, giving him a fierce look. 'I don't care how long it takes. You will be mine eventually. Count on it.'

Then I turned and went over to the couch and picked up the ripped shreds of my dress, draping them casually over my shoulder. 'Well,' I went on calmly. 'It's a lovely day and this is a lovely island. And I've just realised it's been a long time since I've taken a holiday. So… I think I'll stay here for a week or two. If you don't mind, that is.'

His face darkened and he took a step forward. 'Olivia, don't—'

'Don't what? You wanted me to choose, Val, so I'm choosing. And I choose to stay.' I strolled over to the door that led to the hallway and tossed him a smile over my shoulder. 'After all, I could do with a holiday.'

And, before he could reply, I walked out.

CHAPTER TWENTY

Valentin

I DIDN'T UNDERSTAND why she wanted to stay. After I'd taken everything from her. After I'd kidnapped her. Manipulated her into sex. Used her the way I'd used my brother, all to satisfy my own wants and needs.

To satisfy my anger towards a man who was dead.

A man I'd never called Father and yet for some reason a man I'd wanted attention from all the same.

I'd hated him. I'd thought it was Constantine who was like him, not me.

But I'd been wrong. All this time, I'd been wrong.

I let her walk out and I didn't follow, because what could I say? I couldn't love her the way she deserved to be loved. How could I? I'd thought I knew what love was, but I didn't. Another thing I'd been wrong about.

The rest of the day I tried to lose myself in work, but I couldn't concentrate, so I lost myself in exercise instead, trying to outrun the realisation that had frozen me down to my soul.

For once, I felt nothing. My anger was gone; the intense feelings of desire and hunger had vanished.

I'd become my father at long last.

Night came swiftly, as it did in the tropics, and that

was when I saw it—the flames of a driftwood fire on the beach.

It was her; of course it was her.

I ignored her for as long as possible and then, when I couldn't any more, I found myself striding down the jetty towards that fire. I'd tell her to put it out, that was what I'd do, and then I'd walk away. Because, if she wasn't going to, I would. I'd take the first plane out and go back to Europe. Find my brother. Take his company.

I should certainly have felt something about that, some kind of triumph at least, but my heart felt dead inside me. As if a light had gone out.

I was a frozen wasteland.

I found her sitting on a blanket she'd spread over the sand wearing only a silky loose white top through which I could see the delicate little bikini she wore underneath. Her hair was down over her shoulders and she smiled when she saw me, her face lighting up.

The way mine had lit up when I'd seen her for the first time all those years ago.

My chest ached, the ice inside me shifting.

'Come and sit down.' She patted the blanket beside her then picked up a bag of something on the other side of her and waved it at me. 'I've got marshmallows.'

The shifting feeling in my chest deepened into pain.

She must have found those marshmallows in the kitchen, because I'd got them for exactly this reason. To toast them over the driftwood fire the way we'd done all those years ago.

'You need to put the fire out,' I ordered.

'Do I?' She frowned. 'I don't see why. Nothing's going to catch alight.' She picked up a sharpened stick. 'Come on, sit with me. You know I can't do toasted marshmallows as well as you.'

It was true, she never could. I was the best.

The pain began to radiate outwards from inside me and I didn't want it. I wanted the deadness back.

Of course you do. But that's the easy way out, isn't it? If your heart is dead, you can't feel pain.

That was true. Just as if you didn't care, you couldn't be angry.

'If you didn't care then, yes, I might be worried, but that's not the case. You do care. You care deeply and you're furious about it.'

That was what she'd said to me this morning, her gaze direct. As if she'd seen something in me, something that I knew wasn't there.

The pain intensified, because I wanted it to be there.

I wanted to sit next to her. I wanted to toast the best marshmallow and then I wanted to feed it to her. I wanted to have her warm, bare thigh next to mine, and I wanted to talk about foolish things that made us both laugh.

I wanted to give her an engagement ring and see her in a wedding dress.

I wanted to marry her.

I wanted to spend my life with her.

But how could I do that? How could I ask her to marry a man like me? A man who'd been lying to himself all this time about who he was. A man who couldn't even trust himself.

A man who didn't know, who didn't understand, what the word love meant.

I couldn't ask that of her. I couldn't. It would be repeating what her own parents' marriage had been like and I couldn't do that.

She was a star that burned and I... I was nothing but ash.

I turned to go, to head back to the villa, but then I heard her voice.

'Don't go,' she said softly. 'Please stay.'

And I stopped in my tracks. Because those were the words I'd said to her that day on the beach when I'd met her. She'd been so cross to see me and I'd known she was going to leave. I hadn't wanted her to. I'd been desperate for her to stay.

And she had. She hadn't left me. She hadn't left me alone.

A bolt of something hot pulsed down my spine in that moment like lightning, rooting me to the spot.

I didn't know what was happening, but I could feel things shifting around inside me, rearranging themselves into a different shape, a picture I couldn't quite see yet.

I didn't turn, didn't want to move in case I disturbed that picture coming into view, but it was still distorted, still blurry.

'Why are you still here?' I demanded, staring out over the water, impatient because it was just within reach, that picture, but I still couldn't see it. 'What do you want from me?'

There was a moment of silence behind me, nothing but the crackle of the fire filling the air.

'I want you to trust me, Val,' Olivia said softly. 'I know it's hard after what Domingo did to you. I know it's hard to trust anyone. But you can trust me. And you can trust my love for you. That's why I'm still here. I meant what I said. I'm not leaving.'

My anger turned inside me, the frozen wasteland melting.

I wanted to deny that Domingo had done anything to me, but I couldn't. He'd twisted me just as thoroughly as he'd twisted Constantine.

'You think that's easy?' I demanded.

'No.' She sounded very calm. 'I think it's the most difficult thing in the world. It's a leap of faith, Val. But if you never take it, all you're doing is letting your father win.' She paused. 'You never let him win before, my love. Why start now?'

My heart was suddenly hammering in my chest and I couldn't breathe. It was almost as if I was afraid.

'I don't know how to do this,' I found myself saying, my voice hoarse. 'I don't know how to love you. I don't even know if I can.'

'Of course you can,' she said simply. 'You gave me laughter and honesty and belief. You gave me courage. You gave me the strength to be who I am. To embrace it and not be afraid. And what's that if not love?' Another pause. 'I think it's time for you to do the same.'

I couldn't breathe all of a sudden.

I turned around and stared at her, sitting by the fire, watching me steadily through the flames.

Her mouth curved. 'You're proud and bossy and far too arrogant. And you don't like the word no. But you're also protective and passionate. Gentle too, and never cruel. You have so much love to give, I can feel it, I can see it. And you want someone to love you too.'

Slowly she rose to her feet, the breeze catching the hem of her tunic and making it float out behind her. 'You're a difficult man, Valentin Silvera, but you're not a difficult man to love. So, come and sit by me and toast me a marshmallow, and then perhaps make love to me under the stars. We could argue after that about the best way to start a fire, perhaps. Or we could simply go back to the villa and I could show you all the ways I love you.'

She smiled, her face lit up by the fire, every part of

her shining. My little star. 'Then maybe we'll get married the way we always said we would.'

I stared at her, my heart cracking inside my chest. 'How can you say all these things after everything I did? I let you believe I was dead. I kidnapped you. I—'

'You showed me how it felt to be loved.'

I was shaking.

A leap of faith...

Suddenly I was walking towards the fire, barely conscious of what I was doing. The sand beneath my feet was still warm from the hot day's sun as I skirted the fire, coming to stand in front of her where she stood.

'Show me,' I demanded, every part of me aching and raw. 'Show me what it feels like.'

'Idiot,' Olivia said gently. 'It feels like this.' She reached up and wound her arms around my neck, then pressed her mouth to mine.

And, just like that, the picture snapped into complete, sharp focus.

I did know. I *did* know what love felt like.

Love was sitting on a beach throwing shells even when she was angry with me.

Love was arguing with me about building a fire and then letting me sit by it while we toasted marshmallows.

Love was pushing me off a rock and then laughing when I pulled her in.

Love was a first kiss under the stars and wild passion in the sand and her face glowing as she talked about what she wanted for her company and the gentleness of her fingertips on my jaw.

Love was her sitting by a fire with a bag of marshmallows.

Love was my little star, my Olivia.

You can trust her. Of all the people in the whole world, you can trust her.

A shudder went through me, ice melting under the heat of the sun, and somewhere deep inside I felt part of me let the ghost of my father go.

And then I was wrapping my arms around her, holding her tight, kissing her desperately, kissing her as if I was suffocating and she had all my air.

'Livvy,' I whispered when I could finally breathe again. 'I don't know if I can do this. I don't want to hurt you. I don't want to disappoint you. And I'm afraid I'll end up doing both.'

She looked up at me, her eyes shining. 'Oh, you probably will. And I'll probably do the same to you. No relationship is perfect.'

My heart was pounding. I wasn't sure if this was real. 'But I—'

She cupped the side of my face with one small hand. 'It's scary and, believe me, I'm scared too. But we'll make this work because I love you and that's all that matters.'

She was right. Love *was* all that mattered. And right then and there I decided I would do everything in my power to keep her here with me, to make her happy. And not for myself, but for her.

Because I loved her.

I cupped her face between my palms and looked down into her beautiful face. 'I love you, Olivia Wintergreen,' I said, and I made a vow. 'And I will spend the rest of my life arguing with you about the best way to start a fire, toasting you the perfect marshmallow, not getting angry when you push me off a rock, making love to you under the stars and trying to make you happy for the rest of my life.'

I took a breath. 'Will you live with me and have my children? Will you marry me?'

Her face blazed, her eyes the white-hot heart of a star. 'Yes,' she said. 'Yes, I will.' And then she kissed me and I caught fire with her.

And, even all these years later, we're still burning.

EPILOGUE

Olivia

MY WEDDING DRESS was perfect—white silk in a wrap-around style with a sexy slit that went all the way up to my thigh. My hair was loose and I carried some tropical flowers in a small bouquet.

On my finger was the engagement ring Val had bought me, which I adored. A red diamond. The world's rarest diamond colour. Because I too was rare and beautiful and precious, he'd said, and the red was for passion.

He waited for me at the end of the jetty, dressed all in black, and he watched me with all the ferocious intensity a man like him was capable of. Which was considerable.

My Val.

We'd tried to get hold of Constantine the night before, because Val had decided Constantine could keep his company. Val didn't want it. The only thing he'd ever wanted was me.

And all I'd ever wanted was him.

We were married on the end of the jetty and, when I was finally his wife, his kiss just about burned me alive.

So I pushed him into the sea.

Of course he pulled me in after him, but I didn't mind.

Nothing was going to cool the heat between us, and I didn't want it to.

We would burn together until the end of time.

Because it wasn't just me who was a star.

He was too.

* * * * *

COMING SOON!

We really hope you enjoyed reading this book.
If you're looking for more romance, be sure to
head to the shops when new books are
available on

Thursday 23rd
June

To see which titles are coming soon, please visit

millsandboon.co.uk/nextmonth

MILLS & BOON®

Coming next month

CINDERELLA IN THE
BILLIONAIRE'S CASTLE
Clare Connelly

"You cannot leave."

"Why not?"

"The storm will be here within minutes." As if nature wanted to underscore his point, another bolt of lightning split the sky in two; a crack of thunder followed. "You won't make it down the mountain."

Lucinda's eyes slashed to the gates that led to the castle, and beyond them, the narrow road that had brought her here. Even in the sunshine of the morning, the drive had been somewhat hair raising. She didn't relish the prospect of skiing her way back down to civilization.

She turned to look at him, but that was a mistake, because his chest was at eye height, and she wanted to stare and lose herself in the details she saw there, the story behind his scar, the sculpted nature of his muscles. Compelling was an understatement.

"So what do you suggest?" She asked carefully.

"There's only one option." The words were laced with displeasure. "You'll have to spend the night here."

"Spend the night," she repeated breathily. "Here. With you?"

"Not with me, no. But in my home, yes."

"I'm sure I'll be fine to drive."

"Will you?" Apparently, Thirio saw through her claim. "Then go ahead." He took a step backwards, yet his eyes remained on her face and for some reason, it almost felt to Lucinda as though he were touching her.

Rain began to fall, icy and hard. Lucinda shivered.

"I – you're right," she conceded after a beat. "Are you sure it's no trouble?"

"I didn't say that."

"Maybe the storm will clear quickly."

"Perhaps by morning."

"Perhaps?"

"Who knows?"

The prospect of being marooned in this incredible castle with this man for any longer than one night loomed before her. Anticipation hummed in her veins.

Continue reading
**CINDERELLA IN THE
BILLIONAIRE'S CASTLE**
Clare Connelly

Available next month
www.millsandboon.co.uk

LET'S TALK
Romance

For exclusive extracts, competitions
and special offers, find us online:

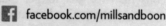 facebook.com/millsandboon

 @MillsandBoon

@MillsandBoonUK

Get in touch on 01413 063232

For all the latest titles coming soon, visit
millsandboon.co.uk/nextmonth